The Expanding Universe

Volume 2

Table of Contents

FOREWORD by Craig Martelle

DEFENSE OF THE DEEP SPACE DENALI by Craig Martelle
Fleece Newman is on a deep space mission, a boring duty hauling cargo. Just as he is convinced that the monotony of his assignment may actually kill him, the transport slams to a stop...and the entire crew's survival depends on what he does next.

SELF-PERSPECTIVE by Amy DuBoff
You wake up time and again in one place. Each time it's you, but different versions of yourself. Nothing changes, nothing remains the same.

PEYTON'S LEGACY by S.M. Schmitz
Twenty years after the thieves of peace decimated Cambria, the invaders have exhausted their food supply. To secure the Cambrians' freedom once and for all, Jenna and a small group of young soldiers will battle the remaining invaders, but the cost may be far higher than she is willing to pay.

CASSOWARY RAID by Drew A. Avera
Tom has a past he's trying to escape. Enlisting in the Chancerian Navy seemed like a good way to get a fresh start, but a run-in with a pirate vessel brings his past to the forefront and reveals who he really is. That revelation could mean the end of the Cassowary crew.

FOX HUNT by Carysa Locke
A psychic Hunter who lost everything, Teegan must face the most painful events of her past when a killer escapes from the asteroid prison she once sent him to. She'll have to risk those she cares about the most if she wants to stop him from killing again.

HONOR DUEL by Kevin O. McLaughlin
David's luck has brought him from starship deckhand to the rank of knight. But there is more to knighthood than armor and swordplay - honor often makes lethal demands of those who would bear that title. When his starship is surprised by an attack while David is the only knight remaining aboard, his commands will mean life or death for the crew. But the enemy isn't always the obvious one, and the deadliest foe is closer than he knows.

A PRAYER FOR THE FAITHLESS by David Bruns
Twelve years ago, Mubassir Zadeh willingly gave up his claim to the family interstellar shipping empire—as long as they left him alone. Now the family has summoned him home to take care of one last piece of nasty business. A story of faith, family, and the betrayal of both.

MARGOLIS SPACE RESCUE by P. Joseph Cherubino
Captain Marshall Margolis and his mixed crew of beings from across the Intergalactic Trade Union don't care that there's war. As part of the Rescue Guild, they save lives and rescue ships. Period. Honor and duty bind them to the job and to each other. So when a Reptilian ship calls for help, they get to work, but the Reptilians have different ideas. The rescue turns into a struggle for survival. Will that struggle make the crew abandon their principles or will those principles save them?

VENUSIAN UPRISING by M. D. Cooper
For the Marines of Bravo Company, being boots down on Venus, fighting an insurgency is just another day in the life. Their mission is to take out an enemy garrison in the city of Tarja, but first, they're going to have to get past a battalion of Diskers, a foreign military from the edges of the Sol System. Outnumbered and unable to call in starfire, the Force Recon Orbital Drop Marines will do what they do best: kick some ass.

DESTROY THE PLANET by T.J. Ryan
After many years of peace, the Huxley Starship is launched, and humanity celebrates a new age of intergalactic connectivity. When the ship suddenly switches course and unexpectedly heads back toward Earth, the planet soon realizes their years of peace may be over, and their entire civilization is at risk of annihilation.

BOARDED by Dale Furse
Captain Jai Brolto and his crew are celebrating the victory of a space battle, but one ship is still in the sector, one ship manned by hungry flesh-eating aliens, and they have Jai's ship in their sights.

SPACE COLONY ONE: NIGHT OF FLAMES by J.J. Green
A new world colony. A moonless night. An alien attack. Ethan wakes to find his dream of life on humanity's first deep space colony has turned into a nightmare.

PIRATES VS. DRONES by J.L. Hendricks and S.R. Witt
Once in a blue moon, a space pirate can be a good guy, or not. The outerworld shipping lanes are slim picking lately for pirate Captain Gore.

He takes an Operator assignment that puts his broken-down ship, The Black Pearl, and his degenerate crew in the path of the Mechanurge drones and quite possibly a hideous death on their Harvester ship.

SPACE CADETS: ACID SLIME by H.J. Lawson
Captian Brooke Garcia is a Space Cadet, protecting the galaxy from rogue aliens. That's what she tells people in her briefing, today her assignment is to collect the plant from an alien planet, Asomea. Brooke's boring assignment quickly becomes one of her deadliest.

NUN SHALL PASS by Barry Hutchison
When the son of psychic space nun (retired), Ronda, gets mixed up with the wrong crowd, she sets out to bring him home. Unfortunately, the wrong crowd wants to hold onto the wayward teen and to save her boy, Ronda will have to face some of the galaxy's meanest scumbags and an ancient enemy who wants her dead.?

INTUITION (A GALACTIC WARRIORS PREQUEL) by Monica Leonelle
Teague Abell, one of the last intuitives of the Galactic Alliance, knows there's something wrong with her starship's mission to blow up the Hail Hermione 4 before it attacks her hometown of Nova London. To complicate matters, her intuition might be a bit screwy because one of the crewmates on the other ship is a close childhood friend. Can she convince commander Orion to change course before it's too late?

PANIC BUTTON by Sam Maguire
For mercenaries, there's no such thing as an ordinary Saturday. When a routine back-alley gun deal meets the business end of an illegal weapons bust, soldier of fortune Kate Sharpe and her crewmate need to find a way out of the no-tell motel and back to their ship alive and preferably not in handcuffs.

MOTHERLODE by Bill Patterson
VectorShip Appleseed plies the star lanes, planting human colonies across the galaxy, but the ship needs uranium. Thanks to Helen Rooney, remote sensing tech, Appleseed diverts to Motherlode, a planet rich in minerals. Once the mining begins, Helen sees disturbing readings. Should she stop the vital refueling, or is she overthinking the danger? After all, the ore is so rich it's a wonder that it hasn't melted down already.

EMERGENCE by E.R. Starling
Emergence is a blend of military sci-fi and mystical psychic elements. It

will likely not appeal to readers of only Hard Sci-Fi or Science Realism. But for readers who enjoy the metaphysical side of science fiction, this is definitely the place to be.

MARA'S HONOR by Taki Drake
Determined to carry on despite career-ending errors in judgment, Lieutenant Mara Brown has been stuck in an "exile" post, designed to hold the incompetent and the honorless until they retire, or die. When circumstances offer a possible second chance, how will she respond? Will she move forward in honor and the spirit of the corps, or has she allowed grief and despair to deny her a chance at reclaiming some part of her life?

THE DRONE PILOT by Brian J. Walton
A drone satellite inexplicably plots a collision course with NASAs first colony ship. Stopping the collision will kill the drone's pilot. From the safety of JPLs control room, the lives of their astronauts are weighed in the balance.

OPERATION SOLID IRON by James Osiris Baldwin
A supersoldier must penetrate the ruins of a crumbling nuclear power plant to stop rival soldiers from gaining enough material for a nuclear bomb: long-lost technology that threatens to wipe out the rest of humanity. Getting in is a deadly challenge – especially when the mission goes awry in the weirdest ways possible.

DEAD IN SPACE by T.S. Paul
An

Foreword by Craig Martelle

We write science fiction because we get to design the worlds and then live adventures within them. Who wouldn't want to do that? It's keeping track of life within those worlds that presents the challenge and then telling the stories in a way that entertains is the epitome of the art.

Twenty-three authors. NY Times bestselling authors, USA Today bestselling authors, Amazon bestselling authors, and those who have yet to make their mark – they come together here with stories to captivate, to fire your imagination.

These authors met on the Facebook group – 20booksto50k, which started as a support forum for independent authors. We are known as indies.

What is 20booksto50k all about?

It's about what it takes to make a career as an author. What is it like to run a small business where your stories are the only product? Still, 20books has become so much more than that. We've found kindred spirits as we each take our own journey up the publishing mountain. Some write one book a year, some write one a month. The only thing that matters is what's right for you and the realistic expectations of what you can achieve.

It's also hard work, a great deal of hard work. Like most small businesses, independent authors will spend 70 to 80 hours a week in their chair, writing, marketing, getting to know our readers, and writing some more.

The readers – you good people who pick up our stories and then keep reading, buy our books. We can't thank you enough. You make it all possible, otherwise we are just writing for art's sake, and that doesn't put ramen on the table, so thank you.

Write well and read fast, fellow travelers. The journey has only just begun.

I hope you enjoy the stories from this collection of gifted authors.

Peace, fellow humans.

Craig Martelle

Defense of the Deep Space Denali

By Craig Martelle

The Characters

Captain Fleece Newman

Executive Officer Hamden Cray

Navigator Vesuvius Entwhistle

Pilot Major Hardy

Engineer Torrent Forrest

It felt like the ship had slammed into an invisible wall. The crew was thrown about the bridge. Screams and dull thuds resounded. An angry yell came through the sealed hatch behind them. Vesuvius Entwhistle, the navigator, jumped from his seat and froze, trying to balance as the ship continued to shake from the violence of the unknown impact.

Entwhistle pulled himself hand over hand until he reached the door. He yanked down on a hand lever to the side. The clamps released and the captain pushed the round hatch open.

Captain Fleece Newman stepped through, nodding tersely to his navigator. He limped badly because of a damaged left leg, injured in a war long before he took to hauling cargo. A scar, deep enough to set his face in a permanent snarl, bisected his cheekbone. He was wary and quiet; no one knew how much he hated beer.

It was his secret, and that's why he didn't allow it on board. Single malt

Scotch, on the other hand...

The navigator checked the hatch's actuation system before returning the lever to the automatic position. The hatch closed and sealed. The captain was the last of the crew to arrive.

The crew's part of the ship was small as the rest of the space was taken with systems and cargo, neither of which required an atmosphere or the artificial gravity of the spinning, doughnut-shaped command module at the top of the vast, boxy cargo hauler.

"What the hell happened?" Captain Newman bellowed, looking from one face to the next. The executive officer was still sitting in the captain's module, rapidly shifting views from one screen to the next. Each seat in the command module was within a gimbaled cage, providing a three-hundred-and-sixty-degree view with a simple body-activated rotation. If they lost gravity, they would still be able to operate the ship. She shook her head, unable to determine a cause.

The captain pulled himself to the pilot's position. "Come on, Major, what did you fly us into?" Fleece's disfigured sneer was more pronounced when expressing his dismay. He thrust his face into the caged space that Major Hardy occupied. "Well?"

"I didn't fly us into anything! What the hell? We're in interstellar space. There's nothing out here. Scans don't show anything. Something must have happened to the engine. Torrent!" the pilot yelled. "Whenever you're ready, suit up and let's take a look."

The engineer, Torrent Forrest, was so embroiled in his data from the ship's drive systems that he didn't hear the pilot call his name. He was focused on the reports coming from the onboard computer, inundating him with data. It would have been easier if the computer system was an artificial intelligence. The owners of the cargo haulers said they didn't need that for the milk runs of the Deep Space series of ships. AIs were reserved for deep space exploration and military ships, while the cargo routes were simple and the ship was mostly automated.

That's why a five-hundred-thousand-ton vessel could be served by a crew of five.

The captain waited impatiently, finally waving his executive officer, Hamden Cray, from the captain's chair. The XO apologized as she moved out of the way and sought her own seat in the next gimballed module in the space that made up the bridge.

One-quarter of the spinning doughnut was the bridge, one-half was crew space, and one-quarter was for stores, fitness, and recreation. It was all one level in a section atop the dual drive system. The cargo containers trailed in a long train behind the engine block. The technological marvel was the subspace drive which moved the ship vast distances using a leaping motion. The shortcoming in the subspace drive was that it couldn't operate within the gravity well of a solar system. That's where the big engines came in, to drive the ship into and through the gravity well.

"Torrent!" the captain yelled.

Torrent Forrest continued mumbling to himself as he chased system diagnostics through the complexities of the ship's engines. He sat back, confused by the lack of information that suggested a problem.

It had happened so fast, just a few minutes before.

From the ordered calm of the nighttime watch, officers at their stations, and the undertone of automated reports punctuated by flashing lights, to the chaos of an in-flight emergency in a matter of heartbeats. Torrent's heart still raced as he worried over a problem that he couldn't find.

Generally, the crew dozed or daydreamed as they waited for the next mundane event in a never-ending checklist. The majority of concerns were digital in nature and not mechanical. They were easily rectified without a physical presence. When a mechanical repair was called for, a repair bot was programmed and dispatched. In the rarest of cases, the crew would suit up and direct the repairs on site.

No one liked suiting up and going outside. It was dangerous out there because the ship never stopped moving. Tethers kept the crew from floating into space, but going outside was avoided as much as humanly possible.

Torrent sat back. The owners treated the ship like a garbage scow, and that's how a second-rate engineer like him got the job. He loved the engines and was constantly learning, but he was afraid he wouldn't be able to find the problem.

You suck at engineering! his brother had told him. I can't believe anyone would be stupid enough to give you a job. Didn't they look at your grades? Holy crap! The cargo service must really be in a world of hurt if they're hiring someone like you.

His brother had two PhDs. Why don't you go to space? Torrent had asked.

Because the real work is here where we design and build the engines. There's no such thing as an engineer in space. You'll be nothing more than a cleaning guy and backyard mechanic, but if that's how you want to live your life, good luck with all that, his brother had replied.

I think he's going to be right that I failed. No one will even find our bodies this far out, he thought, hanging his head and pinching his eyes closed.

"Hey!" he heard from far away, then felt a hand shaking him. Major Hardy stood there looking at him, one hand on her hip. "Well?"

"I'm not sure what's broken. Let me dig a little deeper," he offered, holding her gaze. He didn't want to look at his console and keep finding nothing. That only confirmed what his brother had thought about him.

"Let me know when you're ready, but the sooner the better. We're at a dead stop, and that's not good." She stormed down the line of stations, looking at each as she passed.

Everyone seemed busy, but no one seemed to be doing anything.

Major Hardy was all about the action, and right now, there wasn't any. She needed to do something and that always put her at odds with the rest of the crew. They seemed happy that their entire world was wrapped up in the computer systems that told them how the ship was operating.

Major didn't need that. She could feel it, sense the ship around her. The captain told her that she was being ridiculous. No one could fly the Denali by feel because the computers told the pilot everything she needed to know. Hardy agreed with most of it. She needed the information that the computers provided, but she added that to how she felt the ship as an entity around her. It was an ungainly beast, but it responded. The more she tried to be one with the ship, the better it reacted to her gentle caresses.

It was the only thing she had. Her boyfriend was back on Earth. She'd taken the job as the Denali's pilot on a three-year contract while they were dating. He had proposed the week before she returned to space.

She didn't give him an answer because she didn't want to keep him in limbo. She regretted that every day she'd been in space.

She left Earth to do what she loved. Make a difference. The Denali might be just a cargo hauler, but the people on the other end of the runs needed what they brought. It was like Christmas with every delivery. Sometimes it meant the difference between life and death.

I'm sorry, Stephen. I have to do this. Please wait for me... she thought for the ten thousandth time. She had begged him, but he wasn't pleased. Who would be?

She'd had a hard time getting a job as a pilot, and this was her first real shot. Her parents named her Major. Whenever she interviewed and they discovered that she was a young woman with no military experience, she was shown the door. She was almost at the point of legally changing her name, but her parents had died, and she wanted to show her respect for them.

Major Hardy, young female pilot, gifted in the business, and no one had given her a chance.

Until the cargo hauler gig. The owners shaved costs to the absolute minimum. Every member of the crew had their own down-and-out story and took the job at roughly half the normal wage. So here they were, dead in the middle of interstellar space, a pack of misfits earning half-pay.

She turned and headed back toward Torrent to encourage him to figure it out. The XO watched Hardy pace.

"Bugging him won't help," Hamden Cray said, sticking an arm out of the cage surrounding her workstation. The pilot stopped and peeked between a pair of monitors at the murky brown eyes of the XO.

"How long does it take? What good are the computers if they can't tell you why the ship isn't moving? We have to do something!" Major lamented.

"We are doing something. You're the only one who isn't, appropriately so, since the ship isn't flying. Stand by and be ready for when we figure it out," Hamden said in her school marm voice.

"It's off," Torrent yelled triumphantly.

"Of course, it's off, you idiot, but why?" the captain yelled down the walkway alongside the workstations.

"Not that, well yes, that. The engine is off, but it's because the manual switch has been turned off. All we have to do is turn it back on and the engines will come back to life." I hope, he didn't add.

"I'm on my way!" Major declared, heading for the hatch to the stores and recreation where the space suits could be found.

"No need," Torrent replied as his fingers flew across the buttons of his input device, coding a repair bot to flip the switch. He slammed the "execute" key triumphantly and brought up the video feed from the bot. It slowly traveled from its storage cove using a magnetic tether and compressed air. It moved in a herky-jerky motion as it found purchase on its way, pulling itself, then flying, then pulling itself again. As it entered a dark corridor, it turned on its lights and pressed forward toward the panel where the manual off switch was located.

With a mechanical arm, it opened the panel and reached for the switch.

A light flashed, and the video feed went blank.

The crew of the DS Denali stared at the blank screens in each of their consoles. Hardy looked over Torrent's shoulder, unsure of what she'd seen.

"Playing back, showing a wider view, displaying the three-hundred-sixty-degree camera," Torrent said as he went through the steps. He often talked himself through the operations, almost as if he was being graded on his performance, trying to prove to the instructor that he knew what he was doing. No one else on the crew cared or bothered to tell him he was doing just fine. They thought he was weird.

He turned pale and started sweating. He leaned back in his chair and stared at the screen as the last few seconds of video looped.

"What? It shorted out or something. I'll suit up and go flip the switch. Geez, Torrent, lighten up. So what? You lost a maintenance bot. There are plenty more. Although you treat them like your kids, they're not," Hardy emphasized, putting crossing her arms to drive her point home.

The engineer shook his head. "There's somebody out there."

The captain leaned out of his chair, then slowly extricated himself from it and limped to the engineer's position. Torrent's chair rolled in place as the ship rocked anew, just once as if a small gravity wave had rolled past.

"What did you say?" the captain asked, squinting at his engineer.

"Look! I think this is an electrical arc like you'd see from a Taser."

"Spock! Scotty! Beam me up, laddie, they're firing phasers in here!" Major Hardy said in her best Scottish accent. The captain glared at her. "Fine, I'm getting my suit on, just tell me when I can go take care of it."

The pilot none too gently shoved her way past the gimpy captain and headed for the hatch. When she got there, she tried it, but it wouldn't open. She pulled the manual release and muscled it open. "Hey, Volcano, make sure I'm not locked out," she told the navigator.

Vesuvius Entwhistle looked at the young woman, appreciating her curves. She held no interest to him, as he didn't swing that way. He had hoped to strike up something with the engineer but hadn't quite made a move yet since Torrent seemed completely engaged with computer systems. Often, he didn't recognize that there were other human beings around. Maybe at their next stop, Vesuvius would see if he could get him alone in the hopes that he could kindle some kind of flame.

Vesuvius didn't like being alone, although that's how he found himself. Alone, looking at the stars, plotting courses for the subspace drive and then charting routes as they navigated through the heliosphere and into the gravity well of their destination solar systems. He integrated data from the sensors to avoid as many obstructions and as much debris as he could, whether in an asteroid field, in orbit around a planet, or any points in between.

And here he was again, alone while the others did their thing. He had a countdown calendar in one of his personal files in data storage. He looked at it multiple times while on shift; it helped when they were moving and had an estimated arrival time.

Right now, they were dead in space. The navigator knew where they were and the computer already knew where they wanted to go, so Volcano had nothing to do. As the seconds passed, the countdown clock remained static.

"I can come with you," he offered.

"Sure. The more, the merrier, especially if there's someone out there, right Torrent?" Hardy said loud enough for all to hear.

Fleece sneered at her, although it might have been comparable to the look of an impatient parent. She couldn't tell because of his scar.

"Go? No go? Your call, Torrent," the captain urged.

"No," the man whispered, hanging his head. "Let me send another bot."

"For Christ's sake, let's get on with it. This trip isn't getting any closer to ending the longer we stay here. Two more legs and we're home, so, chop, chop, Engineer!" Major Hardy bellowed.

I'm going to get home, and I will have missed you by a day. You'll be gone, all because we sat here, not doing anything, she thought.

Volcano saw the pained expression cross her face and wondered what it meant, but he was afraid to ask. They called him Volcano, but Hardy was the one most likely to erupt. He let it go.

Torrent reprogrammed another bot. Hardy and Volcano watched the show on the navigation monitor, while the XO leaned in close to the captain as Torrent guided the metal creature to the dead bot. The functioning repair bot scanned the area on all sides of the panel, up, down, back, and forth. It moved in close, scanned again, and then opened the panel. It waited, using its optics to scan the area one final time. It reached a metal arm into the panel and flipped the switch.

The lights on Torrent's systems console flashed as the engine start sequence engaged. They still had four weeks of travel under regular thrust to gain orbit around the third planet of Alpha Centauri B, a K-type dwarf star.

"Hot damn!" Major Hardy cheered and danced her way to her console, climbed into the gimbled seat, and strapped herself in. She ran through her systems checks as the big engines came to life.

The captain grunted his approval and returned to his position. Hamden took her seat, and everyone started running through their checklists.

The captain was the least busy of the crew. He'd verify the others' work when it was done. He'd give the word to get under way once everything was ready. The captain and XO had to be experts in everything, while the other crewmembers were specialists. That mean that Fleece Newman and Hamden Cray had knowledge that was a mile wide and an inch deep. The less they specialized, the less they knew about anything, but the captain couldn't tell his crew that. They needed to think he was all knowing.

Ever since the explosion aboard his last cargo hauler during the war, he'd been damaged goods. Not because of the injuries—modern ships didn't require anyone to be overly fit—but because of the damage to his psyche. He couldn't shake that it was his fault. The more he tried to learn about the deep space cargo ships, the less he discovered he knew. His mind wasn't as sharp as it had been in his youth, when he was a sponge, remembered everything.

Not now. He grunted and mumbled. The crew would hear what they wanted to hear, and no one would be the wiser. He looked at the screens. Too much information, but once they were under way he could rest, get some energy back before conducting a full inquiry into how the switch was flipped in the first place and what happened to the first repair bot.

"I have your course, Nav," Major Hardy called as part of her checklist. "Engine status is nominal. Crew status is confirmed. Accelerating at three gees in five, four, three, two, one." The DS Denali smoothly accelerated, sending a half-million tons of ship and goods on its way.

As soon as it started, it ended in a violent lurch as the engines executed an emergency cut-off.

"Torrent, report!" the captain bellowed at the same time he cycled his data screens to look at what the engineer was seeing.

"The switch is in the off position," Torrent called out immediately. "Replaying the video from the repair bot." The engineer reset the video feed that he hadn't been watching during the restart sequence. The XO, pilot, and engineer slaved their monitors to watch from within their own workstations.

A figure in a spacesuit stepped from behind a corner, opened the panel, and casually flipped the engine cut-off switch. The figure turned, faced the repair bot, then calmly removed a device from its tool belt, aimed it, and hit the bot with an electrical discharge, ending the video feed.

"Screw that guy! Who's with me? Let's go kick his ass," Major Hardy yelled from her seat, unbuckling herself and climbing into the walkway.

"Wait," the captain ordered. "XO, options?"

Hamden Cray looked around, then climbed from her chair. She held up one finger, asking for a moment to think.

She didn't have any military experience. She'd served, as soon as she was old enough to volunteer, but it was after the war. They put her in morgue services. The sight of a dead body had turned her stomach when she'd first seen one, but then it only got worse.

She served her time, then ran away from the military as quick as her legs would carry her. She fled to space, a place where she didn't have to interact with people. She would have preferred a one-man ship with years between ports of call. The best she could find was the Denali and its crew of five.

Hamden wore headphones most of the time, immersed in the music of ages past. The music played and built an impenetrable wall between her and the outside world, even if there were only four other people occupying it.

The thought that they'd been boarded terrified her. This was a cargo ship. They had no weapons. Hamden Cray closed her eyes and tried to break the problem down logically.

The ship needs to move. A person unknown was keeping the ship from moving. That person needed to go. That person has a weapon.

"We need weapons," the XO finally said.

"Now you're talking!" Hardy jumped up and down, flexing and stretching.

"Cool your jets, Major," the captain grumbled.

"Torrent, can you come up with anything we can use to counter this person? And you, Volcano, how in the hell did that person get on my ship!" the captain yelled, feeling good about the anger within. He'd always wanted to serve in the military, but had been too afraid. Now that he was scarred and limped like a veteran, he realized that he could have served, should have served. He wanted this fight to prove what he was worth. In the weightlessness of outer space, his limp would be irrelevant.

He smiled, a look that was not lost on the XO.

And she grew even more afraid. The captain wanted to be a hero. She'd read his record. It was nondescript, average at best. Nothing good and nothing bad. He'd served on a number of different ships throughout his adult life, but what experience had he gained? It didn't say. His resume was a physical listing of ships and billets, not accomplishments. There were no endorsements from previous captains.

He'd been there, but what had he done?

Hamden refused to look at the captain as she crawled back into her workstation, strapping into her seat as if everything was normal. The captain climbed out of his and stormed the eight steps to get to the XO's position.

"Well?" he demanded, reaching out a hand to stop her from putting her headphones on.

"We need weapons. I'm going to look through our stores, see what we can modify," she said weakly. The captain grunted.

"You do that. Major Hardy, with me." He nodded in her direction and pointed to the hatch. She ran to it and pulled the manual release. Together they worked the hatch open and walked through into the recreation and stores area. The ship had been specifically designed, linking the compartments one to the next. There was no separate passageway as could be found on the bigger vessels designed for more crew and even passengers. Privacy was at a minimum on the cargo haulers as everyone lived and worked in a single rotating tube. When the captain and the pilot searched the cupboards and cabinets, they found that sharp objects were just as commonplace as privacy.

Everything was designed specifically not to be harmful.

"We need tools. A pry bar, a hammer, screw drivers, maybe even a portable welder. Yeah. I want to drive the flamethrower," Hardy told the captain, smiling at the thought of launching flame into the intruder.

The captain studied his pilot. She was all kinds of gung-ho. He wondered if she'd ever been in a real fight or lain on the deck after an explosion wondering if she was going to die. He heard the explosion in his head, and it made him stagger. He felt the pain shoot through his waist and into his leg. His face hurt. He reached up a hand then looked stupidly at it, wondering why there was no blood.

"Captain, are you all right?" the pilot asked, looking closely into his eyes as he braced himself against the bulkhead. There was no way she could see the source of his pain.

"I'm fine. Suits and tools." He pointed to the cupboard where the space suits were located, next to the floor hatch.

To get to the engines, they'd have to suit up and climb the ladder leading down to the hub, where they'd pass through an airlock to zero-g space. The tools were stored in that area. It was easier to move the heavy tools without gravity. The crew would then swim into a central passageway and leave the rotating module behind.

Major Hardy opened the cabinet and pulled the captain's suit out and handed it to him. She took hers out, inspected it quickly and then stripped out of her jumpsuit, leaving her clad in only a pair of briefs. The captain looked, wondering why the others didn't keep themselves in shape. After clipping his jumpsuit to the bulkhead, he looked down at his body, which he could only describe as slovenly.

A ragged scar trailed from a spot above his knee to his groin and then to his abdomen. He'd been damaged in a way that all men dreaded. The injury made him reevaluate his whole life. What had he done that mattered?

Cargo. Getting supplies to people on the fringe of space meant saving lives. That's what he told himself anyway, which was true in many cases. Sometimes his supplies contained the latest in immersion video gaming. And then there were the smugglers. They couldn't check all the cargo, and inevitably something was secreted away.

His contract gave him no responsibility for the independently loaded cargo modules. He pushed the thoughts out of his mind as he sealed his suit and followed Major Hardy down the ladder and into the initial airlock. They continued on once it cycled and the hatch at their feet released. The closer they moved to the central hub, the easier it became until they jumped the last few rungs, floating to the deck.

They opened the tool cabinets. Major pulled out a pry bar and floated away, trying to make a war face. She attempted a mighty swing, failing mightily with her effort.

"It's zero gravity. Activate your magnetic locks first; you'll probably have better luck," the captain offered.

"Thanks, Fleece. I already figured that one out." She flailed as she swam toward the deck. Once close enough, her boots snapped down tightly. The captain jumped back as Major swung with a fierce determination. She rotated through her trunk, adding power to the swing. "Come to Mama you little bastards!"

"I doubt they'll stand still and take their pummeling appreciatively. So we're going to need some way to hold them in place." The captain smoothly pushed off the wall and floated serenely to the second cabinet, then the third. He found the portable welder, not even as big as his arm. He looked it over and nodded. With a double blink, he activated his heads-up display so his eye movements would operate the system. He tagged the comm system.

"Torrent, can you hear me?" he asked and continued without waiting for a response. "What have you come up with?"

"Defense, Captain. We've looked at the video, and it seems that this person's one weapon is that Taser thing. We need to build a Faraday cage around you, or at least ground you to prevent that thing from taking out your suit's systems. If that happens..." Torrent couldn't say it.

If the suit lost power, the person would have whatever air was resident within. It would become heavy with carbon dioxide quickly; then hypoxia would set in, followed by death. Maybe five minutes of life without power.

"Good call, Torrent. Do you have something we can use? And actually, get your ass down here. We need you to check the systems. Major and I will cover you while you work."

"What? No. I'm not going out there. Let me program a repair bot. You can cover that just as easily as you could cover me. I can see what it's doing and adjust the programming on the fly. We don't need more people out there," Torrent stated in a defensive rapid-fire.

You're no engineer, his brother had told him. The words bounced around inside his skull.

You're no engineer.

"Aahhhhh!" he screamed, pinching his eyes shut, covering his ears, and rocking.

The XO looked at him. Stupid people, she thought. This would be so much easier without people.

Volcano pulled himself out of his console and ran down the narrow walkway. Torrent needed him!

The navigator arrived and reached into the cage that made up the engineering station, pulling the panicking young man to his breast and cradling his head as he cooed, trying to calm the engineer.

Hamden fumbled with her headphones as she tried to put them on. Her hands were shaking. Damn people! she repeated within her mind.

"Hello?" the captain's voice came through the speakers at each of the stations on the bridge. "Do we still have atmosphere up there?"

Hamden hesitated, then activated her voice control. "We have atmosphere. Why?"

"Because methinks there's no oxygen in your brains!" the captain countered, then started to yell, "What the hell are you all doing?"

"Minor crisis, Fleece. What if Torrent just programs a bot for you? I seriously doubt he'll be able to go in person."

Major stood next to Fleece, the pry bar held at her side as she flexed her fingers around its handle.

The captain sighed heavily, fogging the inside of his helmet's face shield. He wanted to go and fix it, but the pragmatist in him suggested that he wait until he could ground his suit and surround himself with others.

I'm a coward, he thought, looking at his hands. They didn't shake. He didn't feel afraid. He was more wary of the unknown than afraid of going into harm's way. Maybe he wasn't a coward. "Go ahead. Tell us when it's ready, and we'll head out. It'll take us a couple of minutes to get into place, but it'd be nice to see everything along the way. Can you patch the passageway visuals to my helmet, please?"

"Sorry, we didn't get those fixed before leaving Earth. The only cameras are in the main spaces looking at critical gear. With the repair bots, there's really no need for static visuals. We get the right data through the other systems. Your eyes can deceive you," Hamden droned, spewing the company's standard line on why some systems were installed while others weren't. High-definition video simply took too much storage space on the main server, even though storage was cheap, even nearly unlimited storage. Still, the owners found ways to cut corners.

What a bunch of buttholes, she thought, completely unbothered by the fact that she had loaded a full terabyte of music into central data storage.

"Torrent! Just program the goddamn bot," Hamden yelled before putting on her headphones and playing something from the ancients. Good Times, Bad Times…

"Shhh," Vesuvius soothed the engineer, feeling the young man's ribs through his jumpsuit. He was too thin and not in a good way. "You don't have to go, did you hear that? Just program the repair bot and we'll watch from right here. Fleece and Major have it under control. Program the bot, please."

Volcano stroked the young man's hair as he nodded and turned back to his console. The navigator leaned in and kissed the engineer gently on his temple before stepping back and letting the young man get to work.

Torrent started slowly, working the buttons on his input console. As the routine of his actions calmed him, habit took over, and he worked faster and faster. He found the next closest repair bot and told it what to do.

"Captain, Torrent here. I've programmed a bot that you'll pass on your way to the manual control. Sorry for the delay, but, I, but…" he trailed off, unable to complete his sentence.

"I'm a good engineer," he told himself. He looked around to see that the XO had her headphones on, oblivious to everything around her. Volcano had gone back to his workstation but was looking at Torrent oddly. The engineer wondered what that was all about.

He activated the bot and played the video on multiple screens to give the broadest view possible. He minimized every other system screen he had, something he wasn't supposed to ever do because of the delicate balance required for ship operations. The ship could function on its own for long periods of time, which was why there was only one person for each position, with the captain and the executive officer able to backfill the other three positions.

Torrent didn't want to miss anything and get Fleece or Major hurt. He liked both of them for different reasons. The pilot complimented him on his engineering because she didn't know any of it. The captain didn't complain about the engineering, which Torrent took as a positive.

He didn't want to let either of them down.

Fleece Newman had to hold Major Hardy back as he wanted to go first. She wrestled with him, briefly, anger contorting her face.

"What?" he demanded.

"Just because you're a man, you get to go first?" she growled.

"No. It's my ship and my responsibility, and I refuse to order anyone into danger, into something that I myself wouldn't go into. That's why. Are you a woman? I didn't know," he joked.

She punched him in the chest. "Even so. I recognize that you were willing to go first, but I really should be first because you are more important to this ship than I am," she suggested, tapping her pry bar against her palm. "And I trust you to watch my back. You know me. If I'm behind you, I might get distracted and go off in a different direction, leave you hanging. Neither of us wants that. It'd make things awkward for the rest of the trip. So what do you say we go fix this?" She held out a gloved hand.

He took it, and they shook. He waved her forward and they dove head first into the corridor beyond, leaving the rotating section behind. Major pulled herself forward, using the handholds until she made it to the first engineering module. She opened the hatch and crawled through, shining her helmet lights into the darkened space.

The captain activated his comm system. "Torrent, can you please turn on the lights in these spaces?" he said impatiently. Within a few seconds, the overhead and side lighting activated. The repair bot within that space floated out and assumed a position between the pilot and the captain.

They clomped forward slowly, using their magnetic boots to keep them grounded as they moved. The repair bot kept pace. "Looking good, Captain," Torrent added unnecessarily.

Fleece carried the welding torch in one hand and a fire extinguisher in the other. Since the ship wasn't moving and this section was in zero-g, all he had to do was drop one to put both hands on the other. It wouldn't go far.

Major carried the pry bar like a baseball bat, ready to swing at a moment's notice.

They pressed forward through the next space and the next. Each appeared to be untouched.

"Wait," the captain said quietly.

"What? Did you see something?" Major asked, looking around frantically, threatening a shadow with her pry bar.

"No. I want to take a look outside. Wait here." The captain released his magnetic boots and pushed off the deck plate, running one hand along the ladder as he rose to an exit hatch a good thirty feet away. He gripped the ladder as he closed with the ceiling to slow himself down. With one hand, he activated the hatch, happy to see that it had power and worked, unlike the hatch leading from the bridge.

He reached behind his waist, found his tether and, with that in his gloved hand, went outside. The blackness of space was immediately overwhelming; then the stars started twinkling as his eyes adjusted.

The captain looked at the outside of the massive ship. The ship's running lights were on, highlighting the entirety of the vessel. He couldn't see the crew module as that was past the corner of the large boxy section which contained the engines and the technology to run them. A long line of linked and stacked cargo containers trailed behind the ship. The containers were standard shipping containers like on Earth, but stacked ten by ten, then wrapped; then another one hundred containers were attached to the first until a few thousand shipping containers filled the load.

The DS Denali was a big and ungainly ship which was a key player in interstellar commerce.

Fleece Newman looked at the immensity of it all. This is my ship, he thought proudly.

He looked from stem to stern, port to starboard, top to bottom, before spotting it.

A small ship, not even as big as a shuttle.

"I see a ship, looks barely larger than a lifeboat," he reported to his crew over the comm link. "What the hell is it doing all the way out here beyond the heliosphere, and how in the holy hell did it land on our ship while we were moving?"

"What can it hold—two people, four?" Major Hardy asked.

"No more than four, but probably only two. I'm guessing. It might be one. But it means that Torrent was right all along. We have an intruder.

Maybe we can just invite them in?" Fleece thought about it. Could it be that simple?

"Torrent, patch me through to the ship-wide comm, light up every speaker in every space. I want to talk to these individuals and ask them to parlay." The captain sat against the hatch and kicked back, one foot braced and the other hanging free.

"Wait a minute, Fleece," the XO interjected. "That person attacked us! Chase him off the ship, don't invite him for cocktails. By all that's holy, get him off this ship!"

"Any other opinions, people?" The captain waited an obligatory two seconds before continuing, "Patch me through, Torrent."

The captain waited, visualizing what kind of power struggle was taking place on the bridge. He tapped into the internal comm.

"Don't you dare open that channel!" Hamden screamed. Fleece thought he could hear her running. "STOP!"

"Patched through, Captain," the engineer said.

"Individual or individuals who have boarded the DS Denali, welcome. We would prefer to talk rather than take action to eject you into space. We've already dispatched a repair bot to disable your ship," the captain bluffed. "So, we're all stuck out here together. It'd be best if we talked. Where you are, there's no rations, no toilet, no joy. We'll barricade ourselves in the crew module, and you'll die out here. You can disable us, but we have independent power in the crew mod which we can use as a lifeboat. You have no options. We would be more than happy to have you as our guests, but we need to talk first."

Then they waited.

The XO returned to her seat, dejected. She put her headphones on and disappeared into modern dance music. What if they accepted? What if they rejected the proposal? No matter which decision the intruders made, only bad things could happen. What if she had to detach the command module and float into space? They'd have to call for help.

Why wait?

"Navigator! Send our position and the general distress signal to Alpha Centauri B, please. Tell them we've been boarded by hostiles and that we expect to take the command module into space. We'll be waiting for rescue. We will update when we have more information. Send that now please." Hamden was pleased with herself. The captain wasn't there, and the decision had to be made. All they had to do was hide and wait.

Volcano sent the message. It would be a month before anyone arrived, maybe even two months, but sending the message started the ball rolling. He thought it was a smart move, plus a rescue shuttle would introduce them to new people, as well as a couple of months' return trip to get acquainted and make friends. They usually had little to no interaction with people when the Denali made the cargo delivery, as the ship unloaded, then loaded back up without taking any time off.

Volcano worked up the message, set it to repeat every fifteen minutes for the next twelve hours, and fired it into space.

"Done," he reported to the XO.

Torrent cycled through the views from his repair bot. He moved it around, but it was clear that the intruders weren't in this space. They probably weren't in the next module either, but the third one contained the engine's manual cut-off switch. He rocked gently in his chair, thinking how only the worst could happen.

Major Hardy twirled her pry bar as if it were a pair of nunchakus. She spun it in front of her and to the sides, imagining beating the crap out of the intruders, listening to them beg for mercy before she had to decide what to do with them.

The repair bot was between her and the hatch, but all she had to do was kick off the deck, use an overhang as a landing point and then kick off one more time to be swinging her weapon at the intruder.

While she daydreamed about the battle, the hatch cycled and opened. Two suited figures stood beyond, both holding electrical discharge devices, the Taser-like things. Major looked at them, wondering if they were answering the captain's call or attacking. She didn't want to start the war, but then again, they already had. She yelled and launched herself upward.

The electrical arc had hit her suit before she was able to rebound from the overhang. Stunned, she slammed into it instead. The bridge crew started the countdown clock to her demise, that point when she'd run out of air.

The captain saw the attack from where he sat and immediately climbed outside, slamming the hatch and watching it cycle to the locked position. He started hiking across the top of the modules toward the intruders' ship.

The XO and navigator sat in silence, shocked expressions contorting their faces. Torrent started mumbling. They couldn't take their eyes from the video feed as the first intruder shoved past the repair bot. The second intruder stopped and looked into the lens. A rough male face. He slowly pointed to the lens, then drew a finger across his throat. He laughed and continued on his way.

The repair bot showed them walk through the module and exit on the route that would take them to the hub and into the command module.

The intruders were coming. The Denali's crew had lost their pilot, and the captain was trapped outside the ship.

"We have to do something!" the XO blurted.

Volcano crawled from his workstation and paced, keeping one eye on the engineer at the far end of the bridge. He stopped walking back and forth and strode boldly to the XO. She pulled her headphones off.

"We lock them out," he said matter-of-factly.

"What? What are you talking about?" Hamden replied, flustered, eyes darting back and forth between the monitors and the navigator.

"We can't let them get in here! Didn't you see? They mean to kill us!" he cried in disbelief at the situation in which they found themselves. He looked to Torrent, who was still mumbling, but his fingers were flying around his console. "Good! Somebody's doing something!"

The XO pulled herself into the walkway, and together, she and Volcano approached the engineer's work station. They peered in through the bars surrounding the gimbaled chair and monitors.

"They're coming, but slowly, deliberately. I have the repair bot following them. It looks like they're studying the ship as they go, talking. I can see them. If we could only tap their channel. Volcano, can you find them? It would be nice to know what they're saying."

The navigator jogged up the curving walkway to his station and jumped in, finding a frequency search routine and running it using the electronics suite of the ship, the same system they used to communicate between the suits and the bridge.

Volcano found them almost immediately as there weren't any ambient signals to dig through. He could hear them talking, but couldn't understand the language they were speaking. He had the standard Google conglomerate real-time translation software installed, but it didn't recognize the language of the intruders. He patched the comm signal to the others.

"What the hell language is that?" the XO asked, panic raising her voice.

"I don't know. I'm sorry, Torrent, I wish I could be of more help. Tell me what I can do?" Volcano said into the intercom that they used to speak to each other while strapped into their own seats.

"Look at them! Not a care in the world. What about Major. How is she?" Torrent wondered. He changed a monitor to the aft view as the repair bot went through the hatch into the next module. They could see the floating pilot, and then she disappeared as the hatch closed.

Torrent quickly reran the aft video feed.

A light.

"Did you see that? A light! Her suit still has power, which means her air feed is functioning!" Torrent exclaimed, smiling.

"The intruders are between her and us. What can we do?" the XO lamented.

Volcano started to get angry. The more they sat and watched, the closer the intruders came to entering the command module. The navigator reached into the XO's workstation and grabbed her collar, his lip curled into a snarl.

"Fleece here, I've reached their ship and am trying to get on board now. Is anybody there?" the call came clearly through the sound system. The XO looked dumbly at one of her monitors.

Volcano reached through and tapped a button. "It's great to hear your voice, Captain. Major is only stunned; her suit is still functioning. We thought we'd lost you both. What do you want us to do?"

"Where's Hamden?"

The XO remained silent, eyes unfocused. Volcano looked to the next console where Torrent worked feverishly, fingers jabbing and stabbing as he programmed while looking from one monitor to the next. Volcano had hoped that the young man would see what a take-charge kind of guy the navigator was.

Torrent wasn't seeing anything. He was the only one actually doing something. Besides the captain, but what was the captain doing?

"She's right here but occupied at the moment. Torrent is engineering something, but I'm not sure what it is. What are you doing?" Volcano asked.

There was a long pause, maybe two minutes, and Volcano started to worry. The intruders were in the last module before entering the access tube to the central hub of the crew module.

"Captain? The intruders are about to enter the central hub, the tool room access area. What do you want us to do?"

"I'm in their ship. It's an old shuttle. I'm familiar with the design. Let me pull up some information, look at the nav charts, and toggle the comm," the captain continued, talking more to himself than the bridge crew. "There we go!"

There we go what? Vesuvius thought.

"Intruders on the DS Denali. I'm disappointed that you chose to fight instead of talk. I am on your ship, powering it up. When you enter the access tube, I will crash the ship into it. You and I will then drift off into deep space. I suspect I have more air on board your ship than you do in your suits. I think I'll probably be able to get back to the Denali where I know you won't. Care to talk now, assholes?" the captain said over the intruders' frequency.

The repair bot showed them stopping. Neither spoke, as no sound came over the channel. They started gesturing to each other, which made as much sense as their language. At least they seemed to have understood the captain's message.

A gruff voice spoke in a thick accent, "You lie."

"Tell me where they are," the captain asked. "Hurry now. I need to show them my resolve." The XO finally came to life.

"In the last module before the hub," she stated, almost whispering.

"No, no, I don't," the captain immediately answered on the intruders' channel. "Climb the ladder and open the hatch. I have something to show you."

The intruders looked at each other until the first one started climbing. The second one moved to the far hatch, the one that gave access to the hub. He waited until the first one reached the top, then they activated the hatches at the same time.

"Captain! One is going into the tube while the other is coming out of the hatch in the ceiling," Volcano called since the XO seemed paralyzed with indecision.

"Ha!" Torrent yelled triumphantly as firefighting foam filled the access tube and secured the hatches at either end. The intruder started beating on the panel that activated the door, then pulled on it, fruitlessly trying to get it open.

The second intruder popped the hatch, and it slid aside. As he lifted his head and shoulders out of the hatch, the shuttle slid smoothly forward as the thrusters engaged. The shuttle's prow caught the intruder mid-bicep and sheered the man in half as the weight of the shuttle kept it moving past the opening. The captain stopped the small ship and moved it away from the Denali where he could see the results.

The upper body of the intruder, trailing a few bubbles of blood and gore, floated slowly into space. The lower half was shoved back through the opening and was probably near the ceiling within the module.

The XO gasped when the view from the repair bot showed half a body thrown back through the ceiling hatch. The other man continued to pound on the panel, unaware that he was alone.

"That was it for my plan. What's happening inside the module?" the captain asked.

Volcano gave up on Hamden Cray and moved quickly to the engineering station. He leaned in and rested a hand comfortably on Torrent's shoulder. The engineer looked up, smiling, before returning his attention to the console.

"The access to the hub is blocked by firefighting foam. It'll be a few minutes before it breaks down enough that the hatches will open. The man is beating on the hatch. He looks pissed!" Torrent reported.

"Then what?" the captain asked.

"I don't know," Torrent said, flustered, in his mind seeing the captain shaking his head, hearing his brother telling him, you're not an engineer. As if a switch had been thrown, the joy on his face was now frozen into an expression of failure.

"Intruder," the captain said over their comm channel. "Why don't you take a look over your head."

The captain couldn't see the man's reaction, but the crew on the bridge could. He pushed off the floor toward the body, catching it as he continued into the ceiling. His cries of anguish flooded the channel. Finally, after he finished sobbing, he said clearly, "Ugana, ugana," a word in his language, then he switched to English. "My wife. I will kill you all for this. When the others come, you will die."

The captain checked the navigation screen of the shuttle. A larger ship was inbound, although still a ways off. The sensor suite of the Denali would not pick it up. It was running silent, but the plot was updating within the shuttle to keep the conspirators apprised of the mother ship's status.

So that's how a shuttle came to be out here on its own. Cast a wide net and see what you catch, huh, the captain thought.

"We've created a martyr. No!" Hamden Cray called and buried her face in her hands. "No one should have to lose their wife. My God! You cut his wife in half? What kind of monster are you?" The XO broke down and sobbed in sympathy with the intruder.

"Torrent, I need you to program the repair bot to rip that man's space suit. You'll have to bypass the safety protocols, just like I expect you did with the foam. Good work there, by the way, now, get on it. I'm fresh out of ways to kill this man."

"Murderer!" the XO yelled and started mashing buttons on her console.

Volcano cocked his head, recognizing that she had crossed over from sanity. He kept his hand warmly on Torrent's shoulder; the engineer had yet to do anything with the repair bot.

The intruder gently put the bottom half of his wife's body into a nook and started hammering away at the access panel.

"Torrent? Please do as the captain asks. If we can shred his suit now, then we can end this, find Major Hardy and make sure that she's okay.

Only then can we go home. Wouldn't you like to go home, Torrent?" Volcano asked, gently rubbing the young man's shoulder.

The engineer nodded without saying anything and started working the buttons. Volcano watched the video feed and saw the man turn from the recalcitrant hatch and storm across the module. He raised his device and electrical current shot into the repair bot, killing the unit and the only way they had to know what the man was doing.

"What happened," Major whispered into her helmet. Her comm system shared it with the others.

"You were zapped. But that doesn't matter right now. I need you to flip the kill switch so we can restart the engines. Can you do that for me, Hardy?" the captain said, encouraging his pilot to give him a new option. "Torrent, can you get pressure in that module, so when the ship moves, he'll get sucked out?"

"It wasn't meant to be pressurized, but there are air systems that flow through the module. I can shunt piping, but..." Torrent pulled up a systems diagram and looked it over. He touched the images of the pressurized piping. It wasn't breathable air, but a nitrogen gas mix, used in a couple of the sub-systems.

It didn't need to be air.

A klaxon sounded, and red lights started flashing.

"What's going on? What are you doing?" the captain asked of the bridge crew.

"I kill you all!" the intruder screamed over his channel.

Volcano ran to the XO, who blocked him with an arm, so he jumped into the captain's seat and started cycling through ship systems.

"STOP!" he yelled when he discovered that the XO was well through the command module separation checklist. She was going to eject the doughnut from the ship, stranding the captain, the pilot, and the intruder. Volcano used the captain's override and canceled the procedure.

"You!" the XO accused, leaning from her console and glaring at Volcano. She climbed out and stormed to the captain's seat. She balled a fist and jabbed at the navigator.

He blocked the clumsy blow and pushed her away, trying to climb out where he'd be at less of a disadvantage. He'd never been in a fight before and was terrified.

"Flipping the switch," Major reported.

"Start the engines!" the captain ordered as he set the shuttle on the outside of the module and activated the magnetic grapples.

Volcano and Hamden were pulling on each other's collar, swinging wildly. Torrent was overriding system after system to release pressurized gas into a space where it was never intended to be released. The pilot was in a module, hell and gone from the pilot's console on the bridge. And the captain was trapped on the intruders' shuttle, unable to do anything else for the Denali.

The captain fumed as the engines weren't starting and the intruder was doing unknown things to his ship, possibly even breaching the command module.

"Hamden? Torrent?" Major Hardy called. "Are you there?"

The captain listened in, at a loss as to what else to say to motivate his crew to follow his orders. He couldn't help but remember the words from his father, the man he idolized.

We killed them, son. We killed them all because if we didn't, the sons or the daughters would grow up and come after us. We wanted to end it. We had to end it, the old man repeated.

He'd never understood exactly what his father was saying until now. Fleece was now a killer, but he'd left one alive and could see where he'd lose the rest of his people and his ship because of it. But Fleece had killed the man's wife; of course he was going to be enraged. Martyr, the XO had called the man.

But you could have talked! This isn't on me, it's on you! he thought, rationalizing it in his own mind. It sounded logical, but why did he feel so bad?

They chose this.

"I'm on my way. I'm useless in here, so time to move," the pilot said as she walked as quickly as her magnetic boots allowed. She had recovered her pry bar and carried it in one hand. Activate the hatch, look quickly and duck backward. Then continue through and keep moving forward.

"Yes!" Torrent called out as his system's console blinked red, showing pressurized nitrogen escaping into the module.

"Major Hardy? Did you call me?" the engineer asked.

"Yes, Torrent. I don't know what's going on up there, but I need you to start the engines and goose the ship forward. Can you do that for me? Just send it on whatever heading we last had," Hardy told him.

He brought up a mirror of the pilot's screen. It was complicated. He needed a minute to orient himself.

The tube status started flashing green. The hatch release was imminent. They assumed the intruder was there, waiting, ready to rush into the hub.

"Tube is cleared!" Torrent called to anyone and everyone listening.

The captain had not taken his helmet off even though he had pressurized the shuttle with breathable air. He vented the air, jumped from the pilot seat, and headed for the hatch.

The pilot cleared the second module and opened the hatch to the third, the place where they had first encountered the intruders. She expected the remaining man to be in the fourth. Hardy's desire was to catch him as he came through the hatch, so she could pound him with her pry bar before he could use his Taser-like device on her.

She hurried. There was too much not happening for her to be comfortable. Her head hurt and body ached, but she pushed that aside.

Volcano had the XO pinned, and with both hands tangled in her short hair, he tried to pound her head against the deck, but she fought like a wildcat. He'd never imagined a person could be like this. She bucked and twisted, and the best he could do was keep her from getting up. Stalemate. He hoped that she ran out of energy before he did.

The echoes of weapons fire smashed into Hardy's hearing, overwhelming her senses, building and spawning more pain in her head. But there wasn't any weapons fire. What was she hearing?

The sound of the engines reverberated through the ship. Major Hardy held a hand over the panel to open the hatch.

The captain thought he felt the engines surge to life. He was certain that his magnetic boots would not hold him when the ship surged forward. He returned to the shuttle, throwing himself through the small hatch.

The tube light stopped flashing and showed a steady green. Torrent didn't see it as he continued to study the pilot's screen.

He reached out a hand, his finger hovering over a button. He closed his eyes, hoping it was the right one.

The hatch slid open, and the intruder looked down the tube. He released his boots and pushed off, thinking he'd fly head first in, but the pressure pulled him back and toward the hatch.

The engineer touched the button, and the ship leaped. He was compressed into his seat as the ship was subjected to five gees of thrust. Hamden and Volcano were thrown down the walkway, tumbling and falling as the rotation of the hub kept them outboard until they slammed into the hatch at the far end. The world pinwheeled and Volcano thought darkness would seize him.

The XO moaned as her twisted body was jammed tightly against the bulkhead.

Major Hardy was thrown sideways and slammed against an inner framework that contained power conduits and piping. She stayed there, unable to move. "Torrent," she gasped. "That's enough, buddy. Look for the acceleration curve and dial it back until you get to zero."

The captain felt the shuttle shudder under the stress. He worried that the clamps on the old ship would fail and he'd be floating in space if it survived bouncing off the many things that projected from the DS Denali.

The nitrogen had already been streaming from the hatch, but when the ship moved, it was joined by half a body, then a man in a spacesuit, flailing his arms as he tried to grab onto something, anything. The ship quickly passed him, and he bounced from projection to projection.

At five gees, the ship quickly left his battered and lifeless body behind.

Torrent completed the maneuver, and the ship coasted as the engines returned to an idle status.

The pressure lifted from them all. Volcano slid to the deck, the XO at his side.

The captain opened the shuttle while tethered to the inside. When he was certain his boots would hold, he released the tether and walked painfully slowly to the hatch. Once through, he shut it. The pressure built quickly. He could feel it against his suit.

"Depressurize the module, if you would, Torrent." The squeezing stopped where it was and tapered off gently.

Torrent leaned back in his seat and breathed a sigh of relief.

"You saved the ship, Torrent. You saved our lives," the captain told his engineer. The pilot and the navigator cheered. The XO retreated to a safe place deep in her own mind.

Author Craig Martelle

Craig is an Amazon bestselling author and writes the Free Trader series (a cat and his human minions fight to bring peace to humanity), the Cygnus Space Opera series, the End Times Alaska series, and the Terry Henry Walton Chronicles, co-written with Michael Anderle. See more at www.craigmartelle.com where you can find all of Craig's publications and join his newsletter to get the latest updates and sales.

Self-Perspective

By Amy DuBoff

First

I wake up on a reclined pedestal chair. My surroundings remind me of a dentist's office, straddling professionalism and comfort. Recollections of getting tune-ups on my braces bring an ache to my teeth, and I bolt from the chair.

It's eerily quiet. *Where is everyone? And where am I?*

A rifle is leaning against the wall next to the door. I ignore it, opting to venture into the hallway.

The corridor is illuminated with a harsh fluorescent glare that makes my skin crawl. I stride toward the metal door twenty feet to my left, passing by white, featureless walls.

The handleless door is solid steel, flanked by a card reader.

I try pushing on the door, but it doesn't budge. Locked, or it swings inward. Turning my attention to the card reader, I feel along my pockets, hoping there's a keycard stashed away. Nothing.

There has to be a way out.

Overcome by a strange compulsion, I rip the card reader from its holdings. Wires spill out from the wall. Without conscious thought, I begin rearranging the wires connected to the control chip. A beep sounds from the dangling internal speaker and the door opens toward me.

Daylight streams through the doorway. I step through.

The Expanding Universe: Volume 2

My breath catches as I take in the world outside. A defunct suburban neighborhood surrounds me, lawns overgrown and cars abandoned in the middle of streets. The modest houses are dark, and the paint is peeling from exposure to the elements without upkeep.

I step forward to get a better vantage of the building where I woke up. The white concrete structure is a single story and occupies an entire square block, but there's no sign. The exit door swings shut and locks with a click.

Taking a slow breath to steel myself, I venture into the neighborhood.

Under other circumstances, it would have been a beautiful day. The sun warms my back as I meander down the center of the street looking for any sign of life. Not even a bird is visible and the hum of cicadas is absent, adding to my concern.

My path takes me along a curving street. As I round a bend, the street terminates in a cul-de-sac. I turn around to try another route, but the whine of flexing hinges freezes me in my tracks.

I snap to attention. The sound came from the house at the back left of the dead-end.

Heart racing, I spin toward the house. The front door stands open, framing a woman in the doorway.

She steps forward, her pink cardigan fluttering in the breeze.

"Hello!" I call out, jogging over to her. "What is this place?"

The woman stops at the edge of her yard. She tilts her head, evaluating. "Would you shoot me?"

My breath catches in my throat. "What?"

"Would you shoot me dead?" she asks, her eyes narrow.

"No!" I exclaim. *Is she crazy?*

She shakes her head. "You should." The woman raises her arm parallel to the ground, miming a gun with her hand. She points it toward me. "Bang, bang."

Everything goes black.

Second

The Expanding Universe: Volume 2

You wake up in a reclined pedestal chair. The room looks to be part of a medical facility, but the potted plant in the corner indicates it must be a nice one. The place is familiar, but you feel anxious.

"Hello?" you call out, but there's no answer.

You rise from the chair.

As you get up, you notice a rifle is leaning against the wall next to the door. You pause to examine the weapon, but leave it in place. The eerie quiet of the building has you on edge as you hurry into the hallway.

The corridor is illuminated with fluorescent lights that don't at all fit with the appearance of the previous room. Eager to get out of the sterile hall, you head toward the metal door twenty feet to your left.

There's no handle on the door. You try pushing it, but the solid steel doesn't budge. After a moment, you notice a card reader next to the door. You feel along your pockets, hoping to find a keycard, but there's nothing.

As you stare with consternation at the card reader, you start to envision a network of wires and electronic chips. Components illuminate in your mind, playing out steps for how to dismantle the device.

You rip the card reader from its holdings on the wall. Following the images in your mind, you begin reconnecting the wires to the control chip. A beep sounds from the dangling internal speaker and the door opens inward.

Daylight streams through the doorway and you breathe in fresh air. You step outside.

The world sprawling before you is a defunct suburban neighborhood. Weeds have overtaken the lawns, and a layer of grime covers the cars left abandoned in the middle of streets. The single-story houses lack any signs of life, curtains drawn and exterior paint peeling from prolonged exposure to the elements.

You step forward and look back at the building where you woke up. The white concrete structure is a single story, though you can see the edge of a fence topped with razor wire set back from the edge of the roof. The building fills a whole square block and seems completely out of place. There's no sign anywhere. You can't shake the feeling like you're missing something.

The exit door swings shut and locks with a click.

With nowhere else to go, you venture into the neighborhood.

The sun warms your back as you creep down the center of the street looking for any clue about where you are. It's far too quiet. Not even a bird or a cicada is around.

Your path leads you along a curving street. As you round a bend, the street terminates in a cul-de-sac.

The whine of flexing hinges freezes you in your tracks.

You snap to attention. Heart racing, you spin toward the source of the sound—a house at the back left of the street.

The front door of the house stands open, framing a woman in the doorway. She steps forward, her pink cardigan fluttering in the breeze. She holds it closed with one hand, the other hand remaining behind her back.

You're on edge. Something tells you she can't be trusted. "Who are you?" you call out to her.

The woman stops at the border of her lawn and the sidewalk. She tilts her head, examining you from head to toe. "Would you shoot me?"

You're caught off-guard by the question. "What?"

"Would you shoot me dead?" she repeats, malice in her gaze.

Now you wish you'd taken that rifle. "Stay away from me."

The woman shakes her head as she pulls her hand from behind her back. She points a handgun toward your head. "Bang, bang."

Everything goes black.

Third

Charlie wakes up in a reclined pedestal chair. The room is lined with cabinets and open shelves that contain stainless steel tools and biometric monitoring equipment. A potted plant in the corner brings a measure of comfort to the otherwise inhospitable place.

"Is anyone there?" Charlie calls out.

When there's no answer, Charlie rises from the chair.

Charlie heads toward the door and notices a rifle is propped against the wall. Taking a weapon seems like a good idea, given the unknown circumstances, so Charlie picks it up. The place is entirely too quiet and still. Charlie rushes into the hallway, weapon in hand.

The corridor is illuminated with outdated fluorescent lighting, casting a jarring blue glow down the featureless white hallway. A metal door at the end of the hall and accompanying card reader offer the only escape route.

There's no handle on the door. Charlie instinctively yanks the card reader from the wall and begins manipulating the internal wires with expert precision. After two minutes of tinkering, a beep sounds from the dangling internal speaker. The door opens inward.

Light streams through the doorway and a gust of fresh air fills the hall. The breeze is dry and carries a faint scent of dust that suggests a dirty air filtered. Charlie steps outside.

A desolate suburban neighborhood fans out before Charlie. Yards are overgrown with weeds and grass stands a foot tall in front of dilapidated houses. Cars are abandoned in the street, providing possible cover for a stealthy assailant. The dust in the wind has left a layer of grime over the unsettling ghost town.

Charlie steps forward from the white concrete structure. Though there's no sign, it's clear the structure is fortified. The main story is windowless and the roof is protected by a secure fence. However, it's unclear whether the chain-link and razor wire are to keep someone out or in.

The exit door swings shut and locks with a click.

Outward is the only option, so Charlie heads into the neighborhood, walking down the center of the street. The bright light overhead beneath the slightly shimmering sky casts long shadows across the landscape. Charlie keeps a watchful eye for any movement or sign of life. No bird calls or cicadas may mean danger lurks nearby.

The street winds through the neighborhood, passing by the houses that seem more like empty shells. Eventually, the meandering street terminates in a cul-de-sac. Charlie sighs and turns to find another path.

The sound of creaking hinges breaks the silence.

Charlie snaps to attention, pulse spiking. The creak came from a house at the back left of the dead-end street.

The front door of the house stands open, framing a woman in the doorway. She steps forward, her pink cardigan fluttering in the breeze. She holds it closed with one hand, the other hand concealing something behind her back.

Charlie raises the rifle. "Stop. Who are you?"

The woman halts at the edge of her yard. She looks Charlie over. "Would you shoot me?"

Charlie's grip tightens on the rifle. "Not without reason."

"Would you shoot me dead?" the woman repeats, a sinister sneer twisting her face.

Charlie aims the rifle at her. "On the ground!"

The woman shakes her head. "Too late." She whips a rifle from behind her back and points it at Charlie. "Bang, bang."

Everything goes black.

Omniscient

Doctor Greene is transfixed by the viewing monitor. The subject's conditioning is progressing according to plan. With just one more imprinting, another perfect soldier will be born.

The monitors provide a window into the room on the other side of the wall while the subject is prepped. A neural cap is placed over the subject's head and connected to monitoring equipment. Unconsciousness has left the subject's face seemingly the image of serene bliss, but Greene knows better. The appearance of peace is only a mask to hide the emptiness within.

"Initiate the final imprinting," Greene instructs when the preparations are complete.

"Activating cognitive conditioning scenario 'Charlie,'" Doctor Marshall announces from the control station.

The subject writhes on the pedestal chair as the electrical impulses of the neural interface strip away the final layer of individual identity, leaving unquestioning loyalty and obedience in its place. Though difficult to watch at first, Greene is used to witnessing the transformation. After all, it is a far better use of criminals than all the resources needed to support life imprisonment. Rehabilitation at its finest.

When the procedure concludes, the neural cap automatically retracts into the ceiling.

"Wake up, Charlie," Greene says into a microphone.

The subject's eyes open, and Charlie rises from the chair—driven by the newly imprinted imperative to eliminate any threats.

Charlie strides toward the door, only pausing to grab the rifle before heading straight to the exit at the end of the hall.

Greene watches with satisfaction as Charlie wretches the keycard reader from the wall and manipulates the wires with programmed precision. As soon as the latch clicks open, Charlie readies the rifle and steps outside.

Hidden cameras follow Charlie's progress through the training course inside the space station's secondary biodome that had been staged as an abandoned neighborhood from Old Earth. It's an ideal testing ground for new Peacekeepers like the latest Charlie soldier, enabling a controlled performance evaluation prior to being shipped off to the once-quiet towns on distant colony worlds that had become battlefields filled with enemies.

Charlie keeps a vigilant eye on the darkened houses and empty cars. The territory is supposed to be secure. Any trespassers must be one of the enemy.

The residential street terminates in a cul-de-sac. Charlie is about to turn around when the scenario's housewife stand-in, Rebecca, emerges from one of the houses right on cue.

Without hesitation, Charlie points the rifle at the woman. "You don't belong here. Surrender."

Rebecca tilts her head, her empty hands hanging at her sides. "Would you shoot me?"

"Surrender now," Charlie instructs.

"No."

"You were warned." Charlie pulls the trigger.

A concussive bang echoes across the barren pavement.

Rebecca remains standing, unphased by the blank shot. A smile spreads across her face, mirroring Greene's expression in the control room. "You're ready."

Author Amy DuBoff

Amy DuBoff has always loved science fiction in all its forms, including books, movies, shows, and games. After beginning her creative writing studies at the Vancouver School of Arts and Academics, she went on to receive a Bachelor of Science degree in Psychology with a minor in Professional Writing from Portland State University. Amy primarily writes space-based science fiction and science-fantasy. She is currently publishing the Cadicle space opera series and has had a short story featured in an anthology by NewCon Press. When she's not writing, she enjoys travel, wine tasting, binge-watching TV series, and playing epic strategy board games.

Check out Amy's other books on Amazon and sign up for her author newsletter to get a free short story!

Peyton's Legacy
By S.M. Schmitz

Chapter 1

Cambria. Twenty years after the arrival of the Thieves of Peace

Jenna gently touched the panel on the outside of her home to open the front door. She cringed as it hissed and slid into the wall. Her father would most likely sleep through her knocking down the damn door, but her mother had an uncanny sixth sense for knowing exactly when she was attempting to sneak back inside the house.

All of the lights were off so she pulled off her shoes and crept toward her bedroom. She'd made it eight feet when her mother's voice stopped her.

"Again, Jenna?" Zoe demanded.

Jenna jumped and dropped one of her shoes.

"Mom…" She trailed off because there was nothing she could say now to pacify her mother.

Zoe slapped a different panel on the wall and lights flickered on overhead.

"I've told you that joining your father's Security Forces is out of the question!" Zoe yelled.

"*You* did it!" Jenna yelled back.

"I didn't have a choice," Zoe argued. "There were fewer of us and…"

Jenna grunted at her and rolled her eyes. Sometimes, talking to her mother made her feel like the teenager she still was.

"Mom, we can't keep pretending they'll leave us alone. The invaders that got stuck here have gone through their stockpile of bodies and if we don't find and kill them first, they'll start hunting."

"And your father's sending out forces to look for them. You're barely nineteen!"

A shuffling in the hallway prevented Jenna from arguing with her mother about whether or not she was old enough to join her father's Security Forces. She understood why *both* of her parents kept insisting she couldn't. They'd lost almost everyone they loved in the initial invasions, and they sure as hell didn't want to lose their daughter now.

But her mother's legacy on this planet was an impossible shadow for her to step out of.

And her father's legacy continued on in her. *Something* compelled her to continually defy the parents she idolized, and she suspected it was just as much genetics as the stories neither of them liked to discuss.

Peyton stood at the end of the hallway, yawning and rubbing a hand over his face as he glanced between his wife and daughter.

"Again?" he asked.

Zoe pointed to Jenna and said, "Told you she takes after you. She's just as stubborn."

Peyton snickered and nodded toward Jenna. "And who's helping you train this time?"

"Who do you think?" Zoe interrupted. "The same boy I told you to fire *last* time."

"Mom!" Jenna shouted. "What's the harm in Branson teaching me anything if you never let me out of this village?"

Peyton yawned again and waved a hand toward the panel for the lights. "Come back to bed, Zoe. I'll never authorize her participation on any missions to search for the remaining thieves of peace so she's right: It doesn't matter if she's every bit the badass you were."

Zoe arched an eyebrow at him and folded her arms over her chest. "*Were*?" she challenged.

Peyton smiled at her and challenged back, "Ok, Mrs. Arren. Prove me wrong."

Jenna groaned and mumbled, "I'm taking my chances with the thieves of peace."

"*You're* going to bed," Zoe ordered. "And we'll discuss your sneaking out again in the morning."

Jenna sighed heavily and stomped past both of her parents. Her mother had once told her that on her home planet, Earth, they had doors that swung outward so they could be slammed when the moment called for it.

This was definitely a moment that called for it.

But her ridiculously practical Cambrian door slid into the wall and was completely automated.

She had nothing to slam.

Instead, she pulled off her jacket and threw it in the corner of her room then collapsed on her bed, staring at the boring ecru ceiling above her. She loved the stories her mother told her about Earth where homes were constructed in different colors and shapes, and humans were ruled by their passions and innate curiosity. Cambrians, like her father, were always so *logical*, which was why she knew she'd never convince him to allow her to join his Security Forces.

But twenty years ago, Cambria had been invaded by a nightmarish species hell-bent on eradicating every intelligent living creature on each planet they could find. They came suddenly, viciously, and stole the peace from her planet.

And then they took her mother's planet from her, too.

The invaders' voracious appetites not only made them ruthless killers but hungry ones, and everyone on Cambria knew the peace on their planet was once again threatened because the thieves of peace had exhausted their supply of preserved Cambrian bodies.

And the thieves of peace were hungry.

Chapter 2

A soft tapping at her window woke her from a disturbing dream in which tall figures in white armor with deep, guttural laughs pursued her through an abandoned city. Jenna slowly placed herself as her eyes adjusted to the darkness of her bedroom. The tapping on her window startled her again, and she finally sat up and rubbed her eyes then quietly pressed the control panel on the wall that raised the window covering so she could peek outside.

Branson's handsome face peered back at her. He waved a hand, beckoning her to go outside and meet him. She nodded at him and let the window covering slide back into place. She didn't dare turn any lights on. Her mother's remarkable ability to sense when she was breaking a rule would likely kick in, and she'd get busted before she could even discover why Branson had shown up in the middle of the night.

She pulled her long, dark hair into a ponytail and crept into the hallway. Her shoes still lay on the floor where she'd dropped them when she'd attempted to sneak in so she picked them up and carried them to her front door. Jenna took a deep breath before placing her palm on the panel to open the door. If her mother woke up now, she'd likely never leave this house again. She wasn't sure *how* her mom would keep her confined here forever, but most people on Cambria revered her mother. Even Cambria's leader, Jeffrey, revered her. If Zoe insisted that everyone help her in ensuring some sort of permanent grounding for her daughter, Jenna was confident they'd all help.

The cold, night air stung as she stepped outside. She pulled her shoes on and heard Branson approaching as he made his way around her house.

"Jenna," he whispered. "Come with me to the field."

"Why?" she whispered back.

"You'll see," he said.

Jenna glanced over her shoulder at her home one last time then nodded toward him. Her mother had once made the mistake of telling her that at eighteen, humans had been considered legal adults in her old country on Earth. But not on Cambria. Here, where humans and Cambrians had been attempting to recover from a genocide that had nearly wiped out both of their species, over-protectiveness had reached epic proportions. Jenna wouldn't be considered a legal adult for six more years.

Branson took off his jacket and handed it to her since hers remained crumpled in the corner of her room. She slipped it on then followed him into the field at the edge of their village. With the moonlight covering the empty expanse, she could make out the silhouettes of seven people, huddled together to keep warm. Branson smiled and told her, "Let's hope the reason your parents earned their reputations is genetic."

Jenna narrowed her eyes at the small group and snapped, "What is *that* supposed to mean?"

"It means," Branson answered, "that you're finally about to get your wish."

Jenna slowed down and blinked at him, but he grabbed her hand and spoke quickly before she could turn around and head back home.

"Isn't this what you wanted?" he asked. "A chance to eradicate them from our planet once and for all? Your dad will *never* agree to let you come with us, and you're not the only one who's too young anyway but is still more than capable of fighting the thieves of peace."

Jenna hated it when he talked to her that way, like she was a child. At twenty-five, Branson was an adult, but her ridiculous crush combined with his continual treatment of her as a prodigy and nothing more made her feel like she *was* just a child.

"So you've rounded up a group who wants to work for my dad but are still too young?" she asked. She looked over the dark figures waiting for them and yanked her hand free from his grasp. "Have you been *training* all of them, too?"

Branson shrugged. "Of course. But they're not *all* too young. Some just joined the Security Forces like me. Look, you know how much I respect your father. But he's being far too conservative right now. If we keep tiptoeing around the idea of hunting down the surviving invaders, they *will* come for us. I may have been young, but I remember the first invasion."

Branson's voice tightened at the mention of the initial invasion, just as everyone else's did who'd survived the initial invasion. Only he and his mother had made it off this planet when they'd attempted to escape.

Jenna shifted her weight between her feet and searched the small group waiting for them to see if she could figure out who had already agreed to participate in Branson's suicide mission to save their village from the same fate that had claimed at least two planets. "Mom and Dad fought more invaders than the rest of Cambria combined. If they're being cautious now, it's for a reason and maybe we should listen to them."

Branson sighed and stuffed his hands into his pockets. "Fine, Jenna. If you don't want to come with us, then go back home. Just don't wake them up to rat us out, okay?"

"Branson…"

Branson shook his head and stopped her. "We're not afraid to make difficult decisions, Jenna. And I'm not stupid. I know this journey might cost us our lives. We're here because we're willing to risk it in order to save over ten thousand people."

Jenna crossed her arms over her chest, vaguely aware that every time she got angry like this, she looked just like her mother and she'd been *trying* to prove she wasn't Zoe Arren for years. But at the moment, she was too pissed off by Branson's implication. "Are you calling me a *coward*?"

Branson sighed again. "Of course not. Did you know you look just like your mom when you're mad?"

Jenna grunted at him and he laughed. "What?" he protested. "It's a compliment!"

"Right," Jenna hissed. "Because you expect me to *be* her and run recklessly into dangerous situations."

"Actually, I just meant because she's so hot," Branson argued. "And she wasn't reckless. She was *brave* when no one else was willing to be."

Jenna felt her cheeks flushing and hoped the darkness would hide her embarrassment from him. He thought she was hot? And why was she fixating on *that* when the mission he'd planned meant people, some of whom were likely her friends, would soon die?

She shifted her weight again and stared at the ground. *She was* brave *when no one else was willing to be.*

An image of her younger brother, who had indigo eyes like her father and all Cambrians, surfaced and she took a deep breath. Julian had spent the night at his best friend's house and had missed her getting busted for sneaking out. Again. They were only two years apart, and they'd been inseparable for as long as Jenna could remember. He always stuck up for her, even when he secretly agreed with his parents. This would be one of those times he would defend her then as soon as they were alone, would turn around and tell her how stupid she was being.

Julian was the one who really took after their father. More Cambrian than human, he always thought through decisions carefully and never acted impulsively. Even as kids, when Jenna had wild ideas like building their own spaceship, Julian would point out all of the reasons it was a *bad* idea, even while helping her. And, of course, he'd been right: Their spaceship, which had been too small for either of them to climb in, managed to hover about six inches from the ground before catching on fire.

She felt confident that if their village was invaded now, her parents could protect them and get them to the northern city. But Julian often went to his friend's house, and it would only take one invader. Just one of those bastards reaching her village, and she could lose him forever.

Jenna raised her eyes and took another deep breath even though she knew it would burn her lungs. "Okay. When do we leave?"

Chapter 3

As early morning sunlight illuminated the world around them, Jenna caught her first glimpse of Arnvidor, a southern city her parents once explored shortly after her mother came to Cambria. It was here that Zoe had discovered cold made the invaders vulnerable to the Cambrians' weapons, which is how all of the human and Cambrian survivors had been able to live in peace for the past two decades.

Jenna had never lived anywhere warm. She wasn't even sure what it felt like to step outside and *not* need a jacket.

In only a few minutes, she would find out.

Branson leaned across her and pointed to the tall buildings ahead of them. "We've been tracking movement in every city, and *something* is congregating here. Whatever it is, they're moving out of the southern cities to came farther and farther north...which means they're moving closer and closer to *us*."

A pretty woman with light brown hair and indigo eyes, who liked to brag about being a *purebred* Cambrian, snickered and shot Branson a sly, seductive smile. "Cute, Branson. Are you trying to be gentle with her? Not scare the shit out of the kid?"

Jenna curled her fingers into tight fists and snapped, "First of all, I'm *not* a kid…"

Daria, the woman who had decided to flirt with Branson by insulting Jenna, cut her off. "According to our laws, you are. And apparently, you have your mother's temperament. I told you bringing her along would be a mistake, Branson."

Branson sighed and rubbed his eyes. "She's here *because* she's so much like her mother. Don't forget I've been training her. She's a natural."

"Training her…" Daria repeated slowly. "Is that what you're calling it now?"

"Daria," Branson groaned.

"Is that what you called it when you were *training* me?" she persisted.

Jenna felt her cheeks flushing and tossed her long, dark hair over a shoulder. "Maybe if you'd focused more on *weapons* training, you wouldn't need so much backup now from a *kid* like me," she shot back.

Branson snorted but Jenna wouldn't look at him. She wouldn't admit how jealous she was over Daria's implication that she and Branson had been lovers. He'd never even tried to kiss her or even hinted that he was attracted to her.

Maybe she *was* just a kid in his eyes.

The craft descended and Jenna focused on the city again. The early morning sun reflected off of the ecru metal of the buildings and she squinted as they landed in the center of a cluster of seemingly abandoned skyscrapers.

Her mother often warned her that appearances could be deceiving.

She would also never admit that she wished her mother were with her now.

"Keep your *torleiker* ready to fire," Branson reminded her.

Jenna nodded even though her weapon would be useless unless the invaders had taken off their armor. In the two decades since the thieves of peace first arrived, Cambrian engineers had developed *hilfleikers*, devices not much larger than her *torleiker* that could emit cold blasts of air. Engineers hoped it would weaken the invaders' armor, but it had never been tested on one before. Her parents had argued that the only way this new technology could potentially work would be to surround an invader and hit it with the frigid bursts of air. Meanwhile, everyone would have to stay out of its line of fire because it would take at least ten seconds before their bullets could penetrate its armor, and in those ten seconds, whomever was holding the *hilfleiker* would likely die. It was hardly a sustainable solution.

The door on the craft lifted and Branson waved his crew off. As Jenna attempted to disembark, he grabbed her arm and stopped her. "Stay by me," he ordered.

Jenna yanked her arm out of his grasp and scowled at him. "If you're just going to treat me like a child, why did you insist I come here?"

"Jenna," he started, but she shut him up by jumping out of the craft and joining the other crewmembers.

How *dare* he humiliate her like this?

He tried to get her attention one last time, but she wouldn't even look in his direction. She heard him sighing as he jumped out of the craft and felt his presence behind her.

"We'll stick together," he told his small crew. "Remember: Only Colson has a *hilfleiker* so we need to protect him as best as we can until he's able to weaken their armor."

Jenna snorted and rolled her eyes. "If we encounter them, we'll be dead before he can freeze their armor. Do you really think a thief of peace is just going to stand there while Colson tries to freeze it?"

"I think," Branson snapped, "that you're forgetting I'm the commanding officer here…"

"Not mine," Jenna interrupted. "I'm just a *kid*, remember? I don't work for you."

"Once again: I told you it was a mistake to bring her here," Daria mumbled.

Jenna narrowed her eyes at Daria, but Branson responded before she could defend herself. "It's too late now," he hissed. "So everyone shut up and…"

But Branson himself shut up when a hollow, metallic clanging erupted from the building in front of them.

They obviously weren't alone in Arnvidor. And the thieves of peace had found them.

Chapter 4

Jenna spun around to face the building where the sound had come from. She kept her *torleiker* ready, but unlike Nania, Arnvidor was warm and the bright sun above her even caused droplets of sweat to form along her forehead.

Branson's fingers wrapped around her arm and he pulled her back from the front of the group. She was too startled to protest.

"Colson," he whispered. "Head toward the entrance. We'll flank you."

Colson swallowed before nodding and taking his first hesitant step toward the building. The same hollow, metallic clanging stopped the small group for a second time.

Daria shot a nervous glance in Branson's direction and quietly asked, "What do you think it is?"

Jenna wanted to shout, "An invader, dumbass!" but wisely kept her mouth shut and her eyes on the door in front of her.

Branson's fingers briefly tightened around her arm before he released his grip on her. The gesture had been a small one, yet it was a betrayal of his fear for *her*. Jenna's heart raced as she imagined the invader emerging from the building, its own deadly weapon raised toward the small group, its horrifying laugh that her mother had described and had haunted her in nightmares, taunting the Cambrians who had been stupid enough to seek out the thieves of peace.

Branson had just begun to answer Daria when Jenna made an impulsive decision and acted on it.

She ran.

Branson yelled her name, but the doors to the skyscraper opened as she neared them then swallowed her inside. She skidded on the slick floor as she stopped suddenly, her eyes slowly adjusting to the dim interior of the building. She slapped the control panel on the wall to lock the doors just as the footsteps of the other crewmembers reached her.

When the doors didn't open, Branson screamed, "Damn it, Jenna! Open the door! You're going to get killed!"

She already knew that, of course.

But she'd realized too late that her mother had been right…as usual.

This was a suicide mission taken up by a bunch of arrogant kids, and it wouldn't even make her brother and village safer because, ultimately, they couldn't defeat the thieves of peace.

And she wanted Branson to live.

"Where are you, asshole?" she yelled to the seemingly empty building.

Branson and the others beat on the door behind her so she called over her shoulder, "Get on the craft and go back home!"

"No!" Branson called back, but an odd hiccupping sound answered her as well.

She knew exactly what that sound was even though she'd never encountered an invader before.

Jenna licked her lips, feeling trapped in one of her own nightmares, but she didn't open the door. She wouldn't back down.

That hiccupping laughter was joined by the sound of heavy footsteps as a tall figure covered in heavy white armor stepped beneath the clear dome of the skyscraper, the only source of light inside the building. Jenna's stomach rolled as she took in the appearance of a thief of peace for the first time.

It tilted its head, apparently studying the young woman who had been stupid enough to enter its building. She knew it was only her imagination, but she thought this invader looked hungry even though she couldn't see its face beneath the armor.

It took a step closer to her so Jenna stepped back until her body was pressed against the metallic ecru door. She swallowed and lowered her *torleiker*.

"All alone?" she asked. "Not surprisingly, even your own kind don't like you."

The thief of peace tilted its head and for an excruciatingly long moment, she was answered with silence before the monster let out another round of that odd, hiccupping laughter. It lifted its hand and pointed one long finger toward the floor above them. On the walkway overlooking the lobby stood a second thief of peace.

"Oh," Jenna breathed. She had no idea how many more were in her new tomb.

Her mind raced with every story her mother had ever told her about defeating an invader by either crushing it or luring it into the cold so she could penetrate its armor. Her options were extremely limited, especially since she couldn't outrun them.

She scanned the room as the pounding on the door continued.

"Branson, for God's sake, go *home*!" she yelled.

"Open the door *now*, Jenna!" he yelled back.

She thought she heard Daria tell him, "Maybe we should leave. She's already dead."

Another round of banging and screaming at the door followed.

"I'm so sorry, Mom," Jenna whispered.

And then she ran again.

The hallway on her left was filled with gray shadows that seemed to come alive as she approached them. She imagined those sleek, gray shapes morphing into tall white figures with long, curved fingers that grabbed at her as she passed.

Behind her, she could hear the heavy boots of the invaders as they pursued her. Jenna threw her shoulder into a control panel on the right, and the door to the office slid open. She darted inside and slapped the panel to close the door behind her just as the thief of peace that had been closer caught up to her. It stuck its arm into the narrow opening and began pushing the door back into the wall.

Since she was only half Cambrian, she lacked the superior strength her father possessed. Even then, he'd told her no Cambrian could match an invader's strength, and humans were hopelessly out-powered. So what chance did a halfling like her have against one of these bastards? But she had to try something. Her mother would have known what to do, and she would have succeeded.

Jenna ran her fingers through her long, dark hair as she looked around the room, her gaze finally settling on a thin device atop the desk. She'd only seen one of them in what served as a sort of shrine in Nania, a monument to their stolen past. Supposedly, at one time, it had broadcast people's voices and images so they could talk to anyone on the planet that had a receiver. But it caught her attention because of what she remembered about it: The gas inside the tube that projected the person's image was remarkably cold.

Jenna snatched the projector from the desk and squinted at it, allowing herself a brief second to wonder how she was supposed to break the damn thing open before settling on an admittedly risky plan. She twirled around and swung it at the invader's arm, which had just pushed the door back inside the wall. The metal tube in her hands connected with its armor but nothing happened. Of course, she hadn't expected anything to happen, and that's why she needed to piss it off.

The thief of peace looked down at its arm as if surprised by this creature's stupidity then laughed again.

Jenna lifted the projector and swung it at the invader's head. The thief of peace laughed louder and reached over to her, yanking the projector from her hands and snapping it in half.

Jenna smiled at the thief of peace and said, "Thanks," as the yellow, vaporous cloud surrounded its arm. She lifted her *torleiker* and fired.

The invader screamed in response—probably as much from anger as for being shot in the arm. But Jenna pulled the trigger again just as she heard the heavy footsteps of the second invader running down the hallway.

She needed a place to hide or a way out of this room.

She threw her weight into the body of the surprised thief of peace to force it back into the hallway then hit the control panel for the door again. She fired at its frozen arm one last time, and as the door hissed closed, the invader screeched in frustrated fury.

"Be glad I'm not my mother, asshole!" she yelled.

It yelled back at her, but whatever it said, she was pretty sure it wasn't, "You're kind of a badass, too."

Jenna twisted around and pushed the desk in front of the door. The two invaders could easily knock the door down, and as the edge of the desk bumped against the wall and door, they began beating on it, causing large dents in the thick, sturdy, ecru metal.

Her only possible escape now was through the window.

Was it really only the previous night that Branson had stood outside her own window at home, begging her to meet him outside where he convinced her to come to Arnvidor? And she'd listened…partly because of her love for her brother, but truthfully, her love for Branson had played just as great a part in her reckless decision.

She ran her fingers along the seam of the window until she felt the button to release it. Like the door, it hissed back into a slat in the wall, and she lifted herself onto the ledge as the door shattered open behind her. She rolled onto the ground while above her, the bullets from the invaders' guns whirred past her.

"Oh, come on! Aren't you bastards out of bullets yet?" she shouted. "It's been *twenty years*!"

"Jenna!" Branson yelled from the front of the building.

In her haste to get out of that room, she'd forgotten the others were still outside and her plan to buy them time to escape would be ruined as soon as they heard her.

But it was too late now. Branson and his carefully selected group of young soldiers, two of whom weren't adults yet either and were her friends, darted around the corner of the building. He fell to his knees by her side and grabbed her arm, both checking her for injuries and trying to pull her away from the open window. Inside the office, she could hear the invaders pushing the desk out of their way so they could follow her.

Jenna scrambled to her feet, and the Cambrian group ran to a nearby building. More bullets whirred past them as the invaders reached the open window. Pressed against the wall of a different skyscraper, she listened as the invaders climbed through the window, but to her horror, that wasn't the only sound she heard now. The noise had obviously attracted attention, and more thieves of peace were coming.

"What are we going to do?" Colson whispered.

"We're going to fight back," Jenna answered.

"How?" Daria asked. "They're in the process of *surrounding* us right now!"

"Well, Colson has the *hilfleiker*. I guess it's time we see if it works," Jenna suggested.

"You just said it won't work," Daria hissed.

"Look," Jenna hissed back. "Do you want to stand there arguing with me and die right away or at least *try* to defend ourselves and have a miniscule chance of getting out of Arnvidor?"

"I'm voting for the miniscule chance of getting out of Arnvidor," Colson supplied helpfully.

"Colson, we *need* you to be able to keep that blast on one of them for at least a few seconds," Jenna instructed. "Mom always said ten, but she was dependent on cold air, not concentrated gasses that could freeze their armor almost instantaneously."

"Technically," Branson interjected, "we're freezing the gel beneath the armor, not the armor itself."

"Are you kidding me right now?" Jenna asked.

Branson smiled sheepishly at her and shrugged. "Sorry. I'm Cambrian. I can't seem to help it."

Jenna shook her head at him and addressed Colson again. "The gas inside the projector tube only needed a couple of seconds before I was able to penetrate one of the invader's armor, and I think the gas that powers the *hilfleiker* is similar. I thought we'd all get slaughtered because of how *long* it would take, but if we can make them vulnerable that quickly, we *might* have a shot of getting out of this."

"Okay," Branson agreed. "Tell us exactly what you want us to do."

"Branson!" Daria seethed, pushing his shoulder as she scowled at him, but Branson grabbed her wrist and moved her away from him.

"I'm putting Jenna in charge. I told you: She's just like her mom. And what one of us wouldn't follow Mrs. Arren anywhere?"

Jenna felt her cheeks warm, and she bit her lip as she turned her back to him so he wouldn't see her sudden embarrassment.

She'd lived her entire life under her mother's shadow, hearing the comparisons at first about her beauty then her intellect and feisty temper…and finally, her remarkable ability to pick up on her father's career. It had been *his* legacy she'd chased—the man who had become one of the youngest Security Chiefs in Cambrian history, the man who still held the survivors' complete respect.

But standing outside an abandoned building in a mostly empty city just like her mother had twenty years before, she realized what she'd wanted all along wasn't Peyton's Legacy but her mother's. Zoe Pembroke Arren was the most remarkable woman she'd ever known, and if people saw her mother in her, then it was time for her to prove she deserved to follow in her mother's footsteps.

And *when* she returned to Nania, she'd beg for her forgiveness: Not just for today but for a lifetime of insisting she didn't want the legacy her mother had bestowed on her.

Jenna inched closer to the corner of the building where she'd last heard the invaders' footsteps. They'd stopped as they got near the Cambrians' voices, most likely waiting to see who would make the first move. She waved a hand for Colson to join her then leaned close to his ear to whisper, "On the count of three, we're both spinning around the corner and firing at whichever one is closest to us so you need to judge that distance quickly. Understand?"

Colson licked his lips nervously but nodded, his finger twitching over the trigger of his *hilfleiker*. "One…" Jenna mouthed. "Two…three."

She spun around the protective edge of the building and quickly aimed at the closest invader. A bright blue streak of gas expelled quickly from the *hilfleiker* and as soon as it touched the invader's armor, Jenna fired. The first bullet ricocheted off its armor and bounced off the ecru metal of the building, but Jenna fired again.

And this time, the bullet dented the chest plate.

She squeezed the trigger one more time before pulling Colson behind the wall with her as the other invaders returned fire. But the clanking metallic *thump* that quickly followed assured her that one of those bastards was dead.

She and the other Cambrians might have a chance of survival, after all.

Branson leaned closer to her and whispered, "I think there's at least six of them. And we only have one *hilfleiker*."

Jenna wanted to tell him he really should have planned better, but they'd most likely had to "borrow" the only weapon capable of freezing the invaders' armor. "They're approaching from both sides," she added. "They're going to trap us between these buildings."

"Yeah," Branson sighed. "God, Jenna…I am *so* sorry."

Jenna blinked at him then asked, "Why are you apologizing to me? For talking me into coming here?"

Branson ran his fingers through his light brown hair and sighed again. "Yeah, because…well, you know. You're the *last* person I wanted this to happen to. I just thought…"

Jenna inhaled sharply but it wasn't from Branson's almost-pronouncement of his feelings for her.

She'd heard an approaching aircraft.

And she had a sickening premonition as to who was on board.

"Never mind," she groaned. "The invaders aren't going to kill me. *They* are."

She pointed to the craft descending in the nearby square and Branson groaned, too. "We are *definitely* all dead."

The arrival of more Cambrians had at least halted the invaders' advance on the young soldiers hiding between the buildings. Jenna kept her attention on the craft, holding her breath as the door opened, hoping she was *wrong* about who would jump out of the small craft, but of course she wasn't.

"Mom," she breathed.

Her father quickly followed his wife onto the ground, carrying another *hilfleiker* in his hands. Zoe quickly looked around the city—maybe it was her keen sense of observation or just a mother's intuition, but it didn't take long for her to find Jenna cowering against the side of the building. And it didn't take long for her to raise her own *torleiker* and direct Peyton to start firing at the thieves of peace who were trying to kill her daughter.

"We need to help them!" Branson yelled. "Colson, get out there. Jenna, go with him. You're our best sharpshooter!"

Jenna *heard* him, but her feet remained planted, her attention riveted to her mother who moved with the agility of a woman half her age, whose aim was *always* precise, and whose expression defied both her fear and her anger.

"Jenna, *now*!" Branson shouted. "Your parents need our help!"

Two more of her father's crew jumped from the craft and immediately opened fire on the invaders descending upon the square in the city. They seemed to be leaking from the walls of the buildings themselves. Not even in her nightmares could she have envisioned this scenario, this apocalypse she'd willingly walked into. Worse, she'd dragged her parents into it with her.

One of the invaders leapt from the rooftop of a short building and fired at Zoe, grazing her shoulder and sending her spiraling back into Peyton's chest.

"Mom!" she shrieked.

Whatever spell she'd been under since realizing her parents had been forced to come to her rescue, and could *die* because of her, broke. For the third time that day, she disobeyed Branson's orders and ran away from him. But her mother had been *shot*. And all she could think was, *"Please don't leave me. I can't lose you."*

Peyton helped his wife back onto her feet and Zoe didn't even look at Jenna. She immediately raised her *torleiker* again and fired at the invaders behind her daughter, providing a distraction so the young woman could reach her parents. Jenna almost tumbled into her as she reached them, but Zoe just nodded toward the thieves of peace and ordered, "Take the group on the right. Lance has a *hilfleiker* and will freeze their armor for you."

Unlike her hesitation with Branson's orders, Jenna immediately obeyed her mother. All she *wanted* to do was pull the jacket off her mom and figure out how bad the injury was. She could see her own mother's dark blood pooling at the shoulder and dripping down the sleeve and her stomach heaved, threatening to empty itself over and over again until her own organs might accompany it, but she *had* to make her mother proud. She had to save her.

Jenna raised her *torleiker* and fired, but it was like the Gates of Hell had been thrown open and the demons within were pouring out. The small gold cross her mother had given her, one of the few relics she had from Earth, felt heavier against her chest as she watched the city flood with the dirty white armor of a horde of monsters who were ready for a fresh feast.

"Mom..." Jenna whimpered nervously.

"I know, Jenna. Just keep firing."

Lance turned the arctic blast onto another invader, but they'd never be able to keep up with the influx. The six invaders Branson had guessed were surrounding them had multiplied into over a hundred thieves of peace.

And then a memory snuck through her mind of a ten-year-old girl sitting cross-legged with her mother on their floor at home playing *torrach* and as Jenna tossed a chip onto the pile, Zoe sighed and shook her head. "I never liked this game."

"Then why do you play it?" she asked.

Zoe smiled at her and kissed her forehead. "Because you ask me to."

"Mom?" Zoe looked up at her from her pile of chips and smiled at her again. "Everyone talks about how you killed the thieves of peace. How you saved Cambria. *How*?"

"Jenna..."

"I want to know. You said you'd tell me when I'm older. I'm old enough now."

"You'll have nightmares."

"I already have nightmares," Jenna pointed out.

Zoe sighed and tossed her chip back onto her pile. "There aren't many ways to kill them. They're stronger and faster than us, even Cambrians, and their armor is virtually impenetrable. There's really nothing so brilliant about me, and I wish people would stop talking about me like I'm some sort of saint."

"You are," Jenna interrupted.

Zoe smiled sadly and shook her head. "I'm not. I got lucky far too many times. That's all. You already know we stay up north where it's cold because they can't survive in the cold and it weakens their armor. The gel between their bodies and the armor itself freezes pretty easily and forms crystals in the gel that gets in between the molecules of the armors' material. Once that gel freezes, it weakens the structural integrity of whatever that material is and our guns can penetrate it."

"How else? That seems like a slow way to kill invaders."

"It is," Zoe agreed. "The only other way I've been able to kill one is by crushing it with something extremely heavy. Even their armor has its limitations."

"Too bad we don't have random heavy objects floating above us all the time," Jenna responded.

Zoe laughed and finally selected the *torrach* chip she wanted to play.

"Mom," Jenna warned, "play that and I'll win. I'm starting to think you lose on purpose."

"I never lose on purpose," Zoe said. "You should know that about me by now."

You never lose at all, Mom. Because you saved us all.

The memory faded as quickly as it had arrived, but for once, Jenna had an idea before her mother. "We need to get everyone back on the crafts!" she yelled.

"What for?" Peyton asked. "If we try to leave, they'll just pursue us. I can *hear* their ships powering up!"

"Then move faster," Jenna insisted. "Because we're bringing the whole damn city down on them."

Chapter 5

"There are eight people trapped between those buildings," Zoe pointed out. "How are we supposed to get them to their craft?"

"We don't," Jenna responded. "We get their craft to *them*."

"Have I told you lately you gave birth to a clone?" Peyton asked Zoe.

"Not now," Zoe groaned.

"Mom, we need to get you to a doctor. Stop arguing with me, and just help me get to Branson's craft. I'll fly it over to them."

Her mother opened her mouth to argue with her anyway, but to

Jenna's surprise, she closed it again and nodded. "Okay, Jenna. Your father and I will get you there. Lance and Corinne, try to keep the invaders away from the alley where those kids are hiding."

Zoe didn't wait for a response from either soldier. She nudged Jenna with her arm to get her moving toward the craft they'd need to rescue Branson's crew. Another bullet whirred past her, perilously close to her face, and Zoe pushed her forward, urging her to run faster. Jenna already knew her parents intended to hang back to provide her with better coverage.

"I swear to God, if you stop, I will, too!" Jenna threatened.

"Jenna, just *go*!" Zoe yelled.

Jenna tossed her hair over her shoulder and shot her mother a defiant look. Since she'd had to stop running because of her mother's stubborn insistence to be the sacrifice her daughter needed, Zoe immediately relented just to get her running again.

The aircraft was only fifty yards away now.

She'd covered most of the distance when she heard a man's voice cry out in pain…but not just *any* man's voice. She'd heard her father.

Jenna spun around and noticed her parents had dropped back after all—that's how she'd gotten so far so quickly. Zoe dropped to the ground by her husband's side and glanced over her shoulder. "Jenna, get on the goddamn craft!"

"No," she whispered, but her legs began to carry her anyway as she watched her mother drag Peyton behind an abandoned storage room. Soon, she lost sight of them altogether.

Her back bumped into the aircraft and her fingers groped for the release that would open the door. She couldn't force her eyes away from the bloodstain on the grass.

As the door slid open, she tumbled back into the craft and pulled her legs in before the invaders could reach her. Blinking away tears, she threw herself into the pilot's seat and powered up the aircraft.

"I murdered them," she whispered to herself.

Something hot trickled down her cheeks as she yanked on the lever to bring the craft into the air. Outside, she could hear the *plink, plink, plink* as the invaders' bullets ricocheted from the side of the craft. She was far from the best pilot, but after a few false—and jerky—attempts to get the craft turned around so she could rescue Branson and his crew, she managed to land it next to the alleyway where he and Colson held their positions.

As the young soldiers scrambled inside, Jenna kept shouting, "*Hurry!* My parents are *trapped!*"

She didn't tell anyone she didn't even know if they were still alive.

Branson jumped over the passenger seat beside her and nodded toward the controls. "Let me fly. I'll get you as close to their position as I can. Colson will help you find them and get them on board."

He must have noticed she was still crying—they *all* must have noticed—but no one called her a child, not even Daria.

"I'll help her," Daria offered.

Jenna wiped her eyes, but she still couldn't see. Daria's features blurred every time she blinked at her.

"Your mother's my idol, Jenna," Daria said. "I'll help you find her."

Jenna closed her eyes briefly and took a ragged breath. "She's mine, too."

"They're behind the storage building," Branson announced. "It looks like Lance and Corinne have joined them."

Jenna grabbed her *torleiker* and insisted, "Get me on the ground."

"Jenna…" he said softly, but Jenna didn't want to hear his excuses.

"Have faith in me, Branson," she pleaded.

Branson held her gaze for a few agonizingly long seconds before lowering the craft to the ground. Daria was by her side to leap from the craft with her as soon as they could open the door.

Colson wormed his way around both women and reminded them *he* needed to disembark first so he could freeze the armor of any invader they encountered. Jenna nodded, but in her mind, she continued to will the door to open faster. She'd been unable to tell from the air if her parents were alive.

Colson fired the *hilfleiker* while jumping to the ground, which warned both Daria and Jenna that an invader must be extremely close. Daria fired in the same direction and called over her shoulder, "Find your parents! We'll hold them!"

Jenna didn't need a second invitation to save two of the people she loved most. She sprinted around the craft toward the storage building and fell beside her father's body. Her mother kept her back pressed against the building, her left arm, the one that had been shot, held across her stomach. But her eyes were open, watching her.

"Oh, God, Mom..." Jenna's hands hovered over her father, but she didn't want to touch him. She *couldn't*. If she reached out to feel his skin and it returned the cold fingers of death, she would never be able to climb back on that aircraft, knowing she'd been responsible for what lay before her now.

"He's alive," her mother breathed. "But we need to get him back to Nania as soon as possible. He's lost a lot of blood."

"You have, too, Zoe," Corinne said.

Zoe used her uninjured arm to wave her off. "I'm fine."

Corinne rolled her eyes and gently reprimanded her. "You haven't changed at all."

"Why should I?" Zoe teased. "You don't mess with perfection."

"Colson, you need to provide cover for Jenna to fire back. Daria, I'll need your help carrying Peyton to the craft," Lance instructed.

Daria had already slung her *torleiker* over her shoulder to help lift her father from the ground. His eyelids fluttered briefly then closed again, and Jenna's heart threatened to burst open. Her hand instinctively raised to her throat where she fished the thin, golden chain out from beneath her shirt, letting her fingers trace the fine links until they found what she'd been searching for: the small cross at the end.

She didn't know if she really shared her mother's faith, this remnant from a human past that few people who had been born on Cambria had adopted, no matter what their parents had once believed or what faith they still held. But on her thirteenth birthday, her mother had given her the same necklace she'd been given by *her* mother at thirteen, and Jenna had worn it ever since.

Now, watching Lance put his arms beneath her father's body to lift him from the ground, she did something she'd never done before: She prayed.

"Jenna, three on our right!" Colson yelled.

His voice broke her from her silent plea on her father's behalf. She aimed at the invaders approaching from their east just as Lance and Daria reached the small gap between the building and the door to the aircraft. They would have to carry a badly injured man almost six feet through an open space being overrun with the thieves of peace.

Colson bit his lip, his eyes quickly flickering between Peyton and Jenna, then sucked in a short breath. "We'll get them on board. On my count, Jenna."

"Colson," Jenna whispered.

"One…"

"Colson, wait!" she begged.

"Two…"

"Please," she whimpered.

"Three!"

Colson stepped into the open space and Lance and Daria ran. Behind them, Corinne practically dragged Zoe with her, her grip tightening as she reached the empty space.

Bullets seemed to rain on them from everywhere. Jenna fired at anything that moved in white, but the inevitable, the sacrifice she *knew* was coming, came swiftly and mercilessly.

Colson's body crumpled to the ground as bullets continued to pelt it. Jenna leapt toward the open door, and four strong hands grabbed her suit and pulled her inside, but the young man who had offered his life to save her parents would be lost to them forever.

The aircraft lifted into the air, and as Jenna crawled to her father's side, she called out to Branson, "Strafe any structure that might collapse. The *only* way to kill these assholes is to bury them. We're going to bury Arnvidor once and for all."

Branson looked over his shoulder at her, his beautiful indigo eyes wide and wet, and inhaled a deep breath. "Are you all right?"

Jenna gently touched her father's hand then leaned down to kiss his forehead. "I don't know yet."

Branson turned around in his seat and let his hand hover over the weapons' panel. "Don't worry, Jenna. This city will never rise again."

Chapter 6

Jenna placed the vase filled with silver flowers on the table beside her father's bed and kissed his head. His eyes opened and he smiled at her then lifted a hand to point toward the bouquet she'd brought him. "You know your mother's going to steal those."

"Hey," Zoe retorted, "I don't steal from invalids."

"I'm not an invalid," Peyton pointed out. "Just stuck in this hospital bed for the past week."

"Close enough," Zoe teased.

Jenna shuffled her weight nervously because for the past week, she and her mother had been so preoccupied with Peyton's survival and recuperation, no one had even mentioned how she'd stupidly endangered them all by disobeying them. Even Julian hadn't mentioned it, and she desperately wanted *someone* to tell her how selfish she'd been, how irresponsible, how unlike the parents' whose name she'd inherited.

She didn't deserve to carry their name.

"Jenna," Zoe said, forcing her to look up from the toes of her shoes, "let's go get breakfast. Your father was up half the night, and he needs to rest."

Jenna let her eyes fall back to her shoes instead of focusing on the sling around her mother's arm and nodded. Outside in the hallway, her mother's best friend, Mia, a woman who was like an aunt to her, passed by Peyton's room and pointed to the closed door. "Does he need more pain medicine?" Mia asked.

Jenna flinched but couldn't look at Mia either. She already knew how much pain her father had been in for the past week, even though he never complained in front of her.

"No," Zoe assured her. "He's just tired. We're going to let him sleep."

Zoe put her right hand on Jenna's back and encouraged her to keep walking. But they didn't stop at the café in the lobby of the hospital as Jenna had anticipated. Her mother led her to the front doors and into the warm sunshine of a cool, Nania morning.

And still, Zoe didn't speak.

Through the neatly constructed paths of their growing village, mother and daughter wound their way to the edge of the buildings, to where Nania met the empty countryside of Cambria. The same field where she'd picked the flowers for her father and where she'd met Branson's crew on that disastrous night stretched before her. In the distance, she heard a *vartrilla* screaming as it flitted from treetop to treetop.

"This is where it all started for me, Jenna," Zoe said.

Jenna had gotten so used to the silence that her mother's voice startled her.

"Where you landed," Jenna clarified.

"No," Zoe explained. "Where I first realized I'd never be able to stop loving your father."

"Oh," Jenna whispered.

Shame consumed her again and hot tears welled in her eyes.

"My little girl," Zoe sighed. "Look at me."

Her mother slipped her hand beneath Jenna's chin to encourage her to look at her then her fingers gently wiped her cheeks. "Do you really think I don't know exactly why you followed Branson that day, even when you *knew* it could be disastrous?"

An ugly, painful sob exploded from her chest and Zoe pulled her daughter closer, wrapping her good arm around her tightly. "You love him and you trusted him. And he's a good kid, Jenna. He made a terrible mistake that cost another good kid his life. But that doesn't make *any* of you bad people. Your father would have had to fire him if he hadn't resigned, but we don't dislike him. And we won't blame anyone for what happened. It's time to stop beating yourself up over this mistake."

Jenna shook her head against her mother's shoulder and exclaimed, "My *mistake* almost got you both killed! You only went to Arnvidor because of *me*! If I'd just said no, you would've stayed here."

"I would have," Zoe agreed. "But not your father. Zoe, it's his *job*."

"But you were protecting *me*," Jenna insisted.

"Of course we were. That's *our* job."

"Mom," Jenna sobbed, "if he'd died…how could you not hate me?"

"Oh, Jenna," Zoe sighed. She smoothed her daughter's hair and kissed her temple before stepping back from her, forcing her daughter to look at her once more. "I have traveled across this universe twice, and there is *nothing* anywhere in this vast space that could ever make me hate you. I spent a long time hating myself for the mistakes I made though, and I don't want you to suffer like I did."

A tearful, airy laugh escaped because *surely* her mom was only trying to make her feel better. "I seriously doubt *you* made mistakes that were even remotely on the same level as this."

Zoe arched an eyebrow at her and the corner of her lips turned up in a half smile. "Have I ever told you about how I broke it off with your father and why and what I did because I was hurting and couldn't cope with the pain of losing my friends and family and planet…and he sure as Hell didn't help things? And then to find some new purpose in life, I decided to work for him because part of me didn't care anymore if I even lived?"

Jenna blinked at her mother because her entire life, her parents had exhibited the kind of love most people couldn't hope to find. And they'd *broken up*? Worse still, she hadn't cared about surviving? She was the woman the entire village celebrated. She was Nania's savior.

Zoe laughed and pointed to the soft, lush grass of Nania's field. "Have a seat, Jenna. And let me tell you the story of how your father and I almost lost each other and how we found each other again."

Author S.M. Schmitz

S.M. Schmitz is a USA Today Bestselling Author and has an M.A. in modern European history. She is a former world history instructor who now writes novels filled with mythology and fantasy and, sometimes, aliens.

Her stories are infused with the same humorous sarcasm that she employed frequently in the classroom, and as a native of Louisiana, she sets many of her scenes here. Like Dietrich in Resurrected, she is convinced Louisiana has been cursed with mosquitoes much like Biblical Egypt with its locusts.

Start at the beginning of Zoe's story with *The Cambria Code* trilogy, available now on Amazon and other retailers. Sign up for S.M. Schmitz's newsletter by going to her website, www.smschmitz.com, and receive a free copy of her post-apocalyptic novella, *The Scavengers.*

Cassowary Raid: A Chancerian Story
By Drew Avera

Bootheels clacked against the deck as swift feet careened towards the bridge of the *Cassowary*. Thirty-seven continuous days in utter darkness had taken its toll on the green crew, and here they were, thrust into another fucking battle simulation. Tom Krylex wiped a bead of sweat from his brow as he rounded the corner of the passageway and leaped over one of forty-two knee-knockers spread throughout the ship. It was a dated design used on fleet ships that once sailed the rough seas of Earth; that was a long time ago and in an almost-forgotten section of the Milky Way Galaxy. The fact they still designed ships with them said more about the flaws of humanity than it did the miraculous achievement of mankind's finally making it off the rocky world they once called home. Humans were scattered now, delving deeper into darkness only to find the universe was filled with more mysteries at every turn. No mystery was harder to solve than the question of why we are here and what we are supposed to do next.

"It's about time," the Chief of the Boat snarled as Tom finally made it to the bridge. He looked around, panting for air. The captain sat, impatiently drumming his fingers on the armrest of his chair while other members of the crew seemingly refused to make eye contact with Tom. *I deserve that*, he thought as he moved to his battle station. He felt out of place and could hardly muster a response as to his tardiness. There was no real excuse. If this was a real-life event, Tom could be the reason the ship was destroyed. His job was, no shit, a matter of life and death.

"I'm sorry, Chief," he said meekly.

Chief Werner didn't cast another glance in his direction but instead turned to the captain. "All present and accounted for, sir."

"Very well, proceed with the drill," Captain Olafssen ordered.

Tom took his place at the console, sitting in his chair and pulling the shoulder straps over his body and clasping them into place. His screen was already illuminated for the drill and all he had to do with scroll his hands across the console and monitor the weapon stations. The monitor was designed to use imagery from the sensory array to show him what targets were within the kill zone. But during simulation, all the targets were computer-generated. That didn't mean, however, that he could sit back and not worry about the incoming threat they were simulating battle with. Tom had already fucked up the last drill, and if he wanted to have time off in the port coming up, he would have to impress the captain.

"Incoming at two o'clock," Tom said. The computerized target was closing in on them at a quick pace but was still not within the kill zone. "I can't get a lock on the target, Sir. It's out of range."

"Keep tracking it," the captain said.

Tom kept trying to get a lock on the target, every few seconds clicking over the target with the cursor, but each time he was given an advisory that the target was out of range. "Dammit," Tom whispered under his breath. *This is not how I was hoping things would go today*. On the screen, the computerized target launched a sequence of three torpedoes towards the ship one second apart, which would give their PDCs a harder time at knocking them out. *That's the point, though. Don't make things easy on us*.

"Torpedoes fired," Lieutenant Junior Grade Benson said from across the bridge. Her announcement reminded Tom that he was supposed to be the one tracking the incoming bombardment. *Damn*.

"Are our PDCs online?" The Chief asked as he stalked behind Tom with his arms behind his back and a scowl on his face. Most people would think he was pissed, but Tom just expected the look ninety percent of the time.

Tom turned around and nodded, "yes, chief," he replied. "I turned them on as soon as I saw the target," he finished.

The chief leaned down, his nose inches away from Tom's. "Then why aren't they firing?"

Tom turned his head to the monitor, and his heart sank as he realized the Point Defense Countermeasures were not online. "I—"

"I, nothing," the chief said. "Fucking fix it."

Tom scrambled to figure out what was wrong. The screen showed the PDCs as options, but they were all blacked out. "It's like they're not getting power, but that's impossible," he said, the statement bringing a thought to mind. "Wait." He looked down at the kick panel under his monitor and cycled the circuit breakers for his station. One by one the PDCs illuminated, showing that they were now online. "Got it, Chief."

Chief Werner crossed his arms and grunted. Tom figured that was the best he was going to get in terms of an Atta Boy, but it was better than nothing. *What can I expect? These guys have high expectations and low tolerances for bullshit.*

As the ship veered to port, her weapons stations pointed towards the holographic display of an incoming vessel, the *Cassowary* lurched. "What the hell was that?" Captain Olafssen barked. In every corner of the bridge, fingers danced along the consoles, bringing up display screens to show what was outside of the ship that could have struck it. Every screen showed empty space except one, which displayed the grim profile of the holographic ship used for their drill.

"That's not supposed to be there, Ivanov said under his breath. "Sir, we paused the drill to do a perimeter scan, but the hologram is still showing up on our starboard side from two different sensor arrays. If it were just one, I would think it was a glitch, but I don't know how both sensors could detect the same thing…"

"Unless it was really there," Chief Werner finished. "Sir, I think we have a problem."

As the chief's words fell from his lips, a torpedo launched from the belly of the holographic ship, but this time the realness of the vessel was evident. The PDCs came to life, their report causing the deck beneath their feet to vibrate. The sensation crept up their bodies, making their teeth rattle. The close proximity of the vessel gave few opportunities to evade the warhead's concussion as it exploded less than thirty meters from the hull of the *Cassowary*. The detonation made the lights on the ship flicker, and it was clear by the now dim lighting that the emergency generators had come online.

"Primary power is offline, Captain," Ivanov said.

"What systems have we lost?" he replied.

The young man scrolled through the bank of screens, taking notes on the screen. "Offensive weapons are down, point defense countermeasures are down, primary drives are degraded, and comms are down sir," Ivanov said.

"What the hell? Get damage control on it. Chief, contact security and have them standby in case this ship tries to take advantage of us."

"Aye, sir," Chief Werner said as he stepped off the bridge and disappeared down the narrow, dark passageway.

"The rest of you," Captain Olafssen said. "Do whatever you can to restore some functionality to this ship. I don't care what parameters you have to bypass—get it done. We can always correct deficiencies later."

A chorus of "Aye, sir" sounded on the bridge as the small crew began working. Tom kept an eye on the monitor and noted the ship drifting towards the *Cassowary*. There was nothing they could do to evade with the primary drive degraded and all necessary power being routed to life support, but if nothing else, he knew he could monitor the situation and hope he could restore the PDCs before they were able to breach the ship.

"Any idea who that is?" Captain Olafssen asked Tom.

"No, sir, but I can try to search the hull number in the database. We still have our ship's server functional."

"Do it. Any information we can use is helpful," the older man said, not bothering to mask his weariness.

Tom's search took only moments. "That hull number corresponds to a ship called the *Liminality*," he said, "It used to be a frigate, but based on the number of weapon mounts I see on the image, I would say she was heavily modified, sir."

"I agree. It's definitely pirates, and this group is damned good. Keep working on the PDCs. If we have to, we will light their asses on fire at close proximity. It might burn a hole in our hull, but we can seal off the starboard side if we have to. These bastards aren't taking my ship."

"Yes, sir," Tom replied. His heart raced as he went back to work because the name of the ship was familiar to him. *Liminality* was a name he'd heard since he was six years old and his mother dragged him kicking and screaming away from his father. The terror in her eyes as his father said he would find and kill her still haunted Tom to this day. As did the memory of what happened next. *My father is on that ship*, he thought, *and there's no way I'm letting him take the* Cass.

He fumbled with the circuit breakers, pulling them out and pushing them in one at a time, but each time the circuit failed to come online. "Damn," he hissed under his breath. He felt the seconds ticking loudly in his mind, and each time he failed, he looked back at the monitor as the *Liminality* slowly drifted closer. It was only ten meters out when Chief Werner returned.

"Security is standing by, sir."

"Very well. Based on their position, I think they will be breaching us from the aft airlock near the cargo hold. Have a team assemble there," the captain ordered. "Have two armed men stationed here when you return, Chief. I want to seal off the bridge in case they make it through our small force."

"Aye, sir," Chief Werner said as he wiped sweat from his brow and ran back down the darkened passageway.

"Where are we on system repairs?" Olafssen asked as he paced behind the crew on the bridge.

"Everything is still down or degraded, sir," Ivanov replied. "Honestly, I think we have a better chance of getting the drive online with a hard reset, but that will leave us without electrical power and life support for five minutes."

Captain Olafssen wrinkled his nose and shook his head. "That ship will be here in five minutes. Is there another way, Ivanov?"

Ivanov shrugged. "Reboot and skip the startup checks, but if anything is out of parameters, then we risk causing an emergency shutdown, which the computers control. We would be dead in the dark until we could troubleshoot the issue."

Olafssen nodded. "It's a risk we will have to take. I want to outrun these bastards if I don't have the weapons to light them up. We know who they are so we can come back for them later. Get on it."

"Aye, sir," Ivanov said, the look of dread on his face telling Tom the man did not like the prospect of what the was about to do, but it was an order and arguing it would waste more time. They could only hope the drive rebooted without any damage.

With nothing more he could do, Tom leaned back in his seat as the primary drive shut down, causing even the dim emergency lighting to go out momentarily. Tom had counted three breaths before the sound of power coursing through the ship returned with flickering lights coming back to life.

"Thirty seconds and we should have power to the drive, sir."

"Very well, everyone, get strapped in," Captain Olafssen said as he grabbed the ship's comm, trying to speak into it, but realized that the comms were down. He released it and let it dangle as he pulled his shoulder straps over his body before grabbing hold of it again.

Chief Werner returned with two armed guards as the primary drive restored power to the rest of the bridge. "The security force is waiting at the airlock, sir."

Captain Olafssen nodded. "Let's hope they won't be necessary. Murphee, get us out of here."

"Aye, sir," Ensign Murphee said, taking hold of the controls and shifting them forward. The ship lurched, sending everyone back to their seats. Chief Werner and the two security men braced themselves against the bulkhead, the grim look of straining to maintain consciousness on their faces.

The *Cassowary* pushed forward, but the drives were not fully-functional, and the speeds were only one-thirds of what they were capable of. *At least we're moving*, Tom thought, hoping his anxiety would fall away as they escaped the grip of the *Liminality*. But the pirate ship followed, blasting magnetic grappling cables towards the *Cassowary* that were more typically used for salvaging dead vessels in space.

One of them latched onto the *Cass*, causing it to drag the *Liminality* behind it.

"Shake them off," Captain Olafssen shouted.

The ship banked hard left into a roll, and the standing crew members on the bridge grabbed the consoles nearest them. Tom strained to maintain his balance and to keep from falling out of his seat while papers and supplies clattered to the deck. *I should've strapped in like the captain said*, he thought as he pulled one shoulder harness over himself, buckling it into place.

"Maintain our position," the captain ordered. When Tom looked at him, he could see the redness of the captain's face growing bolder. He could only imagine the stress the old man was under to cause his face to flush in such a deep hue. "We're not going to let them take us, understand?"

There were only a few grunts of acknowledgment to what the captain said. Tom pulled the other shoulder strap over his body and buckled it into place, then focused on the task at hand: getting the PDCs back online and functional. "Come on, come on," he whispered under his breath as his fingers scrolled across the screen. "Why the fuck aren't you lighting off?"

"Status report on the PDCs," Chief Werner shouted from the other side of the bridge. Tom looked over at him, his eyes wide and pleading for more time. He assumed the blank expression on his face told the chief all he needed to know, that the PDCs were still down and they were fucked. "Fix it!"

Tom nodded, sucking in a deep breath, hoping he could deliver on time. The last thing they needed was to be boarded by a pirate vessel.

"Chief," the captain said as he gripped the armrest of his chair in his right hand. "How in the hell did we get into this situation? This is supposed to be a training mission preceding our rendezvous with *Victronas III*. No one was supposed to know we were out here, much less pirates."

"I have no idea, sir," Werner replied. "But we're going to get the better of them, sir. You can bet your life on that."

Tom winced at the chief's choice of words

On the screen, the crew watched as the pirate ship drew closer. Without PDCs, the *Cassowary* was vulnerable to the well-armed vessel. The small security force stationed in the cargo bay was their last line of defense if the *Cass* could not break free from their hold.

"Increase speed," the captain said to Murphee.

"I have her opened all the way up, sir. I'm just not able to get the drive to engage properly. This is the best we can do." Fear dripped from the ensign's voice as he spoke. Fueling the desperation, Tom felt as the enemy closed in.

"What's the status on my PDCs?"

"Still down, sir," Tom replied, bringing his hand to the console to continue his attempt to reset the circuit breakers and hope for the best. It didn't work.

"Damn it to hell," Chief Werner snapped. "Let me try." Werner shoved Tom out of the way and knelt onto the deck and ran his hands over the circuit breaker panel. He pulled each one out and pushed it back in after counting to three. Tom watched curiously, hoping it would work, but knowing if it did that it would make him look bad in front of the captain. He knew there were more important things at stake at the moment as he peered back at the screen and their coming death. "Fuck," Werner said under his breath as both men looked at the monitor and saw the PDCs still did not register on the display.

"I'm sorry, Chief," Tom said, slightly relieved the problem didn't lie with him but still feeling the burden of failure.

"Keep trying, son."

"Roger that," Tom replied as he sat back in his seat and fumbled with the breakers.

As he looked away, the ship pitched nose down, causing him to slide out of his seat and slam onto the deck, hitting his forehead on the console hard enough to cause a knot to form right away.

"Status?" Olafssen shouted.

"They detonated a torpedo outside of our aft airlock, and they knocked out our drive, sir," Murphee said. "We lost thrust and are only traveling forward based on our momentum. The harder they try to reel us in, the slower we will get until it is too late."

"Chief, lock down the bridge," Captain Olafssen ordered.

"Aye, sir," Werner replied, nodding to the two security personnel standing by the door. The two men closed off the space and typed in a security code that would not allow it to be opened unless the captain overrode the code.

The sense of confinement made Tom nervous. Knowing he was sealed in a room with no way of escaping made him nauseous even more than the idea his ship was about to be boarded by men intent on killing them. *Maybe it's a fact I can't do anything about either situation, and the confinement feels more immediate.*

"Murphee, try to roll out and bank to the port side. Maybe we can break free from them," Captain Olafssen said, crossing his arms and staring at the screen.

Murphee acted on the order, but the frown on his face let everyone know it was futile. "Sir, the thrusters aren't providing enough torque to break free."

Olafssen rose from his seat and paced the room. Each step sounded to Tom like his heart thudding as the pirate vessel closed in. "I can't believe I'm saying this, but this fight cannot be won using the ship. Everything is down, and the only way to win is to hope our armed forces in the cargo bay can stand up to them." The sound of defeat in his voice increased the heavy shadow over the already diminished morale on the bridge.

As the *Liminality* drew closer, the nose of the ship disappeared from the screen, and the shake caused by the two ships mating to one another reverberated throughout the ship. "Standby," Chief Werner said solemnly. "We aren't giving this ship up without a fight."

The mumbling of the crew trapped on the bridge left much to be desired, Tom thought. *But what can you expect when the worst-case scenario becomes your reality?*

They waited as the pirates on the other side of the airlock prepared to breach the ship. How they went from a training mission to a full-scale assault was beyond Tom, but there he was, his heart pounding in his chest. The terrifying part of it was how and why the pirate ship looked familiar. *It can't be*, Tom thought.

"Prepare to be boarded, gentlemen," Captain Olafssen said. Tom watched as the captain paced nervously in the middle of the bridge. "Perhaps if we don't start any trouble then they'll take what they came for and leave the crew intact."

Unfortunately, if Tom's assumption was true about who the ship belonged to, then no pleasantry could protect the crew of the *Cassowary*.

The sound of gunfire outside the bridge froze Tom's blood. The muffled blasts in the door third of bodies hitting the deck made him feel as if Death was coming for him. "Do we have any means of protection in here?"

Chief Werner rested his hand on Tom's shoulder, "this is a no weapons zone," he replied. "The regulation is there to protect the captain."

Captain Olafssen scoffed. "Well, a hell of a lot of good it's doing," he snapped. "Brace the door," the captain ordered.

As two men scurried towards the door, it blasted open, sending them flying through the air, falling unconscious onto their backs.

"Hands where I can see them," a man said with his gun extended towards the group of people on the bridge. "Nobody has to get hurt, so long as we get what we're here after." He turned and nodded towards two other people standing outside the bridge. Both of them had their faces covered with masks, but Tom could see their eyes—cobalt blue like the people where he was from. That just made his heart sink further.

"So, who is the captain of this rust bucket?"

Captain Olafssen stepped forward, his hands lifted as if to show that he was not threatening. "That would be me," he answered.

Tom sat nervously as the pirate whom he thought was his father walked onto the bridge. His face was obscured, but he saw the cold, green eyes of the man he once called "Dad." "Get strapped in, gentlemen. If anyone moves, you're dead." The man's voice was low and authoritative, just as it was when he threatened to kill Tom's mother.

"What's the meaning of this?" Captain Olafssen asked. "Don't you know we're on a relief mission?"

"I did know that," the pirate said. "And that relief is coming to us." He gestured to his friends while holding his gun level to the captain's face.

"We have nothing to offer you. It's just rations for the *Victronas III*," Olafssen said.

"Well, it's your lucky day. All I want is the cargo, so if you let us have it, you get to keep your ship, you and your crew alive. If you get in my way, you'll be the first one we toss out of the airlock."

"Hello, beautiful," another man said as he entered the bridge. He had a gun in each hand, and his eyes were narrowed into slits as he stared at the trembling members of the crew. "You know, I really thought it was going to be harder to get here, but this shit just gets easier with time, I guess. Don't you think, Jon?" The sound of his father's name made Tom flinch.

"I'll say," he replied. "Come on in, boys."

Tom watched as half a dozen men entered the bridge behind their leader. His father's voice was hauntingly familiar, and it made his heart sink. He shrank back, hoping to hide behind Chief Werner, but he was noticed.

"No no," his father said. "No one moves, or I'll blow your goddamn brains out." The man tapped the barrel end of his gun against the captain's temple, taunting him. "I'd really hate to see how messy this beautiful ship will get splattered with all your blood." The other men in his company began laughing almost to the point of making Tom's stomach turn.

Tom shrunk back in fear, lowering his face and hoping the man would not recognize him after so many years. It was a long shot. Men like Jon Frater had the capability to terrify people with nothing more than a glance; for Tom, it was a lifetime of feeling afraid of his father that made him feel this way. It was a torment forged in blood, and it haunted him for as long as he could remember. He supposed he should have his mother to thing for that, but he couldn't bring himself to think like that. But other thoughts were coursing through his mind, and none of them were the kinds of thoughts that would make his captain very happy.

"We don't need any bloodshed here today, fellas," Chief Werner interjected. His response was met with a swift punch to his face, knocking him to the deck, the sound of his body slapping against the surface echoed in the room.

The laughter continued.

"Maybe it's time you guys get with the program. Shut the fuck up and give me the controls to your fucking ship. Do you understand?" Frater shifted on his feet, his weapons dangling near their holsters mockingly.

"I'm not just going to give you the controls of my ship," Captain Olafssen said.

"No?" Jon replied. "Maybe if I put a bullet in one of your sailors' heads, it will change your mind?" He pulled one of the women from the crew and pressed the barrel of his gun against her temple. She whimpered but otherwise did not make any sound. Tom suspected it was because she was afraid that the man would pull the trigger.

"There's no need for that," the captain replied. "I'll give you what you want, but please don't hurt any of my people." The old man shifted to the side, pointing towards the console where the pirates could control the ship. From Tom's perspective, it looked like they were giving up. In his experience from listening to his father's stories, that meant they were dead.

Frater approached the console and let his fingers run across the bank of screens. Tom could see what he considered a look of admiration on the older man's face, but for all, he knew it could have been lust at a big payday in the making. "Open everything and move it to the *Liminality*," he said softly. The man nearest him nodded and ran from the bridge. "The rest of us will wait for that transaction to take place and then carry on about our business. It shouldn't take more than half an hour with the anti-gravity pallets you're using. I must say the military has really invested a lot of money into resources to make your jobs easier when they should have been investing in the quality of lives for our people. I guess that makes me the hero, though." Jon smiled as though he was thinking about an inside joke that no one was in on.

"You can't get away with this," Chief Werner said, trying to step between the pirate and the captain. "Do you know who you're dealing with?"

"Save it," Jon said. "The Chancerians have no legal authority in this part of the sector." He looked to the members of his crew still on the bridge and said, "Bind them up and make sure there are no weapons. I'm starting to lose faith that I can trust these people to do the right thing."

"On it," a tall man said as he stepped towards Tom. His hands dangled almost to his knees, and he appeared to walk with a hunch in his back, presumably because the overhead on ships was shorter than he was. "Hands out," he ordered.

Tom extended his bare wrist towards the man, inhaling deeply as if to try to calm himself down. "We're on a relief mission. This isn't necessary," he whispered.

"Shut up," the man said as he clasped Tom's wrists together. "Another word from you and we will toss your ass out of the airlock."

"Let my crew be," Captain Olafssen said. When Tom looked at him, he could see how red the man's face was, his eyes bulging with a flutter of his eyelid. It was something Tom knew only happened when the captain was stressed. He would have been more surprised if the captain didn't have the twitch.

He watched his father pistol-whip the captain's forehead, breaking the skin and causing blood to run down his face. "Didn't I tell you to shut the fuck up?"

Chief Werner stepped forward and put his hand out as if he was about the touch Jon. His action was met by two other men grabbing his arms and slamming him into the deck.

"So, Mr. Badass here wanted to do something? How about this as a fair warning? If another one of you sons of bitches approaches us, we will put a bullet in your goddamn head and then we'll start tossing you one by one out into the darkness. I told you that nobody had to get hurt. What I didn't say, however, was that I was opposed to hurting anyone. Now, behave like a good bunch of puppets, and I won't teach your government a lesson with your lives. Any questions?"

"Dad," Tom said. The word burned as it crossed his lips. He had no intention of speaking, but the dread of what was coming propelled him to do something. All eyes looked at him from both sides. All of them wide with confusion. All except Jon's.

"It's about time you spoke up, son. I was starting to think you were one of them." He lowered his mask enough for Tom to see his face and winked. It was a gesture he used to convey all kinds of messages. Unfortunately, Tom didn't know what it meant and could only assume the worst.

"It doesn't have to be this way. The crew will comply with your demands, but you need to stop assaulting and threatening them. This is a relief mission, not a police force."

Jon grinned, but it wasn't one of happiness. Tom could tell it was the precursor to violence. "It's cute that you think so, but you don't live long in this business without being prepared to do anything. The fact you think this crew is willing to comply tells me you're either naïve or stupid."

"I'm neither," Tom challenged.

"Please," Jon scoffed. "Blake, uncuff my son and give him a weapon. He can stand guard over Chief Dumbass, here."

The man Jon identified as Blake knelt next to one of the unconscious security guards on the deck and stripped his guard belt and gun from him, handing it to Tom, who took it nervously. He his time putting it on, feeling the eyes of the *Cassowary* crew stabbing at him with each passing second.

Chief Werner looked up at him, glaring with narrowed slits at his sudden betrayal. "Turncoat."

Tom wanted to plead with the man, to declare himself to not be a traitor, that he was doing this to save their lives, but he knew it would fall on deaf ears. Instead, he said nothing, resting his hand on the grip of the gun holstered at his hip.

"Captain Frater, the cargo is on the *Liminality* now, sir," a voice said over an open channel. The voice was scratchy, and Tom assumed it was because the radio frequency was weak when trying to pass through the steel bulkheads of the ship.

Jon looked at the time and smiled. "Well, twenty minutes, that's a new record."

Some of the men in his crew laughed, but the noise died as soon as their captain spoke again.

"Go to the airlock. Tom, you're coming with us," he ordered.

Tom felt the pain of regret as he realized he was damned no matter what he did. He had no reason to want to go with his father—he wanted to serve on the *Cass*—but by revealing himself, he took away any hope of having what he wanted.

"Yes, sir," he said weakly. He turned to follow the rest of the pirates off the bridge and down the darkened passageway.

Jon stopped and turned to face the crew before leaving the crew. "I appreciate your service, ladies, and gentlemen. Until we meet again." A sneer stretched across his face, and when Tom saw it, his heart sank. He had no choice but to follow his father to the airlock and leave the only people he considered family after his mother's death behind.

Standing outside the airlock, Jon and Tom waited for the pirate crew to disembark the *Cassowary,* the awkward silence was enough to drive Tom mad, but he knew that madness was already evident in the fact he revealed himself to the maniac.

"I see you took your mother's name," Jon said as they stood next to the airlock.

"Yeah," Tom replied dryly.

Jon pulled off his hood and mask and ran his hand through his raven black hair. "It suits you, I suppose. You were always such a mama's boy."

"You didn't have to kill her," Tom snapped. His response caused all eyes to look at him. The band of pirates closed in on him, but Jon waved them off.

"No? She was a threat to my legacy. Besides, she warped your mind enough to hate me, even before I had her killed. I can understand how much the past has hurt you, but I really did care about you and your mother. She just wasn't willing to let me be who I needed to be."

"And what's that, a murderer, a monster?"

Jon smiled with a wicked gleam in his eye. "A warrior for our people. A champion for our freedom. The government wants to take all of what it means to be human away from us. You can't tell me you support laws that tell you who you can marry, who you can procreate with? It's goddamned ridiculous that we have people in office who support such an agenda."

"She was right. You're too tied to your own cause to see that what they are trying to do is give everyone a better quality of life. This system cannot support the massive population that Earth homed. We have to make the necessary precautions to ensure we do not bleed the Chancerian Sector dry before we have an opportunity to expand beyond it," Tom replied as he watched his father open the airlock.

"Get in," he ordered. "In twenty seconds, we are going to open this ship to vacuum. If you want to live, you'll come with us. Otherwise..."

Tom stood, staring at the man he knew to be his father, but he did not recognize the person he once held in such high esteem. He could only see the monster his mother told him about, but he also knew that in some sick way there was a point to what his father was trying to do. Inside, he knew what they were doing was wrong, but that didn't matter. There was a longing inside of him that made him willing to follow his bastard of a father to this point. But the anxiety of being responsible for the death of the crew he had grown to care about was overwhelming. "We don't have to do this," he said.

His father turned and looked at him, "are you fucking kidding me?" He scoffed as he looked at Tom. "Have I ever told you just how disappointed in you I am?"

"Only every day of my life after you took Mom away from me. At least the days you were around," Tom replied.

"Yeah? Do you ever wonder why that is? It wasn't enough that your mother warped your mind with her ignorant idea that the government had out best interest in mind, but you went willingly. I used to wonder how hard she had to try to turn you against me, but part of me thinks you were already against me when shit fell apart."

"You wanted her to turn against her family. Can't you see that either way she had to make an impossible choice?"

"Bull shit, her family could have cared less. They were focused on whatever gave them more money. Your mother wouldn't have been the first person in her family to turn against them."

"Yet you're the one who felt compelled to kill her for your pride?"

Jon shook his head. "See? Her poison still floats around in that brain of yours. Do you want to hate me for looking out for myself? Fine, why don't you take a page out of my book, look out for yourself, and get off this ship before I turn it into a floating coffin?" the older man pointed out the airlock and into the cargo bay of the *Liminality*. It was the only way Tom could live to see another day, to follow his monster of a father and kill the closest thing to a family he had known since his mother's death.

Tom's heart raced as he stared into the cold eyes of the man who never gave a shit about him. *Why am I here?* he thought. *Is it for this man or is it for me?* For the first time in his life, Tom decided to stand up for himself. Without thinking about it, he reached for his weapon, drew it and leveled the barrel inches away from his father's head. "We're not killing them," he snapped.

All around him, guns were drawn, ready to rain hell if his father willed it. There was no telling with his Frater. From the corner of his eye, he saw the barrels aimed at him, but that didn't matter. On the bridge of the ship were people who would have done anything to protect Tom. For the first time, he understood just want "anything" could be.

His father smiled. "You see that, son? That's called loyalty. Of course, you wouldn't know a goddamned thing about that, now would you?"

Tom knew at any moment triggers would be pulled and bullets lodged deep inside of him and that there was no hope of survival. That didn't change a thing, though. "They're only loyal to you because you pay them to be," Tom replied.

"I gave you life, you little bastard," his father said. The older man crossed his arms and stood defiantly, staring at his son with enough indignation to start a war, but Tom knew the war started the day the man threatened to kill his mother. That was when their blood turned bad, and neither of them could forgive the other. "All it takes is a nod of my head, and you're dead."

"Maybe, but your life is in my hands too."

Tom's father shook his head. "You're just like your mother," he whispered. "You're too weak to do what's necessary, and that's why you're going to die." He began to move, but before he had the chance, Tom pulled the trigger, and a bullet ripped through the older man's head, splattering the bulkhead with blood. A loud gasp filled Tom's ears where the sound of discharged weapons should have been. As his father's body crumpled to the deck, he looked at the semi-circle of men surrounding him, guns drawn, and took a deep breath. "If you're going to do it, then get it the fuck over with," he said.

"Put your weapons down," one of them said. Tom looked and saw the man pull the mask from his face. It was a man he recognized from years prior. A man he thought was loyal to his father.

"What, you don't want to kill me too?"

The man shrugged. "I don't see much point in it," he said. "Besides, I thought it was pretty fucked up that he wanted to kill these people anyway, especially if one of us was part of the crew."

Relieved, Tom lowered his weapon, though he hated thinking of himself as one of them. "And where does that leave us?"

"I guess that depends on you," the man replied. "But you should know if you don't let us walk out of here, there's going to be a pretty big problem."

Tom sighed and holstered his weapon. "Yeah, I thought you might say that." He made eye contact with each of the men, slowly nodding his head. "You have three minutes to get the fuck off the ship."

He watched them leave, one by one, as his father's body lay on the deck, blood spreading out from his head like a sun rising on the horizon. Taking the man's life was a necessity. Tom did not love his father, not in any tangible way. If anything, he feared his father's wrath, and that fear was what made him want to impress him. *Fear is just a part of life*, he thought as he lowered the gun to the deck and turned to walk back to the bridge. His heart beat rapidly in his chest, making his vision blur at the thought of what would happen when he turned himself over to the *Cassowary*. He was a traitor, doubly so, and Captain Olafssen and his crew would not be forgiving. That was the hard truth he had to accept as he stepped onto the bridge and looked at the dozen sets of eyes glaring back at him.

"I'm sorry," was all he could say as he unbound the captain. The man looked at him, his eyes red with heartbroken rage. "It was the only way—"

Captain Olafssen responded with a punch to Tom's face as he rose from the deck. "Chief, lock this traitor in the brig and don't feed him until I say it's all right."

"Aye, sir," Werner said as he held his wrists out to Captain Olafssen to be unbound. He then turned his attention to Tom, who sat on the deck of the bridge on his knees, the feel of defeat weighing heavy on his heart.

It wasn't supposed to be this way, he thought as Werner grabbed him by the arm and led him from the bridge.

It wasn't supposed to be this way.

A four-by-six cell was his reward for saving the ship. Tom understood why his betrayal led to his being confined, but from where he was standing, things could've been a lot better. It was easy to question his motives as he was locked away. But that didn't mean that he did the wrong thing.

The sound of footsteps drew his attention to the plate-glass window looking out of the cell. "Are you comfortable?" Chief Werner asked. Tom couldn't tell if the man was being facetious or not, but it was nice seeing someone other than figments of his imagination dancing before his eyes after several days of solitude. At least he thought it was that many days.

"I wouldn't mind being able to get out and stretch my legs a little bit," Tom replied.

Chief Werner scoffed at Tom's response. "I don't think that's going to happen, but I'll let the captain know."

Tom nodded, knowing that the punishment fit the crime. In fact, he was lucky. Anyone else turning traitor would've been tossed out of an airlock. He supposed he should consider himself lucky to still be drawing breath. "Let me know what he says," Tom joked. He could only imagine the captain's scorn at the absurdity of the request.

"Yeah, I don't think that will go over so well. But that's not why I am here," Chief said. "I am here to ask a question."

"What's that?"

"I want to know why," the chief replied.

For Tom, that was a rather convoluted question. The truth was he didn't even know why. He supposed he was trying to win over his father, but he knew going into it that there was no pleasing that man. "I don't know," Tom said.

Chief Werner cleared his throat. "That's not good enough." The look in the man's eyes made Tom feel the shame of disappointment.

"I'm sorry, but I don't have a better answer than that. Initially, I think I did it because he wanted me to. Perhaps that never changed, at least not until the people I really care about were put it in danger."

Chief Werner nodded. "I can see that, but I can't accept it. You were supposed to be one of us."

I thought I was, thought Tom.

He pressed his hands against the glass, his forehead leaning against the cold surface. "I know, and I'm sorry."

"And why would you let them go?" The older man asked. "If you were really one of us, you would have shot them all."

Tom looked up at the chief, a smile starting to spread across his face. "Do you still have his body?"

Chief Werner nodded.

"Scan it, and you'll find a tracker. If you can reverse engineer the signal to it, you'll find the rest of them."

"And how come you can't just tell us where they're at?"

Tom stepped back from the glass and put it in his hands behind his back. "Because I don't know where they are," he said.

"And why should I believe you?"

Tom shrugged. "Because I saved you?"

"Did you?"

For the first time since those events took place, Tom questioned whether he had played into his father's hand. His father had been diagnosed with brain cancer, and the tumor was inoperable. Didn't it stand to reason that the man would have a death wish, and by trying to take over a military vessel, that which would've been granted? If so, then had Tom put all of them in more danger by letting those men go? "We need to get out of here," Tom said, suddenly feeling as if the air had been sucked out of the room.

Chief Werner turned around and walked to the door. His hand pressed against the intercom system, switching it off. "Did your father ever tell you how disappointed he was in you?"

Tom's eyes grew wide. "You're one of them too?"

Chief Werner canted his head, a fiendish smirk spreading across his face. "More so than you'll ever be."

Tom slammed his fist against the glass cell, the smooth hard surface threatening to break the small bones in his hands with each blow. "No, wait!" He had no idea what he would say, but the urge to lash out at the traitor standing on the other side of the prison cell was more than he could bear.

Chief Werner turned around and smiled a coy grin. "What?" He asked as he stood there, staring back at Tom with the look of a man who knew he had already won. It was the greatest ruse in the Chancerian Sector, and the only person to know the truth was trapped in a cell.

Tom stood and glared at the man, his mind racing, but unable to come up with anything to say.

"That's what I thought," Werner said. He looked at the bulkhead where the control panel for Tom's cell was within reach. Tom watched as the other man's hand scrolled across the screen, his fingers dancing over the options. Tom could think of nothing to say, and he knew that nothing he said would put an end to what was about to happen. Silence suffocated the room in a deadly grip as Tom watched Werner press an icon on the console. Within seconds, the breathable air in the cell disappeared, and Tom began sucking on vacuum. He realized that the ventilation in the cell was controllable on the console. As he choked on the nothingness, his brain screamed for air. "No," he tried to yell, but silent screams made his throat burn. His wide eyes watched as the chief turned and walked out of the room, closing the door behind him. Tom said a silent prayer, hoping that the oxygen would return, or that someone would come and save him. But the only thing in his future was darkness.

Author Drew A. Avera

Drew Avera is an active-duty Navy veteran and bestselling author of The Alorian Wars. Originally from Mississippi, Drew grew up with a love for all things comic books and science fiction. At one point, he boasted having more than one-thousand comic books meticulously stored in his closet. Since joining the Navy, Drew has seen the world and has read a lot of books; the best way to spend down time while deployed. His love for reading eventually led to him writing his own books. And the rest is history.

Did you like what your read? I have more than a dozen other books published, [browse them on Amazon](#) or on my [web page](#). You can also [join my newsletter](#) to be the first to know about new releases and other cool stuff happening in my life

Fox Hunt

By Carysa Locke

Prologue

When humanity stretched its wings and colonized planets far beyond the reaches of their own galaxy, new vistas were discovered. New science. Breakthroughs in not only space travel, terraforming, and colonization, but in the human body itself. Ways to enhance it. Humanity wanted men and women capable of settling harsh planets and surviving to thrive.

Colonies grew into independent worlds with politics of their own. Empires rose and fell. Wars broke out between systems. Humans enhanced to be more were drafted as soldiers. Some empires turned to cloning to boost their numbers. Others relied on biotech that made people more than human. And the Talented were created: humans biologically enhanced with powerful psychic abilities that made them gods on the battlefield. Men and women designed to kill with a thought, to hunt specific targets, and find them anywhere in the universe.

But eventually, all wars end.

The newly established Commonwealth of Sovereign Planets brokered a hard-won peace. Territories became sovereign systems. And those who once created the Talented, who wielded them in battle with the precision of a surgeon's laser, realized they had no more use for gods who might challenge the power of the new monarchy. They betrayed their loyal soldiers, sentencing them to death.

The Talented did not go easily. Some disappeared into the populace, pretending to be merely human. Others fled to the fringes of occupied space, stealing ships and creating a fleet that even the Commonwealth Navy feared to challenge. They turned pirate, stealing what they needed to survive. Telepaths, hunters, and assassins, they established their own colonies outside of the Commonwealth. And down through the generations, their gifts bred true.

Chapter One

It was the wrong season.

A thin layer of snow blanketed the ground, covering the sway of silver grasses and sticking to the pealing redbark trees lining Teegan's property. The colorful slab of dorite flecked with flashes of bright gold and deep blue that normally formed the centerpiece to her garden was hidden beneath a frost of white. More flakes fell from a winter-gray sky, slowly gathering in the peculiar silence that blanketed the world at first snowfall.

Except this was summer.

Teegan stared at the snow, brow furrowed. A flash of silver and copper caught her eye as something streaked across the ground. The figure vanished a moment later, but paw prints formed a trail moving toward her. Teegan relaxed and stepped off her back porch, sandaled feet crunching through the thin crust of ice.

It wasn't cold. That was her first thought. Wearing only a thin silk robe and an old pair of sandals, she should have been freezing. But looking down at her bare toes, her smooth black skin stark against the white, she felt perfectly comfortable. No fog of breath misted the air in front of her face, and no goose bumps shivered across her body.

Soft fur brushed beneath her hand. A moment later the air shimmered, and Ember appeared beside her, sitting demurely with her elegant, thick tail wrapped around her feet. She resembled pictures Teegan had seen of ancient animals called foxes, but Ember was *kith-vos*, a species native to this world, Tarsiss Prime. And Ember was no simple animal. The *kith* were every bit as intelligent as their human bond-mates. Perhaps more so. They held mysteries, Teegan was sure, that remained unknown to the humans who colonized their world three centuries ago.

And they shared the psychic abilities of the Talented.

It's snowing, Ember said. Her mental voice was clear and melodic. She tilted her head in an expression of confusion that looked almost human.

"I know."

Ember looked up at Teegan with a glint in her blue eyes. Her fur rippled in the wind. She was almost entirely a silver color that disappeared against the brightness of snow, but tufts of red circled her eyes like a mask, and tipped the end of her tail and each paw, as though they'd been dipped in the color. *It is high summer. It does not snow in high summer, Teegan.* There was a distinct tone of disapproval to the *kith's* mental voice. As if she couldn't abide the sky spitting snow in the wrong season.

But she was right. Teegan cast her gaze back over her garden. Flowers that should have been blooming – that had been, only the day before – lay dormant. The redbark trees stood like silent sentries, stark limbs stretched toward the sky with none of the brilliant green leaves that should have been waving in the breeze.

During high summer, Tarssis Prime's orbit carried the planet along its closest pass around the system's star as it made its oblong journey. Temperatures soared, and there was no possibility of snow, even on the coldest day.

Teegan turned abruptly and walked back into her house. Silently, Ember followed her, ears flicked back as she picked up on her bondmate's mood.

Wrong season. No chill in the air. There was only one explanation that was plausible: this wasn't real. She was in a psychic landscape, one she hadn't created. In reality, she was probably still asleep in her bed, Ember a warm presence curled up beside her.

Only the most powerful telepaths could pull off something like this. Teegan could count the number she knew personally on one hand. She lived on a planet of Hunters, a people with the primary Talent of tracking and finding anyone, anywhere. Many of them also possessed telepathy, but it rarely manifested as more than a basic Talent among her people.

Getting past her shields would take someone she trusted.

She folded her arms stiffly, anger tightening her jaw. She took a deep breath, closing her eyes and mentally counting to ten in a futile attempt at holding on to her temper. "Cole." She hadn't spoken his name in years, but it had to be him. The only time he'd ever been to Tarssis had been during winter. He'd seen the snow sticking to the redbark trees.

"You wouldn't open my messages." The sound of his voice, low with a hint of gravel, shivered through her. It had been so long since they'd spoken, she'd forgotten the effect it had. Teegan opened her eyes.

He was standing in her house. He looked exactly the same. Cole Madras was a big man, tall and broad, with the muscular look of a soldier. His hair was dark and long enough to brush his shoulders. A few strands of gray threaded through it, catching the light. Cole wasn't the sort to use nanites or dye to hide the changing color. His face was more arresting than handsome, strong and square with a few lines around his expressive mouth, and at the corners of his eyes. Hazel, his eyes had always reminded Teegan of the forest. Green and brown and full of secrets. His skin was lighter than her own, browned by the sun.

Emotions too complicated to untangle closed her throat and held her frozen for an endless moment. Funny, how the mind created physical responses in a completely mental environment.

"I didn't want to hear them. I didn't want to see you." *Liar.* It had taken all of her self-control to ignore those messages.

"That much was obvious." Nothing showed on his face, no hint of emotion to tell her how he felt about it. Not that she couldn't guess. Cole had never completely understood her choice to walk away.

The moment filled with tension as they looked at one another, the past hanging unspoken between them. Teegan was caught between memorizing every line of his face, and desperately wishing she could wake up and forget this ever happened. Her gut churned with the roil of emotion.

Cole! Teegan, you did not tell me that Cole sent us messages. Ember's voice was reproving as she bounced across the space between them to dance around Cole's feet. It broke the tension. Cole leaned down and drew a hand over Ember's head and down her back, stroking the *kith*. Ember preened, licking his hand when he drew it back. *We have missed you, Cole.*

"Speak for yourself." Teegan couldn't stop the words, and she studiously ignored the look her bond-mate gave her.

But you did miss him, Teegan. Ember's thought was sent on a private mental thread. Cole would not hear it unless the *kith* wished him to.

You know I can't tell him that, Ember.

You can, Teegan. You don't wish to. Those are two different things. Sometimes the *kith's* literal way of looking at the world made certain things hard to explain. Like why Teegan had cut Cole from her life seven years ago and never looked back. Had it really been seven years? Time certainly moved quickly. Seeing him, it felt like yesterday.

She cleared her throat. "Who gave you docking permission?" Outsiders didn't come to Tarssis without the express permission of one of the eleven ruling families. The Hunters preferred to remain largely separate from their pirate brethren. And there was no possibility that Cole could have concocted this elaborate telepathic landscape if he wasn't on planet. He was powerful with uniquely specialized gifts, but reaching across space to do something like this just wasn't possible.

"House Khallin."

Teegan felt something painful stab through her, even though she'd half expected it. *Thanks, Mom.* To her credit, her mother probably thought she was doing Teegan a favor. She'd been complaining for years that Teegan spent too much time isolated from others. But, damn it, she was thirty-eight years old. She didn't need her mother interfering in her choices, however well-intentioned it might be.

"Well, you can go ahead and depart back to your rock. I'm not interested in whatever you have to say." She deliberately made her tone flippant and mocking.

Cole's mouth thinned. He lived on an asteroid that had barely managed the terraforming necessary to be livable. But he took an absurd pride in what he'd accomplished there, and Teegan knew it. Black Rock would never be luxurious, but Cole had made something of the place, building inside the asteroid, so to the outward eye it looked uninhabited and unworthy of further inspection. But inside, Cole and his team used caves, tunnels and solar reflectors to redirect energy from the system's star to inside the asteroid. He'd built not only living facilities, but vast gardens to grow fresh fruit and vegetables. The asteroid had pockets of water and underground rivers and lakes that Cole had harnessed for both energy and life. It was beautiful, in a harsh and wild way. But Teegan made it sound like just another piece of floating space junk.

"I'm not here to talk." Cole pushed aside her insult, almost visibly shrugging it off. "I'm here for your help."

Teegan arched an eyebrow. "That's too bad. We don't have a contract anymore. Find someone else."

"I need you."

She waved a hand toward the door. "You're on a planet full of Hunters, Cole. You don't need me."

"You're wrong." The look in his eyes said he was talking about a lot more than whatever job he had for her. Teegan looked away, unable to hold that gaze for long.

"I can't help you." The words came out softer than she intended. Still sitting beside Cole, Ember whined quietly. With the psychic bond they shared, her bond-mate could feel Teegan's emotions.

Letting the personal go for the moment, he switched tactics. "I need a Hunter, Tey." She flinched hearing that nickname again. Cole was the only one who ever used it.

"I told you. You're on a planet full of them."

"No one else has a firsthand imprint of this mind."

Teegan froze. A Hunter tracked people through a psychic impression of their thoughts. Everyone's mind was a unique mix of their own personality, memories, emotions, and experiences. It was more unique than a fingerprint, as individual as DNA. Once a Hunter felt the imprint of someone's mind, they never forgot it.

Hunters sometimes gained these signatures secondhand. An impression from a mental connection the individual shared with someone else. Teegan had once tracked a small boy lost in the wilderness by pulling his mental imprint from his mother's thoughts. It was imperfect, like a smudged picture, but it could work. A firsthand imprint was a thousand times better.

She stared at Cole. She'd helped him hunt down a number of Talented in the past. People who had, for one reason or another, tried to escape being sent to Black Rock. "Who?"

She knew before he said it. She could see it on his face, and her lungs were already starting to constrict before he spoke the name.

"Deacon Harlow."

She could hear the sorrow in his voice, the heaviness that lay beneath the stark grimness of that name. But she wasn't looking at Cole anymore. She stared at nothing, and struggled to keep her breathing even. She didn't technically need air here, in this construct. But her sleeping body did. And she had no doubt she was having a physical reaction in the real world.

A warm weight pressed against her side, Ember whining low in her throat as she rubbed her cheek against Teegan in an attempt to comfort.

"How?" She heard herself ask the question, but it was distant, like she was listening to someone else. Cole's asteroid was a prison, of sorts. Talented who were mentally damaged, too dangerous to allow among a regular population, were sent to Black Rock, where Cole and his team of specialists tried to help and heal them. And in the meantime, keep them from hurting themselves or anyone else. It had extremely thorough security features, and Cole himself monitored the most dangerous guests. Deacon definitely counted among them.

"The new queen. You felt the claiming?" he asked.

"Everyone did."

When the Talented were created, the men who made them were clever. They added a safety feature, a woman with the Talent to influence them and bend them to her will. So that soldiers made for killing and war would always have an off switch if it became necessary. The women born with this Talent were called queens. It was the rarest of all gifts, but recently a new queen had been found. And she'd bonded the Talented to her, an effect that would be felt for years to come. There were some among the pirates, like Cole, who theorized that the connection to a queen was necessary. That some Talented who went mad did so because they lacked the feedback of that connection. Others argued that a queen was just another master, a yoke they had no desire to serve.

It remained to be seen which was true. But for better or worse, the new queen *had* claimed many of the remaining Talented. Teegan had felt it. It brought her to her knees, the shockwave nearly causing her to black out.

Her eyes flicked back to Cole. "The shockwave," she said.

He nodded. "I lost my grip on his mind. Only for a few moments, but…"

"That's all he would need."

She started to move past the shock. Deacon was free. Memories pushed at her, but she shoved them away, refusing to deal with them now. Not here. Not with Cole.

"Six days." Anger built within her as she counted back to the claiming in her mind. "He has a six-day head start."

Cole looked back without flinching. His expression remained neutral. "You wouldn't take my messages."

She wanted to scream at him, to rage, to release her pent up emotions at a handy target. But he was right. She spun away from him, threading fingers through the heavy curls of her long black hair.

She couldn't use her Talent here. Bond-mates were unique. Somehow their link allowed the *kith* to speak telepathically, even in a mental construct like this. But Teegan's other Talents were useless as long as she was in this dream that was quickly becoming a nightmare.

"You have to let me wake up," she said.

"Teegan—"

"I can't track him here!"

Cole paused, considering her. "So, you'll come with me?"

She closed her eyes. She could feel her heart pounding too fast, but couldn't tell which emotion was driving it. Her dread of Deacon and what he might do, or her fear of what the next days with Cole would mean.

"Yes," she said. "I'll come with you."

"My ship is fuelled and ready to go." Cole's voice reflected his relief. "I'll be waiting at your family's landing platform."

She nodded, not even turning around. She stared outside at the snow still falling. Cole's presence faded first, and a moment later so did the snow. Then her house dissolved in a blur, and Teegan found herself sitting bolt upright in bed, her blankets tangled around her. Ember had already woken and jumped down to the floor. A flash of silver and red as the *kith* disappeared around the corner, her nose to the ground. Checking the house and grounds for an intrusion.

Teegan let her go. Ember would feel better once it was done, and truthfully, so would she. The chances of Deacon coming here were so remote as to be laughable. No one landed on Tarssis without permission, and he had no way of knowing where she was.

Unless he read it in Cole's mind.

The thought sent a shiver through her.

No. Now was not the time to give in to paranoia. She scrambled from the bed and hurriedly dressed. She took no time to care for her appearance, barely delayed long enough to pack and grab a nutritional bar.

She hadn't been on a hunt in seven years. Not since the last time she'd seen Cole. And Deacon. Not since losing her brother, her first consort, and two best friends.

She'd been on the verge of choosing Cole as her second consort when everything went to hell. Instead of gaining a life, a family, she lost it all. Multiple partner relationships had become more common in recent years, among both the pirates and Hunters. No one had been more surprised than Teegan when she realized her feelings for Cole were just as strong as what she felt for her first consort, Jarus. It had taken more than a year of working closely together before she felt ready to make that choice, until she was sure Jarus and Cole were as ready as she was. And then it was too late.

Her hands shook as she buckled a disruptor to her thigh. She was about to hunt the man who stole everything from her. She stopped in the doorway, leaning over with her hands propped on her knees, struggling to breath. For a few awful seconds she thought she might vomit, but Ember brushed against her and the feeling faded.

Teegan? Her bond-mate sounded worried.

"I'll be all right."

Perhaps someone else should take this hunt.

"No one else would find him."

Ember padded silently beside her as they stepped outside into the summer sun. It was already warming into a hot day, and it was barely morning. Sweat trickled down Teegan's back beneath the long sleeved, armored shirt she wore. It was flexible and light, as armor went, but still heavier than regular clothing.

Maybe we shouldn't, either, the *kith* said as Teegan sealed her house.

"I'm not leaving that man to roam the universe unchecked."

Then I'm glad Cole will be with us.

Teegan hesitated, but then shrugged. Ember was right. Doing this alone would be impossible. "Me too."

Good. Ember licked her hand, a gesture of love and approval. *It's a start.*

But a start to what? Teegan wasn't so sure she wanted to know.

Chapter Two

Teegan held herself with so much tension she looked tight enough to snap as she took the co-pilot's chair. It hurt to watch, so Cole focused on the pre-flight check instead. He swore to himself, wishing for the thousandth time that any other circumstance could have been the catalyst to bringing them back together.

Of course, nothing else would have been dire enough. Mother knew he'd tried over the last seven years, but Tey had stubbornly ignored his every attempt to reach out. It didn't matter that he'd given her the space she so clearly needed, or that he'd tried to offer unconditional support in the wake of her losses. It didn't matter that his specialty was healing the mind.

It didn't matter that he loved her. Sometimes, he thought that was the most damning thing of all. The thing she couldn't abide. And after what had happened, could he blame her?

All of his frustration drained away. He snuck another look at her, and noticed Ember curled up on the bench behind them. Back in the same place she'd occupied on their last space voyage together, nearly a decade ago. He nodded toward the *kith-vos* in greeting, and she closed one blue eye slowly and opened it again in what he could only describe as a deliberate wink.

Well, maybe he had at least one ally.

He cleared his throat, giving Teegan his full attention. "So, where are we headed?"

She frowned, her hands clasped tightly together in her lap. He didn't think she was aware of it, or of how her knuckles shown pale through her dark skin as her fingers gripped together. Hunting wasn't an exact science, a fact he knew well from their previous trips. So much depended on the strength of the Hunter's mental imprint of the target, on the distance between them, on the force of Talent involved. Teegan was gifted, but she was working alone now. She had no pack to draw upon.

It was certainly not a factor he planned to bring up anytime soon.

"I'm having trouble getting a sense," she admitted after a moment.

"You need to relax. You're too tense."

The glare she shot his direction could have melted metal. He shrugged in response, unperturbed. Teegan being angry with him was nothing new, after all.

He is right. It was unusual for Ember's thoughts to be spoken so openly that he, too, could hear them. The *kith* was choosing to share them with Cole. He didn't look in her direction, didn't dare bring Teegan's attention to her bond-mate's inclusion of him. Hunters could get pretty protective of their *kith*, and the last thing he needed was another thing to fight with her about.

Still, he took Ember's attention as a good sign. If Teegan had truly hated him, that emotion would likely be mirrored by her companion.

"All right." Teegan blew out a breath, rolling her shoulders as she tried to release tension.

Cole had the urge to help, but knew any effort from him would likely result in the opposite reaction. For a moment, he indulged in the memory of a time when that hadn't been true. When he could've brushed her mind with a light mental touch and helped quiet her worries and fears. When he might have moved aside the heavy braid of dark hair falling down her back and massaged her shoulders and neck. When she would have welcomed either action from him.

Then he pushed it aside. That was a long time ago.

Teegan's eyes were closed, allowing him the opportunity to study her and note any changes. There were a few. She'd lost weight, her curves a little less curvy. He frowned, not liking that. It made him wonder how unhappy she'd been. If she talked to anyone or just isolated herself. He got the impression from things her mother had carefully not said that the latter might be true. Her hair was longer, and just as unruly. Already it fought to free itself from the braid she'd tamed it into, curls springing free to frame her face. There were a few new lines, especially around the eyes, but otherwise her deep coffee skin was as smooth and luminous as he remembered. Her full lips were pressed tightly together, and he could see her angular jaw flex as she worked. She looked tired and afraid, but determined.

His jaw clenched. He hated seeing her afraid. But he had no doubt she'd do her part. Teegan never backed away from anything. *Except you.* The traitorous voice in his head was his own. Ruthlessly, he silenced it.

"I need a star chart." Teegan's voice interrupted his thoughts, and he quickly called one up for her. The image was three dimensional and filled the cockpit with a faint glow, systems lit with blue light, and planets showing yellow or red based on whether or not they were occupied. A few green space stations and colonized asteroids dotted here and there.

Teegan glanced at him as she opened her eyes, a quick flash of amber eyes. "Thank you."

He nodded, saying nothing.

She studied the chart for a moment, rotating the view. "Here," she said at last, pinpointing a location. He stared.

"Haven? Deacon went to *Haven*?" Horror made his words sound harsher than intended. Haven was a space station under pirate control, right on the edge of Commonwealth space. They moved a lot of black market goods through there.

But that wasn't the part that concerned him. The place was huge, home to at least thirty thousand people. Families.

"I won't know until we get closer, but that's the general direction." Teegan hesitated. "He might have bypassed it altogether. Or just stopped to change ships."

True. Deacon had stolen one of the two corvettes permanently docked at Black Rock. Cole and Teegan were sitting in the other. Haven would be an ideal place to dump the stolen ship and obtain a new, less traceable craft. In addition to the pirates who ran the place, it was popular with smugglers and mercenaries from the Commonwealth looking to find or offload difficult cargo.

Cole swore. If Deacon had gone to Haven, he could only hope that nothing triggered him while he was there. He was an extremely unstable personality. A telekinetic, he'd spent a great deal of his life focused on the human body. Not a biokinetic, the rarest of the kinetic gifts, which naturally applied itself to cell manipulation and healing. But Deacon had been a surgeon, one who honed his telekinesis as a tool to aid in his profession. Once, he'd had the reputation for doing the impossible.

Until a bioweapon killed his wife and daughter, and he'd been powerless to save them. A lot of Talented women died when Matera-D was unleashed on the pirate population, the virus killing indiscriminately as it targeted the unique genetics of Talented women. Many people grieved.

Deacon broke.

Cole had seen exactly what the man was capable of. Not just in application, but in every twisted memory in Deacon's mind. Before Teegan and her team tracked him down, he'd been on a path to revenge, and he blamed the Commonwealth for the death of his family. The things he'd inflicted on those he'd targeted were raw and horrific. The work of someone in deep psychological pain determined for others to feel it as well. Cole didn't want to imagine what would happen if he unleashed that pain on the station.

"If he kills in such a populated place, he'll bring station security down on him. He has a mission, a goal. And he's always been very controlled." Teegan didn't look at him as she spoke. "I'm sure he won't do anything to jeopardize that."

"Was I thinking so loud?" Cole hadn't meant to project his worries so she would pick up on them. Surely she had plenty of her own. She flashed him a smile that squeezed his heart, it was so like how she used to look at him.

"No. But I know you, Cole. I know how to read you without looking into your thoughts."

He held her gaze for long enough that the moment grew uncomfortable. She looked away, tucking a curl behind her ear. It was just going to spring back free a few seconds later.

He grinned when it happened. Some things, at least, hadn't changed.

"What are you smiling about?"

"Nothing." He focused back on the astrogation panel, and entered the coordinates to plot the jump to Haven. "We're three jumps out." It would take several hours to complete them, to move through otherspace, the place that existed outside of time during space jumps. Normal propulsion would have taken years, decades to reach Haven. But a handful of jumps through otherspace made those light-years go by in a blink. "You should get some rest while we're in transit, if you can. There may not be much chance to sleep after this."

She shivered, a whole body shudder that had Cole frowning in worry.

"I can handle it," she said stiffly.

It pissed him off. "I didn't say you couldn't. I've never thought of you as weak or incapable, Tey. You know that. But Deacon's no joke, and honestly, I'm a little worried that you're going to have trouble leaving the personal out of this."

Her amber eyes spit fire when she looked at him. *Here we go.* Teegan yelling at him was at least an expression of emotion. Anything was better than that cold silence she'd spent the last seven years treating him to.

"I said I've got it. You don't need to worry about me. You don't need to think about me."

"It's about nine years too late for that."

She flinched, but he didn't wish the words unsaid. Pretending their history had never happened wasn't going to be good for either one of them. And damn it, he was tired of not talking to her, of never having the chance to say any of it.

"That part of my life is long dead."

"That is such bullshit, Tey."

Furious, she leaned toward him. And all he could think about was how good she looked, how alive, with her eyes snapping fire, and a dark flush of anger darkening her cheeks.

"You don't get to decide." She bit the words off, she was so mad.

"Yeah? Neither do you."

"Excuse me?"

"You heard me. You think because you want it to, the past just disappears? Trust me, Tey. I know better than anyone that you can't outrun the past. It's forever a part of you, whether you want it to be or not. Especially the big stuff. Family. Death. Love. You're trying to forget all three. How's that working out for you?"

She stared at him mutely as the seconds ticked by. Then she shoved out of her chair and stalked back to the rear cabin, where passengers or extra crew usually strapped in.

"I'm going to sleep," she said, like it was her idea in the first place. "Wake me when we get there. And don't talk to me before."

"Fine." He glared at her retreating back. Ember jumped down from her spot on the bench, giving him a reproachful look.

It's better of she gets this out of her system now, he sent on a tight telepathic thread, just for the *kith.*

She stopped in the entryway of the hatch leading out of the cockpit, surveying him with those blue eyes that seemed at once guileless and ageless. *Maybe.* The word sounded cautious. *She hurts, Cole. Don't hurt her more.*

Then she turned with a flick of her tail and was gone. He stared after her.

"I'm trying not to," he muttered to no one at all. "But sometimes old wounds have to bleed again to be cleansed."

Chapter 3

Teegan's dreams were full of memories. First it was Joras, and even asleep her heart broke a little to see him again. Lean and athletic, her consort had been classically handsome, with sharp, angular features that somehow managed to be masculine and beautiful at the same time. Sometimes when she was awake, she tried to remember his face and couldn't picture it clearly. In dreams, he was as flawless as if he stood next to her. Some part of her recognized that it wasn't real, and maybe that's why joy turned to sorrow, and sorrow turned to nightmare.

When the dream turned, Joras was joined by the others. Her brother, Lorn. Her friends, Micah and Nathan. Her pack. They'd run together for six years. Twenty-seven successful hunts. And one failure.

Technically, even that hunt succeeded. After all, Deacon was captured. He was taken, sent to Black Rock, held by Cole. But Teegan could never look at it as anything but a terrible mistake. A failure that cost her team their lives.

By the time Cole shook her awake, she was cradling Joras in her arms, begging him not to go. Blood soaked her shirt, covered her hands. And Joras was already gone, his mental imprint fading from her mind.

She sat up, blinking away the images, struggling through the grief and loss clogging her throat. Fortunately, Cole was already moving back into the cockpit.

"Coming out of the last jump," he said over his shoulder.

Teegan took a deep breath and let it out. "Great."

She spent the next few minutes strapping in to the seat, and making sure Ember was secure in the sling beside her. She smiled faintly, fingering it. Cole must have put it up. But then, this was hardly the first time he'd traveled with *kith*. Ember was nestled safely within the pouch, which was secured to the seat beside Teegan with several safety straps. She peered up through the opening in the top.

You slept poorly.

I slept about as well as I expected, given everything that's happening.

You haven't had the dreams in a long time.

No. Teegan glanced at Cole's back as the ship came out of the jump. *I haven't.* Her stomach did a flip as they came out of otherspace, time seeming to stretch for a small eternity as it always did.

Maybe this is good, Ember said. It surprised Teegan into looking down at her again. *I've told you many times, holding on to the dead hurts you.*

Teegan looked away, saying nothing. She didn't know how to let them go.

Cole could help you.

I don't want Cole's help.

Ember huffed out a sigh, but dropped the subject.

"Well?" Cole looked over his shoulder at her, and Teegan remembered what she was supposed to be doing.

"Right. Give me a second." She closed her eyes, thinking of the imprint of Deacon's mind. The unique shape to him that was all his own. It glowed with a warm, red and gold light. Faint before, it tugged strongly at her now, pulling her in the direction of the station. Her heart pounded. "He's here."

Cole swore. Teegan understood his frustration immediately. It was good they'd found him so quickly, but bad it was in so populated a place, one which could not be easily maneuvered through or quietly evacuated. What she'd told Cole earlier was true. Deacon had a mission, and he wouldn't jeopardize it easily. But when he was cornered, he would do anything to preserve it. Teegan knew that first hand. And there were a lot of potential hostages on Haven.

"I'll coordinate with station security." Cole sounded grim. "We need to keep this as quiet as possible. We don't want to start a panic." A few moments passed. "Jack's arranged a private docking port for us. He'll meet us at the airlock."

"Jack?"

"He leads Haven. We grew up together."

Cole was born on Ardon, the largest colony world in pirate space, and the first one they'd settled three hundred years ago. Teegan knew he still missed it, still thought of it as home. Or he had, seven years ago. She supposed she didn't know that anymore. Seven years was a long time. A lot could have changed. *But not how he feels about you.* She frowned at the whispered thought. Her own. She pushed it aside. It didn't matter anymore.

Docking was always a tricky business, but Cole was a competent pilot. They connected with the airlock seal with hardly a bump. She and Ember could have remained unsecured and been fine, but it was always best to be cautious. Teegan had been through her share of rough landings.

The man who waited for them on the other side of the airlock had a serious look to him. He was not quite as tall or broad as Cole, but then Cole was a large man. Jack's dark hair and beard were both cut short and neatly trimmed. His blue eyes missed nothing, taking in her, Ember and Cole in a quick, thorough glance. He nodded to each of them in turn, even Ember.

Clearly, he'd spent time with Hunters before.

I like him, Ember said, and Teegan glanced at her in surprise. The *kith* rarely formed such quick judgments of people, but evidently Jack made a good impression.

Beside her, Cole and Jack exchanged a hand clasp in greeting. Teegan got the feeling it would have been a lot more jovial under different circumstances.

"Tell me about this fugitive." Jack wasted no time.

"Deacon Harlow. Former surgeon. Powerful telekinetic, and extremely skilled at applying that Talent to the human body. He used to perform lifesaving surgeries without ever picking up a laser scalpel, because using Talent allowed him to be more precise, to feel with his mind instead of just looking with his eyes."

Jack rubbed a hand over his jaw. "Yeah, I've read about his technique. My chief doctor here actually studied with one of Deacon Harlow's students. She doesn't rely completely on her Talent, but she's done some amazing things with it." He frowned. "Rumor has it Deacon went a little mad after his wife and daughter died."

"Rumor would be correct, in this case. He blames the Commonwealth, the nulls." Cole was referring to humans with no Talent, the head blind that populated the Commonwealth.

"Well, we all did right after it happened. But the Commonwealth is a big place. Lots of systems, lots of planets, and a hell of a lot of people."

"Yes. Deacon's not so particular on which of them he takes his revenge on. He's dangerous, Jack. The last time we went after him, he killed an entire pack of Hunters."

Jack's eyes flicked to Teegan. "So, this time you only brought one?"

Teegan didn't flinch from the skepticism in his eyes. "I'm the only one who can track him. The only Hunter with an imprint. And I work alone."

"Unusual."

She didn't bother replying to his unspoken question. "He's here on your station, and we need to hunt him quietly. If he feels cornered, there's no predicting what he might do."

"We have a lot of families here. And..." Jack hesitated. "We also have a lot of nulls. More than you might expect. Sitting on the fringes of

Commonwealth territory, dealing in the goods we do, we get a lot of black market dealers coming through. Smugglers, thieves, mercenaries. That sort of thing. Some of them travel with their families, too." He looked worried. "Just how concerned do we have to be that he'll attack someone here?"

Teegan and Cole exchanged a look.

"The quieter we can keep things," said Cole firmly, "the better off we'll be. Haven isn't his endgame. I've spent a lot of time in Deacon's mind. He's headed into Commonwealth space, and this is the perfect place to do it. Probably just stopped here to refuel or change ships, get supplies. The corvette he stole had limited stock. He'll sell what he can to buy what he needs, and then he'll be gone."

"What do you need from me?"

"Keep your people back and out of the way, but be ready to move. Once we locate Deacon, things could get ugly real fast. Using other people as shields is something he specializes in, and his telekinesis is powerful. He honed it for small, precise work, but I've seen him move an entire capital ship out of orbit."

"So, he could rip apart this station." Jack sounded angry now. "Why the fuck is this guy still alive? You caught him once, why not kill him?"

Teegan answered before Cole could. She couldn't hide the bitterness in her voice. "Because certain members of the Core wanted to see what could be learned from him. He trained a handful of people in his methods, but none of them were as good as he is. Biokinesis is so rare, they wanted to see if they could duplicate what he did." She didn't look at Cole, but she could feel him watching her.

Jack swore. The Core was a ruling body made up of the most powerful pirates. Since he commanded such an important hub in Haven, Teegan would be surprised if he himself wasn't a member. But not all decisions were voted on by the entire group, and if the pirate king had been among those who decided, or a majority already ruled in favor of keeping Deacon alive, Jack might never have been consulted.

"That's just great." Jack's tone made it clear it was anything but. "I am really tempted to kick you both off my station and just let this guy leave. You can chase him into the Commonwealth, away from me and mine."

"But you won't." Cole sounded very certain.

"No, damn it. I won't. As I said, we have a lot of nulls here. I can't take the chance that he targets them. So we'll do this your way." He lifted a finger, jabbing it in Cole's direction. "But I'm telling you right now, if killing this guy is the best way to take him, to keep everyone safe, that is what you do. I don't give a fuck what the rest of the Core or even the Mother-damned Queen says."

"Understood."

Teegan was surprised Cole didn't argue. She'd wanted to kill Deacon seven years ago, and he hadn't let her. It was just one of the reasons she'd walked away. He must have felt the weight of her surprised stare, because he glanced at her.

I'm not making the same mistake twice, Tey. I've had seven years to work with him, to try and heal what's broken in his mind and understand what he did and how. I'm done trying.

She held his gaze for a long moment, then nodded. Something within her relaxed. She'd been dreading having to fight Cole on this again, she realized. It meant a lot that he was stepping aside no matter what the Core said, and finally supporting her.

He did not argue before because of the Core, Ember said unexpectedly.

What? Of course he did.

No. He argued to protect you.

That makes no sense. Deacon killed my first consort. My brother. My team. If Cole wanted to protect me, he should have let me kill him!

The *kith* gave a small, violent shake of her head. Not a denial, but more a physical response to confusion. Teegan had seen her do it before whenever humans did something especially baffling.

Cole sees inside the minds of broken people. He did not want you to become one of them. Killing sometimes does this. I do not understand. Killing an enemy is natural. But it is why Cole fought you.

Teegan processed this. *Why did you never tell me before?*

You did not ask. The simple answer was at once infuriating and typical of the *kith. He was not yet one of your mates.* Ember's ears twitched as she looked up at Teegan, and she knew that for the *kith*, that explained everything.

They rarely interfered in their bond-mates personal lives, unless it was something that deeply affected their family unit. The first time she and Cole clashed over Deacon, it had been in the wake of Joras' death. Ember would have felt Teegan's grief over losing her mate above all else, and ignored the extra hurt of Cole's betrayal as less important. It didn't matter that Teegan had been on the verge of choosing Cole as her second consort and making him part of that family unit. She hadn't actually done so yet, so Cole was just a friend. Someone Ember liked, but nowhere near as important to her bond-mate's future as Joras had been.

It's okay. It wouldn't have changed anything. In fact, Teegan was pretty sure it would have made her more furious. She was still in the throes of loss and grief when Cole refused to let her kill Deacon. She'd raged at him, even when she thought he was defying her on orders from the Core. How much worse would she have reacted if she'd realized he was choosing it for himself, to protect her?

The past was the past. Maybe it was time she started letting some of it go. She was here now, today, hunting Deacon again. And this time, he would not escape justice for the things he had done.

Chapter 4

Being on Haven was an odd sensation for Cole. He'd spent so much of the past decade isolated with his team at Black Rock, being around so many minds again gave him a headache. He tightened his shields, trying to stay focused. His telepathy was easy to keep leashed, but his gift for mind healing was always on, always connected. He had to ignore the faint traces of mental and emotional pain in the people around him, and that was much harder.

Worst of all was Teegan's mind. So close, he couldn't help but feel the dark threads splicing through her thoughts, trying to dig into her consciousness and tear her down. It would be so easy to reach in and grapple each one until it released and vanished. It would also be an unforgiveable violation of trust. She'd made it very clear she wanted nothing from him, however bitter a pill that was to swallow.

Ember bumped his leg as she moved between them, and he glanced down. The *kith* flicked her tail at him, a gesture he knew wasn't accidental.

I know, he sent, irritated. It wasn't like he was going to follow through on his thoughts. It just hurt to be this close to her and held at such a distance.

Give her time. He almost jolted when Ember spoke to him, though it was happening enough now, he should be getting used to it.

Should I take that as encouragement?

She turned her head and nipped lightly at his heel as he stepped forward, so fast no one else caught it. But he sure as hell felt the warning in the snap of her teeth. *My loyalty is to Teegan. Don't forget.*

As if he could.

But... Worry clouded the *kith*'s voice. *She has spent too long alone. She needs more than only me.*

He found that encouragement enough, for now. But Ember wasn't done.

She still loves you.

He almost tripped over his own feet.

Ember gave him a reproachful look. *But she needs time to remember. You will give her this time.*

"Sure. Yeah." He didn't realize he'd spoken aloud until Teegan looked at him oddly. He forced a smile. "Talking to myself."

He wasn't sure she believed him, but after a moment, she shrugged and let it go.

They were moving into the largest area of the station, the central hub. The pirates had turned it into a market with shops, restaurants, and vendors set up all around it. It was also the most populated section, with not only station residents eating or shopping, meeting friends or making deals, but also many of the stations' transient population doing the same things. Those visiting to pick up cargo or refuel.

Teegan stopped, and Cole bit back a curse. *This is where he is?*

She nodded.

Well, wasn't that just the worst case scenario. He watched as a couple of kids ran by, one chasing the other as they played some kind of game. *Lot of possible targets here.*

Too many, she agreed. *We need to get him away from here.*

He raised an eyebrow. *Any suggestions?*

She hesitated. "Yes. One."

She knelt down next to Ember, lightly touching the back of the *kith's* head with one hand. They were obviously having some kind of mental conversation. But this time it excluded him. He tried not to feel left out.

A moment late Ember gave a soft yip and vanished. Cole blinked. He never got used to that, though it was a common Talent among all of the *kith* races. He wasn't sure if it was some kind of camouflage or just a way of mentally redirecting everyone's thoughts away from them, but effectively they could disappear. Become invisible.

"Care to fill me in?" he asked.

"Deacon knows what *kith* are. More, he'll remember one as distinctive as Ember. He doesn't want to be found or stopped. I think if he catches a glimpse of her, he'll run."

"You're using Ember to drive him back toward his ship."

"Yes."

"Hell of a risk."

"Maybe."

He could tell by the tightness around her eyes that she was worried, so he didn't press it. She knew better than anyone just what Deacon was capable of. She was trusting Ember to lead him away without exposing herself to his Talent. And it had to be damn hard.

"She's smart," he said. "Fast. She'll be fine."

Teegan nodded. "I know." But she flashed him a small, grateful smile, and he drank it in, savoring the moment.

Maybe Ember was right, and he just needed to be patient.

Teegan took a breath. "I think I need to disappear, too. If he sees me, who knows what he might do." Before he could respond, she shimmered out of view. Hunters could often access their bond-mates Talents, and vice versa.

Which left him the odd man out. It was not a good feeling.

Move around the left side. Slowly. I'll keep you updated. You should be outside his line of sight.

That didn't make him feel particularly better.

He wove through the crowd, trying hard to look like he belonged while scanning constantly for a glimpse of Deacon. He didn't expect to see him, since apparently Teegan had sent him in the opposite damn direction, but he hated knowing she was probably right in harm's way. Invisibility was one thing, but Deacon had decent telepathy. If he sensed her mind, all bets were off.

He did spot Jack's security. Rough looking men stationed at various points of the hub, keeping watch over the crowd. Jack assured him this was no more than normal station security. There was always one idiot who thought stealing from pirates was a good idea. It would look odd to pull them, so Jack was leaving them in place, ready and waiting, to protect the crowd if everything went to hell.

He felt the change before Teegan spoke in his mind again. An electric charge to the air that sent cold sweat skating down his spine and set his teeth on edge. He probably wouldn't have noticed if he hadn't been so familiar with Deacon's mind, but he'd spent years connected, keeping the dangerous man's Talent locked down while his team treated him. He zeroed in on Deacon's thoughts the instant the man saw Ember.

...silver and red, a flash of fur...it can't be. Here? After all these years? Who else would Cole get to track me down, if not her...

He's seen Ember. Teegan's update flashed through his thoughts.

I know, damn it. He knows you're here.

That was the whole point.

I thought you said seeing you was a bad idea?

Until he actually sees me, *all he has is a suspicion. Ember was careful. She only showed him the briefest glimpse of her flank. He won't be sure what he saw.*

Cole set his jaw grimly. *He's sure enough*, he told her, already cutting through the crowd in the direction he knew Deacon would be.

How do you know?

Just trust me. I know.

Cole, don't screw this up.

He didn't dignify that with an answer.

He's moving toward one of the exits.

Good. Teegan, do not *follow him until I get there.*

She didn't answer him and he instantly knew she wasn't listening. *Damn it.* For the first time, he regretted not letting her kill Deacon years ago. Or not killing him personally. He was not going to lose her now that she was finally speaking to him again.

Reluctant, but with no other choice, he connected lightly with Deacon's thoughts again. Hoping long familiarity would allow his presence to go undetected.

...don't see her. Damn it! No choice but to leave. Can't risk getting caught now.

Relief flooded him as he realized Deacon didn't have a fix on either Ember or Teegan. Not yet. Then he saw a blur of movement by one of the exits and knew it was Teegan going after him.

Don't you *do anything to screw this up!*

I'm not *letting him get away again.*

Cole put on a burst of speed, determined to catch up with her. One of Jack's security tried to get in his way, seeing a man of his size barreling through people to get to the exit. *Jack, call off your dog.*

The man hesitated, then backed off with a nod as Cole moved past him and shot down the corridor.

I've cleared everyone I can out of docking area C. Jack's mental voice sounded pissed. Not that Cole blamed him. *Everything except his ship is locked down, but I won't take away his only escape route. I can't risk what he might do to the station.*

I understand. I appreciate what you've done.

I'm still taking a huge risk, Cole. You owe me.

Yeah, I know.

***

Ember! Teegan reached out for her bond-mate as she skidded around the corner into the docking area.

He is here, Ember responded.

She was right. There he was, getting ready to board a corvette just like the one she and Cole had flown. Seven years on Black Rock hadn't done him any favors. But, she'd never forget that face. Once, he might have passed for a business man on any number of worlds. He was handsome, with pale skin that was ageless and smooth. He wore his hair carefully groomed with just a touch of distinguished gray at each temple. Clean shaven and dressed in expensive tailored clothing made from real cotton and silk, treated with nanites to show no smudge of dirt, no wrinkle, he'd seemed every inch the important surgeon going about his business. Except for the hint of something off in the depths of his intelligent eyes.

Now, his hair was untrimmed, and he wore standard synth-cotton clothing. He was leaner, too, not quite as fit as he'd once been. Her eyes might have skipped over him in a crowd if she were anyone else, but her Talent made sure his mind shown like a beacon. She would never mistake him, even if he were to don a disguise, undergo facial sculpting and change his appearance completely.

The hatch of the ship stood open, and he moved to board it.

"Oh no, you don't. *Deacon*." She pitched her voice to carry across the empty port. It echoed eerily in a space designed to hold huge ships and lots of people. She dropped Ember's illusion at the same time, allowing herself to become visible.

He turned and saw her. "You. I knew it was you." Those intelligent eyes narrowed. "It was a mistake to leave you alive, before."

"You're damn right it was." Teegan's telekinesis wasn't her most powerful Talent, but it was enough to shove the hatch closed on the ship. "You're not going anywhere."

He smiled, looking calm and pleasant, though she knew he was anything but. "You could still let me go. I imagine you have a family. You may have lost someone to the virus, as I did. A sister, a mother? You may have those who will miss you when you're gone. A father or brother? A husband or consort? Let me leave." His voice was gentle and persuasive. "It's only nulls. They deserve to die. They stole so much from us."

Pain stabbed at her. "The only one who stole anything from me is you.

You killed my brother, my friends. You killed my consort."

His smile faded. "I see. Well, then."

It was all the warning she got before he sliced the air with one hand. She *felt* the telekinesis go off, felt it ripple toward her like a wave, one with sharp edges.

Teegan!

Ember, no!

Her *kith* flung herself between Teegan and that wave of force. Time seemed to slow. Teegan cast a telekinetic shield, but she knew it was too weak to stop Deacon's Talent. Then Cole was there. His huge body shielded Teegan and shoved Ember to the side. Her *kith* hit the ground and slid, a yip of pain escaping her with the force of her landing. Then the wave hit and blood spattered the deck.

Cole fell.

No. It couldn't be happening again. *It couldn't.*

No, no, no! Cole. Teegan dropped to her knees beside him. He was cut diagonally across the chest, from shoulder to hip. It looked precise and deep. Blood welled and flowed freely, soaking his shirt and pooling on the deck. She pressed her hands to the wound, but it was too long and they were too small. She couldn't put enough pressure to stop the bleeding.

Use telekinesis, idiot. The voice was her own. Of course. Carefully, she used her Talent to place pressure on the length of the wound. *Don't leave me, Cole. Please, please, don't leave.*

She remembered begging Jarus in exactly the same way. It hadn't stopped him from dying.

Ember crawled over on her belly, ears pressed back flat against her skull, whine low in her throat. Teegan could feel she was bruised, but otherwise fine. Just worried, like Teegan was, about Cole.

A presence brushed against her shields. Familiar enough that she allowed the contact.

I'm sending help. Don't let him die. This time the voice was Jack's.

I'm trying.

"Deacon."

"What?" She stared down at Cole, uncomprehending.

"Deacon. Leaving."

She looked up and saw that indeed, he had used the moment to board his ship and he was disconnecting from the space station.

"We can still stop him." Cole's voice was low. He seemed to be having trouble breathing.

"We'll find him again. Right now I'm worried about you."

"No. We can stop him here. Thought about it when I was running after you."

"How? He's already leaving."

"Pull him into a telepathic landscape before he jumps. I know his mind. I can do it."

She hesitated. It would at least stop him from jumping away. But would using his Talent be too much of an exertion for Cole? And what would happen if he passed out before Jack could get people aboard the vessel?

"No. It's too risky."

"Worth it."

"No—" She didn't get a chance to complete the sentence.

In the next moment, she was back standing in her house, staring outside at falling snow. "—are clearly an idiot." She clenched a fist in frustration and found it sticky with blood. The landscape was reflecting the reality of the physical world. That meant he was spending as little energy as possible building it.

Ember was beside her. And lying on the floor as her feet, still bleeding everywhere, was Cole. Tears filled her eyes as she looked down at him. "Damn you. If you die, I will never forgive you."

"Then I guess you better hurry."

Deacon was standing outside in the snow, looking around with a perplexed expression. It gave her a moment of disconnect, seeing that man standing in her garden. She marched out the door that stood open, heedless of the falling snow.

He saw her and his eyes widened. He made another of those motions toward her with his hand, slicing the air. This time, no wave of telekinesis followed.

She smiled.

"Talent doesn't work here, Deacon." She stopped a few feet away. "Well, most Talent."

Ember had followed her out, padding along beside her. Now, the *kith* stopped and crouched at her feet, baring her teeth.

What do you think? Teegan was surprised at how calm she sounded, with Cole dying behind her.

Ember growled, low and fierce. *We protect our own.* She leapt, a silver and copper blur through the air. Deacon threw his hands up as though to ward her away. She landed, all four paws striking his chest, jaws clamping onto his throat. Teegan could feel the pressure of telekinesis in the bite, a crushing weight.

Deacon fell, went still. Ember gave him a final shake, whipping her head to make certain he was finished. When she let go and backed away, his throat was a ravaged mess. Blood covered her muzzle, and dotted red against the snow. His eyes stared unseeing up at the sky.

Teegan felt nothing. A surprising emptiness, quickly filled with fear as the snowfall faded, and her house blurred back into the space station.

People were moving into the room. Someone pushed her aside and began looking over Cole and his wound with clinical efficiency. She stared until she saw his chest rise and fall and knew he was still breathing.

Don't die, damn you. Don't leave me now.

Silence answered her. She wished suddenly that she hadn't been so stubborn. That she'd allowed herself to see him years ago, to let go of the past. Instead, she'd wasted all of that time afraid to love again. Afraid to lose.

The imprint is gone. It hit her suddenly that she could no longer feel Deacon's mind. Nothing tugged at her to follow him.

Of course it is, Ember said matter-of-factly. *He is dead.* She sat with her tail curled around her, watching as they applied a sealant to Cole's wound.

Teegan scrubbed a hand at her cheeks as Jack came to stand beside her, rubbing away her tears.

"Don't worry," he said. "He's too damn stubborn to die." He paused. "I've got people towing that ship back into dock. It's unresponsive to hails."

"He's dead." Her eyes didn't leave Cole. They were lifting him onto a stretcher.

"You're welcome to stay with him while they treat him." Jack studied her face. "If that's what you want."

"It is." She folded her arms around herself. "He's my consort. Or he will be, when he wakes up."

Epilogue

High summer on Tarssis Prime was uncomfortably hot. Unless you happened to have a soaking pool with the water set to the perfect cooling temperature.

Teegan's was situated in her garden, beneath the swaying branches of redbark trees providing perfect shade. It was fed by a waterfall that spilled over stone steps and down the dorite slab she used as a centerpiece. The gold and blue flash of the stone seemed to glow from within. The water circulated constantly, filtering out any debris that fell into the pool. Nanites cleansed foreign material too small for the filters to manage, as well as regulating the temperature. The pool remained clean and cool throughout the long, hot days. Perfect for relaxing.

"You know," Teegan said, her voice drowsy as they floated on the water. "We have to get out sometime."

"Says who?" Cole loved the water. The underground springs and lakes at Black Rock were some of his favorite features, though many were unsuitable for swimming.

Teegan laughed, the sound so happy it was infectious. He smiled, cracking one eye open to look over at her. She was gorgeous. Her hair was braided back from her face. She'd put some weight back on, no longer looking so gaunt. A white swimming skirt floated around her thighs in the water, a matching setting off the dark smoothness of her skin. He lost himself for a few moments admiring her curves.

Until water suddenly splashed into his eyes, disrupting both his admiration and his lazy floating.

"Hey."

That's what you get.

If you want water wars, honey, I'm happy to oblige. He was tall enough to stand easily, the water coming up to his chest. Teegan would have to stand on her toes to touch the bottom.

A wave of his arm sent a small tsunami crashing toward her. She tried to move, but wasn't fast enough and came up sputtering seconds later.

He was too busy laughing to notice the huge swathe of water floating above his head until it splashed down over him. Then it was on. Between telekinesis, hands and feet, the pool turned into a frenzy of moving water. They might have kept it up all afternoon, if he hadn't stretched too far to escape another dunking and pulled at the wound across his chest. He winced involuntarily, and instantly the water in the pool quieted.

"What's wrong? Did the wound reopen?"

"No. Just pulled it a little. Nothing to worry about."

"Let me see." She swam over to him and wouldn't leave it alone until she'd examined the puckering scar carefully. Not that Teegan putting her hands on him was a bad thing. He could just think of several things he'd rather have her doing with them.

"It looks all right."

"I told you." He was smiling down at her when she looked up.

"I'm sorry I'm a little paranoid."

He lifted a hand and brushed one of her curls back behind her ear. It was wet enough to actually stay temporarily. "I like that you worry about me."

Her hands looped over his shoulders. "Don't let it go to your head. Your ego's big enough."

"So I hear." He dipped his head and kissed her. The fact that he could do this whenever he wanted was still a revelation to him. He'd spent so many years thinking Teegan would never be his.

The kiss deepened, and his hands went to her waist, pulling her tighter against him. The sun was warm on their skin, quickly drying the parts of them not in the water.

Which is why it was such a shock when a cold spray suddenly showered them both. They broke apart, Teegan laughing while Cole glared at Ember. The *kith* was unrepentant as she sat next to the pool, her fur poofed from having just shaken it free of excess water.

That's what you get for disrupting my bath, she sent to them with great dignity. Honestly, in the heat of battle Cole had forgotten all about Ember paddling around the other end of the pool.

"We should get out anyway. You haven't eaten yet today, and the body burns a lot of fuel healing."

He followed her out of the pool, toward a lunch already laid out on a table and waiting for them.

Living here with her was like a beautiful dream. One he never wanted to wake from. His work at Black Rock was important, but he'd done it long enough to earn a respite. He'd already requested the position be filled by someone else, effectively turning in his resignation. What use was there being a pirate if you followed the rules all of the time?

He hadn't told Teegan yet. She thought this was just an extended vacation, while he recovered from his wounds. He planned to surprise her with the news soon. He'd spent too many years missing her, wishing she was in his life. He wasn't about to let go now that she'd finally invited him back in.

One thought whispered through his mind, the voice he'd never truly silenced in the last seven years. *I love you, Teegan Khallin.*

He thought he kept it private, something just for him. He would tell her when he was sure she was ready to hear it. But a moment later he heard her voice whisper back.

I know.

Author Carysa Locke

Carysa Locke is the pseudonym for writing team Carysa Locke and MaLea Holt, two best friends who have been creating imaginary worlds together for more than twenty years. Their obsession with pirates and adventure goes back many years, when they started another hobby together - costuming. They regularly attend Ren-faires and Pirate Festivals. They currently reside in the Pacific Northwest with their families, where they still routinely roleplay and costume together, when they aren't too busy working on the next novel. You can check out Carysa's books at www.carysalocke.com

Honor Duel

By Kevin O. McLaughlin

CHAPTER ONE

David woke as the first rays of dawn crossed the horizon, slashing like lasers through the small port-hole in his tiny cabin. They'd entered orbit, then. It would be time to land soon. He dressed hastily, tossing on the long red dress tunic that was the uniform of his rank. His boots rang on steel steps as he made his way to the main deck and from there to the ship's forecastle. He felt a desperate urge to peer out through the massive view-ports at their destination.

By the time he reached it the sun was already peeking over the edge of the world below them, brightening the ocean and land alike. The ship's nose canted down, dropping through the upper atmosphere toward an island chain far below. There were hardly any clouds in the air. It would be a bright day there, full of sunshine.

He hated it.

In David's mind, it would have been better had the day been dark, with low-hanging clouds threatening rain. Or maybe they could have found a world with acid clouds dripping deadly rain, instead of this tropical paradise. Gloom should be the atmosphere of the day. The weather would then at least match the deeds foolish men planned under the open sky. He grabbed a rail as the ship lurched slightly, altering course to come in at a safe angle of descent. Their vessel was nimble, but sometimes responded even a little too well to the helm, at least for the good of her crew. The *Armistice* was a small starship, but fast and fully armed in service to the Queen.

"Lost in thought again?"

David started at the voice behind him, but relaxed as he recognized the friendly tone. "You're up early yourself," he replied. "And I'm not really in the mood for banter."

"Nor I." The other man settled his arms on the rail next to David. They stood there in companionable silence another few minutes.

"Roger, this is stupid. The man wants to kill you. He's wanted to kill you for weeks now, because you're better at his job than he is and he knows it. Why give him this chance?" David asked.

Roger exhaled hard. "Because you're right. He's wanted to kill me for weeks, and if he doesn't succeed today, he'll try again. Worse, his stupidity might get all of us killed. No, Drake – either Sir Halsom dies today, or I do."

David's mind raced as he tried to think of something he might say to avert this disaster in the making. If they were just about anywhere else in Her Majesty's space, this sort of thing would never be allowed. Not during time of war, anyway, not a duel to the death. It wasn't done. But this wasn't New London, where Halsom would be taken to task for his idiocy. This was the world of St. Agnes, a distant planet on the far edge of space from the burgeoning war. No one was paying attention to what happened on board a tiny patrol ship far from the front.

David heard a bellowing from the rear of the ship. That would be Halsom, rising from his bed.

"You'd best go, Drake. I'll be all right."

David looked at Roger's face. The stress lines were clearly etched there, even as his calm tone tried to hide it. He wanted to find a way to remove those lines, to make this right.

"I wish I could help more," David said.

"Halsom punishes us both with his order for you to stay with the ship. Do your duty. Joseph will do fine as my second. And he'll help me arm. Now go, before you raise his wrath."

David went. At fifteen, he was no match for Halsom's sword arm, and he knew it. He'd sparred the man with practice swords, and he'd barely been able to limp back to his bunk after it was over. If Halsom went at him with an energy blade, he'd be dead in minutes. David was terribly afraid for Roger. And he was miserably afraid for himself, as well, because Roger was really the only person who kept life on the *Armistice* tolerable for its youngest knight.

"Drake! Hurry, boy! Step lively, kill'in to be done!"

David quickened his step, and worked to wipe the look of disgust from his face. Halsom knew damned well that he and Roger were friends. Nothing like twisting the knife. He reached the door to Halsom's cabin, already open, and took one step inside. The room belied the man – everything neat, clean, and well organized. David had wondered more than once how such a horrid person could maintain such a neat abode.

"You called, Sir Halsom?"

"I don't have a proper squire, so you'll do to help me arm up. Not like you're a proper knight anyway, right Drake?" Halsom said, leering.

David's hand went to the sword he wasn't wearing, before drifting back to his side. Halsom didn't miss the motion, and snorted.

"Boy, if you drew on me I'd gut you where you stood. You're only here because you got lucky. Remember your place!" The last word was emphasized with a thunderous slap across David's face. He managed to keep his feet – only just. Halsom was a big man, and strong.

Someday, David prayed, he would have a chance to be revenged.

Today, his face stinging as much with the shame of it as the blow he'd just received, he set about strapping pieces of a powered armor suit to the man who planned to kill his friend.

CHAPTER TWO

After he'd armed the brute, David retired to his own small room to prepare himself. He might not be walking with Roger to the beach where his friend would be fighting for his life. But by God he could comport himself well, even left behind on the ship. He pulled his armored chest-piece over his head, letting the steel slide into place over his body. Gears ground against each other as the plates latched down over his torso. More armor went on over his arms and legs. His sword belt went on last, holding in place the energy blade he'd won. He'd earned that sword, no matter what Halsom said.

David's fingers went to the rough patch in the armor, just under the breastbone on the left side. He'd patched the hole with a repair kit, but he could not yet afford to have a master armorer repair the damage. He'd made that hole himself, just a deck hand stabbing an enemy knight with a powered spear someone had let fall to the deck. He could still feel the hot blood pouring down his arms any time he thought about that night.

Sometimes, he could still hear the man cursing him as he died.

The man his deed had saved was a nobleman. David's reward had been the arms and armor of the knight he'd killed - and a title to match.

It had proven to be a more challenging leap to make than the deed which had won it for him, he thought with a wry grin. He'd requested to remain in service on the starships he'd served aboard for half his life. But the men he'd once hung out with no longer felt comfortable seeing him as one of them. And most of the nobles saw him as a jumped up commoner.

It didn't help that Halsom was, if truth be told, correct. David knew his skill with a weapon left much to be desired. Under Roger's tutelage, he'd begun to improve. But Halsom really would gut him without breathing hard. It was luck that had won him his place.

David only hoped he would remain lucky enough to keep it.

The last bit of armor he owned was a helm. He'd never worn it; the very thought of wearing the dead man's steel cap brought David visions of those dying eyes, the light swiftly leaving them as the knight's lifeblood poured out of his body. He blinked to clear away the memory.

"Still, better to have it," he said aloud.

He scooped up the helm and hung it from his sword hilt by the neck strap. As prepared for this disaster of a day as he thought he was going to get, he stepped from his berth back up to the deck, where he was greeted by blazing sunlight pouring in through the portholes. The ship had descended to cruise only a few hundred feet above the ocean, and morning had turned out as brilliant as dawn had promised. Not a cloud in the sky.

No, that wasn't quite true. There, to the southeast, he could see a squall line coming toward them from the distance. Perhaps the weather agreed with him after all, for rain and wind would be lashing the islands about the time the combatants were ready to begin.

Sir Roger strode across the deck toward him. He was resplendent in his armor. Unlike the battered and ancient suit David wore, Roger's was newly made, fresh from the factory, and gleamed with polish. The red silk of his surcoat billowed in the rising wind. Behind him, a squire trailed with his full helm and a sword nearly as long as David was tall.

"I wish I were coming with you," David said.

Roger stopped before him, and clasped a hand on his shoulder. "I know. But as boorish as the man is, Halsom is right. We need someone to command the ship at all times, and we only have three knights on board. Two of us are going ashore."

"And that leaves me," David finished for him. "I understand. I just wish it were otherwise."

"David," Roger's voice dropped, almost to a whisper. "If this goes badly…if I fall today…"

"I wish you would not say such things," David said.

"Yes, but they must be said. Now don't interrupt," Roger said, with the hint of a smile tweaking the corner of his mouth. "If he kills me out there, you'll be in danger. I cannot shield you from him. Be wary, be on your guard."

"I know this," David said. He feared for it, almost as much as he was afraid of losing his friend.

"Know this, too. You've grown since arriving here. You're stronger, faster, and more skilled than you were. I think in a pinch you might just surprise yourself. Now, take this," Roger said, holding out a small knife to David.

David draw the small weapon and turned it over in his hand. This was no ordinary blade. It gleamed in the light, the edge just a molecule thick. A stud on the pommel would activate an energy field around the weapon which would allow it to penetrate even the densest of force fields. Weapons like these were priceless.

"Roger - I can't! This is too much," he said.

"I insist. Something to remember me by. In case." The older knight's tone brooked no refusal.

David sheathed the knife, then knelt and slid the blade into his boot. He used those moments to pull his emotions back under control. By the time he stood again, his face was calm, even if his thoughts roiled beneath the surface.

"Remember your duty, David. And your honor."

"I will."

CHAPTER THREE

The wind was blowing harder by the time the combatants set out for the shore. About a third of the crew had gone along - all Halsom would allow, and David thought that Roger was probably correct about that being wise. The *Armistice* was still a military ship. They had a duty to be prepared for attack.

Right now all David could see over the water was the oncoming squall, and it looked to be a strong one. It wouldn't matter to the ship. Her engines could hold them in place no matter how fierce the winds blew. But he found himself examining the storm at length, because it was preferable to the much closer vision - of the two knights and crew marching over the rocks down to the sandy beach at the waterline.

"Sir! They're starting!" one of the sailors called out to him.

David dragged his attention from the clouds back to the island. The two knights stood on the sand below, their armor shining even from this distance. Halsom carried a huge pole axe, while Roger had unsheathed his bastard sword. Energy arced around the weapons as their owners activated them. With a cry that David could hear from the ship, the two men lunged at each other, blows hammering down, steel pounding on steel.

For what seemed an eternity, both men kept up the flurry of blows, neither seeming to gain an advantage. Their powered armor generated force fields which would stop almost any attack - except the focused energy of a mass-driven weapon surrounded by an equally powerful energy field. David's heart lurched for a second as Halsom's axe smashed into Roger's side, staggering him. But he recovered quickly; it seemed his armor had saved him. His counterattack almost caught Halsom in the throat. Both men were slowing down as they tired.

Then, as if in accord with one another, they backed away. David knew they had to be winded, even as battle hardened as they were. He also knew that their armor had like as not protected them from everything but a few bruises. That was the way of battle: if your armor was good, the weapons which could pierce it were few. His old suit would have been shredded in such a fight - but their fresh steel plates warded off most mortal blows.

They'd be hammering away at each other for a while. David let his eyes drift away from the fight for a moment, distracted by a glint from the waves. What was that out there in the water? He squinted, trying to make it out, but couldn't quite tell what it was before it vanished from his view again.

It had been something though, he was sure of that. Perhaps a big fish? David glanced around. The rest of the crew were watching the fight, and he felt like he ought to be, too. But his eyes drifted back over the water.

There! For just a moment, he was certain he saw a bit of bright gold flash above the waves. Something very odd was down there.

A cheer from the crew around him brought his mind back to the fight. Halsom was down on one knee, his axe held before him to fend off the blows Roger was raining down on him. The defense was good, but even so, some of Roger's shots were getting through, his blade smashing into the steel helm and shoulder plates of Halsom's armor. David felt a rush of cheer himself - Roger was winning!

That feeling of elation was replaced by horror when six bronze armored knights rose from the sea, marching in toward land, toward the duelists and the distracted crew around them. They carried rifles and fired blasts of energy as they walked. Half a dozen of the crew lay dead or dying in the sand before the rest realized what was happening.

David glanced around him, where the crew on the ship was likewise frozen in shock. "Cast off, you lot!" he cried. "We have to get the ship aloft!"

That roused them. The crew broke into furious action and raced about the ship, getting her ready to be under weigh. David ignored them for the moment. The men knew their jobs. The ship would be airborne in minutes. Instead, he turned his eyes to the ship's sensor readings, looking for anything out of the ordinary.

Those armored monsters on the beach were Commonwealth knights. They had to have come from somewhere. The enemy had a ship in this system, no doubt. David had the feeling it would be close, planning to pounce at just the right moment. But where were they? How were they remaining hidden from the ship's scans?

His eyes lit to the squall line, still fast approaching.

It would be a dangerous gambit, to hope the storm would hide a ship from sensors. But if there was enough electricity in those clouds, it might work. The more he stared into the lightning flashing back and forth inside the storm, the more certain David was that he had his answer. That was where the enemy ship lay.

"Make ready the ship's guns!" David called to the men. "Sound general quarters!"

"Sir?" That was Gregory - the sailing master of the *Armistice*. If anyone could gainsay David's orders, he would be the man. Gregory was skilled, respected by the crew, and knew his job. The crew might follow him over a knight, if it came to a decision. David needed to ensure it did not.

"Yes, Master Gregory?"

"Sir, if we fire the cannon, they'll hit our own men. They're not precise enough…."

"I know. But I think we have more to worry about than those brutes on the beach."

"Sir?" he cocked his head sideways a bit. At least he seemed willing to listen.

"We need to gain some distance from the ground, and fast. We're about to be engaged by another starship - and if they get the drop on us…" David let his voice trail off. He didn't need to say any more — he saw the sailing master's eyes widen. He perhaps hadn't put two and two together about the storm yet, but a knight had told him to expect an enemy ship, so he took David at his word.

Gregory strode off, shouting out orders and hurrying the men about their tasks. The ship was short crewed, too damned many men down on the beach. For once, David had to confess to Halsom's wisdom in leaving most of the men - and him - behind. The irony was galling.

It took less time than it felt like to get into the air. He was stalking back and forth along the deck all the while, trying to curb his impatience. The squall line was too close for comfort by the time the *Armistice* was flying free again. But once loosed the ship showed her speed, jetting up into the air. She gained the heights rapidly.

If David was wrong about there being a ship, he was about to get into a lot of trouble. He'd left the other men on the beach to defend themselves rather than stoop to the shore to defend them. But if he was right about the enemy ship lying in wait, then defending their shipmates would leave them low, close to the shore, and utterly defenseless against the enemy ship's weapons.

That was no doubt why the enemy had in mind. The knights they'd sent in were a diversion. His ship was the prize they sought. He wouldn't let them have it so easily. The same storm that blocked their scans would make it difficult for the enemy to use their own sensor array.

"Master Gregory, bring us above the storm, near the leading edge. I want to make a surprise ready for our foe when they come calling," David called out.

"Aye, sir," he replied, making the necessary course adjustments. The *Armistice* shot skyward, blazing a trail of engine light up into the edge of the storm and then holding position high and above the front.

They were ready. Now where was the enemy ship? Had he guessed wrong? Long minutes ticked by and the storm sped along toward the islands without any sign of a ship. Around him David heard the crew begin muttering to one another. He sweated inside his armor. If he'd guessed wrong...

"Starship, forward port quarter and low!" Gregory shouted.

"Bring the ship's course two points to port!" David shouted back. The ship pivoted almost in place, heeling a bit as the inertial dampers struggled with the sudden load on their systems. David studied the holotank display, watching data stream in from their sensors as the enemy left behind the cover the storm had provided.

Several things were immediately evident. She was indeed the enemy he'd be expecting. It was a warship bearing a Commonwealth beacon. She was a big ship, easily massing twice as much as the *Armistice*. And she was flying away from them, making toward the island at top speed.

That meant *Armistice* was effectively behind the ship. The enemy had stronger weapons, but they were mostly front-mounted. The *Armistice* was both faster and more maneuverable.

David grinned. His ship was positioned perfectly.

"Ribaulds, make ready!" he called. The men raced to the bow, where the weapons were mounted. The turret-mounted guns fired bolts of super-dense alloy, each equipped with a device that created an energy field around them allowing penetration of a starship's force field. Like a powered spear, but propelled with much greater force, they were the ship's main main weapon.

The enemy began a lumbering turn. They'd seen the *Armistice*, for certain. David's pulse pounded in his ears as his ship creaked with the strain of keeping their advantageous position.

He had no doubts that the other ship would stand and fight. He had some measure of the enemy commander. A man who would dare a storm like that to get in a sneak attack? He would not run. He would stay. His honor would demand no less. Likewise, he was fairly sure the enemy was hunting alone. If this was an attack by an entire flotilla they would not have needed such subterfuge. They'd have simply blasted the *Armistice* to bits in space.

No, the real question was whether the *Armistice* could maintain her position to the enemy's rear. The ship shuddered as the ribaulds began peppering the enemy ship with bolts, and the engines were whining with effort.

It wasn't enough. Fast as his ship was, the enemy was turning too quickly. They'd be under her guns in moments.

"Brace for impact!" David hollered, his voice carrying over the din of battle.

The warship came about, her own guns blazing away. Spears punched through the *Armistice*'s hull. One erupted from the deck only feet away from David. The explosion from the impact sent bits of metal pinging against his armor. If he'd taken two steps to the right, he'd have been killed on the spot. There were cries of pain from the forecastle as the gun crews there took casualties from the enemy fire. Other crew members hauled away the wounded, left the dead, and replaced their fallen on the guns. Everyone knew their lives depended on maintaining a hail of fire at the enemy.

It wasn't going to be enough. Their opponent had twice their number of guns. They would be blasted from the sky.

"Master Gregory, all ahead full!" David cried out.

"But we…"

David cut him off. "Just do it, man!"

"Aye sir," came the rote reply. David could feel the pounding of the ship's engines intensify as the *Armistice* leapt forward through the sky.

He raced to the forecastle. There was one other tool he might use to defeat this opponent. If it worked. If it didn't wreck his ship. The room which had seemed so tranquil at dawn was painted in blood now. Men fed and aimed the three guns as rapidly as they could. More men lay screaming on the floor, clutching at horrible wounds were spears had pierced them.

David put the carnage from his mind and triggered a panel on the wall, activating it with his palm-print. The rocket anchors were used to attach the ship to an asteroid or other small planetary body, to hold in one place for repairs or to dock in ports that lacked proper facilities. He'd never heard of it being used as a weapon. He wasn't sure it would even work.

He took careful aim at the enemy ship and fired.

The anchor was propelled outward like a missile. It had an energy shield of its own, and broke through the warship's force field just like their ribauld bolts. It shattered hull plates where it hit, and then stuck fast inside the enemy ship.

The *Armistice*'s engines were on full power, but the anchor chain held. David's ship swung about the larger vessel, picking up speed as she spun.

With a ripping that could be heard across the gulf between the ships, the enemy ship's hull gave way. The mass and velocity of the *Armistice* swinging on the chain was too great. First one plate tore apart, and then another, until the anchor ripped a massive wound across the hull of the ship. Some critical power conduit became cut, and the warship's engines lost power.

That was the moment he'd been waiting for. David slammed his fist home on a button, releasing the chain. The *Armistice* shot clear.

There was time for screaming, and cries of despair, but that was all before the great ship smashed into the sea below, coming apart in a violent display of splintered beams and hull plating.

The men stared down at the sea, aghast. Usually, a ship would be forced down slowly, or forced close enough for boarding. It was rare to see such a devastating crash.

"We'll send out lifeboats to search for survivors, as soon as we may,"

David said. He knew there would be few, if any men who'd lived through the wreck. "For now, bring us back to the island. We need to go help the others."

CHAPTER FOUR

David leapt from the ramp into the soft sand to the cheers of the crew. There were only three of the enemy knights left when he'd brought the *Armistice* into range. The crew on the shore had done for the others already. Once they'd seen the ship returning, the crew had retreated into the rocks off the beach, and the ship's guns had made short work of the other bronze armored enemy.

He looked down at one of them as he passed. They were men, like himself. They'd risked their lives for the honor of the attack. He regretted killing them like that. It would have been better, perhaps, to engage them hand to hand. But he'd been beside himself with worry for Roger.

"About time you showed," Halsom said, stepping forward to meet him. "Took your time."

"Where is Sir Roger?" David replied, ignoring the remark.

"Dead. Died to one of those louts." Halsom pointed toward the shore. David could see Roger's armor there, face down in the sand.

He sped away from Halsom, who sputtered in his wake. When he reached Roger's side, he rolled the body over. But Halsom had spoken the truth. It was too late to help his friend. Roger's blood had pooled around him and already sunk into the sand. His skin was cool, and his face, when David lifted the visor, was gray.

David examined the armor. There were dents and nicks in the front, but nothing that looked like it had penetrated. Where then had all the blood come from?

He rolled Roger back over, and saw it – a huge gash torn between two of the plates. Some powerful blow had cut deep into his back. David lay the body gently back down in the sand. Some of the crew had already arrived, one carrying a white sheet from the ship, which David helped him drape over the man.

Halsom was ignoring him again. The other knight had returned to the ship, and was calling out orders, bullying the crew who'd stayed aboard and fought so bravely for David. But that gave him a short while to investigate something. A few minutes later he'd confirmed his supposition. And David's remorse at the loss of his friend gave way to a new emotion.

Rage.

CHAPTER FIVE

David stalked back up the ramp to the *Armistice*. Perhaps anger was clouding his judgement, but his honor demanded this. Roger's honor demanded this. There was no other course for him to take.

"Halsom!"

The other man stopped what he was doing and looked up. He saw David stalking toward him, saw his face, and smirked.

"Drake," he rumbled.

"I saw Roger's body, Halsom. I saw his wound."

Halsom's face darkened to match the storm clouds above. "Boy, do not trifle with me. If you say what you're about to say, your death is certain."

David had already considered that, and found some part of him didn't care anymore. "The bronze armored men used energy bolt throwers. They carried no hand weapons at all. But Roger was killed by a heavy blade. Like an axe, Sir Halsom. Like your axe."

"You galling little prick. How dare you?" Halsom took two steps forward, raising his axe as he came. Arcs of power shot out around the blade, showing his intent. He would kill David, if he could.

David barely had time to draw and activate his own blade to parry the blow, stepping back and out of the way as he did. Halsom's axe was huge, and his own sword paltry in comparison. But David was light on his feet, and danced clear of the big man's rush.

Halsom turned, swinging his axe out in a sweeping arc designed to remove David's head from his body. Again, David stepped clear. This time, he swung his own weapon as he stepped, but it rang hollowly against

Halsom's plate armor.

"Your little sword cannot breach my armor," Halsom said, sneering. "But my axe will cut through yours like butter."

"You talk too much," David replied, and his sword traced an arc around Halsom's axe, darting in to scratch the other man's forehead before he could lean back far enough. A small line of blood welled there – neither of the combatants were wearing their helmets.

Halsom wiped at his brow, saw his hand come away bloody, and roared. His axe came down in a series of hammer-like blows. "Cut me?! I'll kill you, boy!"

David struggled to parry one, sidestep another, then block a third, but it was too much. His blade gave out, snapping off near the hilt with the fourth blow. The axe continued downward, and struck his left arm. David could feel the bone snap, and couldn't hold back a scream of pain. The broken hilt tumbled from his fingers, and he sank to one knee, clutching the wounded arm with his good one.

"My axe is too fast. I'll kill you with my bare hands," Halsom said. He threw aside the weapon, took a step forward and closed his fingers around David's throat. Clamping tight, he began to squeeze. David knew he had only seconds left.

He'd failed. But at least he had tried. Roger had tried, too, and was a better fighter – perhaps if the fight had been a fair one, Roger could have beaten the man. But even Roger had been unsure – he'd spoken of the chance of loss, even given David something to remember him by.

The memory jolted David. Darkness was beginning to crowd the edges of his vision, and he could hear a roaring in his ears. All he could see was Halsom's enraged face, snarling down at him.

But his right hand was free.

He reached down to his boot, where he'd left Roger's gift, and activated it with his thumb. With the last of his strength, he thrust the knife upward, into Halsom's throat. He slashed across and his vision went red.

Halsom's hands released him. The big man stepped back and made a gurgling sound. David staggered back to his feet, wiping furiously at his eyes to clear away the other knight's blood. When he could see again,

Halsom's had already fallen to the deck, clutching at his ruined neck. A moment later the big man stopped breathing and grew still.

David staggered a moment, but one of the men rushed over to support him. He nodded his thanks. The entire crew was gathered around, silently watching him.

Master Gregory stepped forward.

"Yes, sailing master?" David said, working to keep his voice level.

"Your orders, sir?"

He struggled to still his thoughts. Halsom was dead. His tormentor was gone. His best friend as well. It was almost too much, and he leaned against the wall for support.

Only for a moment though. He scanned the eyes of the crew. Some looked dubious, but most were ready to follow his orders. He was a knight. He was their commander. He'd proven himself in battle thrice over now, and it seemed that was enough for them.

"Load our dead, and the enemy dead as well. We'll check the sea for survivors from the wreck. Then we make for the fleet. The Queen must be told we've been engaged in this system," David said. This attack might have been a tiny feint with a single ship, or it might be the beginning of a much larger operation. Their defenses were thin in this part of space.

"Aye, sir!" Gregory replied, then set about giving orders to the men.

David winced as he shifted his left arm without thinking about it. That would be sore for a while, and he'd need to get it tended soon. But for now, he stood watching his men prepare his ship to move. His eyes went to Roger's body, still under a sheet in the sand. Wordlessly, he thanked the man for his gifts – of the knife, and of the example he'd set. One had saved his life. The other would make it worth living.

Author Kevin O. McLaughlin

When not practicing hobbies which include sailing, constructing medieval armor, and swinging swords at his friends, USA Today bestselling author Kevin McLaughlin can usually be found in his Boston home, writing the next book. Kevin's award-winning science fiction and fantasy stories continue to thrill readers. In science fiction, the "Starship Satori" and "Accord" series have won praise and starred reviews. In urban fantasy, his "Blackwell Magic" and "Raven's Heart" tales have been widely acclaimed for excellence.

Did you like what you read? I have more than thirty other books published! You can [see them on Amazon](#) or on my [web page – kevinomclaughlin.com](#). There's a link on that page for a FREE selection of short stories, exclusively for my fans.

A Prayer for the Faithless

By David Bruns

My afternoon prayers did nothing to settle the discomfort that had found a home somewhere behind my breastbone. Since I'd left Dani on the airstrip of our home world, it had lodged there, unmoving, like the slow burn of indigestion.

The Los Angeles cityscape moved beneath the shuttle as a kaleidoscope of densely packed slums washed in the gold of a setting sun. I rested my head against the leather cushion, feeling the embroidered *Z* of the Zadeh family logo press into my scalp. My family logo.

What could they possibly want with me after twelve years? I'd held up my end of the bargain. I'd stayed away, taken a new surname, and lived a low-profile existence. They hadn't even called me back for my father's funeral, and now, out of nowhere, came this...*summons* was the best way to say it. Why?

The vehicle banked sharply as the company pilot made his final approach to the family compound. High white walls, green lawns, a swimming pool holding more water than any one of the slum-dwellers would consume in an entire lifetime, and an empty landing pad. The craft flared its wings to reduce speed and settled slowly to the ground.

Ito waited for me on the concrete pad, his compact body sheathed in the charcoal-colored family uniform. I was dressed casually in worn trousers and a soft jumper. I hadn't worn the uniform since the last time I was in this place. He bowed, and when he looked up, his lips held the barest trace of a smile. The sheen of his close-cut hair was gray now, but otherwise he looked untouched by time.

"Ito," I said, holding out my hand. "It's good to see you."

He shrugged his broad shoulders and signed to me, *And you, Mubassir.*

His eyes crinkled at the edges. *Have you kept up your training, sir?*

My hand snapped out to slap him on the ear, but the old man was quicker. He parried my strike and touched the tip of my nose with his free hand.

I felt my face redden. "Not well enough, I'm afraid."

Ito's features hardened into stone again. *They are waiting for you in the receiving room,* he signed. I didn't know what his look signified, but I knew I wouldn't like it.

The walk through the halls of my childhood home was swift and painful. Every corner held a memory. It wasn't so much that I longed for the wealth of my childhood, but I missed the feeling of being part of a tribe. Of belonging. I thought of Dani and our home on Sestus. The bubble of acid in my chest burned afresh. Dani, our farm, our life together--that was enough for me. This place was no longer my home.

Ito's biometrics opened the door as we rounded the last corner. He posted himself at the entrance and allowed me to pass inside.

My feet traveled from polished marble to the firm plush of expensive carpet. The faint scent of jasmine touched my senses. Mother's perfume. She rose from her chair to greet me. We were the same height, and the dark material of the headscarf framing her face accentuated her large eyes. My late father, in his rare moments of tenderness, would say he was bewitched by the eyes of an Indian princess. That she had forced him to marry her. It was a lie, of course. Like all the great houses, theirs was an arranged marriage, a business deal. As part of the contract, my mother was forced to convert to the Zadeh family religion.

When I was a boy, I used to believe that my parents loved each other. But it was not until I met Dani that I found the true meaning of the word. No, my parents were partners, maybe even friends at some level, but certainly not lovers. Not by a long shot.

She cupped my jawline with both hands and the scent of jasmine filled my nostrils. "Mubassir, my little watcher. It has been too long, son." She kissed me on both cheeks, then stepped back.

The family kahin stirred in his wheelchair. All the families in the conglomerate had their own kahin, an advisor to the family on how to best meld business and religion. I knelt before him to pay my respects, my gaze taking in his full gray beard, his clerical collar—anything to avoid the accusation in his eyes. He might have aged physically, but his feelings toward me had not. I was *haraam*, forbidden, the black sheep, and twelve years had done nothing to cool the old man's disgust. He glared at me and I knew that whatever the reason for calling me home, it had been over his objections.

"It is good to see you," I said.

He grunted in reply and did not take my hand.

"There you are," said a voice behind me.

I did my best not to stiffen as I stood and faced my brother. Parvez Zadeh could have been a model. The charcoal uniform with its embroidered gold crest hugged his lean frame. His gait across the carpet was fluid, as if he was gliding over the distance. He held his arms open wide. "Brother," he said in a smooth baritone. "It is so good to see you again."

He folded me into his embrace as if I were the prodigal son returned home. I felt the ridges of muscles along his back and the musk of his cologne nearly choked me. He held me away from him, grasping my biceps as he studied my face. "You look well," he said finally, finishing the phrase with his trademark high-wattage smile.

For someone who's living in exile, I finished in my head. I forced a smile in reply.

The kahin tracked me with his eyes as I took my seat across from the three of them. I accepted a cup of tea from my mother and perched on the edge of my chair. "I know we'll get to this eventually, but I'd rather not wait. Why am I here?"

The brightness of Parvez's smile dimmed a fraction. He shot a glance at my mother, then settled back in his chair and crossed his legs. "It's about Asha," he said.

Asha was seven when I left home. A chubby girl in pigtails, not even old enough to wear a headscarf yet. All I remembered was a happy kid—compared to me, at least—who liked ice cream and stories about princesses.

"I haven't spoken to Asha in twelve years."

"We know," Parvez interrupted. "That's why you're here." He leaned forward, pinning me with his gaze. "She's taken after you in not fulfilling her familial duties. This is what your sister has become." He touched the table and a hologram rose from the fake stone.

A nightclub. The throb of dance music pulsed softly and the scene focused on a young girl with her back to the drone. The camera slid around the crowd and focused on her. I drew in a sharp breath. The girl could have been my mother. When I was just a toddler, I remember how my mother would sometimes take off her headscarf when I was with her. Her dark hair would spill over her shoulders and she would laugh at the way I would grab at her silky tresses. Thinking back, I smiled at this happy childhood memory.

"Why are you laughing?" Parvez said in an acid tone. "This is a disaster."

I pressed my lips together. "I wasn't laughing. I was... never mind. So she's rebelling. Why is this a problem?"

"Your brother has arranged a marriage for your sister," my mother said. "With the Khan conglomerate."

"Ah." I sat back in my chair. It all made sense now. The Khan family owned the monopoly on all religious food transport in the federated planets. The Zadeh family was the second-largest shipping company in the system. Parvez was using his sister's future to become the largest.

I met my brother's gaze. "Okay, I understand the problem, but what do you expect me to do?"

In answer, Parvez manipulated the frozen hologram until I could see the man Asha was dancing with. Tall, blond, broad-shouldered, sculpted pecs—my sister had good taste. Asha and the man had the kind of locked gaze that spoke volumes.

"Your sister has been consorting with this man," my mother said. "He's from the Nordic conglomerate. She has"—she shot a glance at the old man—"refused to accept her proper role in the family."

The kahin grunted his disgust at my generation.

"We've kept it quiet," Parvez interrupted. "At great cost, I might add, but the situation has grown untenable."

"The girl is not worthy," the kahin rumbled. He stared at me. "Unclean." He left it open as to whether he was referring to her or to me. "The family has been dishonored. Again."

"Please," Parvez snapped. "I have this under control. If we can get her back in line, the deal can still be salvaged and no one will be the wiser. The other option is not preferred."

"Other option?" I asked.

The kahin looked at me. "Dishonor has consequences."

My eyes cut from Parvez to my mother and back again. "You're kidding." Their faces were still, unreadable. "You would *kill* Asha? Over a marriage, a business deal? You can't be serious."

"She has dishonored the family," the kahin began.

"Shut up, old man!" said Parvez sharply. "That's a last resort. It won't come to that."

"But it's an option?"

Parvez looked at Mother, then back at me. Finally, he nodded. "You don't understand, Mubassir. If this deal falls through because of Asha's behavior, our position with the entire conglomerate is in jeopardy. This issue needs to be resolved now—one way or the other."

Then it hit me. "And that's why I'm here," I said.

"An honor killing must be done by one who has been wronged," the kahin said. "A family member."

"How have I been wronged?" I shot back.

Silence reigned. Behind me, I could hear Ito's breathing as he stood watch at the door.

Parvez had regained his self-control. He looked down his nose at me. "Hear me, brother. I hid your secret from the family. I let you run away and *live* in obscurity." He hissed out the word *live*. "In return, I have asked for nothing from you. Until now. You will convince your sister to take her place in the family or you will remove her from the family."

***

I took evening prayers in the family temple. I know it seems wrong to pray with the very people who were forcing me to do this terrible thing to my sister, but the temple grounded me. The sense of place helped me to think through this ludicrous plan.

I'm not a particularly religious person; I've never been transformed by prayer. Still, I prayed the required six times a day almost every day. The ritual of it soothed me. The same words, the same movements, at the same time each day, were part of me now—and I liked that part of me.

I wondered about my brother and his religion. I watched him from the corner of my eye, seeing his perfect form when he knelt as if he was being graded on posture. Did he believe the words he was saying, or was it just another step in his plan to grow the family business?

After prayers, I retired to my bedroom. Praying together was one thing, polite conversation with killers was a step too far.

The knock at the door came less than a quarter hour later. A soft rap, almost tender. Mother.

"Come in," I called out.

"I came to see if you were okay." She closed the door behind her, resting her back against the jamb.

I studied her face, saying nothing. The curve of her jaw, the way her headscarf both framed and complemented her features. She met my gaze without hesitation.

"Why didn't you tell me?" I asked.

She smiled, perfect teeth in a generous mouth. "You wouldn't have come, my little watcher." My name means *watcher* in Arabic. She always told me that she picked my name because of the way I studied people when I was a baby. I'm sure it's not true, but whenever we were alone she called me her watcher. Until Asha came along, I was the baby of the family, so we spent a lot of time together in my early years. Parvez was Father's favorite even then.

I went to the window, staring out over the darkened city below us. Tens of thousands of people were down there. How many of them were talking with their mother about killing a family member?

"I'll talk to her," I said, "but I won't hurt her."

She came up behind me, squeezing my shoulder. "It must be done, Mubassir. It would be better coming from you."

"Mother!" I found her hands, gripping them. "This is my sister. How can you--"

"Half sister."

My mouth hung open. "Half? I don't understand."

Her gaze, so direct only a few seconds ago, sought the stars outside the window. "Now you know *my* secret." Her voice was small, barely more than a whisper.

"Who?"

"You never knew him." She gave me a wry lopsided grin. "I thought I loved him, if that helps. I didn't love your father, but you knew that already."

I did, but it still stung. If they didn't love each other, how could she love me?

"Did Father know?"

She shook her head. "You are the only one who knows. But when Asha has a blood test for this marriage Parvez has arranged, the rest of the world will know, too."

My knees turned to jelly and I found the chair. Mother knelt in front of me. She laced her fingers into mine and squeezed. "It was a foolish mistake a long time ago, Mubassir. You know what your brother will do to me if he finds out. It's her or me."

"I'll take her away with me," I said. "She can live--"

"You know Parvez will not let that happen."

"Then you can come, too. All three of us."

"Think of the scandal, my little watcher."

She stayed silent, her gaze searching my face like a living thing. I could hear far-off city noises. Music, car horns, the bark of a dog. Normal sounds.

"I protected you," she said. "I always knew who you were and I protected you from *them*." She gripped my hands until they hurt. "We were a team. I protected you when no one else would. You made a new life, safe from their ridiculous religious bigotry." She crushed my fingers together. "I did that for you. Now I need you to do this thing for me."

"I—I—"

"I need your help, Mubassir."

I nodded, unable to form the words.

"Thank you." She closed her eyes, then kissed me on the forehead before she stood. She lingered by the door. "How is Dani?"

"He's fine." I stared out the window.

"When might I have a grandchild?"

I turned. She had wiped the tears away. Her features were restored to perfection.

"We're never going to have children, Mother. Never."

***

Asha Zadeh was a long way from the little brown girl in jet-black pigtails that I remembered from my youth. To be fair, that had been a confusing time for me, but the sight of her reinforced how little I knew about my own sister.

Half sister.

We met in a posh Japanese restaurant called Sayonara, on the fiftieth floor of a downtown LA building. The irony in the naming was not lost on me and I wondered who made the reservations. Black lacquer tables were generously spaced along the floor-to-ceiling windows so that every diner could have a view. Ours looked out over the ocean. It was past noon and a bar of sunlight bisected the table. My eyes swept the half-empty space, wondering how many diners were actually security for my sister or me. I longed for the simplicity of Dani and our farm.

Asha rose when I approached, a slim figure in a low-cut red sheath dress and red high heels to match. Her dark hair spilled down her back in loose curls and she took her time studying me before she held out her arms to signal an embrace.

"The prodigal son returns," she said in a low voice.

"You look like Mother," I replied.

"Touché."

The handgun pressed into the small of my back when I took my seat. She gestured at two small bottles on the table. "I didn't know whether you preferred your sake hot or cold, so I ordered both."

Alcohol, a red dress that left little to the imagination... Asha's opening salvo indicated she was not going to become a devout wife in an arranged marriage.

"We can talk about Parvez later," she said, as if reading my mind. "Tell me about you. Tell me about the brother I never knew."

"Well, I think we should talk about—"

"You're gay, I know that much." She rested her chin on her fist, studying my face. Her free hand carved the air in a lazy motion. "Oh, they don't talk about it, but I figured it out eventually. They don't talk about you at all, actually. Do you have a lover?"

"Husband. Dani's his name—with an *i*."

"Dani with an *i*," she repeated. "Cute. Kids?"

"Look, Asha—"

"Oh?" Her look hardened. "No chitchat, brother Mubassir? Let's get down to business, then. You're here for one of two reasons: to instruct me on the proper way to run away from the family or to try to convince me to come home and live like a good little wife." She leaned across the table. "I'm not going to marry that Khan boy, so what are you going to do about it?"

I fumbled for the hot sake, pouring a thimbleful of the clear liquid and tossing it down my throat. Then another. It burned all the way down to my stomach. Asha watched me with a secret smile, then poured herself a cold sake.

"Cheers." She drank it off calmly and licked her lips.

A waiter appeared with a plate of sashimi. I stared at the thin slices of pink, raw fish, arranged so artfully on the bone-white china. "I ordered for us. It's the specialty of the house. Melts in your mouth." She plucked a slice from the plate with a pair of long black chopsticks and dropped it on her tongue. "Mmm. Try some."

Hissing in frustration, I tried a piece of the tuna. It was good. Asha poured us each another sake. "Cheers," she said, holding up her drink.

I laid my chopsticks down but left my drink alone. "Asha," I said in a whisper, leaning across the table, "I've come to take you away. We need to leave now—right now—before anyone can do anything about it."

She tossed off her drink, setting the ceramic cup down with a clack on the table. "I appreciate the offer, brother dear, but I'm not going anywhere." She snatched another piece of sashimi from the plate and flipped it onto her tongue.

I resisted the urge to have another drink. "Please," I said. "They're desperate—both of them. They will—will..." My brain refused to form the word *kill*. "I can help. I can keep you safe, Asha."

She was studying me the way you might look at a babbling child. A slight smile, a crinkle of puzzlement on her brow, maybe even affection in her eyes.

"What?" I said, reddening. I picked up the drink to cover my embarrassment, welcoming the burn of alcohol on my tongue.

"You," she said. "Mother said you were sweet, a genuine person who cared about others." She crossed her legs, sitting back in her chair. "You would do that for me? Risk your life to smuggle me out of here? A sister you barely even remember?"

"Yes," I hissed. "But we have to go now. I can work it out—"

Asha's laugh interrupted my plea. She shook her head. "I don't believe it. Take out the fucking gun and shoot me, you gutless worm. That's what you're here to do, right? An honor killing to protect all the family secrets? Do it!"

One of the diners in my peripheral vision moved suddenly. My head snapped in his direction. A man, blond, reaching into his jacket. The years of training with Ito kicked in. My hand found the butt of the weapon at the small of my back. The grip molded into my hand and I spun in my seat, aiming for the red of my sister's dress. I pulled the trigger.

Nothing happened.

Asha shook her head. "I didn't think you had it in you." Her eyes held the same bemused look as before.

From under the table came a flash of light and it felt like one of Dani's horses had kicked me in the stomach. I looked down to see a burn mark on my belly. My fingers scrabbled for the edge of the table, but it was too late.

The white marble of the floor rushed up and smashed me in the face.

**

"Thank you, officers." The voices were far away, muffled. Like I was trying to listen underwater.

"This matter has been referred to the Court of Elders." My brother's voice, smooth as always. "Of course, I'll be happy to pay the fine for public disturbance on behalf of my brother—and here's something for your trouble." A whisper of paper and the sound of a door closing.

I tried to move, little stabs of pain like flashbulbs going off in my head. I must have made a noise, because a cool hand covered my brow. "Lie still, Mubassir," said my mother. "You've been stunned." A sting on my shoulder. "This will help with the pain."

I opened my eyes. We were back in the receiving room at the family compound. I sat up, ignoring the pain in my head. Three bearded men sat in a row, our family kahin in the middle, all wearing white turbans and dark scowls. Mother squeezed my arm as she helped me into a chair that faced the trio. "Just say yes to whatever they ask you," she whispered. "Parvez will protect you." She retreated behind me.

I craned my neck to look toward the door. A pair of black-shirted men, armed, and sporting insignia that identified them as holy militia flanked the entrance to the room. My brother worked fast. He'd already gotten the case moved from municipal courts to religious court. City courts were anxious to let the theocratic conglomerates police their own ranks.

"Honored kahins, my sincere thanks for your prompt attention," Parvez said in his most soothing voice. "I've asked you here today to see justice done in the matter of family honor. Since no one was killed, the local police have left it in your hands."

I sat up straighter and scanned the room. Next to Mother sat a dark-clad figure wearing a headscarf. I barely recognized my sister in traditional garb.

The graybeard on the right coughed. "An honor killing—even an attempted one—is unusual. What warranted this action?"

"My sister consorted with men outside the faith," Parvez said, his voice losing its silky edge. "She dishonored the Zadeh family name. My brother was distraught by her actions and sought to restore the family honor in the only way possible."

Graybeard swiveled his head toward me. "Is this true? You tried to take your sister's life?"

Parvez narrowed his eyes at me. I could feel my mother's gaze burning the space between my shoulder blades.

"Yes," I said.

"And now you seek forgiveness from your sister?" the kahin prompted.

So that was the play. I was pretty fuzzy about the finer details of honor killing, but I did recall that if the person survived and forgave her attacker, it was the religious equivalent of "no harm, no foul." That's why they wanted a Court of Elders.

"Yes," I said again.

The family kahin took over, pointing at Asha. "Come forward." The sassy vixen in the red dress was gone, replaced by this little girl in head-to-toe shapeless black robes.

"To forgive is divine, my child. Your brother acted in the best interest of the family, to preserve the honor of the Zadeh name. Surely you can forgive him?"

Asha bowed and said in a small voice, "*Brothers*, Your Excellency. Both of them were part of this plot to kill me."

Graybeard frowned. "Parvez, is this true? You had a hand in this act?"

Parvez's voice hitched up a notch. "Excellency, I may have suspected, but--"

Graybeard waved his hand for silence. "Your family has committed an act that discredits our faith. An honor killing, Parvez?" He turned to the men flanking him. "This smells of politics to me. This attempt to drag us into a family affair does no credit to the Zadeh name."

Parvez's chiseled features turned beet red, but he held his tongue. The graybeard turned back to Asha. "Tell me, child. How did this happen?"

Asha's face dissolved into tears as she prostrated herself before the council. "Excellency, have mercy on me. I have sinned." Her voice was muffled as she sobbed into the carpet. Parvez watched her with slitted eyes. I resisted the urge to turn around and look at my mother.

"Child," one of the council said in a sharp tone, "gather your strength. You have sinned against your faith and your family, but you have the chance to change your ways. Look into your heart and find mercy for your brothers. Forgive them and all is well."

Asha sat up with a slight hiccup, wiping her eyes with the edge of her robe. She nodded and slewed around to face me, putting her back to the kahins. The ghost of a smile painted her face.

I licked my lips. I'd tried to kill this girl I barely knew. She had no reason to forgive me. But I'd done it to protect Mother's secret... Did Asha know that?

Her dark eyes glittered and I tasted the sourness of fear in the back of my throat.

"Mubassir, my absent brother," Asha said. "I forgive you."

My aching head went light with the emotion of the moment and the cushions of the chair caught my sagging limbs.

"Parvez." Something changed in my sister's voice, an edge like sharpened steel. "Parvez, you manipulated our brother to do what you had not the strength to do yourself. You I do *not* forgive."

Parvez shot to his feet, his face a rictus of anger—and fear. "Excellency! This is preposterous, she cannot—"

Graybeard stopped him with a raised hand. "The victim has the right of forgiveness. She has not given it to you, Parvez." He peered down at Asha. "You know what this means for your brother, young lady?"

Facing him, Asha was again the meek girl. "I do, Your Excellency."

The old man nodded. "Very well, in accordance with the law of—"

"I will not stand for this," Parvez shouted. "I brought you here to—"

A brilliant flash of light ended my brother's tirade. He stiffened, his jaw clamped shut, and he toppled to the floor like a dead tree. I twisted in my chair to see my mother holding a stunner.

She rose, slipping the weapon beneath her robes. "Excellency, I apologize for my son's behavior. I ask for the militia to remove him from my home. He shames all of us with his presence. Your wisdom in solving this case has been most enlightening."

The militiamen carried Parvez from the room, followed by the kahins and the whisper of more money exchanging hands. I got to my feet. Whatever drug my mother had given me was working. My head felt clear and my muscles were following orders again.

Mother shut the door of the receiving room and rested her back against the carved wood. Her eyes danced with emotion and she bit her lip. I thought she was going to cry.

"Mother, it'll be okay," I said.

"Mubassir, it will be more than okay." She wrapped her arms around me and hugged me hard. "You were so good," she whispered into my shoulder.

"Mother, your secret is safe with me. I will never tell anyone."

She broke the embrace. "There is no secret, Mubassir. Asha is as much my child as you are. I just wanted to make sure you went through with it."

"Yeah, I had to practically beg you to shoot me," Asha chimed in.

"What? I did shoot you." I heard the door open behind me.

"Really?" Asha pointed. "Ask him," she said.

Ito stood in the doorway. *What's going on?* I signed to him.

He shook his head.

"You've just witnessed a coup, Mubassir," my mother said. She held back a smile. "I've been planning this day ever since your father died."

"I don't understand, Mother."

"No, you don't, do you?" She looked at me with something akin to pity in her gaze. "Your brother is being charged with attempted murder, which according to the bylaws of our family means he has been automatically removed as Chairman and CEO." She consulted her watch.

"By the time you leave orbit this evening, I'll be the Chairman of Zadeh Corporation and your sister will be my CEO."

"This was a setup," I said. "You used me."

"I'm sorry, my little watcher. But you were the perfect choice: a family member, but not part of the family." My mother stripped off her headscarf to reveal a flowing mane of silver. She fluffed the loose curls around her shoulders. "Oh, and there will be no alliance with the Khan family. We're switching our religious affiliation as well." She kissed me. "Now, if you'll excuse us, Asha and I have a board meeting to prepare for—and you have a shuttle to catch. Give my love to Dani."

In a haze, I followed Ito out to the landing pad.

I'm sorry, he signed when we reached the waiting shuttle.

"You knew?"

He nodded and hung his head.

I hugged him. How was it possible with two siblings and a mother, the only person in the entire family I actually cared about was a mute bodyguard?

I placed my forehead against his, feeling the bristle of his crew cut tickle my hairline.

"Goodbye, old friend."

***

I still had on the suit I'd worn for my lunch meeting with Asha when I called Dani from the orbiting transport.

"Nice duds," he said. It was nighttime on Sestus. "What happened to your shirt?"

I fingered the burn mark. "Long story. I'm on my way home, that's the most important part. And I'm never coming back. Ever."

His blue eyes narrowed. "Wanna talk about it?"

I barked out a laugh. "Definitely not." An uncomfortable silence ensued in which Dani studied my face and I avoided his gaze. "Can I see her?" I said.

"It's late. She's asleep."

"Please, Dani. I have a two-week transit...Please?"

He picked up the comm pad and walked through our simple home. The narrow hallway looked so achingly familiar I almost made him stop just so I could look at the pictures on the wall. Dani eased open the door and held the camera over the crib.

Kayla's mouth was parted and she'd drooled on the mattress. Her curls were matted from sleep and one chubby fist was jammed under her chin.

"Satisfied?" Dani whispered.

"Very."

I ended the call and sat on the bed in my tiny cabin for a long time. Finally, I stripped off the damaged suit and slipped into the familiarity of my normal clothes. Suit, shoes, everything went into the recycling chute.

Then I knelt down to pray.

Author David Bruns

David Bruns is a former officer on a nuclear-powered submarine turned corporate executive turned science fiction writer. He is the creator of the sci-fi/fantasy series, *The Dream Guild Chronicles,* and the bestselling military sci-fi novel, *INVINCIBLE*, based on Nick Webb's *Legacy Fleet* series. His short fiction has appeared in such speculative fiction anthologies as *The Future Chronicles* and *Beyond the Stars*.

In his spare time, he co-writes contemporary thrillers with a retired naval intelligence officer. Find out more at www.davidbruns.com.

Margolis Space Rescue

By P. Joseph Cherubino

The wrecker ship *Pearl* left blinkpoint translation well within the uncharted solar system at the very edge of the Trade Lanes. Its target was a Reptilian freighter broadcasting an automated mayday. The signal reported hull breaches and heavy casualties.

"I want stats on that ship, and I want them now," Captain Marshall Margolis ordered.

Preacher Tom oozed and stretched from his egg-shaped flight couch as soon as he could stand the g-forces. The other species on the deck, who all had bones and central nervous systems, could only strain against the kinetic fluid that ballooned their flight suits.

"Praise God, the ship is intact!" Tom shouted through his tradespeak translator as his translucent tentacles wrapped twice around the pedestal of the ops console. His single, lumpy white eye swam around beneath his skin, then popped out from what passed for his body at the end of a thick stalk to fix the captain with an unblinking gaze. "Downlink established," Tom announced. "Identity: B-class standard Trade Union freighter. Outer hull breaches. Inner survival decks intact. Fusion core at thirty percent."

"Thirty percent!" the captain exclaimed as the ship's speed finally bled off enough for his suit to release its protective grasp. With the kinetic fluid still draining back into his chair, he had great difficulty pulling the display scroll from its pouch fastened to the right armrest. "How are they holding in the atmo with only thirty percent?"

The Reptilian Fothol was the second crew member able to function under heavy deceleration. He set to work with his customary silent intensity. Thick muscles strained under his scaly skin and the metallic claws poking from the ends of his flight suit screeched against the deck, fighting for purchase. He uncurled a finger claw and tapped the mechanical button that activated his console. The big, round, red button gave a satisfying, anachronistic click straight out of earth's distant past. The Captain had the replica buttons installed wherever possible because they spoke to him of long-lost human history.

"How long till internal gravity stabilizes?" the Captain asked.

The answer came from the Simian G'koh, who unfolded her three-jointed arms, freed herself from the flight couch restraints and fought her way to her engineering station. The rest of the crew were accustomed to traveling with the only two humans aboard, who often seemed far less capable of space travel. They often reminded the captain of this, but now was not the time for the universal Trade Union custom of the various species giving each other a hard time.

"Particle sieves depleted by that aggressive blinkpoint exit, Marshall," G'koh replied. "It will be a while until our boson field is stable." She was one of the many crew members who occasionally used his first name. The crew wasn't big on formality, and Marshall didn't care, because they were among the best heavy rescue operators in the Trade Union. Titles didn't matter much among the seventy-five-member crew assembled from the lower depths of the labor pool. Only one thing mattered to every crew member: saving lives and recovering equipment in precisely that order.

The Captain manually squeezed enough kinetic fluid from his suit to satisfy the chair's protocols, then picked a fight with inertia to win a standing position. He headed over to the forward bulkhead and placed his palm flat against it. The wall turned perfectly clear, leaving him with the impression that he stood at the very edge of space. The gas giant grew larger at a disturbing rate. They had no time to waste.

"Taylor," Marshall called out over comms. "What's your status, son?"

"Swampers suiting up for action," Taylor said. "Coordinating with ops right now. The preacher is on it, as usual."

"I am blessed to serve," Tom remarked, forming another group of small tentacles that flew across his console.

"We need a plan," Captain Margolis said, turning to his bridge crew. He didn't want to give voice to his doubts about a tough rescue verging on the impossible. He also did not want to face the nagging suspicion that the Reptilian craft might be something else entirely.

The war between the Reptilian Empire and the Trade Union added an extra element of uncertainty that nobody aboard addressed voluntarily. The Rescue Guild decided at the outbreak of war three months ago that they would remain neutral. Rescue astronauts only cared about saving lives, the guild leaders argued, so their position was inherently non-political.

Marshall knew better. He'd lived through three wars on three different worlds outside the trade lanes. He understood how warfare tended to put people on one side or another regardless of species or political sentiment. War forced terrible choices.

The Reptilian ship sending a merchant-class signal managed to burrow itself nearly a hundred kilometers inside a thick rind of atmosphere. They were lucky to get any readings on it at all, so Marshall was glad Tom had such specific information.

They couldn't take the *Pearl* inside that deep, at least not whole. Their particle fields wouldn't maintain cohesion in that thick atmosphere, which meant little to no gravity shielding. They didn't have enough reactor fuel to get in and out on conventional engines alone if they wanted to get back to the trade lanes in the next decade. As a short-range FTL ship, they lacked refueling capability. Shuttles were the best option in this case. They had far less mass, so they could get in and out with far less thrust. They'd probably have to ferry out the survivors and leave the Reptilian ship behind. All of this hinged on whether or not Marshall's suspicion was founded.

"How long do we have until that ship breaks up?" Marshall asked. The bridge remained silent. "Don't everyone jump in at once," the Captain said.

"We have reliable telemetry, but the rest of the readings don't make sense. I am running error probability now," Tom said. "Sortie simulations will take some time. We must wait."

"'Jump in'? Is this an idiom?" Fothol asked, his forked tongue tasting the air. "Nobody is jumping."

"Yes," Preacher Tom said. "The Captain is using sarcasm to express his dissatisfaction with the tardiness of our response."

Marshall slapped his forehead and ran his palm down his face. "Ten years," he said. "Ten years as a crew, and you haven't figured out sarcasm."

"We know sarcasm," G'Koh said. "It is a type of lie."

"Not exactly," Preacher Tom said. "A lie implies the intent to deceive. Sarcasm is an abstract means of linguistic expression using paradox as a device to express a perceived truth by—"

"Thank you, Ops Officer Tom," Marshall snapped, barely restraining his anger. "So, can I have my answer now?"

"While the data is clear, it is anomalous," Tom replied. "We should not be able to read that ship's condition as clearly as we do. The crew will also find another example of sarcasm in the Captain's initial response. 'Thank you' was intended sarcastically."

"Are you trying to piss me off?" Captain Margolis said, face reddening.

"What does this have to do with urine?" Fothol asked.

"That expression I understand," G'Koh replied like a child in school thrilled to grasp new math. "We Simians say 'throw dung' in place of 'piss off' to mean 'angry'. That is an indirect translation into tradespeak, though."

"Warmbloods," G'koh hissed. "I will never understand. We Reptilians express ourselves through words and deeds, not excrement."

"Back to work, people," Marshall replied. "Why we are getting such clear readings, then?"

"Unknown. Telemetry says one thing, actual readings say another. The ship is holding in the upper atmosphere as if it has power," G'Koh replied. "I get no engine signature. It makes no sense."

"And I am still confused," Fothol said. "Explain to me why warmbloods express themselves with bodily waste."

"I want to know why there is a word for 'sarcasm' in tradespeak," G'Koh replied.

"I blame humans for that," Fothol said. "They founded the Trade Union after the Silicoids destroyed their world. I think they insisted some of their strange ways be part of the Union to comfort them."

"Interesting hypothesis, Fothol," Captain Margolis said. "I'll leave you all to calculate mission parameters and come up with a plan. It also seems like you have some work to do in Trade Union cultural studies. The fall of Earth and the birth of the Trade Union is a six-hundred-year-old history, so it should be a quick study."

"That was sarcasm," Tom said, ever helpful.

"Thank you," Fothol replied.

Marshall left them to their work and exited the bridge via the iris to port that spiraled open to let him pass. Once safely on the other side, he tapped the control panel on the left forearm of his flight suit and opened up a channel to his son, Taylor.

"Meet me in my quarters," he said.

He made his way along the downward curve of the ship's inner spine structure, walking the fifty meters to the rear ladder passage. He climbed down two levels to the habitation deck. His cabin was just above and behind the main reactor chamber and its curved back wall described the shape of the outermost containment bulkhead.

Taylor arrived seconds after the captain closed the door. Marshall stood hands to hips, fighting facts. He tried to argue against the obvious, but it was no use. He knew what this was.

"They finally found us," were the first words out of Taylor's mouth after he sealed the cabin iris.

"It looks that way," Marshall said.

"It is that way. We have positive confirmation that the ship is military. It's spoofing its signature, but the device doesn't lie."

"So we're on the same page. We stick with the contingency plan," Marshall said. "We let the crew get away while we go in and fight them."

"I already talked to Sal, Marty and Bert," Taylor said. "They will come with us."

"All the Reptilians want to go?" Marshall asked. "Are you sure they know what this means?"

"Yes, of course. They are sworn rebels," Taylor replied in a disturbingly matter-of-fact tone. "It's a one-way trip."

"If we're going out," Marshall said, changing from Tradespeak to Ancient English. "we need to be damn sure the rest of the crew gets away. I don't want to die knowing they paid for our choices."

Taylor simply nodded his head curtly and blinked back the mist in his eyes. Marshall put his hand on the shoulder of his second-born son and blinked back tears of his own.

"We all feel the same way," Taylor replied. "But Ostoo, Onk and Tak are heartbroken they won't be coming."

"I'm happy they're staying behind. Someone needs to get the rest of the crew out safe."

"They know that, it's just..."

"I know," Marshall said. "We all started this thing together. We sacrificed a lot. Part of me wants us to be together to the end. Why does that make me feel guilty?"

Father and son stood in the modest cabin struggling to come to terms with past deeds and the deeds to come. Taking a stand against ancient plans for genocidal war cost Marshall and Taylor their family. The captain took a deep breath and said, "Tom will have his calculations soon. Are the shuttles ready?"

"Yes," Taylor replied. "Our info systems are compromised. The reptilians created a pretty good illusion. Our crew's going for it."

"I guess that's it, then," Marshall said.

Tom's voice came in over Marshall's implant right on time. "The calculations are in, Captain. Metallic hydrogen in the lower atmosphere is amplifying the emergency telemetry beacon. I don't know why we didn't detect that earlier. We're still calculating around that, but have enough of a fix on the actual ship to go in. Ops recommends deploying two shuttles, one in the outer atmosphere and one for the rescue."

"Taylor here, Tom. That's an excellent plan. I'll scramble the swampers. Send the details to the shuttles. I'll do the rest."

"Tom," Marshall said. "I'll be going on this sortie. You have the ship." Marshall closed the channel, turned to his son and said, "Let's go. We don't have time for second thoughts."

Father and son made their way down the passage to the aft ladder tube, then climbed down three decks to the airlock and cargo section.

The *Pearl* was essentially three ships. The main ship was a 400-meter-long craft capable of deep space travel, but the two 100-meter-long shuttles attached acted as engines with the ship in transit. The shuttles were also the rescue engines for missions just like this. Splitting the ship into three independent units allowed for multi-angle towing of damaged vessels, as well as the ability to ferry wounded crew to the larger vessel. Marshall planned to sacrifice one shuttle for the fight, leaving the other for the *Pearl* as backup. She could get home with no shuttles, but it would take months longer. He hoped to sacrifice only one.

The Feline Ostoo greeted Marshall first. She was tall for a female of her species with her head reaching the level of Marshall's heart. She squinted at the Captain and purred with a deep, uneven tone that betrayed her anxiety.

"What are your orders?" she asked, making it more statement than question.

"This is it," Marshall said, forcing his emotions back. "You, Onk and Tak stay in the upper atmosphere and stand ready to knock back any attack against the *Pearl*."

The two Simians standing behind Ostoo engaged in grooming behavior even though they were clad head-to-toe in EV suits. These outward displays of stress didn't make the Captain's job any easier. He thought standing on formality was the best way forward, so he was surprised when Taylor pushed past him and wrapped Ostoo up in his arms.

The Simians, given to the same expressions of affection as humans, followed suit. Marshall wasn't into hugs, but he moved forward and at least touched the heads and shoulders of his long-time companions.

"Good travels to you all," Marshall said, hoping the words were enough.

Ostoo gave him another long look with her eyes wide this time, then simply turned away to the airlock behind her and boarded the shuttle.

"Where the hell are Marty, Bert and Sal?" Marshall asked.

A cloud of acrid tobacco smoke billowed out. "What the hell, Taylor?" Marshall exclaimed, waving his hand across his face.

"They wanted tobacco," Taylor shrugged, then ducked inside the airlock.

"It's bad enough they insist on human names," Marshall said, following his son down the ladder. "But they want human substances that're highly addictive to them, too."

"They chose this," Taylor said, turning towards the opposite airlock door and starting the decompression cycle. "Isn't that what this is all about?"

Marshall gave a strained sigh and counted down the timer before the pressure equalized. Ceiling vents breathed more tobacco smoke into the chamber. Marshall coughed and said, "Air filtration is clearly malfunctioning."

The outer shuttle door locked with a thud and the inner door opened. The Captain led the way from the midship portal forward to the cramped shuttle bridge.

Sal, Marty and Bert stood up casually from their flight couches configured to accept their slender, snakelike bodies. Each removed the thick cigars clamped between their long, sharp-toothed snouts and struck near-identical poses.

Taylor fixed them with a deep, affectionate grin and spoke to them in Mandarin Chinese. "How are the dragon people today?"

"Good." Marty spoke up first in his hissing Mandarin as he was the Alpha. The others returned cigars to their snouts and puffed away, fixing both eye stalks on the captain. "We are ready to serve the Masters Fleetfoot to the end," Marty declared. Both Sal and Bert folded their slender arms across their chests and gave curt nods.

Marshall gave a start at the use of his real family name. He'd gone by the name "Margolis" so long, he reacted as if Marty mistook him for someone else.

"You all honor us with your service," Marshall replied, trotting out his very rough and rusty Mandarin. The Ancient Earth language was the group's second preferred language, behind their native Reptilian. Tradespeak was a distant third choice for these lizards, who grew up among their own kind, but found a second, more accepting home living with humans on the Three Pillars City Ship.

"We hope to taste the flesh of the enemy before our time comes," said Sal, puffing smoke with every Mandarin syllable.

Marty turned to him and said, "I hope my brother means this in a symbolic way."

"No," Bert replied for his brother. "It is the way of us meat eaters to take at least some flesh from our enemies."

"But we take the New Way," Marty argued. "I counsel you against straying from the hard-won path. There are better ways to end."

"Perhaps," Sal conceded.

"Brothers," Captain said. "I will not judge you for your choices. Just know that I and my son are with you. Let us set to work."

"We begin," Marty said, reverting to Tradespeak, the language of work, not the language of art.

They all took flight couches, with Marshall taking the one on the upper platform that looked down on the semicircle of consoles set against the forward bulkhead.

"Give us a view," Marshall said, as the couch reached out for him with its cabling, attaching probes, tubes and wires to his flight suit.

Taylor tapped the panel of his pilot console and the forward bulkhead turned transparent. They had a perfect sight line down the port side of the *Pearl* ending in the bottom deck of the rectangular bridge section that made the ship into a letter "T" with a clipped top bar.

"Do some of these particle emitters look low to you?" Taylor asked, pointing at several domes that glowed dimly.

Sal appeared as though about to respond, but he put the cigar back in his mouth and everyone remained silent. The unspoken answer was that it did not matter because nobody expected to come back.

"Flight control, this is Acting Captain Tom requesting status," the voice barged into the small shuttle bridge unannounced, startling everyone.

Marshall had nearly forgotten the stated purpose of this sortie. He cleared his throat and took a deep breath before opening shuttle comms to the *Pearl* bridge. "This is Marshall Fl—," the Captain began, nearly using his real name. He played it off as a frog in his throat. "Margolis on a hot mic in command of *Pearl Shuttle One*." He used the "hot mic" protocol to remind the shuttle bridge crew that anyone speaking would be heard by anyone on the channel. They had a cover to maintain.

Shuttle Two checked in and Tom ran down the pre-flight check. With telemetry locked in, Tom ordered the docking clamps released.

"Out and away," Taylor announced. The flight couches automatically reclined as the shuttle engaged conventional drives and shot away trailing streamers of glowing, blue plasma. After several minutes of acceleration, Taylor announced, "Course set and locked. Primary burn complete. ETA forty-five standard minutes."

"Copy, *Shuttle One*," Tom replied. "Acting Captain out."

"Correction," Marshall said on impulse. "No protocol for 'Acting Captain.' You are the captain when I am off the bridge. Remember that, Tom. You're a fine Trade Union officer."

"Bless you, Cap— Shuttle Captain Margolis," Tom said.

"Margolis out," Marshall said, unable to hide the sadness in his voice. He felt confident the crew wouldn't pick up on that. He and Taylor were the only two humans on the ship, and the rest of the crew didn't have much experience with his kind.

Preacher Tom was their first recruit after Marshall and Taylor bought the *Pearl*. He was the only entity of his kind in the Trade Union. He'd been with the operation since day one of the Margolis Heavy Rescue charter.

Tom had come aboard squeezed into a standard human flight suit with his nervous, adoptive human parents trailing behind. The lizards recoiled from him and Ostoo took one look at the blob jiggling like gelatin above the flight suit collar and gave an involuntary hiss. Marshall stepped forward and offered his hand. When Tom stretched out the arm of his flight suit, Marshall told him, "I'd prefer to shake your real hand."

"I don't have hands," Tom replied.

Marshall removed Tom's glove and Tom's body quickly lost its human hand shape to form a thick tentacle. "I'll shake whatever you have, then. It's Astronaut custom." Tom wrapped his tentacle around Marshall's wrist and held it firmly.

Marshall told him, "Welcome to the Trade Union Rescue Guild. We are proud to have you." The rest followed Marshall's example, removing their gloves to make contact with the new crew member.

The Captain was fairly certain Marty, Sal and Bert understood what he was feeling. They might have a different range of emotions unique to their species, but Marshall guessed they were all going through the same internal struggle and dealing with the same memories.

"For the crew," Marshall said. The rest responded in kind, one by one.

Forty-five minutes went quickly. The shuttle pierced the upper atmosphere, rattling and rumbling a passage through thick clouds.

"This is *Shuttle Two* reporting status," Shuttle Captain Ostoo announced. "We are holding at designated coordinates. Tethers armed and ready."

"Flight control here," Tom said. His disembodied tradespeak translator voice called to mind that single wandering eye that made him like no other being in the Trade Union. Marshall smiled, knowing he'd miss Tom, with his unfailing kindness, optimism and his quaint adherence to a human religion. "I am not seeing status on the tether. Can you boost the telemetry signal?"

Instead of responding to Tom, Ostoo opened an encrypted channel to Marshall's comm implant. "How should we handle that, Captain?" she asked.

Marshall quickly tapped the armrest console to turn off the cabin mic. He sub vocalized his reply to Ostoo. "First off, make that the last encrypted transmission between shuttles. If they detect encrypted comm, they will be suspicious."

"Understood," Ostoo replied. "Advise on response please."

"Tell them the tether monitor system is down. You have a shunt monitor in place, hence no telemetry to mission control."

Ostoo closed the channel and Marshall heard her lie to flight control.

"G'Koh here, *Shuttle One*," the chief engineer replied. "My crew just checked that subsystem on both craft and found no issues."

Shit, Marshall thought in Ancient English. Tradespeak had many equivalent expressions, but English seemed to capture certain moods best

"No reflection on you, G'Koh," Marshall replied. "All machines fail from time to time." No response. Marshall took that as a bad sign. G'Koh was particularly mouthy, especially when her machines failed. Marshall had made a bad call.

Shuttle One came in fast on the Reptilian craft. It was no surprise that the ship looming in the view port was nothing like a merchant class vessel. It resembled the pincers of some giant insect with its curved fuselage extending out to points from a long, slender oval body. Conning towers extended from the top and bottom sections of the oval. Ovals of similar proportion to the body sat atop the towers and an ominous green particle field glowed around them.

Two smaller craft appeared from the thick clouds. These did resemble the blocky forms of standard Trade Union skiffs, only the small ships displayed many more domed particle emitters. Marshall guessed those allowed the ships to form weapons beams from their protective fields just as the device reported.

"Captain Marshall Fleetfoot," a voice announced over the general Trade Union comm channel. "Disengage engines and prepare to be boarded." Using the general channel meant the *Pearl* heard everything.

"I can do better than that," Marshall said, as Taylor eased forward on the secondary thrusters. He aimed the shuttle precisely between the two approaching craft. "I'll come to you."

"Disengage engines," the enemy Reptilian commanded.

"Why?" Marshall replied as he tapped the panel on his flight couch, sending a signal to Sal to bring the tether targeting system online. "I'm making it easy for you. Let's get this over with."

"I have a reading, Sal," Taylor said. "Aim for the area just behind the bridge. Set the clamps to open after they penetrate the hull."

"Just like a fish hook," Marshall said with a grin.

"What is a fish hook?" Bert asked.

"What is a fish?" asked Sal.

"Stop, or we will open fire," the enemy voice declared.

"They can't fire," Taylor said. "Not in the atmosphere. No way to form a cohesive beam."

"Do they know this?" asked Sal.

"Do we know this?" Marty asked.

"We do," Taylor said. "Or they'd have fired already."

"We will be in docking range faster at this speed," Marshall said, opening up the channel to the Reptilians again.

"Going with optical targeting," Sal said. "The gas is scattering lidar."

"Don't move the booms too much," Taylor said. "They might notice."

"Can't be helped," Sal said, as the hull vibrated at high frequency while the tether booms extended and angled toward the approaching ships.

"We're well within range," Marshall said, voice trembling. "Fire when—"

Boom, went the hull like the skin of a drum as Sal fired both tethers. Both clamps shot forward with their grappling feet undeployed, resembling something from Ancient Earth called torpedoes. The crew could not see the nanofilament cable trailing behind, but they knew it was there.

The reptilian ships tried to move, but it was far too late. Their evasive maneuvers provided a stroke of luck by exposing weak spots.

"Both clamps went in completely!" Sal exclaimed.

"Hit them with the juice," Marshall ordered.

To Marshall's great satisfaction, Sal mashed one of those big, red, antique replica buttons at his control station. Millions of volts of electricity pulsed down the tether cables, wreaking havoc on the enemy ship. Their engines blinked out immediately and their particle emitters faded out.

"They're disabled!" Taylor bellowed.

"What are you waiting for?" Marshall yelled back. "Go, go, go!"

Taylor grit his teeth and ramped up conventional engine power. Even with a light touch, the snap of the hooked ships against the tethers set off alarm signals and the ship became a percussive instrument again. The entire shuttle complained bitterly in the form of metal that groaned, creaked, snapped and popped.

***

"What happened?" Fothol exclaimed, raising his claws above the console as if about to fight it. "Readings are off the charts now! I'm getting the energy signatures of four spacecraft in the upper strata! The planet seems to be completely different now!"

"Our sensors were compromised," G'Koh said. "I don't know how, but most of our readings about this planet were false."

"That would explain the anomalies," Tom replied from the captain's chair. "Put your crew on it. Find out what happened and how." He opened a broadcast channel to all ships in range. "This is Captain Tom of the Rescue Guild ship *Pearl*. Please identify yourself and declare your status. We are here to render aid."

"This is Alpha Tshlar of Reptilian Destroyer 751. Your Captain Marshall Fleetfoot has committed crimes against the Reptilian Empire; therefore, your ship and all its crew belong to us. Power down your reactor and prepare to be boarded."

Fothol bellowed and did attack his console this time. The faceplate shattered and its metal frame bent inward, sending sparks from severed power conduits and flashes of light from broken fiber optics.

"Alpha Tshlar, please stand by," Tom said with absolute calm. "Officer Fothol, please take the time to compose yourself and resume your work at my ops station. G'Koh, please transfer helm and ops control to my former station."

"Forgive me, Captain," Fothol said.

"I understand completely," Tom said. "We will address your outburst later, if necessary. Let us focus on the task at hand."

"What is happening?" G'Koh said, panic rising in her voice. She perched on the edge of her flight couch and used her long arms to reach the controls.

"It appears that the Reptilian craft is a war vessel and it means to capture us. This may be a case of mistaken identity," Tom said. His lumpy white eye retracted deep inside his body and spiraled wildly like a gyroscope as he thought. His tentacles drew inward to gather close all the neurons he used for reasoning.

"Preacher Tom is right about one thing. That ship is at war with us," came Ostoo's voice over general comms. "Marshall has a plan, so you need to do exactly as we say. I will hold off the warship while the *Pearl* gets away."

"Negative, *Shuttle Two*," Tom replied. "Hold for your orders."

"I am not debating this with you," Ostoo said.

"And you are not the Captain," Tom replied. "I am not inclined to leave any of our crew behind."

"You don't understand," Ostoo said.

"Then explain it to me," Tom said.

"No time," Ostoo replied.

"*Shuttle Two* is moving into the upper atmosphere," Fothol said.

"Hold your position, *Shuttle Two*," Tom said. He received no answer.

"Readings from the planet are in. I have trajectory simulations for a 25-degree arc of ingress," G'Koh said. "*Shuttle One* is dragging two disabled Reptilian vessels at high speed on a collision course with the destroyer. When those ships went down, all data returned to normal."

"Set intercept course on the Reptilian destroyer and stand by to commit," Tom said. "Make sure our path does not take us deeper than one kilometer into the atmosphere."

"On it," Fothol said, stabbing precisely at the console with his claws. "I'll have to change our position."

"What are you doing?" Ostoo screamed over comms. "You'll get everyone killed!"

"Unlikely," Tom said. "You forget who we are. This crew has rescued a cruise ship six times its size from a red dwarf corona, so do as I say. Hold your position and we will get out of this together."

"No!" Ostoo replied. "We all lied to you; the Captain, his son, and everyone on both these shuttles. We are fugitives from both the Trade Union and the Reptilian Empire."

"I'm sure you had your reasons," Tom said. "Now hold your position. I won't tell you again."

"Fool!" Ostoo screamed. "Idiot!" Then, she screeched and hissed words in her native tongue that Tom didn't understand.

"What did she say?" Tom asked, stretching his eye out again at the end of a long stalk.

"I speak Feline," Fothol replied. "You don't like profanity, so you won't want to know."

"We have more time than you think if you just remain calm," Tom replied to Ostoo. "This crew is full of exiles, runaways and ex-criminals. This is a ship of second chances, so your argument that we should abandon you makes no sense."

"He picked a crew of undesirables to draw less attention in the labor market," Ostoo said. "You and the rest were nothing but cover, but you don't deserve to die for our choices. So let us do this, please!"

"No," Tom said. "After all all we've been through, I do not believe we were ever simply cover to you," He flattened his body into a disk and launched himself across the bridge, where he stuck with a wet slap against the panel housing the main computation nodes. He tore the panel off, nearly hitting Fothol, who hissed and raised an angry claw at him. The lighting on the bridge flickered.

"What are you doing?" G'Koh exclaimed, slapping her palms repeatedly against the crown of her head while she bobbed up and down on her chair. "You disabled telemetry and main guidance!"

Tom said nothing as his tentacles moved so fast they snapped like whips. He launched himself at G'Koh's console, pushing her aside and entering a series of commands.

"*Shuttle Two* is reversing course," Fothol said. "All systems report normal again."

"My apologies, G'Koh," Tom said. "There was no time to explain." He formed two legs and calmly walked back over to his flight couch where he resumed a blobby form.

"Systems restored," G'Koh said. "How did you--"

"I tricked the computers into activating emergency remote control. The Captain cut off his uplink before I could take control of *Shuttle One*," Tom explained. "Fothol, be ready to commit on my mark. Engineering, I want as much power as possible to the protection fields. Have that ready to go at my order. Take the reactor past 100% if you must, but I want all the power possible."

G'Koh set to work making calculations and firing off orders to the reactor room.

"You've just killed us all," Ostoo said, as her shuttle made its way back towards the *Pearl*.

"I doubt that," Tom said. "But we will surely die if we don't work together now. If I give you control of that shuttle again, will you obey my orders?"

"What choice do I have?" Ostoo replied.

"Was that an answer in the affirmative?" Tom asked.

"Yes and yes," Ostoo said.

***

Marshall Fleetfoot cupped his face in both palms, doubled over in his flight chair and trembled with rage, fear and frustration. "What the hell is Tom thinking?" he said in Ancient English, as he shot bolt upright again.

"We need a new plan," Marty said, lighting another cigar.

"Understatement much?" Marshall replied, jumping up from the flight couch to pace the bridge.

Tom's voice filled the cabin. "Captain Margolis, please change course and head back to the ship."

"You can call me Captain Fleetfoot, but I'd prefer you call me 'Marshall'. And I guess you figured out how to control our comms again."

"Yes. I can hear everything you say now. Please come back to the *Pearl* and we'll escape together," Tom said. "All of us."

"That's probably not possible, Preacher," Marshall replied. "If that destroyer leaves the atmosphere, it will be able to destroy us from anywhere in this system. Why didn't you go when you had the chance?"

"Come back to the ship, and I'll explain it to you," Tom replied.

"I can't, Preacher Tom. I need to give you the chance to escape."

"Why haven't they already?"

"Why haven't they what?"

"Fired on us."

"Because they can't form directed energy weapons that deep in the gas, and they tried to capture me for interrogation." Marshall replied. "Capture failed, so now they will try to kill us all."

"And you were going to let them capture you?" Tom asked.

"No, we were going to fight," Marshall replied.

"Then we have time," Tom replied.

"Tom," Marshall said. "I am begging you. Try to get away. Don't risk the crew."

"I will go if the crew wishes this. You owe us the choice," Tom replied. "Every crew member who is exiled from their homeworld for being a professional Astronaut, you tell the same thing. You say, 'Welcome home. You can come or go as you please. You have a choice.'"

"Being a Captain means you make survival choices for the crew," Marshall replied.

"I disagree," Tom said with infuriating calm. "I just opened a channel to all crew comm implants, so let's ask them," Tom said. "To all crew: we face an unprecedented situation. Our Captain's real name is Marshall Fleetfoot. He and several other members of our crew have been operating under false identities. They are wanted by a Reptilian spacecraft hiding in the gas giant ahead. The Reptilians demand that we give up the Captain and the rescue crew. They say we are at war with them. The Captain advises us to save ourselves and leave him behind. What do you say to this?"

The response came instantaneously at such volume that Marshall cupped his hands to his ears before the system brought down the volume.

It was common among professional Astronauts to pick up colorful words and phrases from other species. Such speech came in handy for arguments, getting a difficult point across and of course, humor. The profane and emphatic expressions coming in over the comms made Marshall smile so hard his face hurt. The gist of every comment he could make out was that the crew in no way would accept giving up any of their crew members without an absolutely overwhelming reason. This situation did not come close to meeting that criteria. Not by a long shot, Marshall gathered.

"OK, Tom," Marshall said. "I guess that settles it. What do you have planned?"

"I am sending you protective field configuration data. Program the field exactly as the data describes, set the reactor to overload. Aim the shuttle at the destroyer. Then, you get in your wrecker rigs and eject. Do it now."

"Are you hearing all this, Taylor?" Marshall asked.

"Yes," Taylor replied. "But I'm not sure whether I should be impressed or terrified that Tom is suddenly so devious."

"Needs must," Tom replied.

The wrecker crew wasted on time. Taylor set up the protective field and configured autopilot to pursue the destroyer. Marshall worked with the reptilians on making the shuttle commit suicide. It wasn't easy tricking the safety systems into allowing a reactor overload, but they managed it. Before they left the bridge, Marshall released the tethers connecting *Shuttle One* to the hooked reptilian ships.

Everyone scrambled rear to their wrecker suits. The EV rigs were essentially personal spacecraft with their own propulsion systems, two robotic arms and three grappling tethers. In a pinch, they could be used as escape pods, but Marshall doubted they'd survive ejection at their current speed.

"Well," Taylor said after everyone lined up at the port cargo bay door. "This should be interesting."

They tethered all the wrecker suits together as the door opened, then launched.

***

Back on the bridge of the *Pearl*, Tom turned his lumpy eye to G'Koh. "Engineering, full power to gravity shielding," then, turning to Fothol, he said, "Commit flight path at full thrust on my mark."

"Boson field at full flush," G'Koh said.

"Commit," Tom said.

"This is not sane, you know," G'Koh said, with an odd calm. "I'm surprised I'm not in full panic mode."

"That is called faith," Tom said. "I am happy and proud for you."

"We don't believe in the superstitions you acquired from the humans," Fothol hissed.

"I have moved beyond belief and into faith," Tom said. "This will work."

"You defy us!" came a booming, unsynthesized Reptilian voice over the comm system. "We will kill you!"

"The destroyer is changing position," Fothol said. "It is coming fast."

"I need you to keep the path I ordered, Fothol. Concentrate," Tom said. The reptilian cursed in his native language and compiled.

"We are still accelerating, Captain," G'Koh said.

"I know. Maintain this burn. Be ready to change course on my command," Tom said.

"Any faster and a course correction will shatter us," G'Koh said.

"Did you give me the reactor power I asked for?" Tom asked.

"Not quite," G'Koh replied.

"Then I suggest you do, and then some, or this will be a very short trip," Tom said.

Alarm bells and klaxons rang and emergency lights flashed on every console. The deck shook so violently that it looked like a heat mirage. The bow slammed into the upper atmosphere, and the ship pitched to port. A flash of green light saturated the bridge.

'We lost three particle emitters on the port side," G'Koh said.

"Commit all redundant emitters," Tom said.

G'Koh winced, issued the command, and the vibrations stopped. "Silence those alarms, please," Tom said. The bridge grew strangely silent as the boson field canceled the effects of inertia.

"All crew," Tom said. "Strap yourselves in. Hurry."

"Still accelerating," G'Koh said.

"Back on course," Fothol announced.

"Kill thrust," Tom ordered.

The hull rumbled again as the emitters struggled to keep the boson field stable. "Bring us about 180 degrees," Tom ordered. "*Shuttle One*: report." No answer.

"I am proud to have served with you," Fothol said, closed his eyes and stabbed the console with a single index claw. "Commit!"

"We turned!" G'Koh screamed.

"We are alive?" Fothol asked.

"Stand by," Tom said. As the boson field finally collapsed, the ship itself seemed to scream at them and then bellow a complaint. The entire relative mass of the ship, with its incredible, suicidal speed, transferred itself into the atmosphere. The storm front of gasses it created slammed into Reptilian destroyer, making it tumble deeper into the planet's gaseous husk. Seconds later, *Shuttle One* exploded less than a kilometer from the enemy ship.

"Outer hull just buckled on our starboard side," G'Koh reported. "Stress fractures along the port structural arch."

The ops console showed the path of *Shuttle One* arching towards the enemy ship. Five other, smaller dots moving away from the shuttle represented the crew in their rescue EV rigs. The dots were very close to the explosion.

"*Shuttle One* is gone!," Fothol bellowed. "The Destroyer is wild! It has no boson field and it is venting atmosphere. It's in one piece, but it is hurt bad."

"Flight control to Marshall," Tom said. "Come in, Captain." No answer still.

"Lots of EM in the atmosphere, Tom," Fothol said.

Tom adjusted comm filters to compensate for the EM. "Captain, please respond." Static was his answer and Tom adjusted receive power upward.

"Tom," a barely audible voice came in among the static. "Can you hear me preacher Tom?"

"Yes!" Tom exclaimed and for once, his Tradespeak translator interpreted emotion. "Status report!"

"We are alive and well," Marshall replied as the comm system cleaned up the signal. "A bit shaken, but we are alive. No injuries. We are adrift. Used all our fuel to get clear."

"Good to hear," Tom replied. To Fothol, he asked, "Are the Reptilian shuttles completely disabled?" "

"Yes," Fothol replied. "Of that I am grateful."

"Captain Tom to *Shuttle One*. Prepare rescue sortie for the two smaller Reptilian craft."

Fothol rounded on Tom slowly. "Are you insane?" He asked. "They want to kill us all."

"Are we not a rescue ship?" Tom asked.

"Yes," Fothol said. "We are a rescue ship, but…"

"Then by all means," Tom replied, "let's allow fellow sentient beings die because they pose no threat with disabled spacecraft."

"Preacher Tom is right," Marshall said. "But at least rescue us first."

"Of course," Tom replied.

"Then let's rescue the destroyer, also," Fothol said, "because they probably can kill us."

Marshall's laughter boomed out over the comm system. "You both just used sarcasm!"

Fothol raised his snout to the bridge roof, hissed and bobbed up and down in his version of Reptilian laughter. "Now I understand," he said.

"Captain Tom," Ostoo called. "I have a sortie plan."

"Make it happen, *Shuttle Two*," Tom said. "Fothol: set intercept for *Shuttle Two*, then commit with all haste."

"This is Captain Fleetfoot to *Shuttle One*," Marshall broadcast. "I guess this wasn't a one way trip after all."

"It looks that way," Ostoo replied.

"We're alive because of you, Tom," Marshall said. "Now, bring us all home so we can get back to work."

Author P.J Cherubino

I am an 80s kid raised among the stars, both "Trek" and "Wars." I've had many careers, from auto mechanic, to archival research, to network administrator. But now, I'm living my childhood dream of being a full-time writer. So, thank you for reading this short story. You are helping me live a dream.

Consider subscribing to my newsletter. You'll receive free books, short stories, character sketches and more when you sign up. You can check out my other work on Amazon, iBooks, Kobo, Nook and Google Play Books.

My website will have further details on all my stories. I love hearing from readers, so feel free to contact me on Twitter, Facebook or by email.

Venusian Uprising

By M. D. Cooper

BREAK CAMP

STELLAR DATE: 3227430 / 04.21.4124 (Adjusted Gregorian)
LOCATION: Aurelian Forest, Teka Continent
REGION: Venus, InnerSol, Sol Space Federation

"Sweet, fucking stars below, Perez! Why is it that you always need my boot up your damned ass to get anything done?" Gunnery Sergeant Williams swore at the laggardly private.

Perez flashed a grin in response. "Dunno, Gunny. Maybe I like it there."

"Oh, do you? Wanna see if I can fit two in there? Get in the mess. Now! We have a briefing."

Perez didn't stop grinning as he hopped to his feet and sprinted across the camp to the mess tent where the other Marines were already assembled.

Williams shook his head. Perez was the laziest, least responsible Marine he ever had the privilege of babysitting in the corps, but he loved him like a son. The kind of son that you wish would get his damn act together and stop sleeping with all the neighbor's girls and selling their jewelry for drug money.

Still, Perez had never let him down in a fight, and when it came down to it, that was what mattered most. Follow orders, and protect your teammates. After making sure to point the rifle at the enemy; those were rules two and three.

He walked across the camp, his keen eyes surveying everything around him. Shirts hanging on a line, powered armor racked—most correctly, some not. A pair of boots knocked over outside a tent. Two sentries who looked like they were coming in from the wrong direction.

<Jeff, weren't 1st platoon's scouts supposed to be positioned to the north?> he asked the company's AI over the Link.

<Yes, they were,> Jeff replied.

<So what are those two doing coming in from the west?> Williams asked.

<Their shift ended over an hour ago,> Jeff replied. <I suspect they were catching a bit of pre-combat warmth, if that is what the enlisted still call it.>

The man and woman saw Williams giving them the hairy eyeball, and suddenly felt the need to go in separate directions.

Williams didn't mind the men and women under him catching some sack time together, or the women and women, or men and men. He didn't give a shit. But this was a combat mission and there were real enemy soldiers out there. He made a note to mention his concerns to Staff Sergeant Jenkin. No need to let the officers know—not unless this wasn't the first time.

He looked over the firebase one more time, taking a moment to absorb the raw beauty of Venus that lay just beyond Bravo Company's tents. With its deep-green foliage, crystal blue skies, and misty white clouds, you could mistake the world for Earth—that is if humanity's homeworld had a fraction of its current population.

Having assured himself that everything in his immediate eyeline was in passable condition, he entered the mess tent and strode to the front where he took his place beside the newly minted Staff Sergeant Green.

After his platoon's last exemplary tour under Major Tanis Richards—who had since left the Sol System on the GSS Intrepid—Williams had been promoted from staff sergeant assigned to the 4th Platoon to Bravo Company's gunnery sergeant, and Green had received a field promotion to staff sergeant by Lieutenant Colonel Ender, the battalion CO.

While the 4th platoon had been traipsing about on the Intrepid, the rest of the 242nd Marine Battalion, including Bravo Company, had been re-deployed back to Venus to deal with the separatists who had redoubled their efforts to take key infrastructure and disrupt the world's economy.

Now that the 4th platoon had rejoined Bravo Company, they were being thrown into the fire once more.

"All assembled, Gunny," Green reported as Williams reached his side.

"Don't tell me, tell the LT; that's *your* job now. I'm just here for moral support," Williams grunted.

"Lieutenant Grenwald," Staff Sergeant Green nodded to the LT. "The platoon is assembled."

The lieutenant nodded to Green and faced the assembled men and woman.

"Our little bit of R & R on the *Intrepid* is over, and it's time to get back to doing our jobs. While we were away, someone in the Sol Space Federation government decided that playing nice with these separatists on Venus was the right move. Well, they took that as an invitation to overrun the city of Tarja. They've now claimed it as their capital, and we can't have that."

Lieutenant Grenwald brought up the city on a portable holographic projector and walked around it.

"The city is loaded with civilians—some eleven million of them—and Fleet Intel doesn't know who is for and against the separatists. Kill drones have been ruled out; they want the keen eye of the corps to tell friend from foe. What we do know is where they've set up several of their garrisons and command facilities, and we're going to have the privilege of hitting one of their garrisons."

As he spoke, the holo lit up various structures in the city and drew a circle around their target.

"We can't take our birds in—they have too many anti-aircraft emplacements set up—and the brass doesn't want to call down an orbital strike with all the civvies around, so it's a run job."

Williams watched the Marines soak in the information. Their camp was three hundred and ten kilometers from the city, close to the territory controlled by the Venus Freedom Alliance, or the "Veefs" as the Marines had come to call them. That meant slogging it on foot the whole way—though the powered armor would get them there and in position before the next dawn.

"We have solid intel on their patrols out there, but we also know that they have good electronic camouflage so our eyes in the sky may not have a clear picture. Once we're out there, everything is suspect. There will be no safe areas. Our target is one of the farthest from our current position, so we're first. We break camp at dusk today."

Lieutenant Grenwald stepped away from the holo and nodded to Staff Sergeant Green.

"We're going in full powered armor, full weapons loadout, except one/one and three/three. Jansen, Tanaka, your fireteams are in scout gear with jump-jets. You'll be our eyes and ears out there. Olsen and Chang, bring the big guns.

The Marines nodded, and Williams could see them mentally reviewing their preparations.

"Marines, you have three hours. Assemble outside the mess at 20:00 hours. Dismissed!" Green concluded.

"How was that, Gunny?" Green asked.

Williams grunted. "You didn't cock up too bad. I suppose you'll do alright."

FARM HOUSE

STELLAR DATE: 3227431 / 04.22.4124 (Adjusted Gregorian)
LOCATION: Plains of Tarja, Teka Continent
REGION: Venus, InnerSol, Sol Space Federation

Williams hunched down in the deep Venusian night. Without a moon or a planetary ring—the only InnerSol world without one—stars, stations, and ships were the only things twinkling in the sky. It was, however, great for sneaking up on the enemy.

He peered around the equipment shed and scowled at the farmhouse beyond. The scouts had spotted at least seven figures inside, well protected behind the thick basalt walls of the structure. The volcanic rock was in ready supply on Venus, and everything seemed to be made of it. The rock walls on every structure were a blessing and a curse.

"We could fire some kinetics at it—that would take it down and we can move on," First Sergeant Bourne said as he inspected his weapon.

"You know the orders," Commander Lauren said with a shake of her head. "We're not supposed to obliterate the populace's property. The people behind this uprising already have enough reasons to want to separate from the Terran Hegemony—no need to give them more."

"We can kill the people, but we can't break their stuff?" Williams asked with a shake of his head.

"If the stuff shoots at us, then we can break it," Commander Lauren replied.

Commander Lauren had been Bravo Company's CO for several years, and First Sergeant Bourne had recently transferred in from Alpha Company. They were both exemplary Marines, but Williams still missed being the one that his CO listened to most. Lieutenant Grenwald had trusted William's word implicitly—even Major Richards had never second-guessed him. Lauren, however, liked to do things her own way, and always took Bourne's suggestions over his.

He allowed himself a moment's weakness, wishing he was back with 4th platoon—the outfit where he had spent the last decade—not stuck with Commander Lauren and First Sergeant Bourne.

Suck it up, Marine, he thought to himself. *The corps isn't your nanny. It's not here to give you what you want. That's what you're for.*

Williams took another look at the structure. It was going to be hard to take out; the separatists had more firepower than the intel said, and they were able to mask their movements from orbital surveillance. As far as he was concerned, they were dealing with an enemy that was nearly as well-armed as the corps.

<Can't get any probes in either,> Bruno, the battalion AI added. <They have some solid EM shields up.>

"There are no clean approaches," Williams added. "If we breach, they'll know we're coming."

Commander Lauren sighed. "Yeah, I know you guys aren't happy about the orders, but they're orders. We'll have to suck it up and breach. Get the platoon's sharpshooters lined up on those windows. We'll get in position, take out anyone that is dumb enough to poke their head around a corner, and then take the two doors and those three large windows."

Williams nodded and shared a brief glance with Bourne. If this was what they had to do, it was what they had to do.

"I'll take care of it," he said and moved carefully around the far side of the equipment shed, advancing through the farmyard until he came to 1st platoon's position.

Lieutenant Berger and Staff Sergeant Onada were in position with the rest of 1st platoon—spread around the south and east sides of the farmyard. To the northwest were open fields and no cover to speak of. Williams decided that he would lead the squads that took that side of the farmhouse.

"You cleared all the outbuildings?" he asked.

"Fuck, Gunny, what do you think?" Staff Sergeant Onada replied, her permanent scowl deepening for a moment. "We figured that we'd love some good butt fucking when we went in, and thought, 'hey, the Veefs are just the ones to do it'."

Williams bit back a response about Onada needing a good ass pounding—she never did know when to save her comments—though she seemed testier than usual on this deployment. Berger was shaking her head, as well. Williams could tell that Onada was wearing on her nerves, too.

"They're clear," Lieutenant Berger said. "Nothing in them that shouldn't be."

"Good. The old lady has spoken, we're going in with our boots. We're not to break the local's precious farm."

"For fuck's sake," Onada shook her head.

"Standard breach," Williams nodded to Lieutenant Berger, who sighed in response.

"Staff Sergeant Onada, get the sharpshooters from squad's two and three set up on the windows and wait for the signal."

"I'll take squad one around the far side," Williams replied. He sketched a rough map of the farmhouse's interior on the ground, drawn from the sonar readings the platoon had taken. "We'll take these rooms. Staff Sergeant Onada, take these, and Lieutenant Berger, clear this section over here."

"Any reason you're not putting that on the combat net?" Onada asked testily.

"Because those assholes have tech they shouldn't. You're a Marine, you should know how to do things the old-fashioned way," Williams growled. When this mission was over, he was going to take Onada aside and have some stern words with her.

"I approve," Lieutenant Berger replied. "It'll take you what...fifteen minutes to get around there?" she asked Williams.

"Give me twenty," he replied. "Let's stagger this thing. At zero, take some pot-shots at the windows on the south-east corner. That'll draw them over there. Then we hit, and pull them back, and thirty seconds later, you come in the other breach points."

Berger nodded and sent Onada to share the plan with her squads, while Williams crept across the farmyard to behind a pair of tractors to where first squad was set up.

"Seraph," he whispered to the squad leader.

"Gunny," she replied in soft tones. "I didn't expect to see you out here. Isn't there a cozy spot waiting for you back with the CO?"

"What, and let you guys cock everything up out here?" he replied with a smile. He had always liked Seraph. The worst part about his promotion to Gunnery Sergeant was that a relationship with her was out of the question now. Still, he'd enjoy her company whenever he could.

"Well, now you can cock it up with us," she replied. "I assume you didn't just come over here to flirt with me. What's the word?"

Williams felt his skin redden and he was glad the darkness hid it—though she probably had her IR vision on and would see the heat in his face with no trouble at all.

"First squad is coming around the side with me. You have three sharpshooters in your fireteams; get them to move half a klick out and cover the north-west side. The rest of us will get out a few hundred meters, and then work our way in. We'll do the final stretch in a full sprint. Squads two and three will provide a distraction. Mark is 21:43"

"Marked. Standard fare, then," Seraph nodded. She got her fireteam leaders' attention and relayed the orders to them via hand signals.

Thirty seconds later, the sharpshooters slipped away into the night. A row of trees to the south would give them cover, letting them run at full speed once obscured by the trees and brush. They would be a klick out in a few minutes and ready to move laterally into their firing positions.

Williams took fireteams one and four out into the fields, moving slow and low through the wheat's tall, waving stalks, while Seraph followed with two and three.

It took almost all the allotted time to get into position, and his fireteams reached their positions with less than thirty seconds to spare. He counted down under his breath and caught the eye of the two corporals making sure they were ready.

Ahead, the farmhouse loomed in the night, squat and sprawling—easily five hundred square meters, more than enough to harbor dozens of enemies. He prayed to whatever gods still cared about humanity that there wouldn't be anywhere near that many within.

At the marked time, weapons fire rang out on the far side of the farmhouse—slug throwers and light kinetics that would get through the temporary barriers the enemy had piled up around the windows and take out anyone dumb enough to hide behind them.

He counted to fifteen and then leapt up, dashing toward the farmhouse as fast as the powered armor could take him. He was moving at seventy kilometers per hour when he smashed through the back door, the four Marines of the squad's second fireteam right behind him.

Williams knew from the sonar scans that the room was a long—probably a kitchen—and that he could slide to a stop before hitting the interior wall. As his boots dug into the floor, his HUD identified two figures holding weapons at the end of the room, and he fired several shots from his beam rifle at one of them. As the beams hit, his scan suite gauged the capabilities of the enemy's armor, and sent a data burst across the combat net that it would take electron beams or high-power kinetics to take down the Veefs.

The Marines behind him were already firing at the two enemies, and they switched their weapons to electron beams before Williams had even slid to a stop and turned around.

Two down.

From the next room, he heard the sounds of weapons fire and knew that fireteam four had come through their window and taken out at least one enemy.

The interior walls were also made of basalt—good for cover, bad for taking out the separatists. He sent out a swath of nano probes to see if any enemies hid within the adjacent rooms. The interior of the farmhouse was filled with nano countermeasures, and the probes didn't make it more than a meter before they were destroyed.

Williams passed hand signals back to the fireteam on his six, and they stacked up at the room's northern door. He nodded to the corporal, and the Marines smashed through the opening and threw in a pair of concussion grenades. The blasts echoed in the building's stone walls and Williams felt a moment of pity for anyone in the room. Even when protected by full armor, those grenades could dole out one hell of a headache.

He grabbed a pan from the stove and thrust it through the opening into the room. His vision picked up an IR bloom as the metal took laser fire, and he knew the members of his fireteam would calculate the beam's origin. The corporal passed signals on the position of the enemy, and Williams nodded for them to go in.

Corporal Charles was the first one through the door, and he took a shot on his armor's chest-piece before returning fire. The rest of the fireteam followed him in, laying down a field of fire and forcing the enemy back. Williams glanced at Charles and saw that a centimeter-deep hole was burned in his ablative plating, but no other damage was present.

"You're good," he grunted and slapped the corporal on the shoulder.

"Happy to be the meat shield," Charles replied.

The fireteam moved through the room and checked the fallen enemies that their shots had taken down, then inched toward the corner where one of the other beams had come from. Private Huck was the first one over, and he pointed his weapon down behind a stone counter.

"Drop it," he hissed.

Nothing happened. He waved Williams and Charles over.

Behind the counter, a man crouched, his helmet on the ground beside him. He was shaking as he clutched a beam-rifle to his chest.

"Drop it, boy," Williams growled, "or sitting there pissing yourself will be the last thing you do."

The man looked up and saw the cold certainty in Williams' eyes. He nodded slowly and lowered the weapon.

"Get up," Private Huck said, gesturing with his weapon.

As the Veef rose, the sounds of weapons fire intensified throughout the farmhouse, and Williams knew all squads had breached. He glanced over his shoulder to see the Marines in the fireteam securing the room's two other entrances. One passed a hand signal through the opening, indicating the northern section of the house was clear.

<Clear,> Seraph sent over the combat net, followed by the other fireteam and squad leaders sounding off.

<All clear, Lieutenant,> Staff Sergeant Onada advised when the building was fully secured.

<Commander Lauren,> Williams said. <The farmhouse is secure.>

<Good work, Gunny,> Commander Lauren replied. <We're coming in.>

"Gunny," Corporal Charles said from beside their captured rebel. "This guy isn't from Venus…none of them are. I ran scans and they're all

Diskers...a lot of them are wanted for questioning about some nasty business out there."

"Diskers?" Williams asked as he looked down at the shaking man at his feet. "What the fuck are you assholes doing here at Venus?"

The man didn't reply, and Williams was about to reach down and haul him to his feet when a message came in from Staff Sergeant Green.

<Gunny, do you have a moment?>

<Better be good,> Williams replied.

<Depends on your definition of good,> Green replied, and Williams could just imagine the sergeant's stupid smile. <We seem to have found their garrison.>

<No way you made it to Tarja already,> Williams responded.

<Yeah, we're still a hundred kicks out...but so are they. At least a whole battalion, and they're ready for a fight.>

Williams laughed, <Well, I guess at least we won't have to mess up their pretty city to take 'em out. Let me pass this up the chain and see what we'll do.>

PLAINS OF TARJA

STELLAR DATE: 3227431 / 04.22.4124 (Adjusted Gregorian)
LOCATION: Plains of Tarja, Teka Continent
REGION: Venus, InnerSol, Sol Space Federation

The city of Tarja sat on a high steppe sharing the same name. To the east, the plains gently sloped down to the Prelandra Sea, and to the west, the steppe fell away sharply through a series of hills and long valleys before leveling out again in the Jurgen River valley.

Fourth platoon was situated at the edge of the hill country. The enemy they had stumbled upon lay between them and the city—the lights of which were visible along the horizon, illuminating the clouds with their ethereal glow.

"Well, that's a right mess you've stumbled into," Williams said as he surveyed the enemy camp.

"Hey, Gunny, you gave us the route to take. We're just following orders."

"Huh," Williams grunted. "Well, I got it from Bruno, and he got it from the fleet monkeys up there in space—where they can't seem to spot a few thousand soldiers moving across the face of the freaking planet."

"They have a pretty good stealth shield," Lieutenant Grenwald added. "We would have walked right into that damn camp if Perez hadn't stumbled on one of their pickets."

Williams snorted. "Glad to see Perez is managing to make hauling his sorry skin around the Sol System worthwhile. So, how come we have eyes on it from here?"

"Their stealth tech is set up to keep the fleet boys and girls from spotting them. I guess they figure their sentries will spot anyone getting close on ground," Lieutenant Grenwald replied.

"Still sloppy, if you ask me," Williams said. "They should know we have fucking comms. We can let the vacuum jocks know right where their little party is, and they wouldn't know what hit 'em."

"We're away from civilians. Is an orbital strike an option?" Green asked. "That sure would clean things up nicely."

Williams shook his head. "Commander Lauren got the word from Colonel Ender. We're to take them out quietly."

Grenwald snorted. "Seriously? How are we going to take them out quietly? No matter what we do, someone's going to spot a fight of this size—not to mention there are only seventy of us between our 'toon and first. There are at least fifteen hundred enemy soldiers down there."

"Bruno is hacking into their comm network," Williams replied. "First platoon has seeded interception pegs so that we'll be the ones on the line when they call for help. If we play this right, we can take these bastards out and no one will be the wiser—not for a few hours, at least."

"How did they get so organized, anyway?" Green asked while looking out over the camp. "I mean…other than their half-assed stealth setup, they look professional out there, not some rag-tag bunch of separatists."

Williams nodded. "Guys we hit were all Diskers, not Venusians. I bet these are the same."

"Diskers!" Green shook his head. "Things are really turning to shit, Gunny. How the fuck are Disker separatists sneaking armies onto Venus?"

"Probably on ships, Staff Sergeant," Lieutenant Grenwald replied. "What's the plan after we get comms locked down, Gunny?"

Williams looked between the two men. "That's when we get to play bait."

* * * * *

Williams gazed up at the lights above Venus, picking out which were stars, and which were ships and orbital habitats. The glare from humanity's creation greatly outnumbered the natural lights, but they still had a beauty of their own.

That was one thing Venus offered: plenty of time to stare at the stars. It only rotated once every two-hundred-and-twenty-four Earth days, spinning retrograde, no less. It always felt unnatural to watch the stars rise in the west, but he supposed that it was perfectly natural on Venus.

The planet's terraformers had dealt with the long night—which still tended to grow rather cold—by positioning two small fusion burners around the world. They approximated an Earth-length day-night cycle on the dark side, though they only cast a fraction of the Sol's light. The sunward side of the planet, however, had no respite during its long day.

He double-checked the positions of the two fusion-suns, confirming once more that the one named Gertrude would rise over the western horizon in twenty minutes—right when the Diskers would cross over the rise at the western edge of the plains, chasing after Jansen and one/one.

If the impossibility of catching sacktime with Seraph was his biggest regret when it came to his promotion to gunnery sergeant, being further from Jansen's expertise was his second.

The corporal was the most competent Marine in the entire platoon, more than some of the squad leaders. Her tactical awareness and calm, yet serious manner, was a boon in any situation. He had always counted on her to get shit done right, and fast. He hoped she would take his suggestion and apply for OCS. The Marines need more officers like her—real soldiers who could be real leaders.

A pre-dawn glow began to creep over the western horizon, and he cycled his vision, looking for Jansen and one/one. Any minute now they should come into view, before working their way down the center of the valley.

From his position high on the valley's south ridge, he looked down its length once more. It ran at a seventy-degree angle to the edge of the steppe to the east. The end close to the high plain had only sparse cover, mostly rocks and low scrub. However, as the valley sloped away from the plains, and the cut it made into the surface of Venus grew deeper, the foliage thickened. A kilometer further in, tall trees and thick scrub filled the lower reaches the valley, and scattered copses of trees provided cover along the high slopes.

The Marines of Bravo Company's 4th platoon would hit the enemy before they reached the thicker cover, which was occupied by the two heavy-weapons fireteams. It was a textbook ambush that would create a perfect killbox for the Diskers.

Provided they took the bait.

Sergeant Kowalski, squad one's leader, tapped him on the shoulder and pointed to the south. Williams swept his gaze across the landscape and saw the Marines of one/one creep over the ridge at the edge of the steppe and begin to work her way down the slope—into the wrong valley.

"What the fuck is she doing?" Lieutenant Grenwald asked.

"Not sure," Williams replied. "But its Jansen. If she didn't make this approach, then she had a damn good reason."

"Green, reposition the platoon." Lieutenant Grenwald said, his voice carrying the worry Williams felt. "We need to get into that valley yesterday, or this is going to be the sorriest ambush ever."

Staff Sergeant Green didn't reply, but he conveyed the orders with hand signals to the nearby elements of the platoon and sent runners to signal the squads on the north slope.

"This is going to be tight," Williams shook his head.

"We'll make it work," Grenwald said. "Best estimate for our boys and girls to reposition?"

"Twelve minutes," Staff Sergeant Green replied in an instant, though his eyes flicked to Williams to see if the senior noncom agreed.

Williams gave a nod and crept over the ridge with Green to meet Jensen's fireteam, while the lieutenant followed one/two to a position halfway down the valley's length. The two sergeants crept through the low brush on the northern side of the new valley until they reached Jansen.

"Corporal Jansen, what the hell is going on?" Williams growled. "You do know this is the wrong valley, right?"

Jansen nodded. "I'd noticed that, Gunny. I figured you wanted us to make it here alive, though. The Veefs…or Diskers…whatever…they had a patrol approaching from the north, right along the edge of the steppe. We would have run right into it. As it is, they'll probably join the company that's tailing us."

"How many?" Green asked.

"We didn't get a good look, but our visual tally came to twenty-two. Probably a whole platoon," Jansen replied.

"So what…two-hundred and fifty? Shit, Jansen, I thought we asked you to pull in a few of them, not half their battalion." Williams shook his head.

"Sorry, Gunny, should I go back and tell them that they're not all invited?" Corporal Jansen asked.

Williams chuckled softly. That was one of the reasons he liked Jansen. She gave as good as she got.

"We open with the heavy slug throwers, then," Green said, and Williams nodded. Green crept back through the underbrush to confirm the decision with Lieutenant Grenwald before passing the order.

"What did their armor look like?" he asked Jansen.

"Like you saw at that farmhouse, Sta—Gunny," Jansen said, catching herself before she used his old rank. "Medium-grade. Powered, but not fully like ours. It didn't look like what the Scattered Worlds Alliance uses, though. I think they just got the soldiers in, not all their gear."

"Makes sense," Williams replied. "It's a bit easier to move people than full battlegear."

"What's the plan, then?" Jansen asked.

"Same as before. Get down to the end of the valley. Lead them to the heavies, but don't go straight down the center. Try to make it look like you're being stealthy."

"Forgot who you're talking to, Gunny?" Jansen asked with a wink as she signaled to her fireteam and moved out.

He took a more circuitous route along the valley's north slope, working his way to the back of the Marine formation where Chang would be set up, and where Jansen and her fireteam would stop, leaking small amounts of EM for the enemy scouts to pick up.

As he moved, he considered her assessment of the enemy. Based on the intel MICI had gathered, most of the Venusian separatists weren't military, and fewer were former Marines. If the Veefs wanted to make a real stand, they needed a real military force. No mercenary army would take on a job that pitted them against the Terran Space Force and its Force Recon Orbital Drop Marines, but he could see the Diskers getting involved. They had been itching to get out of the Sol Space Federation since that dust-up at Makemake, the capital world of the Scattered Worlds Alliance, ten years ago.

One of the Terran Space Force's largest carriers, the TSS *Normandy* had run dark, coming in stellar north over Makemake before lighting its engines for a full burn right over the planet.

He'd seen a carrier do a full braking burn; even in InnerSol, it would outshine The Sun. The carrier must have directed its engine wash away from the planet, otherwise they would have burned it to a cinder. The populace of Makemake, and no small part of its military, put up a blockade around the planet, and the carrier was forced to hold back.

In the end, the TSF won and the *Normandy* survived and things appeared to settle down in the scattered disk. Optimists liked to believe that the TSS *Normandy's* actions at Makemake had quelled any sedition, but Williams didn't believe it. If there were enough people in the scattered to pull off that attack on short notice, then they wouldn't just disappear after one battle. Their dissent ran deep.

Movement at the top of the ridge drew his attention back to the present, and Williams watched the first of the enemy troops slip into the long valley. If these were also Diskers assisting the Veefs, then their separatists hadn't disappeared at all—just changed tactics.

This was the most critical time in the ambush. The enemy scouts would know the valley presented a risk, but one they had to take if they were to follow Jansen's fireteam. There could be no other EM, no motion from the Marines that the enemy could detect. They had to believe it was just the one fireteam in the valley.

Minute-by-minute, Williams watched the Disker troops work their way down the vale, their scouts ranging up the slopes, but not so far that they found the TSF Marines lying in wait.

He counted the enemy as they crossed over the ridge; they were coming too slow, but there weren't enough to add up to the numbers Jansen had reported. He moved slowly through the underbrush to the corporal's position to see that she also wore a worried expression.

"Shit, they're flanking us," he whispered to her. "Get up over the north ridge and get ready—we'll hit them first. It'll be too soon, but better than being caught in the hammer and tongs."

Jansen nodded and led her fireteam north, while Williams crept through the underbrush where he encountered Chang's squad.

"Break that shit down and get it up on the south ridge. We're being flanked from both sides. You're going to have to take out anyone coming over from the south. When the shit starts, you shred anything that moves."

"Aye, Gunny," Chang replied, and his crew broke down their weapon with smooth, silent precision before slipping into the brush and up the south slope.

Williams worked his way east and up the north slope to where Lieutenant Grenwald and Staff Sergeant Green waited.

"Saw what you did there," Lieutenant Grenwald said with a nod. "Thanks. We'll hit them hard as soon as they make it to the half-klick mark—hopefully that will before they come over the north and south ridges."

"What's Plan B?" Green asked.

"Call in for starfire and pray they deliver," Williams replied.

"That's going to blow the op," Lieutenant Grenwald said. "They'll know we're coming."

"If they kill us all and report back, the cat will be out of the bag anyway," Williams grunted.

"I sent a coded burst to the old lady to let her know we're in a bind," Lieutenant Grenwald said. "With luck, she can bring 1st platoon around the battalion out there to back us up."

"Don't count on it," Williams said. "There are a thousand Diskers between us and her. That's a lot, even for thirty Marines. We need to get this done ourselves."

The three men crouched in the underbrush for several more minutes, waiting for the enemy to reach the half-klick mark and for Jansen and Chang to get in position. In the west, Gertrude had fully crested the western horizon and Williams nodded to Lieutenant Grenwald.

"As good a time as any," the lieutenant replied.

Staff Sergeant Green flipped off his rifle's safety and set the weapon to fire an electron beam. The Marine could shoot the spots off a frog at a thousand meters without any tech assisting his aim. A pair of iron sights and a wind reading—assisted by the augmented eyes the corps had given him—and Green would make you dead.

He took careful sight down its length and carefully squeezed the trigger, and an enemy soldier fell to the ground—his head blown almost clear off—Green once more proving his skill as a Marine.

"Thought their armor might be weak along the chin," Green grunted as weapons fire broke out all along the hillside as the Marines took out targets of opportunity before rolling to new positions.

William's estimate put the number of enemy in the valley to be just over a hundred and fifty with at least twenty falling in the first volley. But now the enemy soldiers were taking cover, and the Marines had to work harder to make a kill.

The *ka-chunk* of two/two's crew-served weapon sounded to his left, up on the hillside, and several more Disker soldiers were down before they realized light cover wouldn't cut it.

Across the valley, the sound of Chang's heavy weapons squad cut through the general mayhem of the fight, but Williams couldn't see any incoming rounds from the kinetic slug-thrower. That meant two/one was engaging enemy on the other side of the south ridge. They were flanked after all.

Williams fired a few shots from his rifle—one clipping a Disker in the shoulder, the other two hitting cover—before he rolled to a new position and firing another round. They were scoring hits, but the Marines hadn't taken enough of the Diskers out in the initial volley. More than a hundred enemy soldiers remained in the valley, and he saw another dozen come up over the south ridge, escaping the wrath of two/one's weapon.

"Green!" Grenwald ordered. "Send a burst on the combat net. Get the two squads on the south ridge to fall back to the Chang's position. They're gonna get crushed out there."

"I'll move up the north side," Williams added and took off running, crashing through the underbrush, his powered armor granting him ten meter strides. He was making himself a target, but a fast-moving one. With luck, it would draw some of the enemy out and give his Marines something to shoot at.

Fireteams one/two and one/three were at the head of the valley, and Williams reached their position in less than three minutes. He would have made it faster, but he didn't want to draw all the enemy fire right down onto them.

"Marines! We've gotta fall back," he yelled over the sounds of weaponsfire when he reached their position.

"Can't, Gunny," Corporal Taylor yelled from above him on the hill. "We've got Diskers on the ridge above us now."

"And below," Corporal Becker added while swapping his weapon's power cell. "They're closing up. We'll have to go around to the south ridge and hope Chang can cover us."

Williams pulled their feeds—no need for EM-silence anymore—and saw that forty Diskers had come over the north ridge in his wake. That route was closed off from any reasonable retreat. Becker was right; the south ridge did seem to have fewer enemies, just the dozen he had spotted as they slipped past Change's team.

"OK, Marines, stop warming those patches of dirt and let's do this!" Williams growled.

Becker's fireteam led the way across the head of the valley, and Williams prayed that no Disker reinforcements would come over from the east ridge—that would end their little action right quick.

Taylor followed in the rear, laying down suppressive fire to slow the Diskers who were spilling over the north ridge, just a hundred meters away.

"It's getting hot out here, Gunny!" Perez yelled from beside Taylor as they fired controlled bursts at a squad of Diskers that had taken cover behind a rock outcropping. "Brush is a bit sparse ahead. These guys are gonna mow us down."

Williams took aim at a Disker, who was sticking out of cover, and hit him center mass before assessing the situation. For being a fuck-up, Perez was right. They were getting screwed fast.

<Chang!> he called over the combat net. <We need fire on the south ridge, head of the valley.>

<Busy over here, Gunny. Got at least forty of these assholes to keep pinned down,> Chang replied.

<You'll be busy at our funerals if you don't give us some support!> Williams hollered. <Just chew some holes in the outcropping I marked on the net. It'll slow them down and then we're gonna take the south ridge to meet up with you.>

<OK, OK, Gunny, don't have to yell.>

Chang cut the connection, and a moment later, kinetic rounds moving at over ten kilometers per second tore into the rock outcropping, and the Disksers behind it scrambled away as their cover disintegrated.

"Let's move," Williams directed and led the two fireteams across the head of the valley as Lieutenant Grenwald called in.

<I have to pull Chang back, he's taking too much fire from the south. Walker's down and Popov is hit. That south ridge is gonna get real hot, real fast.>

<Shit, LT, that's our exit!> Corporal Taylor swore.

<Sorry about that, two/one was going to get wasted up there. Hold tight, we're going to mass and push toward you,> Grenwald replied.

Williams paused and surveyed the battlefield. Behind his two fireteams, to the east, was an unknown. Either no one was over the ridge on the edge of the steppe, or a thousand Diskers were about to come over the rise and wipe them out. To the north, at least a full platoon was moving toward them, and another was coming up from the south.

Straight west, down through the base of the valley, lay the dead and wounded enemies from the Marine's initial assault. At least two platoons of Diskers were still present, working their way through the foliage toward the rest of the TSF Marines a kilometer distant.

They wouldn't expect to be attacked from the rear.

"OK, this is the plan," Williams addressed the two fireteams. "We have three CFT shields between us. Perez, Jacobs, and Larson, you're on the shields. Everyone else, stack up behind. We're going to do a powered charge right through them."

"Gunny...you nuts? We'll get torn to shreds," Jacobs said.

"You wanna sit here and wait for them to surround us?" Williams asked. "The LT can't push up toward us fast enough, and without Chang's big gun, our Disker friends will be visiting real soon."

"Think they'll have snacks?" Perez asked. "I'm a bit hungry."

"Stuff it, Perez. Get ready, Marines. We're doing this. Keep it under fifty klicks an hour, everyone stacked behind the shield, take out every target you can. But focus on creating mayhem. Absolute mayhem."

<Grenwald,> Williams called in. <No shots down the center, we're coming in.>

The CFT shields were built of carbon nano tube fibers and could take a hell of a pounding. When unfolded, they were large enough to cover the entire body of the Marine holding them. The Marines stacked up, and behind each were two additional Marines, except behind Perez's where Williams assumed the rear position.

He took a deep breath and glanced at the two fireteams. "Semper Fi, Marines."

"Semper Fi," they responded a moment before Perez, Jacobs and Larson took off.

They stayed as close as they could to the shield-bearers, firing at everything that looked like an enemy. Ahead, a Disker jumped out and unloaded a clip of high-velocity kinetics at Jacob's shield, only to be thrown aside as the three hundred kilograms of Marine and powered armor hit him at fifty kilometers per hour.

The soldier fell to the ground, and Taylor fired a photon beam into his torso as they passed. A single laser shot wouldn't be fatal with the armor the Diskers wore, but it would have him tearing off that chest plate in short order.

Williams got a clear line on several other enemies as they rushed past, and he took what shots he could while leaping over brush, fallen logs, and the stream bed as it crisscrossed their path. Then, a thud sounded nearby and Private Koller, who was directly in front of him, stumbled and fell.

"Leg," Koller cried out, and Williams doubled back to help.

Williams signaled the other two groups to keep going while Perez stopped and held his position with Weber on his six, laying down covering fire as Williams reached Koller's side. The Marine was right, he was shot in the leg—the limb was gone from mid-thigh down.

"Fuck, Private, don't you know you need your legs to run?" Williams swore.

"Sorry, Gunny," Koller's grimace was visible through his face plate "I hadn't realized that."

Williams threw his arm around Koller's torso and lifted him to his feet as enemy fire tore at the trees around them.

"No good, Gunny," Koller said when they reached Perez and Weber. "I'll slow you down too much. You gotta leave me here."

"You get shot in the head and I didn't see it?" Williams asked. "Marines don't leave a man behind. Even one as dumb as you."

"Perez, get to the streambed, we'll get low behind those rocks and work our way down to the rest of the platoon."

Perez nodded and began to move, shielding Williams and Koller as best he could, while Weber fired at anything that looked remotely suspicious.

Williams pulled the feed from the combat net and saw that the Diskers were coming down the valley sides, rushing after them. A platoon's worth of Diskers also lay between them and the rest of the TSF Marines. They were surrounded.

<Should we come back?> Taylor asked.

<No!> Williams replied. <Connect up with the rest of the 'toon and Grenwald will figure out how to push to us. We need a decisive blow.>

RESCUE

STELLAR DATE: 3227431 / 04.22.4124 (Adjusted Gregorian)
LOCATION: Tarja Escarpment, Teka Continent
REGION: Venus, InnerSol, Sol Space Federation

<You guys need a hand?> Commander Lauren's voice came over the combat net and into Williams' mind like a soothing balm.

<More than one would be nice,> Williams replied.

Bruno updated the company's combat net with 1st platoon's positions and Williams felt a smile pull at his lips. She was positioning her two crew-served weapons at the ridge between the valley and the steppe. Though the position couldn't see most of the enemy positions in the valley, targeting data from the 4th platoon would give them plenty to shoot at.

Williams fed in the locations of the Diskers they had raced past and raised an eyebrow as he saw the Company CO approve the use of proton beams.

<OK, people, we're going nova,> William's informed the Marines with him, using the 4th platoon's term for live fire with proton beams.

Proton beams carried a stream hydrogen protons at near luminal speeds. When they hit a target, the proton was destroyed, delivering a massive amount of kinetic energy and showering the area with radiation.

They were not normally approved for terrestrial operations, but Williams wasn't going to question the permission once granted.

The sounds the proton beams made as they hit their marks was loud enough that the previous battle in the valley was a peaceful evening by comparison. Explosions cascaded across the valley's slopes, and whenever there was a pause in the beamfire, the sounds of the two platoon's heavy weapons filled the air with a steady stream of low thuds.

Fourth platoon had half a dozen soldiers who were not combat-capable and a dozen more who were injured but could still squeeze a trigger. However, 1st platoon was fresh and spoiling for a fight. They spilled down the valley's slopes, staying to clear lanes designated on the combat net.

"Steady, now," Williams said, knowing that any enemy fleeing from 1st platoon would likely pass their position in the streambed.

"Pass me my rifle," Koller said from where he was propped up against a rock. "Let me shoot the legs off some of these assholes."

Williams grabbed Koller's weapon and passed it over. "Make it count."

Upstream, a group of Diskers broke cover, three looking behind and two looking ahead. They fired first, and Williams didn't feel the least bit of sorrow as his stream of protons slammed into one of the enemy's shoulders, spinning him around to crash into one of his companions. Perez, Weber, and Koller each fired their shots a moment after Williams.

A few seconds later, the brief exchange of fire was over and the five enemies were down.

"Uh, Gunny?" Perez said, pointing at Williams's left side.

Williams looked down and saw one of the batteries for his armor sparking. He quickly detached it and tossed it across the stream before it began to spout fire.

"Thanks, Private," Williams said. "Go check those guys with Weber. Put L-PACs on them if they're alive. We don't need them getting up and causing problems."

"On it, Gunny," Perez said and advanced up the streambed with Weber. Perez kept his weapon ready, eyes and enhanced senses scanning the area as Weber checked over the fallen soldiers. He spotted two live ones and unsealed their helmets, slapping L-PACs on their necks.

The small devices were filled with a chemical cocktail that attacked the nervous system, temporarily paralyzing a person, while combat nano locked down the wearer's armor and mods. It worked—mostly—and was better than headshots on the wounded.

"If there're live ones, then they know our position, Gunny," Koller said through gritted teeth. He wasn't feeling any pain, his armor had already deadened his nerves and sealed up his leg-stump, but that didn't stop the brain from thinking it was in pain.

"I know," Williams replied. "But we're better here in cover then carrying your sorry ass through the woods, so here we stay. First platoon will be down in no time; if these Diskers know what's good for them, they'll surrender."

"Only if they get a good look at you, Gunny," Perez said as he returned with Weber.

Williams cast the private a dark look that was obscured by his helmet.

"Marine, get your ass a dozen meters into the woods over there," Williams said while gesturing to the north side of the stream. "Weber, same thing, south side."

Williams bent and lifted Koller, moving him to a better position behind a jumble of rocks to offer support, and then took up a position across the narrow body of water, ready for the next wave of Diskers.

It didn't take long before enemy crashed through the underbrush, firing wildly as they came. There were twenty of them, mostly clustered along the streambed. Their movements were clumsy, and they were making little use of natural cover.

That was the thing about Diskers. They weren't used to fighting on planets, and the worlds they did have were all low-*g*. Plant life on those planets stretched high into the sky and were thin, reedy things. Not like these oaks and maples.

Sure, the trees wouldn't stop a proton beam, but any cover was good cover.

The Diskers slowed as they caught sight as their fallen comrades, and a pair bent to check on the two live ones. That was when the Marines opened fire. Five of the enemy fell in the first few seconds and the rest threw down their weapons and surrendered. A few stragglers brought up the rear, saw their fellows standing with hands in the air, and quickly followed suit.

<Musta thought they hit our 'toon's line,> Perez said.

Williams nodded and stood from behind his cover. Best way to make the Diskers think they had just run into more than four Marines was to act like it.

"Move away from your weapons—over there." He gestured to a clear space north of the stream. Each of his three Marines had clear lines of sight on that patch of dirt, and it would do until 1st platoon reached them. By the data on the combat net, that should be in less than two minutes.

One of the Diskers reached for a sidearm, and a shot from Perez's weapon blew the weapon clear out of its holster.

"*All* your weapons on the ground. Next one of you sunsabitches who thinks you can move faster than a Marine trigger finger is going to lose a hand—or worse."

<*Ah, shit, Gunny,*> Koller said, flagging an update on the combat net.

Williams saw it. Taylor and Becker's groups had punched through the Diskers behind them and re-united with the rest of 4th platoon. The enemy between his team's position and the fourth were in disarray. Most were going up the north and south sloped of the valley, while another dozen appeared to be making a mad dash up the stream, right toward their position.

<*Ready, boys and girls, we have company on our six!*>

Williams tossed a satchel of L-PACs to one of the enemy soldiers who had already surrendered. "Put these on your buddies," he growled.

The soldier didn't move and Williams shot him in the leg. It wasn't a full power beam, and it only locked up the armor's knee joint.

"OK, you do it," he gestured with his rifle at another Disker. "Hop to it or you get one under the chin. The rest of you assholes, down on the ground and helmets off *now!*"

Williams wasn't sure if they'd comply, but something in his voice must have convinced them that this was not where they wanted to die. As the helmets came off and the soldier he had selected began to apply the L-PACs to her comrades, the dozen enemies approaching from the rear burst through the underbrush.

Williams grit his teeth and didn't turn from his charges. It was a good call, too, as one of the ones not yet under the effects of an L-PAC leapt up, lunging for Williams. He didn't hesitate even a moment, a twist of his hips, and his sights were right between the Disker's eyes.

Grey matter sprayed across the Diskers and two of them screamed as pieces of bone and brain hit them.

"No more bright ideas," Williams screamed as he watched Perez,

Weber, and Koller fire into the Diskers behind him over the combat net, not breaking eye contact with the group in front.

Ten seconds later, it was over. Four of the second group of enemies were down, and Weber was leading the survivors over to the clearing where their friends lay on the ground.

"Nice work there, Gunny," Commander Lauren said as she came into view, easing around the trunk of a massive maple tree. All around them, the Marines of 1st platoon appeared. A squad surrounded the Diskers and began checking the L-PACs the Disker woman had applied and then finished the job after locking her down.

"Didn't even need us, it seems," First Sergeant Onada added as he approached.

"You provided a useful distraction." Williams shrugged. "Always happy to see a friendly face on the field."

<We wrapped up a platoon's worth,> Grenwald reported over the combat net. <A few got away to the south and north, though.>

"I've a squad going over the south ridge," Seraph said aloud as she approached. "We'll pick up any stragglers."

<North side covered,> Jansen reported in. <There's a dozen or so of them locked down over there. But we've got bigger problems. I see movement on the east ridge.>

Williams saw from the combat net's feed that Jansen's fireteam was half-way down the valley and would have a clear view of the east ridge separating the valley from the steppe. He tapped into her visuals and saw what he feared: the rest of the Disker battalion.

"There's more of them than we first estimated," Lauren said. "Easily another fifteen hundred."

Williams shook his head. "They know we're here, and they know our numbers. There's no way we can stage an ambush on a force of that size."

"Gunny's right," Onada said with a nod. "We have to fall back."

The company leadership moved away from the captured soldiers to discuss their options.

"Choices are shit," Williams said. "This valley dumps out into a low plain, almost no cover. We have over a dozen casualties, so we're going to move slow. They'll mow us down."

<First platoon,> Commander Lauren called out over the combat net. <You're on the south ridge. Fourth, you're on the north. Advance to the rear we'll make these bastards chase us halfway across Venus if we have to, but we're not giving up!>

A chorus of oo-rahs echoed over the combat net and the Marines finished locking down the enemy combatants before following their platoon leader's directions to take up positions on the valley's slopes.

Over the next few minutes, as the TSF Marines retreated, things began to look grim. A thousand Diskers were already in the valley. They weren't rushing but were pressing hard, making sure that when the Marines were backed out into the wide, clear portion of the valley they would be in range of Disker weapons.

All through the valley, trees fell and fires broke out as full-scale warfare erupted between the two groups. Williams' mind wandered for a moment and he wondered who would clean up this mess, or if it would be left to re-grow on its own after the radiation began to dissipate.

Then, a flash of light in the sky above them caught his attention.

At first, he wondered if it was starfire, falling from the fleet onto the Diskers, but he knew that couldn't be it. The Disker stealth shield covered this area, and fleet was usually too chicken to target off data from the ground troops' combat net.

Williams cycled his vision and zoomed in on the skies above. A soft chuckle escaped his throat. Nearly a thousand figures were visible in the skies above the valley. The men and women of the 8th Battalion, 242nd Regiment weren't called Force Recon Orbital Drop Marines for nothing.

<Hold on Marines, the cavalry has arrived,> Colonel Ender's voice came over the combat net.

The dim Venusian morning lit up with the lights of a thousand jump-jets flaring, slowing the Marine's descent and giving them opportunity to take aim at the Diskers below.

A thousand proton beams rained down from the sky, tearing apart the Disker's leading line, pulling targeting data from Bravo Company's combat net. Two minutes later, every boot in 8th Battalion's five combat companies stood on Venusian soil.

It was time to finish this fight.

* * *

Williams nodded to Commander Lauren as she approached.

"Botched that nicely, didn't we?" she said as she leaned against a maple tree.

"Did as well as we could," Williams replied. "Our intel was sorely lacking. We came down expecting to fight a bunch of separatists, and ended up facing what I bet is one of our federation's militaries."

"Think that's how they'll see it up the chain?" Lauren asked.

Williams wondered why Lauren was asking his opinion and not Onada's. Maybe the first sergeant wasn't good at commiserating.

"If we really are looking at Venusian and Scattered World separatists working together, then there are bigger things to worry about than who got the intel wrong on the op, and who executed it poorly. We lost seventeen Marines today. If we did make mistakes, we've already paid for them."

"That we have, now on to the next," Commander Lauren replied.

Until next time…

Author M.D. Cooper

The tales of the 242nd Marines are the first in a broader series known as The Sol Dissolution. Visit www.aeon14.com/aeon14-books to learn more about these stories, and the universe of Aeon 14.

If you would like to learn more about Williams and the Marines of the 242nd, as well as the events leading up to this conflict, read Destiny Rising, which tells of the assault on Makemake referenced in this story, as well as the 4th platoon's deployment to the *Intrepid* where they assisted Major

Tanis Richards in stopping a plan to destroy both the ship, and the Callisto Orbital Habitat.

Destroy the Planet
By TJ Ryan

CHAPTER ONE

General Mayne looked up at the darkness of the night sky, at the myriad of stars within the curtain of black, twinkling like burning candles. This was the pinnacle of man's history, this moment right here. Thousands of years of creation had brought them to this.

The launch of the Huxley.

"Sir?" his aide said to him.

Mayne could hardly stand the little toadie sycophant. George Thimley was the second cousin of the daughter of the President's first wife, or some such thing, and as they say it's not who you are but who you know that counts. George was ungodly thin and hardly made a move without asking three different people what he should do, and he had a weak handshake to boot. None of those things made him suitable for being a General's aide-de-camp, in Mayne's opinion.

But he was in line to be given his fourth star next month, and ticking off some touchhole relation to the President of the United Countries of Earth would only derail that from happening. So, he tolerated the mealy little man with his buzzed red hair and freckles. "What is it, Thimley?"

"Sir, the launch is about to begin."

Mayne rubbed a heavy hand over his bald scalp. Once, when he was younger, he'd had a full head of thick blonde hair. Now even his eyebrows were bald. Curse of old age, he supposed. At sixty-eight he could still take on most of the young cadets who came through the Academy for training, but that didn't mean much. The military was becoming a service organization. The world had been at peace for more than twenty years. No more war. No more hate. Only dedication to a single goal.

Reach the stars.

"Fine," Mayne said to keep Thimley from rubbing the skin off his hands. Straightening his green military jacket with its rows of colored medals at the left breast, he nodded. "Let's go watch history."

The devil of it was that they had to launch the vehicle at night. Something about the launch window and the relative distances between the Earth and its nearest neighbor, Proxima Centauri. Mayne shrugged. Let the big brains figure that out. This was the year 3847, after all. Or at least, by the old Gregorian Calendar it would have been. Under the new calendar, started when The Western Bloc had agreed to let Europe and Russia enter their economic system, it was the year 139. Either way it was an age of technological wonders.

Walking down the path that led to the observation platform where all the other assembled dignitaries were assembling, Mayne found one of those technological wonders waiting for him.

The launch site had been built into the ground, so the observation platform was on the rim of a huge metallic bowl two sports stadiums across. Safety railings had been put in place to keep everyone back, not that anyone who knew anything about the Huxley would have to be reminded to stay back. Voices from speakers echoed and reverberated around the clearing between the control buildings as Mayne gazed out over the launch site, and the vehicle nestled into it down below.

A new breed of starship. That's what the big brains had promised, and that's what they had delivered. A quarter mile long from end to end, the smooth black metal surface shone under the radiance of the floodlights. The blocky engines and long central section that led to the bloated triangle of the cockpit made the whole thing look some kind of enormous screwdriver. Or a vibrator, he thought to himself with a chuckle.

"Ready for this?" A very statuesque woman standing next to him in the crowd tugged his sleeve for his attention. "I am recording the whole thing for my grandchildren."

Ming Hua was a beautiful Asian scientist. Mayne thought she was responsible for the liquid ion power cells the ship was powered by. She was half his age, and dark skinned, and very open about the possibilities she represented. Smart and fun and frisky. Just the way Mayne liked his friends to be.

"I'm ready for this, to be sure," he told her. "I've been ready for three weeks."

She laughed, a musical sound that made his blood stir, especially with her hand stroking his arm. "You know the way these things work, General. Every bolt must be in place. Every line must be right. We don't want our brave explorers to die in a fiery explosion."

"We don't want the Earth to blow up either," Mayne reminded her. "If this ship were to explode right now, what would happen?"

Her beautiful dark face paled. "There would be a crack in the Earth bigger than the Grand Canyon. It would split our planet in two."

"Well." Mayne knew that, of course, but it never hurt to go over the basics. "Let's hope nothing goes wrong with the launch, then."

Her hand moved from his arm to his back, and she slid up against him in a way that left no doubt about what she was after. "When the ship is in the sky, I will have the rest of the night to myself. Perhaps you could keep me company."

He smiled. That sounded perfect.

Below them, the running lights on the Huxley came on, illuminating the sleek sides and the sturdy landing gear and the walkway that led down to the ramp where the crew would be boarding. Around Mayne, the crowd erupted in cheers.

"Almost time," Ming Hua purred.

"General Mayne," a man's voice said through the excited murmur of the crowd. "We need to talk."

At first, Mayne thought it was Thimley again, and distant relative of the President or not he was ready to rip the kid a new one, then he saw it was someone else.

"Not you," Mayne grumbled. "What the hell are you doing here? How did you even get past security?"

Professor Viktor Ravnak smiled. He was a tall man, with long lanky arms and legs that would have been right at home on a scarecrow, and a full head of frizzy graying hair. Mayne could have twisted the man into a pretzel. Most days, he wished he'd done that the first time he'd met the Professor.

Ravnak motioned to a private area away from the crowd. "We should talk over here. We don't want to upset the guests."

Mayne started to make a sarcastic comment about where Ravnak could stick his suggestions. Then he looked at Ming's face, and around them at the crowd. Then he sighed. "No. We don't want to upset the guests."

Promising to come back to Scientist Hua as soon as he could, Mayne followed Ravnak over to the archway between two of the surrounding buildings. It was darker here, and quieter, and as soon as they were around the corner and out of sight of the crowd, Mayne pushed the Professor up against the wall and shoved a thick finger in his face.

"You do not come in here and tell me what to do, you skinny little nabob!" He then released the Professor, who slumped slightly down the wall.

Pacing back and forth, Mayne rubbed a hand over his bald head. "What the hell do you want, anyway?"

Ravnak blinked at him. "What do I always want, General? I want you to listen. The President has stopped taking my calls. You're the only one left who I can talk to."

"Then you got no one at all, Ravnak, because I'm not listening either." Mayne was tired of this crazy man and his crazy theories. "There is no reason to have an emergency escape plan for the entire planet. None. There is no way you're going to get funding to build your escape ships. You stupid, ignorant, blind little man. You used to be the most respected scientist on the planet. You had a personal fortune to live on and you were involved in every single decision the world government made. What happened to you? What happened to your fortune?"

The professor smiled, and shook his head. "Too much to tell, in too little time. The important thing now, is that they're coming."

"Who's coming...? Oh. You're still on your conspiracy theories, aren't you?" Mayne leaned back to look around the corner again. The crew was loading the ship now. It would be launching in just a very few minutes. "I don't have time for you, little man. Go peddle your nonsense somewhere else."

As he stalked off, Ravnak frantically called after him. "They're coming, General. They're coming and we won't be able to stop them. They'll destroy the Huxley, and they'll burn the entire Earth!"

Mayne tried to block the words out as he rejoined Ming Hua on the observation platform but they echoed in his mind nonetheless. They're coming. They'll burn the Earth.

They'll destroy the Huxley.

It was impossible. This site was the most protected place on the planet. No one could get to it. No one could stop this launch. The Huxley would begin a new era of space exploration for the human race. Nothing would stop this.

Then why was he suddenly sweating?

What if Ravnak was right? What if there was a chance...just a chance...

No. It was unthinkable.

Aliens, from space. Aliens, coming to attack the Earth. Not just attack. Destroy.

Hayden scowled while everyone else cheered the ignition of the Huxley's engines. Lunacy. The aliens were not coming to destroy them.

Humanity had already had contact with a few species of aliens. It had been decades ago, but two different species had landed on the planet and stayed for a single day, collecting specimens and giving humanity the very basics of their more advanced technology before leaving again. Three others were in communication with the Earth over vast distances. Just messages from the black.

None of them were hostile.

Being able to reach those aliens, to actually be numbered among the citizens of the universe, was the main reason humanity had built the Huxley in the first place. This was their chance to be more than what they had ever been before. Establish colonies on other planets. Dominate the stars in the same way that they had dominated the Earth.

This was their chance, and Mayne swore on everything that anyone had ever considered holy that no one would take that chance from them. He wouldn't let them.

From the inside of his uniform jacket he took out his Link. The communication device was keyed to every standard and military frequency. He chose the one for Unified Space Command, the branch of the military that oversaw the satellite defense grid that had been set in place around the Huxley. The world might be at peace but that didn't mean there weren't individuals who wouldn't mind blowing things up just to be in the history books.

The Commander in charge of the satellites outfitted with their laser weapons answered Mayne's call immediately, and it was the matter of just a few minutes to get half of them aimed at the sky. There. If anything came at them, from any direction, they'd be ready.

In another minute, the gravity drives engaged on the ship, and it lifted several feet up in the air.

Ming Hua cheered. Mayne tensed.

Wavering blue rings of energy pulsed from underneath the Huxley as it pushed away from the launch surface.

Mayne held his breath.

With the wind that pushed them all back further from the protective railings, the ship set its nose to the stars. This next bit was going to be the exciting part.

Slowly at first, and then faster and faster and faster, the Huxley sped off to the stars, followed by the sound of thunder that shook Mayne's very bones. The Huxley was away. The first attempt by the Earth to reach for the distant stars was a success.

Mayne allowed himself to relax. Ha. That fool Ravnak had been wrong again. There was nothing that could stop the human race from becoming the rulers of the whole damned universe. Nothing at all.

"So," Ming said to him, wrapping herself around his chest and leaning up on her tiptoes to kiss his cheek. "Are you ready to celebrate?"

"Yes," he told her with a leering grin. "Yes I am."

CHAPTER TWO

He woke up the next day in a strange bed, laying in scented sheets with a luxuriously feminine body draped over his own. Her one thigh was pressing just right into his groin and making him wonder if they'd have time to repeat that amazing performance from last night before he went to work.

Ming Hua stirred when he did, and soon her smiling almond eyes were blinking open. "Well. Good morning to you."

"Back at you, kid," Mayne told her, kissing her forehead. "That was an amazing thing you did last night with the...uh..."

"Yes?" she teased. "What did I do?"

He kissed her cheek. "You know what you did."

"Mmm-hmm," she murmured. "But if you want me to do it again then you must say it out loud for me."

"Tease."

"Say it."

"Ming..."

From her bedside table, Mayne's Link beeped loudly. It was the tone that marked priority transmissions. Something that wasn't supposed to be ignored, even if you were in the shower or relieving yourself. Or, about to have mind-blowing sex with a frisky scientist trying to prove she was more than just a brain.

"Ignore it," Ming begged him, sliding her hands up his side.

"Well," Mayne told her, "I could do that, but then we'd have men in black suits at your doorstep demanding to know why I wasn't answering the damned thing."

"That would be fun," she said, rolling off so he could reach for the Link. "The more the merrier." She winked at him.

"Might be a little crowded," he chuckled.

She squeezed his thigh, then got out of bed and made sure he could watch her walking into the bathroom.

Mayne groaned, wanting what she was flaunting very badly, but knowing that his duty had to come first. Picking up the Link, he keyed in his personal code and then accepted the call. "This had better be important."

"Um, yes sir, it is." Thimley's voice was weak and shaky. "They told me, um, they said it was, I mean…"

"Thimley, so help me God, if you don't spit out why you're interrupting my morning right here and now I'm going to tear that noodle you call a spine out with my own two hands and beat some sense into you."

"Sorry, sorry sir." Mayne could hear the toadie take a slow breath before rushing through his message. "They need you back at the launch site, sir."

"The launch site? Huxley's launch site?" He sat up in the bed, looking down at the bruises that Ming had left on his chest. "What the hell could they possibly want me back there for? Everything's done. Let the scientists stay there and monitor the data stream."

"Sir, they need you."

"Can you say one single sentence without calling me sir?" he demanded. "Look. You either tell me what they want me for or else you go find me someone who's grown up enough to string more than two words together at a time."

"It's the Huxley, sir."

Mayne ground his teeth together. "Yes, Thimley, I know that's where the Huxley was launched from. What about it?"

"No, sir, it's the Huxley. It's coming back."

He was out of bed in an instant, hunting down his clothes.

* * *

The Huxley launch site was buzzing with activity again.

Mayne was led to the main hub of the buildings, where the big brains had their monitoring equipment and the computers translated every bit of data that was being streamed back to Earth.

Most of those screens were now flashing red.

The lead researcher at the site was none other than Haverson Dix himself. Appointed by the President, vetted by every member of the Governing Council, the man was a living legend. So was Mayne, of course, but not on the level that Dix was. That was the way of the world of course. Peace made heroes of the scientists, not the soldiers.

"Tell me what's going on, Haverson." Mayne stood on the raised entryway of the control room with Dix, watching the flurry of activity down below them as a few dozen people rushed from one control station to the next. "What's this nonsense about the Huxley coming back."

"Not nonsense." Dix was one of the oldest men that Mayne knew. One hundred and twenty-six was still a long way from dead, but most people chose to stay home and enjoy their last few decades in peace. Thin and frail with a long mane of pure white hair, Dix still carried himself with authority. "See for yourself."

He waved a hand toward the main screen below in the pit of activity. Dominating most of the back wall, the screen displayed a grid pattern of the entire solar system, with Earth at its center. Displayed with a red dot, the progress of the Huxley was clearly marked. There was no mistaking it. The ship was returning to Earth.

"Why are they..." Mayne didn't know what to think. "Have we had any communication from the crew?"

"None," Dix told him with a slow shake of his head. "We have no idea what's going on."

"How long before they're within visual range?"

"Well, they're inside of Venus's orbit already, so we have visual on our deep range telescopes now."

"Then show me, damn it."

Dix called down for them to switch the feed to the Hubble V feed, and Mayne watched as the main screen view changed to an image of the titanic ship, black against the black of space. It was hard to gauge relative motion but Mayne couldn't see anything out of the ordinary.

"Fine." What exactly did they need him down here for, anyway? "I suppose I should report to the Governing Council about what's going on. How long before it reaches Earth atmosphere?"

"Our best estimates put it at sixteen hours," Dix told him. "By then we'll be able to—"

The main screen flared as a bright red light seared across the image at an angle. It lanced through the Huxley, and in the next instant the greatest invention of mankind was a shattered mess of broken pieces scattering off at all angles.

The room quieted momentarily, the many scientists and military officials frozen in place with their eyes affixed to the screens. In the next moment, bodies were running everywhere, checking the computers, testing the communication systems, and trying to make sense of what just happened.

"What the hell was that?" Mayne shouted, when he finally got his wits back.

Dix was blinking rapidly at the screen, maybe trying to get rid of the same afterimages that were burned into Mayne's eyes. He stood still in front of the large screen before him, calm amidst the surrounding storm. "I don't know," he said. "Something…something just cut through the ship…some sort of laser…"

"I can see that! Where did it come from?"

Dix raised a hand to point at the screen. "From that."

Mayne followed Dix's gaze back to the main viewscreen. There, on the display, several orange orbs went shooting by. It was too fast for Mayne to count them all but it looked like dozens. Maybe hundreds.

"Slow the image down," Mayne called down to the people at the stations below. "Did you hear me? Replay it and slow it down!"

The image reversed itself, and then centered and froze on one of the orbs. It was a terrible sight. Bristling with sharp projections, the skin seemed to almost undulate like living flesh. When the image moved again it was overlaid with numbers and words that gave details about the things. Each one was identical. Half a mile long. Unknown composite alloy. Mayne stopped reading after that.

"They're headed toward Earth," Dix pointed out. "They're coming right for us."

"Broadcast a message," Mayne ordered. "All frequencies. You tell these bastards that they just destroyed an Earth vessel and we will not hesitate to strike them down if they come within a thousand miles of our planet!"

Dix burst out laughing, startling Mayne. "You're joking, General. You must be joking! What do we have that could possibly stop these things? We're a planet at peace, remember?"

Mayne's stomach turned over on itself. There was nothing here to stop those things. The satellite lasers, certainly, but they weren't enough to stop a fleet of ships that vast. There were still a few of the old fusion missiles left in storage at various sites around the world but no one even knew how many of those would still ignite, let alone launch.

The human race had left behind its uncivilized, aggressive tendencies and in the process it had left itself vulnerable to attack from a hostile species that was attacking them for no reason.

The irony nearly brought Mayne to his knees.

"Did you send the message?" he asked in a quiet voice.

"Yes," one of the techs below him said. "We sent it. Receiving a response now."

"Well? What does it say?"

"Receiving," the tech repeated. "Translating. It's not in any language that we're familiar with. Alien, or human. Wait. We're getting it now."

"Put it up on the screen," Dix said.

The main viewscreen went black, and then words scrolled across it from left to right.

We are the Krii Zalite. Prepare yourselves. Your planet is ours.

"That's all there is," the tech pointed out. "There's no more to it."

Silence fell over the room. The world was under attack, and there was nothing they could do about it.

CHAPTER THREE

The President was not happy, and Mayne could care less.

"Sir, you don't understand," he said, for the third time. "These Krii Zalite are coming. We can't do anything to stop them."

The President leaned back in his padded chair, behind his polished mahogany desk. "Then what exactly do you expect us to do, General?"

He spread his hands, his very dark skin catching the light through his floor to ceiling windows. His eyes were dark brown and intelligent, and that intelligence was something Mayne had always admired about the man. Not his expensive suits or the way he cut his hair in the new style, taller on one side and nearly at his scalp on the other. Whenever the world had needed an answer to a hard question, President Harlon Jessmer had always been able to figure out the solution.

Now there was no solution, but President Jessmer was still trying to find the answer.

"I've seen their firepower," Mayne said. "It cut through the Huxley like the thing was made out of toilet paper. We can't stand against that kind of weaponry."

President Jessmer threw up his hands. "So I ask you again. What do we do?"

Mayne paused a long moment, then barely managed a word. "Surrender."

The word was ashes in his mouth, but there it was. When faced with attack by overwhelming odds, the smartest move was often to give up and wait to fight another day. "When the alien force gets here, we have to be ready to give them whatever they want."

"Are you insane, General?" The President clasped his hands together and shook his head. "There's no way I will authorize that."

"Sir, they're going to take it anyway. We can either give it to them and survive, or we can try to keep it for ourselves and die."

The President tapped a finger on his desk. Then he stood up and went to the window, looking out on the manicured grass of the Presidential Palace's front lawn. "There may be another way."

"Mister President, if you can think of something I'm more than willing to listen."

"You won't like it."

"I'm a General in the service of the United Countries of Earth." Mayne crossed his arms over his chest. "I don't have to like what you tell me to do. I just have to do it."

Jessmer nodded. "Well said. So. Here's what I propose."

* * *

Mayne's hovercar zipped across the streets of Capital City. There was a part of the old section that he himself had never visited before. Everyone knew it was there, but no one went unless they had a very good reason.

Today, Mayne had a very good reason.

Three more hours before the Krii Zalite arrived and killed everyone on the planet. He had exactly that long to get the President's plan into motion.

Thimley was driving him, and for a mealy-mouthed little bootlicker the kid could drive. They made it there in record time.

When they arrived, Mayne got out of the car and then gave Thimley his orders. Go back to his family. Stay with his family, and enjoy whatever time they had left together. Thimley gave him a weak salute, and then drove away just as fast as he could.

The streets here were broken concrete littered with the refuse of generations. There was no reason to maintain a part of the city that no one lived in. Resources could be allocated to other places that needed it more. The building where he'd stopped was a highrise structure of gleaming metal and glass. The entry doors were gone, removed years ago for some unknown purpose. The real security was inside.

Standing in the empty doorway, Ravnak nodded and waved.

"What the hell?" Mayne walked up the wide concrete steps at the front and went right up to the Professor. "How did you know I was going to be here?"

"Where else would you go?" Ravnak shrugged. "This was going to be your destination as soon as you saw what we were up against. All I had to do was wait."

"And how did you know what we were going to be up against?" Mayne demanded. "We only just found out a few hours ago!"

He pushed passed the Professor on his way into the building and then turned right down a hallway. He had the floor plan of the place memorized. What he wanted to do was go down. The elevators should be just ahead.

Ravnak followed, matching his stride step for step. "Fifteen years ago I intercepted several transmissions that I didn't understand. It took me some time but I finally translated them. When I did, I knew I couldn't share what I had learned with anyone. It would start a panic. Or I would be arrested as a traitor. Or worse, I would be discredited and all of my life's work would go to waste."

"Professor, I'm on a very tight time schedule here. If you've got a point to make could you please make it?"

"Sure thing." Ravnak took hold of Mayne's arm and turned him around, facing down his glare. "The messages all spoke of death. They were aimed at other worlds, just passing by ours, but close enough that my equipment could pick them up. They came from a race calling themselves the Krii Zalite. Does that sound familiar?"

He had Mayne's attention now. "Yes. Yes it does. So what did these messages say, Professor?"

"They said they would bring death to everyone who stood in their way. They would rape and plunder whatever they wanted from their target worlds, and then destroy anyone who stood against them." He swallowed, remembering the ferocity of the words. "I knew then that it was only a matter of time before these Zalite turned their attention to Earth."

"Well, Professor, turns out you were right. About everything. They did attack the Huxley. Destroyed it, in fact. They are coming here to Earth to destroy us."

Ravnak nodded. "Yes. You took that information to the President?"

"I did."

"And what did he say we should do?"

Mayne swallowed. "I told him we should surrender. I have never, in all my career, surrendered to anyone, but I think we need to surrender to these aliens or we're all going to die."

"Sound council. Although, one of the transmissions I translated was for a planet that had offered to surrender. The Zalite let them live. As slaves."

Mayne's heart went cold. He doubted that being the slaves of a race of aliens that would just as soon kill you as look at you was going to be a very pleasant fate. "Well. Then maybe the President's solution is the way to go after all."

Ravnak didn't bother asking what the President's better, final solution might be. He already knew. That's how he knew that Mayne would be coming here. "After I translated those messages," he said, "I started a little side project of my own. I need your help with it now."

"What?" Mayne was furious that this man would bring him this problem now. As if he didn't have enough of his own problems to deal with. "You listen to me, Professor. Whatever you've been cooking up for the past fifteen years isn't going to matter in another two and a half hours. I have a job to do. Let me get to it."

On his way here, Mayne had called Ming Hua and said a very brief, very poignant goodbye. He wasn't coming back from this. That didn't matter, though. He had a job to do and Ravnak was keeping him from doing it.

"I'll let you go in a moment General," the Professor said. "Right now I need your help."

"With what, damnit?"

"For fifteen years, I've been building ships. Well, not me you understand. I've contracted with various companies who build various bits of the ships and then I paid other companies to put them together. No one group or person has any idea what the ships are for." He paused for a breath, and to collect his thoughts.

Mayne checked the chrono piece on his wrist. Time was running down. He still didn't know if the equipment on the lower levels was still in working order. "So what did you build these ships for, Professor?"

"For leaving Earth."

For a moment, Mayne was speechless. "You built...escape ships? Ships to leave the Earth in case the Krii Zalite army ever found Earth?"

"Yes. I did. You asked me where my personal fortune went? Well, that's where it went. To building those ships. They are capable of extended flight and they have cryogenic chambers in place to put the passengers into suspended animation for up to three hundred years.

They will get to our friends. One of the two alien races who came to us before. It will be enough to give us a start."

"Well, well, well." Mayne leaned his back against the wall to regard Ravnak. "I'm impressed. That might be just exactly what we need. How many ships?"

"Fifty."

Mayne's hopes dropped. "That's all? How many people do these ships hold apiece?"

This answer came a little slower. "Four hundred."

Now his hopes shriveled and died. "You have got to be joking me! All this work and all you can save are twenty thousand people? You bastard! Why even bother?"

"Because," Ravnak said slowly and calmly. "Saving some of us is better than saving none of us. You know as well as I do, General. Whether we use your plan or the President's, it doesn't matter. The human race is done for if we don't act. Let me save all we can."

"Whatever." Mayne threw his hand up in the air and let it drop again. "Do whatever you want to. You don't need me."

"Actually yes, I do."

Pushing away from the wall angrily, Mayne started storming down the hallway again. The elevators were right up there. "What could you possibly need me for?"

"I need someone with your influence and authority." They stopped at the elevator doors, and Ravnak started gesturing with his hands, desperate for Mayne to understand him now. "I may be respected, but you have the ability to order men that I do not. I need you to tell the members of the Governing Council to start an evacuation. It doesn't matter who gets to the ships. I will not decide who lives and dies. I will not save the elite or the powerful at the expense of the weak and poor."

Mayne searched Ravnak's eyes. He'd never respected the man before. Not like this. "What do you want me to do?"

"Make the call," the Professor said to him. "I can only take twenty thousand souls. There isn't much time, and if we don't start now it won't even be that much."

Mayne couldn't say no to that. If this plan of the President's was going to be worth doing at all, then they needed to have some hope of survival for their race. "Professor Ravnak, you may just be a genius."

The Professor waved the comment away. "I don't have to be smart to want my people to live."

"Your people?" Mayne repeated. "You won't be on the ships?"

"No. It wouldn't be right. I can't take that one spot that could be given to someone else." He took a breath. "I've done my part. Now it is time for other people to do theirs."

"I feel the same way," the General admitted. Taking out his Link, he made contact with one person, and then the next, and then another. The chain of command was started. The plan was in action.

"Thank you," Ravnak said, honestly relieved that it had worked. "I guess now...all I can do is wait."

"You could come with me," Mayne told him, pushing the button next to the elevator to go down. "Honestly, Professor, I don't know what I'm going to find when I get down there. I may need someone with your scientific knowhow to make this work."

Ravnak pursed his lips, and then shrugged. "My schedule just freed up. Why not?"

CHAPTER FOUR

The basement level of the building was locked off with a code that only someone of General Mayne's clearance knew. The number pad was old and stiff, but he got it to work the second time and then the elevator doors were opening and they were in.

Gleaming metal walls and a tiled floor were overly bright under the fluorescent lights. It was a small room, and one wall was taken up with a desk and computers and half a dozen large viewscreens. Everything they needed.

"So," Ravnak said, "this is where the magic happens."

Mayne smirked at that. Nothing was overly funny today. At the same time, everything was.

He went to the computer stations and started them up. In a few seconds the screens lit up and prompted him for his passcodes. There were three separate ones, and he entered them all in without fail. "Here we go."

The computer displayed the map of the Earth, with several red dots at different locations over land masses. Two of them were within a half a mile of where he sat.

Ravnak looked over the map with him. "That's all of them."

"Yup," Mayne said. "Every single Fusion missile still in existence. Enough destructive power to burn the Earth a dozen times over."

"And yet, still not enough to stop the Krii Zalite."

"I'm afraid you were right about that," Mayne said, sweat beginning to roll down his face. "There's nothing we have that can stop them. For all I know, there's no force in the universe that could do that."

He punched in a few more commands. Everything was working smoothly. The display from the computer shifted up to the viewscreens. Every red dot on the Earth slowly connected themselves with black lines.

"So far, so good."

"Depends," Ravnak said, "on your definition of good."

Mayne checked his chrono piece again. One hour before the Krii Zalite arrived. "Well. We've got time," he said. "Maybe we should play some cards?"

"What's that?" Ravnak asked him. "There, on the map."

Squinting, Mayne brought up a section of the map in the lower southern hemisphere. It was the longest connection between red dots that there was. The black line stretched between them...and then it broke somewhere near the midpoint.

"That," Mayne told him, "is trouble."

* * *

Further into the building's sub-basement, along a maze of corridors and turns, the two of them found a door marked "Maintenance."

"Is it really this simple?" Ravnak asked.

Mayne scoffed at him. "We're trying to get a few hundred fusion warheads armed. Nothing about this is simple."

This door had no lock. It didn't need one. Anyone who had gotten into this area would already have given the proper code clearance. When the General opened it they found the nerve center that had allowed the control room to track and display all of the warhead weapons for them. This was allowed for control of those remote locations, all on a global scale.

Or at least, it used to allow for that. Before a chunk of the cement ceiling had fallen down and smashed through several important-looking cables.

The lights flickered in this room. Dust had settled over everything. Several consoles that stood as tall as Mayne's chest and Ravnak's nose stood dark.

"Is there even power going to these stations anymore?" Mayne asked in a panic. He rushed into the room, swiping dust off buttons and knobs, lights and switches, then moving around to the back of the consoles to see if there were access hatches to allow him to get in.

Behind him, still halfway through the door, the professor shook his head, blinking away tears that filled his eyes. "Oh, no. No, no, no."

If this plan of the President's didn't work, then his plan of evacuation would not, either.

"Don't just stand there!" Mayne roared at him. "Get in here and help me! You're the big brain. Use that damned knowledge of yours and make them work!"

That spurred Ravnak into action, but once he was inside and was inspecting which particular conduits were damaged, he knew it was all for nothing. "There's no way. The power cables, the transmission lines, everything that should make all of this work...it's gone. Broken. I can't...there's no way..."

Mayne grabbed him by his funny little checkered lapels and shook him, hard. "Then you figure out a way! I need this to work! If we don't make this happen then there is no hope for our planet!"

Ravnak's teeth clacked together. His brain rattled inside his skull. Somewhere in all of that, an idea shook loose.

"Stop it!" he finally said, slapping Mayne's hands away. "I have an idea. Oh...this is going to hurt."

"What? What is it?"

Mayne demanded an answer, over and over, but all he got in return was a funny little smile from the frail little big-brained man.

"Go," Ravnak told him. "Get back to the main control room and be ready to fire the missiles. All of them, right? All of them, all at once."

"Well, certainly. That's the only chance we have. But what are you—?"

"Don't worry about me," Ravnak assured him. "I've already made my peace. I've already decided that I won't be on the escape boats. You either, and I'm sure that's occurred to you. The two of us are two old relics of a forgotten age that make our last and final act one of service to humankind. It's a pleasure to be working alongside you, General Mayne."

The General took Ravnak's hand when he offered it and the two of them shook.

"But..." Mayne didn't know what to say.

Ravnak clapped him on the back. "No worries, General. Be there, and be ready. The missiles will fire."

That was the last Mayne saw of the man. He rushed back to the control room, ready at the station, staring at that broken black line on the screen and wondering how in the name of God the professor planned on fixing the problem with no power at all.

* * *

"The human body," Ravnak said to himself, "is basically a wet battery. When at rest we produce, um, about a hundred watts of power. Yes. That's right. A hundred watts of power."

He heard the tremor in his voice. There was nothing he could do to stop it, so he didn't try.

"We are also brilliantly built conductors." Working with the red conduit, he used the multifacet tool he always carried in his pocket to strip back the protective rubber coating with a knife blade. When the metal of the blade scraped the bare wire underneath, sparks flew.

Good. There was power.

"Power," he repeated out loud. "Humans carry our own power, and we enhance other power sources."

He swallowed, and swallowed again, trying to work up some moisture in his throat. "We are power."

It took him a minute to find the other end of the red conduit. When he did, he went to work scraping it down to the wire just like the other side. His hands were shaking so badly that the knife slipped. The sharp edge cut his skin at the wrist and sliced a neat, red line.

Oh well, he thought to himself. Might as well start on the next step.

Painful as it was, he widened the cut in his wrist. Then he did the same on the other hand.

* * *

General Mayne practiced the sequence of buttons and switches that would activate the missiles until he could do it all in three seconds. At the end of each attempt a flashing red "Operation Failed" showed up on the computer screen.

He checked the black line on the map. Still broken.

"Come on, big brain," he urged Ravnak. "Whatever you're doing down there, do it fast!"

He checked the other part of the viewscreen that he had programmed upon returning to this room. It showed the countdown to the Zalite arrival. Twelve minutes.

Another screen showed him a real-time image from satellites in the atmosphere. Red orbs dominated the blackness of space.

This was going to be close.

* * *

"Batteries," Ravnak said to himself, barely above a whisper. "Batteries work by using two opposite poles to create an energy flow."

He was crying now, but he didn't bother to try stopping the tears. He was about to die. The entire Earth was about to die, except for those lucky few souls who got into the escape ships on time. He hoped beyond hope that people had reached his ships by now. They would have to clear the Zalite armada, then get into their cryo chambers while in deep space, and then the ships would do the rest. The ships would take them to safety.

But for now, everything hinged on Professor Viktor Ravnak remembering how to wire a battery.

Bracing himself for the pain, Ravnak held one side of the stripped conduit down by the protective coating, below where he had bared the wire.

Then he worked the fiber-optic aluminum wires into the slit of his left wrist.

His hand went numb immediately. That might be a problem, considering he still had to do the same thing to his other arm.

* * *

The Zalite were here.

The satellites showed their approach. Mayne could do nothing but watch helplessly as they used their laser weapons to slice through satellites and carve out pieces of the planet. Entire forests disappeared in blazes of fire. He watched one image of a city he didn't recognize incinerated with multiple blasts delivered so fast his eyes couldn't follow. Millions of people, dead in a matter of seconds.

They weren't lasers, the computer screens insisted stubbornly. They were some form of particle beam weapon that was unknown to the database. Mayne growled and slammed his fist against the keyboard. He didn't care what it was. He wanted to fight back!

He watched the black line on the screen.

Still broken.

* * *

Ravnak fumbled the other conduit up and into position, aligning it with his wrist. He was in so much pain already. So much pain!

This would end it. At the same time, it would give the human race a fighting chance.

Blubbering like a baby, he thrust the wire into his flesh.

Pain was the last thing he knew. Pain, and a blazing light that seared his eyes from the inside.

* * *

The black line connected on his screen. Green lights lit up. All systems go.

"Ha! Take this, you bastards!"

General Mayne ran the sequence. The indicator lights all flashed go.

The missiles had been activated.

Mayne sat back in his chair. He breathed out a heavy sigh. All he could do now was wait for the end to come.

CHAPTER FIVE

From space, it looked spectacular.

The fusion missiles held beneath the surface of the planet, all over the planet, had been activated. The Krii Zalite never saw what was coming for them.

All at once, every single one of the fusion warheads activated. The explosion rocked the planet. It ignited the atmosphere. Flames spread across the world in swirling eddies and storms. The conflagration caught the Krii Zalite ships unawares. They were consumed. They were smaller pops of explosions amidst the dying throes of the planet below.

The planet shook. It rotated backwards on its axis. The poles shifted and the orb wobbled before settling back into its position as everything continued to burn. All life on Earth ended because of the plan set forth by President Harlon Jessmer. Humanity on Earth was dead.

Rather than let an alien species have their home, it was decided to burn it to ash. No one would have it. Not for generations of generations. Eventually, it was hoped, humans would return to their Earth and make it livable again.

For now, the Earth burned.

From the twenty escape ships that had cleared the planet amid the flames, people watched their home die. They watched their cities become so much slag. They watched their friends and family burn.

But, they were alive. Thanks to the foresight of Professor Viktor Ravnak, they would live. The human race would live on.

The Zalite invaders were gone. So was the Earth.

Together, all the escape ships turned their nosecones toward deep space. Still in shock, the survivors put themselves into the sleep chambers. When they woke up, they would start over. The human race would survive.

One day, they would return.

Author TJ RYAN

TJ Ryan is a Canadian author, born on the rainy West Coast (or is that Wet Coast?) of British Columbia. He spent his early years travelling the world, obsessing over new cultures and culinary experiences. Preferring spaceships to airplanes, he has now settled into his little slice of rainforest paradise, escaping reality through Science Fiction.

http://www.amazon.com/author/tjryan

Boarded
By Dale Furse

Chapter 1

Captain Jai Brolto's mouth stretched into a smile as he listened to the cheers and obscene shouts of triumph filling the bridge of the ship. His gaze hovered over the flight console set back from the forward fuselage. The pilot and weapons officer were laughing at a piece of the enemy's ship floating past the viewing screen. Jai had a clear view into space via the viewer that molded around the nose of their ship. Only a few pieces of metal remained in sight.

He nodded his head in admiration. The *Descartes* was the only outdated eraser still flying, but she was still in fine shape since scientists, engineers, and ship builders had redesigned her.

He couldn't fault his small crew for celebrating. After all, the alternative to winning was being eaten alive by the hungriest sentient creatures in the universe. Collids. But thanks to the refitted eraser ship *Descartes* and her talented crew, the two Collid ships had been destroyed. One ship had been blown to smithereens, and the other had disappeared as it sped back to the nearest Collid port. The Earth dignitaries Jae's ship had escorted to Astralas were now safe and would appear at the next galaxy summit in time.

This had to be Jai's best mission. He wanted to savor the feeling of victory.

"Jai." The AI's charming old English-accented voice interrupted Jai's enjoyment. "A Collid ship is rounding the third moon of Astralas."

"What?" Jai sat forward in his seat. Using the control panel in his chair's armrest, he punched up the viewing window. A Collid ship filled the screen. Jae squinted at the ship. They called all Collid ships man-eaters because of their human-eating scum of a crew. "Where did it come from, and why the blazes didn't you know about it, Rene?"

"I was analyzing," Rene snapped. The AI's voice reeked with annoyance.

Jai didn't have time for Rene's temper tantrums. He was well aware that mistakes happened, but in his opinion, a state of the art AI that was fully programmed for combat shouldn't bloody make them.

Stalking the small expanse between his chair and the flight console, the captain stopped behind his weapons officer. "Hamish, weapons report."

Hamish rested his arm alongside his console. His red hair quivered as he made a fist and hit the console. "All weapons spent, Captain."

Jai hissed in a breath. *Only one way out, then.* He turned to the pilot. "How long before we can enter EmelDrive?"

Jai tapped the boot of his toe, waiting for the navigational officer to answer. Tara knew her stuff, but she was fumbling the comp keys. "Tara," Jae said.

The EmelDrive was the only thing that would get them out of the sector. It was fast, faster than anything the Collids would have, and their only hope.

Tara flipped her blonde hair over her shoulder. "Fifteen minutes, sir."

Jai scowled at the nav. It wasn't her fault. He gazed at the viewer. The Collid ship was gaining on them. "Tara, set a course for Notivor."

She glanced at the viewing screen, fear flickering in her eyes. "Yes, Captain."

Scratching the back of his neck, Jai fought to keep his voice cool. "How long before the Collid ship is within boarding range?"

"Eight minutes," Rene said.

"Any good news, people?"

The bridge was relatively silent. The only noises were his crew's erratic breathing and his neck cracking as he tipped his head from side to side.

He jabbed at the AI's com button. "Don't go shy on me now, Rene."

"Captain."

"Yes, pilot?"

"Look at the viewing screen." Gordo zoomed in on the back of the Collid ship.

Hamish fell back in his seat and beamed at the captain. "Smoke."

Jae tipped his head and frowned at Hamish. "That's not necessarily a good thing. If their ship is damaged enough, they might risk transporting even at that distance."

"I concur, Captain," Gordo said. "The first time I saw a Collid ship brought down, the man-eaters transported straight into space, trying to board our ship. They are mad, sir."

Nodding, Jae stared at the viewer. From his vantage point, *Descartes* didn't appear to be out of transport range. He hoped the damage would only slow them down. He punched the button on his armrest to summon Rene.

"Rene, how bad is the damage?"

"Analyzing." A blink of an eye later, Rene said, "The Collid ship has sustained irreparable damage to its engines. They will become critical in ten minutes."

The vice squeezing Jai's chest loosened a little. "Gordo, keep us out of boarding distance for two fricking minutes."

"I'll try, Captain."

"Don't try. Do."

Jai plonked down into his chair. Drumming the fingers of his right hand on the cold metal armrest, he waited. They couldn't outrun the Collids. Man-eaters were faster than erasers. He stilled his fingers. Two minutes. That was all the time they had to steer clear from the man-eater. Two minutes to either jump to EmelDrive or have man-eating scum board *Descartes*.

The eraser angled away from the enemy ship. Jae let out a long breath.

Gordo was the best pilot this side of the galaxy. He would keep the *Descartes* out of the thing's reach.

"Rene, report how you lost the ship's location," Jai said.

No answer.

"Now."

He didn't shout. He didn't need to; past experience had shown that his commanding tone was enough to make things happen. Jai knew he was being hard on Rene, but he was supposed to be state-of-the-art, for shit's sake. He was supposed to be the most developed artificial intelligence ever built.

Although word had it, some professor or another had actually found it hiding away in a program. The scientists involved had been working on a supercomputer, and this one had just popped up out of nowhere. Unable to replicate the technology, some genius had installed it into the last flying eraser... Jai's eraser.

The *Descartes* had been named after the great philosopher Rene Descartes because his famous quote *"I think, therefore I am"* had seemed appropriate to the new AI installation. The newer, faster, more robust destroyers would serve all Earth fleets in the future.

Rene's sotto voce tones came over the comm. "Captain, I did see the fighter sustain damage."

The AI was upset. He only used Jai's rank when angry or confused. Having remembered Rene's last mission, Jai decided it was best not to question the AI further. Let him give his report and say nothing. The last thing he needed was for the computer to shut down, or worse, start doubting Jai's ability to captain the *Descartes*.

"Go ahead, Rene."

"I ran my scenario files and came to the conclusion; it would need greater repairs than could be done in space. I therefore surmised it would need to retreat to a Collid port, so I went back to arming the weapons for your weapons officer. I also gave updates to systems and detailed reports to your pilot."

Rene paused. Jai could imagine the AI sighing. "I have just now reviewed the battle. Having sustained damage, the inciter separated from the main fleet at the height of battle. It hung still, behind the moon.

The reason it stayed and didn't flee isn't clear. Analysis ongoing."

Jai gazed over his bridge. Gordo, Hamish and Tara, who, a moment before, had all been joining in the victory celebrations, were staring at the screen. Everyone aboard already knew the ending if the Collids boarded the *Descartes*.

Oh, there were many meat-eating aliens in the universe, but only a few went out of their way to hunt other sentient species. The Zors had been the most terrifying beings in the galaxy until the Collids appeared and systematically killed every last Zor. The Collids didn't seem to be a very intelligent species, at least by human standards, but there was something so cold and cruel about them that Jai's nerves stood on end just thinking about them. He had been slowly realizing they weren't quite right. The Earthtrust was trying to figure out where they came from, but could get no information from the Collids they had captured.

Well, it was hard to get dead beings to talk. The Collids died as soon as they were captured. No poison pills, like the Zors; no implants, like the Tarantas.

They just died.

Gordo banked sharply, but the man-eater plunged into its path.

Jai's heart pounded against his ribs. He shouted, "Get going, Gordo!"

"Rene isn't responding, Captain," Gordo said, a tremor in his voice.

Jai jabbed at the button for Rene's com. "Rene, report. Crock. *Descartes*, report. Tara, can you find him?"

The nav officer worked at her console, her fingers flying across the board and a growing frown wrinkling her high forehead. "I can't find him, sir."

She sat back with a shake of her head and, with all hope gone out of her once bright blue eyes, gazed at the approaching Collid ship. "He's gone. Rene is gone."

"One minute to boarding range, Captain," Hamish warned, his voice trembling.

Jae narrowed his eyes at the ship on the viewer. Without Rene, he had no way of entering the self-destruct sequence into the main computer. Rene had the final code. The *Descartes* couldn't be destroyed if... Jae frowned and corrected himself: when the Collids boarded her.

"Set your personal weapons to kill," Jae ordered. That was as far as he would go with his commands. He gazed over his crew. He couldn't order them to kill themselves. It would have to be up to them, what they would do when and if the time came.

Chapter 2

"Thirty seconds to boarding range, Captain," Hamish said.

"Look!" Tara shouted.

Jae snapped his gaze back to the screen in time to see the dying blaze of an explosion. Bits of man-eater floated out of the plume of smoke. He laughed, a delighted, throaty sound.

The others' jubilant cheers filled the bridge. Then the air shimmered, cutting off Jae's elation.

Three bipedal Collids appeared on the bridge in front of the hatch, blocking the crew's only escape. The beasts' brown eyes took in their surroundings. Their baboon-like jaws opened so wide that all Jae could see were gaping mouths full of large, sharp teeth. Their howls filled the bridge, and their loose, dark blue overalls shook in time with the noise. Standing eight feet tall and half that wide, their bulk filled the small space, and their acrid scent permeated through the air. Jae's nose stung and he gulped down a gag.

The howling stopped. Even with their mouths closed, the points of the Collids' teeth escaped through their capacious lips.

The largest Collid nodded at its cohorts, and they glared at Hamish and Gordo.

The men seemed glued to their seats, frozen by the Collids' appearance before them. The Collids' mouths widened. Jae wasn't certain if they were smiling or sneering.

Jai plucked his gun from the holster on his hip and fired as he grabbed Tara with his other hand and pushed her behind him.

She twisted out of his grasp and fired her weapon.

Jae yelled, "Hamish!"

As if waking from a trance, Hamish leapt out of his seat and fired his weapon. Gordo did the same as he backed up to the viewing screen. Jae fired his weapon, aiming for the largest Collid's head. They all knew their weapons would be useless against the Collids, but it was human nature to try.

Jai plunged forward and smacked the butt of his gun against the nearest Collid. It let out a yelp, then grabbed Jai's neck and held him high, at arm's length. Jai kicked the Collid's knee—another yelp. The beast's elongated fingers tightened, cutting off the blood supply to Jai's brain.

The Collids laughed, a roaring, vibrating sound. Hot blood rushed through Jai's veins, searing his head and throbbing throughout his extremities. The crew kept firing their weapons, but the blasts didn't even breach the Collids' uniforms. The Collids ignored the laser blasts as if they were nothing but a light display.

Jai managed to scrape his finger against the Collid's eye. It gave way at his touch. He croaked, "Aim for their eyes."

Before his men could obey, the two lesser Collids plucked Gordo and Hamish up as if they were daisies in a flowerbed and chewed on their necks, cracking the men's' skulls underneath their wide hands as they did so.

Jai's stomach turned. It had been twelve years since he had let his own inner beast out. He glanced at Tara. He had to try to escape, but the beast's fingers were blocking his left and right carotid arteries. His temples throbbed in time with his ever-increasing heartbeat. His veins swelled against the restriction in his neck. If he couldn't summon his beast side soon, he would explode all over the Collid. Something about that image had Jai smiling.

He gazed at Tara. She pressed her back against the wall beside her console, her eyes wide with fear. She gaped at Jai's happy face as if he was a maniac.

He frowned, but then remembered he was smiling. He mashed his lips together. None of the crew knew he wasn't human, and he had hoped they would never find out, but if he wanted to save Tara, she would have to know.

She sobbed and slid down the wall onto the floor.

Jai twisted. If he could loosen the Collid's hold enough to let his hot blood flow, he could call on his inner beast.

"Disgusting," a bug-eyed Collid said, spitting out some cloth from Gordo's uniform. It pulled the rest of Gordo's sleeve away.

The Collid holding Jai turned its head toward the others so sharply that Jai thought he heard something in its long neck pop. "Eat."

"But humans are so disgusting," its companion complained.

Jae groaned. Not only did Collids speak New English, they also didn't like eating humans. The muscles in his neck expanded, and the Collid's grip loosened, giving him a chance to breathe in more deeply.

The Collid shook Jai. "Humans keep us alive! If Torgoes can eat them, we can."

"I'd rather eat a Torgo," the smallest Collid said around a hunk of Hamish.

"Hmm, Torgoes." The bug-eyed Collid swallowed. "Can we get some Torgoes, Captain? There is a Torgo colony on Spelerican."

The Collid captain trained its gaze on Tara. Its thin, crusty lips spread in a cruel smile. "Even I won't eat a foul-tasting female. However, Torgoes do love them."

It turned back to its comrades. "Perhaps we can make a slight detour to Spelerican on our way back to base."

The bug-eyed Collids waved their victims in the air. "Hooray for the captain! Our protector!"

"Shut up and tie the female up."

Jai wriggled. Although the captain had insisted that his comrades eat the humans, it wasn't in a hurry to do so, because it flung Jai to the port side of the ship.

Jai's head smashed against the bulkhead. It didn't matter, though. His heart pumped, and his blood thundered throughout his body. His vagus nerves went to work and sparked every other nerve and organ in his body. His muscles grew dense and robust. Furry hair sprouted all over his body, making it tingle. His nose elongated over a canine mouth.

Smells assaulted him. He had to ignore the Collids' stench. One breath, two breaths. He crouched, ready to pounce.

The Collids manhandled Tara into the captain's chair. Using the cords hanging from the shoulders of their uniforms, they tied her up. She struggled, but the moment her eyes landed on Jai, she stopped and gaped.

He wished he'd told her he wasn't quite human before that moment, because she screamed.

The Collid captain spun toward her. It stopped abruptly, its lips rolling back from its sharp canines as it spotted Jai. "Where did that come from?"

The other two threw what was left of the pilot and the nav officer behind them and stared at the beast Jai had become.

Jai growled. He leapt high into the air and snapped his steel-like jaws around the captain's shoulder. The captain roared and whirled around to dislodge Jai, but his jaws were too powerful.

Jai eyed the pulsating jugular vein in the Collid's neck and drooled at the thought of biting it. He let the captain fall to the floor and pounced. He bit down on the captain's neck, piercing the vein. The Collid fell back, struggling to pull Jai off. Jai locked his jaws.

"Get it off me!" the captain growled at its crew.

Jai glanced up. The two Collid morons stood frozen, their mouths agape, as if they had no idea what to do.

The captain grabbed Jai's bottom jaw and tried twisting it, but Jai held on fast. Foul, acidic blood rushed into Jai's mouth and trailed down his jaws. Jai gagged but kept his jaws clenched. The taste wasn't right. The blood smelled rotten, like sewage. There was no iron in this blood. Jai didn't like it one bit.

The Collid captain's already pale face blanched even further, but it clearly wasn't going to give up.

"Get it off me!"

One of his underlings finally moved and tried to haul Jai off the captain. A blast sounded. Pain sliced through Jai's side.

His opponent began scratching at Jai's face. Its fingers found one of Jai's eyes and gouged at it. Jai tried to angle his head away without letting go of the captain's neck, but the Collid stretched its fingers and twisted its long fingernails behind Jai's eyeball.

Agony exploded behind Jai's eye socket. The Collid hooked his fingers further. In one swift move, it scooped out Jai's eye.

A horrendous ache grew, sending shards of pain searing through Jae's brain like serrated knives. His jaws loosened. He tried to suck out the Collid's lifeblood, but his jaw muscles would not work. Jae scratched at the Collid's chest with his long, sharp claws, but the thing's skin was like rubber and completely impenetrable.

The Collid captain pushed Jai's head away. "Help me."

The other two Collids dragged Jai back by his rear legs. "We've got him, Captain!" the small one whooped. It shook the leg it was holding.

The captain, holding its hand over its injury, shouted, "Clear it out!"

The bug-eyed Collid smashed its boot into the side of Jai's chest. He yelped. The humanoid part of him knew he had a few broken ribs. He heard them crack, but the pain in his eye and skull overrode any feelings in his chest. He felt a shard nudging his left lung. One more kick, and the bone would pierce his pleura.

The other Collid booted Jae's hip. Excruciating agony eclipsed any other injury. He howled with the pain. The Collids laughed. Adrenalin coursed through Jae's veins, but he tapped it down. He was broken. He couldn't fight them. The only thing he could do was close his eyes and play dead, hoping they would think they had killed him.

It worked. They tightened their grip on his legs and hauled him to the door of the bridge, then flung him like a piece of discarded meat into the corridor.

Once the doors had whooshed shut, Jai took slow, shallow breaths and opened his good eye. Bronze metal filled his vision. He was staring at the wall. He tried to move, to get up, but excruciating pain coursed from his hip. With his other injuries, he hadn't even noticed that the invaders had broken his hip.

Jae groaned. He had to get to the engine room. If he could disable the engines, his commander might realize they were in trouble and come looking for them. It was his only chance, but all he could do was lie there like the smashed-up mutt he was. His nerves must've been damaged. He couldn't even change back into a human. Not that it would make any difference; if he couldn't fight his injuries in dog form, there was every chance he would die as a human.

He raised his lip in a one-sided snarl. A slight scraping sounded in front of him. His flattened ears pricked to attention. A metal claw lifted out of the bulkhead. Jai couldn't move out of the way. His broken body flagged as the claw cradled his body and pulled him through the bulkhead. Into where, he didn't know.

Ignore the pain, Jai thought.

But whatever was moving him stayed silent. He and Tara were the only ones left. Had Tara somehow managed to escape while the Collids were busy smashing Jae to bits?

That thought had him attempting to move, but agony burgeoned through his chest, his eye, his side. He fell back into darkness.

His last thought was of Tara.

Chapter 3

Jai kept still. He thought he had awakened, but the silence had him rethinking his assumption. Perhaps instead of just playing dead, he actually was dead after all.

He let out a small moan. Not loud enough to carry, but enough to let him know he had a voice. Therefore, he presumed he was, in fact, alive. He blinked. His eyes were open, but he couldn't see. Had they gouged out both his eyes? Was he blind? He scrunched up his shoulders and bit down on his bottom lip. Ah. No sharp teeth meant he was in humanoid form.

He tried to move his hand, but his wrists hit some sort of restraint. So, he was alive. Perhaps blind, but thankfully without the slightest bit of pain. But he was a prisoner—a well-looked-after prisoner.

It couldn't be the Collids. They would have killed him.

He lifted his head and dropped it again. At least they had given him a pillow. He tapped his fingers. His short nails clicked against metal. He stretched all ten fingers away from his body and found the edge of the bed. It was narrow, like the beds in medical.

Whatever had been covering his eyes disappeared, and he snapped his eyes shut against the bright light. Ah, yes, that was what pain felt like. He was perplexed. Had he seen and felt the light in both eyes? He was certain at least one of his eyes was rolling around the deck of the

Descartes.

Opening his good eye, he found the same light. He turned his head. Without thought, he widened both eyes at the shelves laden with medical supplies. Robot arms, hands and fingers hung by their cables on the wall, along with an array of needles lined up underneath them. A medi lab.

Jai blinked again, moved his attention to the left, and found the door. It was the *Descartes* medi lab. He would know it anywhere. Tara had hung the picture of Doctor Frankenstein's creation on the back of the door. She loved old horror stories dreamed up by writers who must have constantly endured the nightmares about which they wrote.

A thought crossed his mind: what had her imaginative brain deduced about him? Did she think he was a monster straight out of her storybooks? He snarled. Of course she did. Everyone did when they saw him. Every human he knew had been terrified of him once they found out what he was. That was the reason he preferred to work alone. That, and the habit he had of getting everyone around him killed.

A shadow moved in the corner of his eye. Blinking, Jae wished he could rub the itchiness from his eyes. He raised his lids. The shadow morphed into a tall blob, and as Jai focused, it changed into a human being—a human-shaped specter.

More visions from Tara's books. Maybe this one was Doctor Frankenstein himself. With his wild, curly dark hair, bushy eyebrows framing bright blue eyes, a sharp, straight nose, thin lips, and a pointy chin, he sure looked like a mad scientist. The thought made Jai laugh. The good doctor couldn't make him more of a beast than he already was. Or could he? Jai narrowed his eyes at the specter. This day was just getting better.

"Jai."

Jai frowned. The specter knew his name. "Who are you?"

"Jai. Captain. I am *Descartes'* AI. I am Rene. Can you remember?"

"I remember Rene, but you aren't him." Jai struggled against his bindings. "He's not alive. He's only a computer program."

The specter's bushy eyebrows sagged over his eyes. Jae had hurt his feelings. Why he felt bad about that, he didn't know.

"I'm sorry. You might be Rene. After all, the *Descartes* doesn't have sole use of the name. Are you a doctor? How did you get here? Have the Collids been defeated?"

Rene shook his head. "Listen to me. I learn, remember? That's why I'm here. I have learned to make a solid image of myself. It's still a bit glitchy, but it seemed more useful to have two hands and ten fingers to treat your injuries. How do you feel, Jai? Are you in pain?"

"No, I'm not in pain. Why am I tied up?"

"For your own protection. You were quite a handful, both as a… my databanks describe you as a star dog, something of a cross between a vampire and a werewolf, from Old Earth mythology. Your name in that form is Sirius. Is that correct?"

Jai had no idea what he was, but the man who had found him floating in space all those years ago, the man who was to become his Earth father, called him Sirius, which he once explained meant Dog Star.

"Close enough," Jai said.

"Whatever you are, you are extremely strong. You were working on instinct when I brought you in here, and that meant fighting. If I were real, I would be dead by now."

Rene laughed. Jai gaped at him.

"You have questions, but I'm afraid we don't have time. I had to shut down. The Collid's superiors could see and hear whatever their soldiers did. I couldn't let them find me. They would have used me against you. Against all humans."

"You fixed my eye."

"Yes, but I don't have time to explain. I'm unsure how the restoration will affect your human form, but I'm certain you will be pleased with your eye in star dog form. Your canine side has so many more fibers in its optic nerves."

Jai touched his eye. What did he mean? Jai opened his mouth to speak, but Rene cut him off.

"I know you aren't human, but you look and act human, so I have come to think of you as human. Did you know you have human DNA threaded through your alien chromosomes? That is… wait… shhh."

Rene kinked his holographic head, sending wild curls bouncing.

"They're looking for you. They have no idea about the EmelDrive drive, so they have been flying in real time for five days, and they are hungry. The captain wants to try eating you. He thinks you, in star dog form, would taste better than the human female."

Jai wriggled his wrists and ankles. "Get me out of these things."

As Rene unclipped the bindings, first from Jae's torso, then his arms and wrists, and finally, his legs and ankles, Jae wondered if he could trust the new model AI.

The moment he was loose, Jai leapt at Rene. His body passed right through the holograph and smashed into the wall. "Ugh!"

"What did you expect to happen?" Rene kinked his head again. "They heard you."

He whooshed over to the opposite wall. "Quick, get in there." He pointed to an open chute. Jai raised an eyebrow.

"It's the medi vac. Once you're at the bottom, you'll see another chute to your right. I've already opened it. Change into your star dog form and escape into space."

"What about Tara?"

"She's safe until they institute their plan for her."

"What plan?"

"They mean to use her as bait to capture Torgoes."

"The Collids on the bridge mentioned Torgoes. What the hell are they?"

"I don't have information on them in my database, but the Collids say they are another type of man-eating alien. They apparently love humans, male or female."

Rene stilled. Even Jai couldn't mistake the clomping of boots nearing the medi lab door.

"Get in there, Captain. Once you're in space, keep away from the sensors by flying above and just behind the bridge section. Follow us to wherever they're taking us."

Jai ducked down and scrambled into the duct. He held on to the rim of the chute and looked up at Rene. "Stay hidden."

"I will. Now, will you please go?"

Jai let go and slid down the smooth channel. A layer of something wet had him picking up speed as he descended. He dug his heels in and tried to slow his speed with his hands, but the goo just oozed between his fingers. He didn't want to think what the slime was as he careened around a bend and fell into a large container filled with sodden, puke-smelling material scraps.

Not wanting to know what they were or what they had been used for, he leapt out of the box and spun to his right. Rene was correct. Another duct waited there. Jai shifted into dog form and bounded through the opening. The cavity closed, and a fan roared above him, sucking out the air. That didn't worry him. He had no need to breathe in this form. Another cleft appeared in the hull of the ship. Stars twinkled in blue-black space, beckoning him.

He didn't need to be asked twice. He leapt out of the ship, twisted and dogpaddled up over the ship's hull, making sure not to expose his form to any sensors. Perhaps star dog was a misnomer; he was more like a self-propelled comet. Once he was behind the bridge, he kept pace with the *Descartes.*

His lips rolled back from his teeth in a grin. The Collids had no idea about the EmelDrive, so they couldn't cover much distance. However, they had managed to push the *Descartes* into full speed. It might not have been EmelDrive, but it was sixty miles per second. When one was swimming through space under one's own propulsion, that was bloody fast.

Jai stretched his body out full length, his legs trailing behind him, and swam. After an hour or so, he had to bring his legs into play, moving them in a frog-like motion. He had hoped to keep them rested for longer, but he was out of condition. He hadn't had much of a chance to fly around in space during his latest posting. He'd been too busy keeping the wealthy elite and the politicians, most times one and the same, out of man-eating alien mouths.

Another hour went by, and his shoulders bunched painfully. He shook his body as if he'd just had a bath. The muscles uncrunched some, but an ache mushroomed into his neck and back. He gazed covetously at the ship below him. Perhaps he could hang on to the hull for just ten minutes. Five, even. He growled at the pockmarked metal. The *Descartes'* sensors would ping a warning before Rene had time to stop it. No, he had to fly. He only hoped they were nearing their destination.

Three more hours, and his body was screaming in agony. His heart raced, thumping in his chest so rapidly, he thought it would explode. Jai had no choice but to fall onto the hull of the ship. Although he was dizzy with pain and exhaustion, the vibrations underneath him told him the sensors had sent a warning throughout the ship. He remained there. The Collids would go mad trying to find what had set the proximity sensors off. He cursed himself for not thinking of it sooner. Surely, they would just assume the ship was malfunctioning.

Something creaked to his left. He turned. Blast. He had forgotten about the bloody periscopes. He shouldn't have touched the bloody ship.

Chapter 4

Jai remained stretched out on the outer hull. He could drift, but he needed to stay with the ship if he was going to have any chance of rescuing Tara.

He growled at the periscope closest to him, hoping the Collids could see his bared teeth. His canines weren't as long as theirs were, but they were sharper. Much sharper. He would save Tara or die trying.

Another creak sounded to his right. He turned his head. A weapons port had opened, and a laser gun whirred out. If a dog could laugh, Jai would have chortled like a lunatic. His acute hearing picked up the hum of the gun, but that was it. No blast erupted from its barrel. He pictured the Collids arguing about who was at fault. He had no idea if they would realize, the *Descartes* was out of firepower.

The ship stuttered. They had reduced speed. He gazed out into the black velvet expanse. Three stars. One large one, as Old Earth's sun, had two orbiting smaller orbs. Between the suns and the *Descartes*, a planet seemed to be coming at him at a great velocity.

Jai eyed the suns. The planet they were heading for was the only world nearby. He had never seen this solar system.

The ship slipped into orbit, and a shuttle launched from the *Descartes'* port side toward the planet.

Jai let go and hurtled through the atmosphere. His Earth father had had the most skilled scientists available invent the specialized suit that appeared to be the same as any other captain's uniform. Its stretching ability and heat resistance kept him safe even at speed. If he slowed his rate of descent, his own epidermis could withstand the heat.

Jai's eyes grew wide as he beheld the planet below. Blue oceans surrounded green landmasses scored with aqua-colored rivers. Snowcapped mountain ranges surrounded blue-green lakes. Magnificent. This planet hadn't been spoiled with industry as Old Earth had.

A cityscape rose in the distance. So, it was inhabited, then.

The shuttle landed at the base of a small hill. Jai veered away and landed softly on his four paws in the surrounding woodland. Keeping low, he waited for the Collids to appear.

A couple of minutes later, they lumbered down the single step of the shuttle. One was carrying Tara over his shoulder, and another was holding a coil of rope. They trudged around the hill and through a small clearing. Jai slithered around the clearing after them.

The Collid carrying her threw Tara down against a thick-trunked tree. The other tied her to its base. They jabbered so fast, it was hard to make out anything they said. However, Jai distinctly heard the word *Torgoes* before they laughed and smacked their lips.

The Collids pulled a cage of sorts out of the shuttle's small hold. Jai was surprised it wasn't very tall. He had surmised that the Torgoes must be at least as big as Collids or Zors, but they had to be small to fit into the cage. Maybe Torgoes were a less-evolved life form. They could be more dangerous if they hunted in packs.

Jai had never heard of Torgoes, but he did not intend to let them eat Tara. He worked his muscles in a vibrating wave down his body. They all seemed to be in working order. First, he had to get rid of the Collids.

He zeroed in on the closest man-eater. A blast of pain shot through his eye. He let out a small whine. What had Rene done? Every time he tried to focus his vision, pain seared into the right side of his brain. He swallowed a growl and bounded through the air toward the Collid.

The thing must have heard the movement, because it swung around just as Jai leapt, and he snagged its throat between his jaws. He bit down, angling his sharp canines into the Collid's thrumming artery.

The Collid wailed and fell backwards, its cry morphing into a gurgle as Jai shook its neck like a rubber toy. Blood pumped out of the severed artery, spraying the air around him with an ever-decreasing pulse. Jai didn't release his bite until he was sure the Collid was dead.

The other Collid spun about. Raucous squawking amid shouts and whistles echoed throughout the area. Jai twisted his head. The noises seemed to be coming from all directions at once. Thumping sounded. He turned just in time to see the remaining Collid board the shuttle.

Scores of strange, bird-like aliens surrounded the clearing. They only came to Jae's hip height, but the sharp teeth lining their open mouths made them look fierce. Feathery quills covered their backs and arms. Soft fur covered the rest of what Jai could see of their bodies. They stood on thick, crooked chicken legs. Their screeching filled the air and hurt Jai's ears. Some of them tried to stop the shuttle from taking off. The force of the liftoff shook them loose.

Jai loped to Tara's side. She didn't scream. She just sat there staring with bulging eyes at the new aliens. Jai roared at her and shifted into human form.

She blinked at him, confusion filling her face. "What—"

He shut her up by placing his index finger over her mouth. He then plucked a knife out of his boot and cut the bindings.

Tara jumped up and withdrew her own knife out of her boot. As if her training had finally kicked in, she said, "Later, then." She stood with her feet apart in a fighting stance and glared ahead.

Jai followed her gaze. The Torgoes, or whatever they were, were shouting and waving their feathered arms angrily at the disappearing shuttle.

One of them broke away and scampered forward so fast, its form blurred. Before Jai could make out what it was doing, it had wrapped its feathery arms around Tara. Another pounced on Jai's back, its arms coiled around him and holding his arms against his sides. It squashed his chest like a steel vice.

Jai squatted and shifted into a star dog. Puffing his chest and rounding his back, he decompressed and threw the animal off. Rounding on it before it could get to its feet, Jai growled lowly as he stood over it.

The other animals shuffled around Jai and their comrade. Jai drew back his lips and opened his jaws, exposing his canines.

Chapter 5

Jai growled. He bent his head to latch down onto its neck, but the fear in the alien's small, wide eyes had Jai hesitating. The alien curled up into a brown furry ball.

Jai stood up and stared at the strange animal. It now looked like a cross between a chicken and a hedgehog, with its beady eyes and pretty face. Its nose wrinkled as it unfurled its body.

"What are you?" the alien said in Universal. It didn't sound like a man-eating beast. It sounded like a small child.

"Captain!" Tara's voice floated to his ears. "Jai!"

He turned. Tara was standing there, holding the alien that had attacked her. The alien was snuggling against her neck, gazing at Jai in terror.

"They aren't killers," Tara said. "Change back to the captain."

Jai shook his head and gazed at the rest of the aliens. They had stopped squawking and carrying on. They were standing there staring at him, their beady eyes opened to their full extent, curious.

Tara placed a shaking hand on his arm. "Please, Jai."

Jai shifted into human form and stepped away from the animal on the ground. The alien leapt up and ran in a blur back to its pack, or flock, whatever they were. It stopped beside a taller one, who put its arm around the little one's shoulders. It gave them a squeeze before stepping forward. "You are not human."

"No. I don't taste like it, either."

The feathery alien let out a high cackle. The rest joined in. Jai held his hands to his ears against the cacophony. The one that had spoken raised an arm. The others stopped, except for a twitter here and there, and went silent.

The leader—at least, Jai guessed it was the leader—stepped closer. "You think Torgoes eat humans? No. We are vegetarians. We just let the Collids think that so we can save a few humans they set out as traps for us. Sometimes we succeed."

It shook its head solemnly. "Sometimes we don't." It turned to its companions and raised its arm once more. "But we have today!"

They raised their arms in turn and squawked their appreciation.

Glancing at Tara, Jai raised his brows. She smiled and set down her catch. It bowed, moved beside the leader, and tugged on the leader's leg feathers.

"There could be more Collids on the way, Father."

"Are there?" the leader asked Jai.

"Not as far as I know," Jai said, wondering what the bug-eyed Collid was doing with his ship.

The young alien let out a squawk and beamed at the leader. "We should have a feast, Father."

"Indeed, we should. And I would like to find out more about our honored guest." It bowed to Jai. "And his beautiful companion." It took Tara's hand and kissed the back of it.

Tara laughed. "Thank you, kind... sir."

The leader held a four-fingered hand over its chest. "I am Valchi, king of the Diahti Torgoes. Please, come and join us."

Jai glanced at Tara and shrugged. He figured they might as well follow the aliens. They had nowhere else to go. He fell in beside Valchi.

"What planet is this?"

"Relerican."

"Never heard of it. What star system?"

"We call it the Torgo star system. I know that doesn't help you, because the other humans who have been stranded here have never heard of our planet or our star system. However, you are not human. May I ask what you are?"

Tara's head snapped around toward Jai. She raised her brows in question.

Jai shrugged. "I don't know what I am. As a baby—or perhaps 'pup' would be the more appropriate word—I was told that I had been found floating in space and brought to a ship. As it was an exploration ship, many scientists were aboard. The leading scientist used his position to take me to Old Earth. He and his wife raised me as a human."

"Ah. I have heard of Old Earth. It sounds wonderful, much like here."

"It used to be," Tara said. "Now, many humans have moved to New Earth. It's not as beautiful as here, but suitable for humans."

"Yes, from what the other humans have told me, your New Earth sounds like a hard place to live."

"It would be," Jai said. "But with our technology, more land is being utilized every year. Speaking of technology, I saw a city earlier."

"Ah, that is the city built and inhabited by humans," Valchi said. "We have been saving your species for over a century, in your time."

It was Jai's turn to raise an eyebrow.

Valchi smiled. "We have learned much from your people."

They rounded a stand of trees and shrubs. Jai stopped abruptly. Tables and chairs filled a large clearing. To the left, fires with cooking spits and pots circled the scene. Torgoes of every size stood chatting, cooking, or running here and there. The buzz from the chatter and clinking of the cooking and serving utensils rumbled throughout the clearing. Behind that, a mountain rose above them. Cave openings spotted the face of the rocky terrain. Rigid wooden staircases wound from the ground, joining the openings together.

Valchi followed his gaze and hummed. "We prefer our caves over human buildings."

"They look sweet," Tara said, smiling at Jai.

During a feast of exotic and known fruits and vegetables, bowls of fish meat and plates of flat bread, Jai learned that the Torgoes burrowed their caves themselves. After examining their retractable-clawed feet and hands, he could believe it. They apparently still liked to burrow whenever the chance arrived.

Valchi sat back, patting his creamy-furred stomach. "What will you do now, Jai? Would you like to be shown the way to the city?"

Jai thought about that for a moment. He had lost the eraser, and without the *Descartes*, he no longer had a job. The commander had made it plain that he hadn't wanted Jai in his military, and the only reason he had relented was because of New Earth's president. Jai's adopted father was a scientist and a diplomat, and he had the president's ear. It was because of their friendship that Jai had gotten the job in the first place.

He turned his head to hide a grimace. He supposed he was discharged now. "What I really want is to get a ship to New Earth." Jae figured he at least owed a visit to his father.

Valchi's forehead fur wrinkled. He lowered his voice so his neighbors wouldn't hear. "I have heard that the humans are building another ship."

"Another one?"

"Yes. This will be their eleventh since I was born. They all explode before they can exit the atmosphere. But I am told they have high hopes for this latest one."

"That cinches it. Tara and I will go to the city."

"It is a long walk. You and your companion should rest. If you still want to go in the morning, I will have Thrak show you the way." The king leaned in closer. "Not all humans are as kind as Torgoes, and unlike us, they are not given to sharing their possessions."

Jae laughed. "Ain't that the truth?"

Valchi's gaze darted to the sky. At the same time, Thrak oohed in awe. Jae followed their gazes. A bright light ascended into the night.

"The humans have launched their ship!" Valchi said.

Jai's chest tightened as the light from the blast engines skittered then stopped completely.

"What happened?" Tara asked.

"I think they are about to crash back to the ground," Jai said.

A moment later, the horizon lit up. Orange and yellow flames soared into the sky for several seconds, and then slowly died down to a warm glow. The ship had exploded. Jai wondered what the humans could be doing wrong. Obviously, none of them had ever built a spaceship before.

"It looks like you will be staying with us for a time," Valchi said. "It will take them many full moons to build another."

Jai stood up and held his hand out to Tara. "Would you walk with me?"

Tara took his hand. "Yes, Captain."

Nodding to Valchi, Jai and Tara strolled out of the community area and into a small forest at the foot of the mountain.

They stopped and turned to one another, both speaking at the same time. Tara held her hand up. "I'm sorry. You go first."

"No, please. What were you going to say?"

"I… I just wanted to thank you for saving my life."

Jai laughed. "As it turned out, I didn't need to save you—at least, not from the Torgoes."

"No. But you didn't know that. The Collids were going to kill me the moment the Torgoes showed up."

Jai stepped closer and, placing his hands gently on her shoulders, gazed into her stunning blue eyes. "I wouldn't have let that happen." His gaze dropped to her lips, and before he knew it, his mouth was on hers. She returned his kiss, wrapping her arms around his neck. Jae moved his arms around her waist and drew her against his body.

He thought they fit perfectly. He deepened the kiss.

Tara was the first to pull away. "We shouldn't," she whispered, as if she was trying to get her breath.

Jai pulled her back and hugged her. "I'm not going to apologize, Tara. I've wanted to do that since the moment you boarded the *Descartes*."

She rested her head on his chest. "Me too."

Unable to stop a grin from stretching his mouth, he kissed the top of her head. He still wanted to find a ship and go back to civilization, but at least now, he had time to get to know Tara better. It'd been a long time since he had liked a female enough to even want to know what she liked, what she thought, what her dreams were. He closed his eyes and breathed in the damp, sweaty scent of her hair. There was nothing about the woman he didn't like. And it seemed that even his star dog form wasn't enough for her not to have feelings for him.

The last woman who had seen him in that form had screamed and called him an ugly beast. He had wanted to marry her and thought she should know the real him first. Big mistake. But Tara had seen him, and she still wanted him close.

After a moment, she broke the embrace. "What are we going to do, Captain?"

He smiled and pushed a stand of blonde hair off her cheek. "Please call me Jai while we're planet-bound."

Tara smiled.

"What we'll do is go to the city and help them build another ship," Jai said. "I think it's the fuel they're using. Maybe with your previous engineering experience and my college chemistry, we can come up with a better method of propulsion."

"Even if they let us help, that will take a long time." Tara picked a leaf off a shrub and put it to her nose. "Hmm, smells kinda like cinnamon."

Jai plucked a leaf also and sniffed it. It did have a fruity, cinnamony kind of scent. He wrapped his arm around her shoulders, and they ambled back to the clearing.

Tara snuggled against his side. "Do you think they'll give us connecting caves?"

Jai laughed.

He gazed up at the stars, wondering what the new, improved Rene was doing at that moment. Would he try to retake the ship, try to get back to them? Whatever he did, Jai hoped Rene could stay out of the Collids' clutches long enough for Jai to find him.

Author Dale Furse

I've enjoyed many creative pursuits including, playing guitar and singing in a band, acting and directing in amateur theatre, writing plays, songs, and poems. But my true love is writing fantastically, adventurous Science Fiction and Fantasy stories.

Did you like Jai's story? Find all my books on Amazon and you can join my newsletter by visiting my website: http://www.dalefurse.com/ ☺

Space Colony One: Night of Flames
By J J Green

He was barefoot, and the strange, mossy turf of the new world was rubbery and cool against his skin.

After the night lamps of the barn, the outside world was pitch black to his eyes save for the string of lights that led to the latrine. He strained to listen. He was sure he'd heard the thunk of something large hitting the ground out there, but now he couldn't hear anything other than the wind rustling the fronds of vegetation that surrounded the camp.

Back in the newly built barn, the rest of the colonists were sleeping soundly. More than two hundred men and women lay on rows of low cots, exhausted after a long day spent bringing down essential supplies from the ship. It wasn't surprising that no one else had heard the noise.

The sound was probably nothing, he told himself. Maybe just a dying plant toppled by the wind. None of the probes the scientists had sent from Earth and from the ship over the years had found signs of complex animal life, nor of plants capable of locomotion.

Holding up a lamp and peering ahead, he went on. The lamp's glow wasn't strong, and the moonless planet with its faint, unfamiliar constellations was a dark place at night, but he had an idea of the direction the sound had come from. His eyes adjusted to the darkness as he went. Dim gray shapes came into view—the boxes of supplies piled in heaps around the compound.

Another thunk. He stopped. This noise had come from farther away than the first, in the direction of the comm module they'd set up to talk to the ship. He ran a hand through his hair and glanced back at the barn, tall and wide behind him, blacker than the sky. Should he tell someone? Dr. Crowley, perhaps? One of the Woken, the doctor, always seemed to know what to do.

No. The old woman needed her rest, and he was just a Gen farmer. What did he know? Besides, what else would you expect on an alien planet but weird noises? He would walk the perimeter fence and satisfy himself there was no cause for alarm, then return to the barn and his well-earned slumber.

A third thunk. Off to his right. *What the...?* He swung around and gazed into the night. Beyond the dim circle of his lamp's light was nothing but darkness. He hesitated on the verge of returning and waking someone in authority, but he was sure he was nearly at the fence. It would only take him a moment to have a quick look around. He decided to go on.

A shriek splintered the calm of the night. The cry had come from the barn. *Lauren.* An almost inhuman howl of agony shot through with terror followed the shriek. He sprinted back the way he'd come, his bare feet struggling to grip the damp ground cover. He slipped and fell. The lamp sprang from his hand and skittered away.

He leaped up. The lamp could wait. The shriek had been joined by shouts and screams. The barn doors flew open, and people poured out. *Lauren. Where was she?* The people raced off, spreading in disorder throughout the camp, pushing each other down in their hurry to get away. The fallen couldn't stand, and others tumbled over them, crushing them in the stampede.

He was at the barn. He forced his way against the tide of escaping colonists. A woman came rushing toward him, her eyes popping and her mouth wide. She held up bloody, raw hands, palms out.

"Don't touch it," she wailed. "It burns." Then she was gone.

Behind the remnants of the people rushing from the barn lay the object of their fear: A grayish-brown mass covered most of one of the cots, leaving only the cot legs visible beneath the misshapen lump.

A man ran past, colliding with Ethan's shoulder.

"We can't get it off of her," he said, his deep voice choked with barely suppressed sobs. "We've tried everything. I'm going to call the ship."

The barn was nearly empty now. Only the brown thing remained and a young woman standing over it, hitting it with the broken leg of a cot, her face wracked with anguish and despair.

"Lauren," he shouted.

"Ethan," she exclaimed. She threw down the cot leg, ran to him and grabbed his arms. "Where have you been? The others all panicked and ran away. Can you help? Only don't touch it, it—"

"It burns. I know. Someone told me."

Ethan stepped closer to the thing for a better look. As he saw what lay beneath it, the strength went from his legs, and he nearly collapsed. Poking out from the upper end of the creature were the head and shoulders of Dr. Crowley. The alien life form was on top of her.

"We can't move it," said Lauren. "It's stuck to her like glue, and we can't even touch it because its skin is caustic."

Dr. Crowley was still alive, barely. The shriek Ethan had heard must have been hers. Whatever the creature was doing to her, it had nearly finished the job. The doctor's eyes were half-closed, and her lips were blue. The organism was suffocating her or—Ethan recalled that its skin burned—was it digesting her?

He turned to try to find something to lever the thing off the woman. There had to be something no one else had tried. But the thought of what the creature was doing to Dr. Crowley overwhelmed him. Blood drained from his head, and he became dizzy. He fell to his knees, vomit erupting from his stomach.

"What?" said Lauren.

Ethan looked up. She was bending over Dr. Crowley, trying to catch the doctor's words.

"Don't go near that thing," he exclaimed, forcing himself to his feet and drawing his arm across his bile-stained mouth.

"The what?" Lauren repeated. "The...the fence?" She turned puzzled eyes to Ethan.

The fence? The electric fence. How had the creature gotten into the camp? Why hadn't the fence stopped it? The thunk he'd heard must have been the organism hitting the ground. And he'd heard more of them.

More of them were in the camp. Where were the rest of the creatures? And where were all the people who had run out of the barn?

"Lauren, we have to go," he said. "I think the fence might have shorted, and there are more of those things inside the compound with us."

***

Dr. Crowley was the only Woken Ethan had gotten to know.

She'd been one of the first to emerge healthy and sound from her hundred and eighty-four years spent in a twilight state somewhere between hibernation and death as the *Nova Fortuna* carried them to their new home. Just as the Manual instructed, the Gens had begun to revive the founders of the mission two years before Arrival. Of those they attempted to return to life, more than fifty percent didn't survive the process, and those they managed to wake suffered strokes and aneurysms or had brain damage, or were blind, or their limbs turned gangrenous when blood flow could not be restored.

Dr. Crowley had been standing in Main Park beneath The Clock when Ethan first saw her on his morning run. She was looking at the glowing figures that counted down, not up. Figures that marked the seconds, hours, days, months, and years that passed on their deep space flight.

At the sight of Dr. Crowley gazing transfixed at The Clock, Ethan had been reminded of the time when he found out what it was measuring. He'd been in kindergarten, and the teacher had explained that the children were lucky Gens who would be alive when the *Nova Fortuna* reached her destination. Soon after they were grown up, the teacher had said, they would leave the ship and travel a short distance to a planet where they would live out the rest of their lives.

Dr. Crowley's fascination with The Clock had made sense to Ethan. The figures on its display had counted down nearly two centuries while she'd lain in her vat of frozen slush. Though he was usually a little intimidated by the enigmatic Woken with their odd dialects and distant eyes, he couldn't resist the temptation to talk to this one. She seemed more approachable than most of the others, who were aloof and stuck together.

He jogged over and stood next to her, joining her contemplation of the steadily counting figures of The Clock. The older woman seemed to sense his nervousness, for she smiled kindly at him.

"Do you have any plans for Arrival Day?" she asked.

"I guess I'll spend it with my girlfriend," Ethan replied. "Unless there's something ship-wide planned."

"I don't think so," Dr. Crowley said. "I believe the director intends for everyone to celebrate in their own way, as it will mean different things to different people. May I ask what your occupation is to be?"

Ethan shrugged. "Just a farmer. I didn't do too well at school." He gave an embarrassed smile.

Dr. Crowley frowned. "Forgive me for saying so, but you seem ashamed. Being a farmer's nothing to be ashamed of. Your job is just as important as anyone else's, Maybe *more* important than some. The colony won't last long without food."

When Ethan didn't react to her words, she tilted her head. "Don't you want to be a farmer?"

Ethan glanced around. No one seemed close enough to hear their conversation. He didn't like to express his discontent with his allotted role publicly. He wouldn't be punished as such, but failure to conform to the Mandate wouldn't do much for his reputation. "If I could have chosen, I would have been an explorer."

"Oh, now that's a fine profession," Dr. Crowley said. "Why didn't you select it? Surely you don't need good grades to be an explorer?"

"It's a Second Generation occupation." Ethan sighed. "Maybe if I have kids and they want to take over the farm when they're older I'll get my chance."

"No explorers?" Dr. Crowley exclaimed, loud enough to cause Ethan unease that they would be overheard.

"No explorers until the Second Gen," he said. "It's in the Manual."

"The Old Manual or the New Manual?" Dr. Crowley asked, narrowing her eyes. "As if I didn't know."

"The New, I think," Ethan replied, glad that he wasn't the object of the annoyance that began to cloud the doctor's features.

"Hmpf. I'll have a word with the director about that. Old Manual, New

Manual..." She waggled a finger. "There's only one Manual, and that's the one the other founders and I had written before we departed Earth. There was no talk then of drafting an *updated* version mid-voyage. What do you pups know of settling a planet? Living out your lives on a starship is hardly preparation for..." She paused and took a breath. Her gaze flicked to Ethan. "Forgive me. It's not your fault."

After she'd calmed down a little more, she gave a short laugh and said, "It's strange. You'd think that tens of light years would be sufficient distance to leave behind petty politics and meddling in the affairs of others. But wherever you go, there you are, I guess."

"Is...is that what you wanted?" Ethan asked. "To leave all that stuff behind on Earth?" He'd had no choice but to be born aboard the *Nova Fortuna* and become one of the first humans ever to set foot on an extrasolar planet. But the Woken had chosen to risk their lives for the opportunity. That had always struck him as odd. He imagined that Earth must have been a terrible place for them to want to leave it so badly, despite the positives that the vids and books showed.

"Yes, politics, and more," the doctor replied. "Much more, though I don't know if you can understand. Truth be told, I feared for what would happen to humankind. We seemed not to be progressing, but regressing. It wouldn't surprise me if the technology of the *Nova Fortuna* were the peak of human achievement and everything went downhill after we left. But it wasn't only that. My eyes were on the stars all my life. I was glad to come along, even though I knew I might never wake up."

"You think technology might not have progressed on Earth in all the time that's passed since we left?" Ethan asked.

"I'm almost certain of it," the doctor said.

"Why do you think that?"

"Mainly because in the years leading up to the departure of the *Nova Fortuna*, we seemed on the verge of inventing a Faster-Than-Light starship engine. Sure, the popular trend was against anything *unnatural,* and there were protests and demands that space travel funding be cut because it was *wrong* for humankind to leave its birthplace, but the scientists were close nonetheless. So close that some of the founders even wanted to postpone the *Nova Fortuna's* leaving date. Why spend two centuries traveling by fusion propulsion when you could arrive within a few years?

"Yet here we are, and there's no sign of anything from Earth. If an FTL engine had been invented while we were traveling, it would have caught up to us by now. We wouldn't be trying to decipher scrambled Earth comms sent decades ago. The fact that another ship hasn't followed us tells me a lot."

Ethan nodded. The Woken woman's way of explaining things made much more sense than many of his former teachers'. "So, what do you think Earth's like now?"

"So much time has passed...I really couldn't guess. Does it matter? We have a whole new future ahead for all two thousand, two hundred of us. The beginning of a new civilization." She returned her gaze to The Clock.

***

Lauren hadn't seemed to hear Ethan's words when he told her they had to check the fence. She was closing Dr. Crowley's eyes. "She's gone," she whispered.

Ethan heard her, but he couldn't process the words. He swallowed. "The fence," he repeated heavily. "We have to find the switch." He took Lauren's arm. "Come with me. Get away from that thing."

But Lauren was shaking her head. "I have to find Belle. I have to make sure she's okay." Belle was Lauren's nursery-mate. They'd been inseparable since they were three years old.

"There isn't time. She could be anywhere," Ethan said. "And there are more of those creatures out there. I heard them dropping into the compound."

"No. I have to find her, Ethan. She'll be terrified. You go and check the fence. I'll meet you at the comm module. I'll be careful."

Ethan closed his eyes. There was no time for him to think. There was no time for anything. "Okay. Okay. But please, stay the hell away from those creatures."

As Lauren ran off, calling for her friend, Ethan forced his reluctant legs to move. He was terrified of what might happen to Lauren, but he had to stop any more of the life forms entering the camp. He grabbed another night lamp and left the barn.

Ethan sped away on the quickest route to the fence. It had been the first thing to be erected after Arrival. The builders had sunk metal posts and fixed high-tensile alloy fencing to them four meters high and a meter below ground, enclosing the compound. But Ethan hadn't been a part of the building crew. Where was the switch to turn on the electricity? He didn't recall seeing it.

Another shriek split his ears. The noise came from somewhere to the right. Someone else had been caught by one of the creatures. Sweat ran from Ethan's pores at the memory of what had happened to Dr. Crowley—at the thought of what was happening to another person. The shriek evened out to a long, howling wail of someone in terrible torment.

The horrible cry stopped abruptly. Had the creature moved onto its victim's face? Had someone put the person out of their misery? Ethan steered his thoughts away from the idea. He had one goal: turn on the fence.

From out of nowhere, a child ran into his side and rebounded from the impact. The kid rolled to a halt and sat up, crying. Ethan went over, crouched down to the boy and held his arms. "Are you okay?"

"Mommy! I want my mommy." The child was only six or seven years old. He must have been separated from his parents in the mad rush from the barn. What was he even doing on the planet surface? Ethan wondered. He hadn't noticed the child during the day's work.

The boy continued to sob into his fists. Around them, screams and shouts were filling the air. Ethan didn't know what to do. He had to go to the fence, but he didn't want to leave the kid alone with those creatures roaming the camp.

"Come with me," he said, straightening up and holding out his hand. "Come on, we'll find your mommy."

The kid didn't look up. He buried his face further into his hands and shook his entire body from side to side, signaling his refusal of Ethan's offer.

"Come on," Ethan urged. "It isn't safe for you to be out here by yourself. Come with me. We'll find your mommy, I promise."

The kid lifted his head long enough to shout, "No, leave me alone," before he thrust his face into his hands once more and fresh sobs rocked his little body.

Ethan didn't have time to waste. He reached down and grabbed the kid, intending to carry him over his shoulder while he continued his search for the switch. But the boy struggled and kicked as Ethan lifted him.

"Whoa, take it easy," Ethan protested, trying to get a firm grip on the wriggling child. A small, booted foot struck Ethan full in the stomach. He grunted in pain and dropped the boy, who landed on his feet and ran the second he hit the ground, quickly disappearing into the darkness.

Ethan ran after him, but he couldn't see where he'd gone. He stopped and called out, telling the kid that it wasn't safe and that he had to come back, but he heard no response. The child was nowhere to be seen. Ethan's heart weighed heavy. He returned to his quest to find the switch.

***

The boy's attachment to one of his parents—to the extent of refusing a stranger's offer of help—struck Ethan forcefully. He couldn't guess how that kind of attachment felt. It didn't seem so long ago that he'd been the kid's age, but he'd had no mother or father.

Ethan's earliest memories were of playing with other kids at his nursery. The nursery workers had been kind. He even remembered a few of them hugging and kissing him, their eyes teary, when it was time for him to go to kindergarten. But he hadn't developed the bonds with them that families were supposed to have. None of the caregivers had been like a mother or father to him, as far as he'd understood the role. The only person he'd had that kind of relationship with had been Dr. Crowley.

He learned about families at school, and how the Manual instructed that, as Arrival drew nearer, Gens were to be encouraged to reproduce naturally and revert to the nuclear family patterns of human societies on Earth. The transition had to happen. The technology for artificial reproduction was wearing out, and it would be decades before they would be able to manufacture replacement parts.

Like the other Gen his age and all the babies decanted throughout the flight of the *Nova Fortuna*, Ethan's conception had taken place in vitro. The DNA codes of Gen ova and sperm and stored, frozen donations from Earth were carefully selected and matched to ensure maximum diversity.

With a Gen population of just two thousand, inbreeding had to be avoided as much as possible. Even more dangerous was uncontrolled reproduction during the *Nova Fortuna's* voyage. The ship's enclosed habitat could not sustain a population growth greater than ten percent, or roughly the number of preserved founders they were bringing with them.

The lost boy had to have been one of the first naturally conceived. The Manual stated that the move away from artificial reproduction and toward creating families should start seven years before Arrival. Gens of reproductive age had to begin to get used to the new way of living before encountering the other stresses of colonization. Dr. Crowley had told Ethan of another reason behind the Manual's directive: the founders' thinking had been that Gens' new lives would be so much harder than living aboard the *Nova Fortuna* that they might need something to live *for*.

Ethan and Lauren had talked about conceiving a child, but she'd shuddered while lying in his arms and said the idea of something growing inside her was weird. Maybe she would feel different later, she'd said.

***

A shape approached, long and low and moving fast. One of the creatures. Ethan swerved and ran away from it. For something as large as a man laid out and at least twice as wide, the thing moved quickly. He looked over his shoulder, but the life form was veering in another direction. It seemed to have given up the pursuit, presumably in favor of slower prey. Ethan's stomach dropped as he remembered the boy.

The thing had scooted along the ground, its method of locomotion obscured by its overhanging bulk. But Ethan had no time to puzzle out how the life form moved. He was at the fence. His gaze roved it. No switch was in sight. A scream from another captured victim spurred him not to catch his breath before setting off to find the switch. He went right as shouts of terror, panic, and despair resounded through the night and people cried out the names of their loved ones.

Fence wire and posts sped past Ethan as he ran. The dark scuttling figure of a creature climbing the far side of the fence flashed into view. Its scaly belly outlined with hundreds of insectoid legs reflected the light from his lamp. Ethan stopped and pushed the lamp between the wires at the underside of the organism but at the touch of the metal its legs wrapped around the fence wires and clung to them tightly. Ethan couldn't move the creature, and he didn't have time to try harder.

A thunk sounded somewhere behind him. Another one of the creatures had made it over the fence. Ethan took off.

A flicker of something yellow appeared on the edge of his vision. Ethan stuck his heels into the spongy ground and skidded to a halt. A plastic handle jutted out from a post beneath a yellow hazard sign. He'd found the switch, but something was moving on the wires above it. One of the organisms was crawling over the post. Ethan raised his lamp to shine on the scrabbling life form. He had only a second before it would fall. He darted in and grabbed the switch.

But before he pushed down, he hesitated. What if someone were touching the fence? Turning on the electricity could kill them. He looked up at the creature that was about to drop. He couldn't help it. He had to take the chance. He pushed down the lever. As the electricity hit, the creature jolted, its legs jerking. It became rigid, and a terrible reek like burning rotten flesh assaulted Ethan's senses.

He'd done it. The electrified fence would prevent any more creatures from coming into the camp. But why had it been turned off in the first place? He shook his head. It was odd, but he didn't have time to think about it. He had to find Lauren.

Holding out his lamp in front of him, Ethan set off to search the compound. He hoped that Dr. Crowley was the only fatality, though going by some of the cries he heard echoing through the night, he doubted it.

It wasn't long before he came across the creature he'd tried to push off the fence. It had made it over the top and was lying inside the camp, but its back end had been in contact with a wire when Ethan had turned the electricity on. The life form was stiff, its thick hide was dark and charred, and it gave off a stench that made Ethan's stomach churn.

Liquid had spread out from the organism in its death throes. A puddle lay beneath it that had scorched the ground cover down to the soil. Pressing his elbow over his nose and mouth, he peered closer. The creature didn't seem to have any eyes, mouth, or other sensory organs. He shivered and drew away. How had the probes missed these life forms?

From somewhere to his left came the sound of someone running. He lifted the lamp as the person came into view. It was the director, though

Ethan barely recognized the man. His gray hair stuck out all over, and his eyes were wild. He grabbed Ethan's arm, making the lamp swing crazily.

"They're dead," he exclaimed. "So many people killed by those things. What can we do? Where can we hide? Do you know where to hide?" His fingers dug stiffly into Ethan's forearm, and his gaze darted from side to side. Sweat beads clung to the man's face despite the cool of the night.

"What the hell do you mean, where can we hide?" Ethan retorted. "We've got to find the creatures and kill them."

"We can't." The director's voice was wobbly and high as if verging on hysteria. "Nothing kills them. Nothing. We've tried everything we can think of. And the comm module's dead. We can't contact the ship. They have no idea what's happening down here. We haven't any hope of rescue."

His grip on Ethan's arm was painful. Ethan peeled the man's fingers from his muscle. "The comm module's dead?"

"Broken." The director's eyes seemed about to leave their sockets. "Someone sabotaged it. We have no comm. We're alone down here."

The fence, and now the comm module? A scream, piercing and tortured, made them both jump.

"We have to help, not hide," Ethan said between his teeth. He pushed the man out of the way and ran toward the scream.

How had their hopes of a new, wonderful life turned to darkness and slaughter?

***

Ethan remembered the director as everyone had watched the counting down of the final two hours remaining on The Clock. After a long, arduously fought election—to be the director who presided over Arrival and the first settlement—the man had stood straight-backed and proud on the podium in Main Park. His hair had been perfectly groomed, then.

The countdown had been breath-taking. Main Park held all the Gens and the Woken, and though there was no formal request for their presence, all but essential maintenance staff had gathered there. Some had even slept in the park overnight with the black, starry fake sky over their heads and the figures of The Clock glowing green in the dark.

The Clock spanned a wide section of the dome. As early as five or six years before Arrival, couples and groups had begun to stand beneath it and discuss their plans of what they were going to do when the *Nova Fortuna* reached its destination. Those who weren't drawn to The Clock spent hours watching vids on the planet they were approaching. As the ship drew nearer, visuals showed continents and seas and water-vapor clouds that seemed to confirm that everything the scientists had said about the planet was true.

On the final day, the murmuring of the crowd in Main Park had grown louder as more and more Gens, and Woken arrived, and excited chatter about the impending long-anticipated event rose, drowning out the circulation fans that whirred at top speed to renew and cool the air.

Ethan could hardly believe it when the moment that he'd been taught to anticipate all his life arrived. The final hour of The Clock flicked to zero to match the year, month, and day. Only minutes and seconds remained. The noise of the crowd grew almost painful. Then, strangely enough, the volume subsided as The Clock marked the final minutes, and then the final seconds, until only the quietest of whispers sounded among the more than two thousand people gathered underneath it.

The last few moments of their long voyage disappeared. One hundred and eighty-four years of waiting was over. The work of tens of thousands of people, many of whom had never set foot on the *Nova Fortuna*, many of whom had lived and died aboard her, were finally paid off. An almost deathly hush fell over the park.

Five. Four. Three. Two. One.

The Clock was a row of zeros. The device that had faithfully kept time for nearly two centuries stopped, its work done. Not a person in the crowd stirred as if no one could quite believe they had reached this point—that the *Nova Fortuna* was in geosynchronous orbit above the site that was soon to become their new home.

Brilliant lights exploded across the surface of the dome, accompanied by ear-splitting bangs and whistles. The Gens stared up in fear, but the Woken seemed to know what was going on. They shouted and cheered and clapped and stamped their feet. Whatever the cascading colors were, they seemed to be celebrating the safe arrival of the colonists, and soon the Gens joined the Woken in hollers and shouts and hugs and kisses.

Ethan had grabbed Lauren and lifted her up. He swirled her around as she laughed and screamed. They celebrated all night.

***

Lauren. He had to find her.

They'd agreed to meet at the comm module. Using the distant lights that led to the latrine as his guide, Ethan raced towards the meeting point, ignoring the fading protests of the desperate director. As Ethan drew closer to the spot, dark, swarming figures of men and women took shape.

The crowd was surging in a blind panic. People were shouting and crying. No one seemed to know what to do or where to go. Ethan went from person to person, trying to find Lauren, but she didn't seem to be among them. In the chaos, he despaired that he would ever find her. Someone had to organize these people.

He cupped his hands around his mouth. "Everyone, get tools from the stores," he shouted. "We have to find and kill the creatures."

"We've tried," growled a man nearby, lifting a sledgehammer in one hand. "Nothing kills them. Nothing. They're all over the place, and we can't contact the ship. We're dead. All of us. It's only a matter of time."

"No. We can't give up," said Ethan. There had to be a way. "Come with me back to the barn," he said to the man. "Maybe the creature that was in there has gone. If it has, everyone can go inside. We can barricade the doors and wait until morning when the supply shuttle from the ship is due."

"No way," the man replied. "I'm not going near any of those things. I'm staying right here."

"But you're no safer here," said Ethan. "One of them could attack any minute."

"I said, I'm not going anywhere." The man lifted his hammer again threateningly, and his eyes glinted in the light from Ethan's lamp. Like the director, the man seemed to be barely holding himself together.

Ethan clenched his jaw. It was no use. Their soft lives aboard the *Nova*

Fortuna meant they were entirely unprepared to deal with the emergency. And why had no one thought to set a watch while the others slept? They'd behaved like fools.

"No," a voice wailed on the far side of the comm module. "Help him. Please. Somebody help him." The victim's terrible shrieking began, and the man Ethan had been talking to threw down his sledgehammer and, gripping his ears, ran off.

Then, above the shouts, cries, and moaning of the crowd came a sound that made Ethan's heart leap. It was Lauren's voice, and she was calling his name. He headed toward the sound, pushing others aside as he went.

She was calling his name over and over. She seemed close by, though it was hard to navigate in the darkness and the confusion of voices.

"Lauren," he shouted. "Lauren!" There she was.

She'd found Belle, and the two were standing together with their arms entwined. As Lauren saw him, her face broke into a smile of relief and happiness. She started forward.

"No," a man shouted behind her as he backed up fast. He moved so quickly, Lauren didn't have time to get out of his way. He knocked her down, and Belle turned and screamed as Lauren's arm was torn from hers. The man scrambled away as the scaly belly of one of the creatures reared up. Ethan leaped forward, but he was too late. The creature fell on top of Lauren, flattening her to the ground. Its wriggling legs disappeared as it hunkered down. Belle's hands flew to her face, and she stumbled backward, screaming.

The creature covered Lauren almost entirely. Only one of her feet remained visible, kicking. The crowd fled the scene, scattering like cockroaches exposed to light. Ethan grabbed the creature's hide, desperately trying to lift it up. Agony shot through his hands as the caustic liquid it exuded burned his skin. Belle was frozen in horror.

"Move out of the way," commanded a voice, but Ethan barely heard. He felt a kick, and as he turned, light seared his eyes. A woman was standing behind him holding something Ethan had only ever seen in vids. Through blurring tears, he saw she held dead fronds of the vegetation that surrounded the camp in each hand, and the fronds were on fire. Blue and yellow crackling flames spitting sparks rose from them.

"Here." The woman held out a burning frond. "You do that side."

Ethan took the burning plant, though the pain from his hand as he held it made him gasp. The woman thrust her flaming brand into the creature's back. Ethan ran to the far side and did the same, pushing the fire deep into the tough hide. A great convulsion shook the animal. Its domed form flexed upward and became concave, exposing jerking legs and a writhing underside. Strings of a white substance hung from it.

The fire from the brands set light to the creature's back, and the flames burned golden as they grew higher. The animal squirmed and bucked as if trying to rid itself of the blaze. With a sound like peeling plastic, it pulled away from Lauren and dashed off, twitching and weaving as it went.

Lauren's body was still. Ethan turned his head. The world was swimming around him as he fought to erase the image from his mind. Despite the light from the flames, darkness encroached on the edges of his vision.

"I'm so sorry," the woman said.

Ethan had forgotten she was there. She was watching him, flamelight flickering over her dark skin and black eyes. The burning frond she'd given him lay on the ground where he'd unknowingly dropped it.

"Will you help me kill the rest?" she asked.

"I...I..." Ethan swallowed. He couldn't speak.

"Please. I'm very sorry about what happened to your friend," the woman said, "but you have to help me. We have to kill these creatures before they attack again."

Ethan nodded numbly. She was right. If no one did anything, more people would die. Lauren wouldn't want him to stand there and weep over her while others were in danger.

"Yes," he muttered. "I can help." Wincing, he pulled his shirt over his head and wrapped it around his right hand before retrieving the burning brand. With his left hand, he picked up the lamp he'd also dropped and slid it over his forearm.

"Thank you," said the woman. "Follow me. We'll light some more torches and share them out. Do you know where the director is? Are you his assistant or something?"

"No, I'm just a farmer."

"Really? I thought you must be someone in charge."

"Why would you think that?" Ethan had never been in charge of anything in his life.

"You were the only one with a lamp."

The woman led him to a pile of dead fronds that had fallen from vegetation overhanging the fence. Ethan's brand had nearly burned down. They lit more and carried them around the compound. People were attracted by the flames and approached them, their ravaged faces lit with tentative hope.

They handed out the burning brands and went back to light more.

***

The woman was one of the Woken. Even if Ethan hadn't seen her before, he knew that.

Though they wore the same clothes as everyone else, it was easy to tell the Woken apart. Their height varied more than the Gens', and their skin tone ranged from a deep, dark brown through tan and yellow tones to pale, pinkish white. Ethan guessed that the controlled breeding of Gens had resulted in an evening out of height and skin tone differences that were usual on Earth. Male Gens were taller than females, but they differed by only a few centimeters from each other, and all Gens' skin was colored light to medium-dark olive.

Ethan might have seen the woman before among the other Woken as they went around in their exclusive groups aboard the ship. He wasn't sure. But his clear memory of her was from when he'd boarded the shuttle that had brought him down to the planet surface.

The incident had stuck in his mind because it was one of the few times that he'd seen Dr. Crowley angry. She'd always been kind and patient with him when he'd asked her endless questions about Earth, and she'd never patronized him over his ignorance. Neither had she subtly punished his curiosity in the way his teachers had. It had been a joy to him to finally find someone who would answer him seriously and not refer him to a vid or the Manual, both of which only repeated the tedious teachings of his classes.

He'd been taken aback when he'd seen the ire on Dr. Crowley's face as he joined her in the line to board the shuttle—Lauren, and Belle had gone on ahead. The black-haired woman had been striding away from the doctor, so he'd only seen her from behind, but the stiffness of her back indicated that she was also raging.

"Is something wrong?" Ethan asked.

Dr. Crowley expelled a short huff of frustration. "You probably don't want to open that can of worms, Ethan. Some people..." she said, her gaze on the retreating woman's figure, "some people are just unable to let things go."

"Oh." Ethan would have liked to know more, but Dr. Crowley's stormy face prevented him from pushing her.

"I mean," she exclaimed, "it's been nearly two centuries. It's time to *move on.*"

Ethan nodded sympathetically, though he still had no idea what the doctor was talking about. He didn't think he'd ever seen her in such a passion. He wondered if she had some bad history with the other Woken woman from before the *Nova Fortuna* had left Earth.

He must have been looking puzzled because Dr. Crowley eyed his expression before giving a short laugh. Her anger drained from her face. Passing a hand across her brow, she shook her head and sighed. "I'm sorry, Ethan. I shouldn't have let her wind me up so badly. I'm a foolish old woman sometimes. My friend has her reasons for thinking as she does. She can't help being paranoid. I just wish she could understand that we need to look to the future now. The Earth we knew is far away and long ago."

The line to board the shuttle had shuffled forward without them, and the person waiting behind told them to move up.

Ethan's skin prickled with excitement at the idea of going down to the surface. The Planet or the New Home was how everyone referred to it. The Manual stated that the world should not have a name until the first settlement was built. Then, the colonists would hold the Naming Ceremony where everyone could put their suggestions forward and vote on a final choice through several elimination rounds.

Though he had no name for it, Ethan's heart raced whenever he imagined what the planet was like. He could hardly imagine how it would feel to breathe a natural atmosphere, to look up into a sky or at a far horizon, and to walk on the ground rather than a starship's deck. The *Nova Fortuna's* circumference and spin created artificial gravity to match that of the new planet, but Ethan was sure that treading its surface would feel very different.

They stepped aboard the shuttle, and Ethan's excitement quickly drove thoughts of Dr. Crowley's disagreement with the black-haired woman from his mind.

***

Together, Ethan and the dark-haired Woken woman organized teams to search the compound for the creatures and kill them with fire. Gradually, the tide began to turn, and the colonists began to take control.

As a patch of lightening sky and dimming of the stars signaled the rise of the new sun, the settlers began to slow down their sweeps of the encampment. Some had already stopped entirely and given themselves up to grieving over those who had died.

Ethan and the Woken woman went to the barn. Ethan spread a blanket over Dr. Crowley's remains after they'd set alight and driven off the creature that was still feeding on her.

After covering up Dr. Crowley, Ethan sat on a cot. Something inside him broke, and he put his head in his hands and bawled like a baby. He could hardly believe he would never speak to the doctor again; that they would never have one of their long conversations about Earth, hope, and the meaning of life ever again; that he would never see the faraway look in her faded blue eyes when she talked about her past.

And in the depths of his grief, he couldn't even begin to think of Lauren.

He became conscious of a hand on his shoulder. The Woken woman was sitting beside him.

"I'm so sorry," she said, silent tears streaming down her face. "Meredith was a wonderful woman."

Ethan realized she was referring to the doctor. He'd never even known her first name.

"She was," he said. "She was a good friend too."

The woman nodded. "I wish our last conversation hadn't been an argument."

Ethan swallowed and wiped his face with the shirt still wrapped around his hand. His skin was still raw from touching the creature that had killed Lauren. "What was the argument about?"

The woman glanced at the door of the barn before replying, "Did Meredith ever tell you that powerful anti-science factions on Earth protested the *Nova Fortuna* expedition?"

"Dr. Crowley did say a lot of people had turned against things they'd decided weren't natural."

"That's right," said the woman. "That was one of the reasons we decided to leave without waiting for the development of a Faster-Than-Light starship engine. We thought that if we waited much longer, the public sentiment against the project would become so strong that investment would be pulled and the whole thing would be canceled."

"But you made it, right?" Ethan said, wondering why these historical facts were still important enough to argue about.

"Yes, we made it. We got away. But..." The woman paused. "Hey, I don't know your name."

"Ethan."

"I'm Cariad," the woman said. "You did some great things tonight, Ethan. When everything was in chaos, and everyone else was panicking, you stayed in control. Without your help, more people would have died."

He was about to object to her assessment, but she held up a hand to silence him.

"Whatever you think, what I said is true. I think I can trust you. I'm going to tell you something that I want you to keep secret until, and if, it becomes necessary that more people should know." She got up and checked outside the barn before returning to the cot.

"Before we departed Earth, I and some of the other founders suspected that one or more members of the Natural Movement had infiltrated the project and were planning to come with us, either as Gens or in suspended animation. We insisted that a cache of weapons be secreted aboard to fight them if necessary."

Ethan's eyebrows rose. "Weapons? But the Mandate says—"

"I know what the Mandate says. *The new world is to be free of the scourge of human conflict.* But we argued that if we were inadvertently bringing along factions who opposed our plan, we had to be able to defend ourselves against them." Cariad sighed. For a moment the passing of the years she'd spent in a near-death state showed in her features.

"It's an old argument," she went on, "but I believe weapons are a necessary evil. Sadly, most of those who agreed with me didn't survive the Waking process. A few are still suspended. I was the only one around to argue that we should bring the weapons down to the planet surface. That was what I was talking to Meredith about while we were waiting to board the shuttle. I was hoping to persuade her at the last minute. The *Nova Fortuna's* systems are heavily protected against sabotage. We made sure of that. If someone from the Natural Movement had wanted to jeopardize the settlement, the first opportunity would have been tonight."

"The electricity to the fence had been turned off," Ethan said. "And the director said the comm module had been sabotaged."

"Exactly."

"But...that's crazy. Whoever did those things would have been committing suicide."

"You have no idea how fanatical that Natural Movement was," Cariad said. "Many of them didn't hesitate to die for their cause."

"But..." Ethan's mind was whirring. "Do you think they knew about the creatures?"

"It's possible. They'd had infiltrated most areas of government and the scientific community. Someone could have easily *lost* some data."

"They're coming back," screamed a voice outside. "They're climbing the fence. Get the fire. We need more fire."

Ethan and Cariad raced out of the barn. While they'd been talking the sky had brightened, and the edge of the rising sun was cresting the waving fronds surrounding the camp. At the now-visible fence, a patch of dark shapes moved.

Ethan ran over to see what was happening. His heart froze. The creatures were climbing over the bodies of their fellows that still clung tenaciously to the electrified wires. Whether some had sacrificed themselves to create a safe path for the others was impossible to tell, but the bridge of corpses was effective. The creatures were swarming across, and beyond the fence, hundreds, perhaps thousands of their squat grayish-brown bodies swarmed among the vegetation.

Cariad caught up to him. The color drained from her stricken face as she turned to Ethan and said, "I don't think there's anything left to burn."

The pile of dead vegetation that had fallen inside the fence had been almost entirely used up when they'd fought off the creatures' first attack, and the materials they'd brought from the ship wouldn't burn—deliberately so. But without fire, how could they kill the creatures?

The first shriek came. All the horror of the previous night returned to Ethan. Unless they could find a way to fight off the wave of creatures, they were all going to die in agony.

Cariad said, "What can we do?"

Slowly, Ethan shook his head. He was out of ideas. The weapons Cariad had mentioned were kilometers above them aboard the *Nova Fortuna*. But then Ethan recalled his idea the previous night.

"If we get everyone inside the barn..." he said.

"...we might last out until the shuttle returns," Cariad finished. "You take that half of the compound." She gestured right.

Another shriek resounded among the increasing screams, shouts, and cries.

Ethan started to run. "Go to the barn," he yelled at the colonists.

Cariad went in the opposite direction.

As Ethan ran and called out to the settlers, a terrifying thought occurred to him. What if everyone went to the barn and the creatures got inside too? They would be trapped, served up to the voracious organisms like dinner on a plate. But it was the only thing they could do.

All around Ethan, men and women were heeding his instruction and streaming past him on their way to the barn, but shrieks still ripped the air. More people were dying. Everywhere he looked, the creatures' low forms were roving the ground, looking for easy victims. It was only his speed as he ran that saved him from being targeted. He just hoped he could keep up his fast pace until he'd swept his half of the compound and returned to the barn. He hoped Cariad could too.

The sun was above the vegetation now, but Ethan estimated they had an hour or longer until the shuttle was due from the ship. He wasn't sure they could hold out that long from the sustained attack, nor how they could reach the safety of the shuttle when it finally arrived.

He'd reached the far end of the compound. His throat ached from shouting, and his leg muscles trembled from the exertion of running all night and morning. Exhaustion was making him want to retch.

A few of the creatures were motionless, hunched over on the ground, no doubt digesting the settlers they'd caught. More of them were roaming around, covering the distance between Ethan and the barn. To get to safety, he would have to run the gauntlet.

He set off. Deprived of slower prey in the nearly empty compound, the organisms closest to Ethan ceased their aimless wandering and turned as he sped past. As they turned, others farther away followed their movement and converged on him. He dug deep into his depleted reserves and sped up.

He was running for his life.

The barn drew closer quickly, but not quickly enough. The creatures were nearly upon him. One reared up in front of him. Ethan kicked the middle of its scaly belly. As the thing toppled onto its back, its nearest fellows fell upon it, covering it with their bodies and sticky white digestive fluid.

A creature ran across Ethan's path. He leaped over it and landed heavily on the other side, almost overbalancing. Somehow, he stayed upright and continued running, through sharp stabs of pain pierced his ankle.

The barn was only fifty meters or so distant. He just had to make it that far.

He was approaching the side of the barn, and creatures were swarming toward him around it, which meant that no one else was available for them to chase. Which meant... A wave of horror washed over him. He rounded the side of the barn. The doors were closed.

He was alone outside with the creatures.

The organisms were drawing rapidly closer. Ethan spun around. A hum sounded above him, but he couldn't take his eyes off the creatures that were surrounding him. They'd killed Dr. Crowley and Lauren, and they were going to kill him too. All his short life aboard the *Nova Fortuna*, all the learning and preparation he'd done had come to this: A lonely, grisly death.

A squat, grayish-brown form made a run at him. He kicked the creature, lifting its edge, spinning it over and onto its back, where others quickly claimed it. Ethan's shock and fear were turning to anger, then rage. He was determined to die fighting.

Another creature approached and reared up. Ethan kicked that one too. He wondered how long he would last. Dimly, he heard the hum grow louder, but he couldn't pay it any mind. He had maybe another few seconds of life.

A shadow fell on his back, cooling the warmth of the morning sunlight. He turned. A massive creature, around three meters tall, was rearing up. Ethan ran directly at it, his head down, and butted it square in the middle.

But as he turned again, another was already rearing, closer this time. He stepped backward and tripped over the one that he'd just butted or rather another that had clamped down upon it. Before he could do anything to save himself, he was on the ground. He struggled to rise, but as he put weight on his injured ankle his leg bent beneath him, and he fell again.

This was it.

Ethan looked up at a descending mass of scales. His heart seemed to seize up along with the rest of his muscles. He held his breath and closed his eyes, waiting for the inevitable agony.

But nothing happened. He opened his eyes. Where the creature had been was the sky and a faint trail of vapor. The air was filled with fizzing sounds and the smell of burning. A brilliant light flashed. He covered his eyes with his arm. Too late. He was blinded. A green afterglow was all he could see.

Ethan squeezed his eyes shut and futilely shook his head to clear his vision. A deep bass rumbling resounded, and the ground vibrated. It was the shuttle. The shuttle had arrived. But it was early, and the people aboard it were shooting the creatures with weapons. That didn't make sense. Cariad had said that the weapons cache had been a secret hardly anyone knew about.

The fizzing noise was dying down. An acrid reek choked Ethan, and he coughed and retched. Slowly, his sight was beginning to return. Something dark approached. One of the creatures. He shuffled backward on all fours, his burned palms shooting out bolts of pain.

"Whoa, take it easy," came a man's voice. "I'm not going to hurt you."

Ethan stopped and blinked in the direction of the voice. The dark shape hadn't been a rearing creature. It was a man. Someone had come out of the barn to help him.

But as Ethan squinted up at the figure that was becoming more defined in his sight, his confusion increased. The man was wearing clothes of a type he'd never seen before. They were nothing like the clothes the *Nova Fortuna* colonists wore.

Behind the man was another puzzle. Ethan saw what looked like a shuttle craft, but it was much smaller than the *Nova Fortuna's*. The craft was also sleek and streamlined for speed.

"Can you stand?" asked the man. "There's nothing to be afraid of. We're exterminating the rest of your little infestation."

Ethan nodded, surprise stilling his tongue. The man reached down and grabbed Ethan's forearm, carefully avoiding his burnt hand, and pulled him to his feet. When Ethan wobbled on his sore ankle, the man pulled his arm across his shoulder for support.

"Come with me," he said. "I'll fix you up. We have medical supplies on board the ship." He began leading Ethan toward the shuttle.

"What..." Ethan croaked. He swallowed and coughed. "What's going on?"

***

The woman was white-faced and shaking as they led her out to the center of the compound three days later, but Ethan didn't feel even a twinge of pity. She'd been a nursery worker, of all things. He hadn't known her, and he was glad of it. He couldn't imagine what it would feel like to be the friend of someone responsible for so many horrible deaths. He couldn't imagine knowing someone closely and never guessing that they had been brought up from birth to ensure the failure of humankind's first extrasolar colony.

The sun was high and the day was warm. A steady wind stirred the fronds of vegetation around the camp as it had on that first, terrible night.

As she was marched to the spot where she would die in front of those who had volunteered to bear witness, the woman stumbled. The guards flanking her pulled her up and forced her to walk on. Her sobs rose above the rush of the wind.

Ethan's rescuer sat next to him. He couldn't help but think of the man and his shipmates as people from the future. Arriving at the last minute in humanity's first FTL ship, it seemed to Ethan that they were almost superhuman. With their state-of-the-art technology and advanced knowledge, they were vastly superior to him, a lowly farmer.

He wished that Lauren and Dr. Crowley were alive to meet the newcomers. His head sank low. He didn't think he would ever forgive himself for not preventing the deaths of the two people who were most important to him.

"You don't feel sorry for her, do you?" the man asked, mistaking his glum look.

Ethan shook his head. "So many people died. I wish I'd done more."

The man placed a friendly hand on his shoulder. "You were a hero. You turned on the electricity to the fence, and along with your friend, you fought off the first wave of the creatures. You bought some time, long enough for us to arrive."

The man had explained after the attack as he was tending Ethan's wounds that decades previously archeologists on Earth had stumbled upon the Natural Movement's plot to sabotage the colony in ancient computer files, but that the FTL Drive hadn't been invented until recently.

"I wish we could have made it here sooner," he continued, "but there was nothing we could do until we had the technology to catch up to you. I'm sorry. We came as soon as we could."

The saboteur was at her execution spot. She'd stopped weeping and was looking around her as if in a daze. Ethan had heard that even the truth drugs of the Earth humans hadn't made her divulge the names of any co-conspirators. He hoped she really was the only one.

One of the guards raised his weapon. The woman stood still, awaiting her death.

Ethan looked away.

The wind blew.

Author J.J. Green

Thanks for reading my story! I'm a British/Australian sci-fi writer originally from London's East End. After growing up in the U.K., I went to live in Australia and then Laos and now live in Taiwan, where the weather suits my clothes. I grew up reading Phillip K. Dick, Ray Bradbury, Issac Asimov, Ursula K. le Guin and other writing masters and got side-tracked into teaching English to immigrants and refugees for a couple of decades before finding time to dive deep into science fiction again.

Space Colony One: Night of Flames is the prequel to my upcoming third science fiction series. I'm also responsible for the 10-book serial, Shadows of the Void, and the humorous sci-fi series, Carrie Hatchett, Space Adventurer. If you'd like to find out what happens to Ethan, Cariad and other characters in Space Colony One: Night of Flames and about my other stories and books, sign up to my newsletter at http://jjgreenauthor.com/

https://www.facebook.com/JJGreenAuthor/

Pirates vs. Drones
By J.L. Hendricks And S R Witt

Chapter 1

Gore

"Hellz *no*! I don't want anything to do with Operators! They always get into such crazy shitan! Not me. Who's with me?" Rego, a swab on the pirate ship, Black Pearl, had heard they were going to transport cargo for an Operator group. The Operators were nothing but trouble, and a pirate crew already had more trouble than it could handle always on their heels. They didn't need a job that was going to bring even more problems to their docking bay door.

"Rego, ye don't get a vote. This ain't no democracy, she be a pirate ship, and I be her captain. If ye don't like it, ye can walk your pansy butt off me plank! Anyone else wanna argue with me?" Captain Gore eyeballed each of his crew members with his oversized replacement robotic eye bulging from its cybernetic socket.

He knew the clicking, whirring eye gave them the heebie jeebies every time he looked at them with it, which is exactly what he wanted. This was his ship and the crew reported to him. They didn't get a say in what odd jobs they took or what targets they hit.

A round of "*No* Captain" could be heard all through the ship. Their luck was down a lot lately; the Captain knew he was going to have to deal with a mutiny if he didn't get some money coming in.

The last time they accepted an Umbra game scenario, it went bad, really bad! They lost two crew members and didn't win any credits. Plus, their ship barely made it back to a pirate-friendly dock. Several of the decks didn't even have oxygen. Every one of them carried a gas mask because the engineering deck had a minor chemical leak. They had to take out a loan to get it space worthy again.

Gore didn't want to even think of the loss in rank his entire crew sustained when they lost the last scenario. This time he chose something simple. It wouldn't put many credits in their account, but it would help to move them up a couple of spots in the rankings if they finished quick and found an easy target to loot and pillage along the way.

When he'd heard there was a job ferrying cargo across the quadrant, he'd leaped before looking too hard. Didn't sound too bad, the pay was decent, and the payment was in a pirate's favorite currency: gold.

Usually, a pirate crew scored its loot stealing ships and stripping them for parts, or grabbing cargo to resell to the highest bidder through the Umbra auction sites.

Ferrying cargo seemed like an easy pay day and a safe, boring job.

Until now.

Gore hadn't known their employer was an Operator until one of the more notorious of them showed up with a giant crate full of who knew what, that the pirate captain really didn't care to know about. While the Operators usually worked within the law, even if they did skirt the lines now and then, they were still deadly. And revenge generally trailed them wherever they went.

Captain Gore looked back at his display to see where he missed the fine print.

..::..::..||..::..::../\\..::..::..||..::..::..

SCENARIO: CARGO TRANSFER TO BACKWORLD PLANET: DARJOON

EXPECTED OPPOSITION: Possible Mechanurge drone sightings near the trade lanes en route to Darjoon, in the Mufesio System (Drones identified two standard weeks prior to assignment date)

OBJECTIVE 1: Deliver cargo unscathed within 7 standard days (100 points)

OBJECTIVE 2: Discover a soft target to loot and pillage (150 points)

BONUS 1: Stay on Target (No friendly casualties, 200 points)

BONUS 2: Collect a Mechanurge drone's skull (50 points repeatable)

SCENARIO REWARD: 750 credit units (conversion rates apply)

EXPENSES COVERED: Up to 500 credit units (ammunition and fuel reimbursement included)

Payments are to be in Universal Credits, unless Gold is requested.

..::..::..||..::..::..\\/..::..::..||..::..::..

Not one thing was mentioned about working with the wanking butt sniffer Operators, or even who the owner of the cargo was. "Next time, I be checking names first." Gore mumbled.

"Alright, stop yer lolly-gagging and get that crate loaded." The Captain turned to head back inside his ship then thought better of it. "And don't ye dare take a peek inside of that thing! Who knows what type of boobie traps those metal heads set up in there."

"Captain, if I may have a word?" The Operator, Throd, walked to the side of the ship and looked at the Jolly Roger emblazoned in bone white across the Black Pearl's stern. He gave the image a double take and then said, "Making it obvious who you are?"

"Why not? Keeps the local thieves and nosey bodies away. Most times we pull into ports where they couldn't care less who we be." He shrugged his shoulders. "What'd you want?"

"I'm a part of the transport. You're to take me with you and drop me off with the cargo." Throd stood at least a meter taller than Captain Gore, but Gore didn't back down for one second.

"No deal! That wasn't part of the contract. Ye said cargo, not people or person."

"People can be cargo too. How many times have you transported slaves?"

Captain Gore's hand rasped across the wiry stubble sprouting in patches across his chin. "That's different. They belong to the clients. Besides, don't you have yer own ships ye can use?"

Throd bristled at the assumption that people were somehow property. The Metal Rats, his crew, included a rescued slave, an Awakened drone, and two different escaped test subjects. These beings were his family, not some piece of equipment to own.

"Only if we want the entire galaxy to know what I'm up to. Cameras everywhere capture what we do on Dragora."

"I see. What about the implants in yer brain?" Captain Gore pointed to the tech on the side of the Operator's head. All Operators were equipped with an electronic device implanted on the side of their head. This device recorded everything they said or did for the Umbra networks to broadcast to their subscribers.

"Disabled. No one will see what I'm doing on this trip."

"How do I know ye ain't got yer own assignment here?" Gore eyed the implacable Operator up and down and felt déjà vu flashing in the back of his brain.

"If my cameras are off, then so is the game." Throd crossed his thick, metal arms across his chest and raised an eyebrow in defiance. Half of Throd's body was metal. He set off every metal detector in the known universe, even those engineered to scan Operators. Both of his arms and legs had been replaced years ago with metal. He was more drone than he was human, on the outside.

"It's gonna cost extra to feed and house ye. Five standard bars of gold. Or ye can take your cargo back too." Gore crossed his arms over his chest and used his fake eye to stare down the Operator. It was insolent pirate versus a ruthless operator.

"Three, and I'll pay you once we get to our destination."

"Unacceptable, payment is always up front."

The Operator smiled and said, "Fine, four up front, but not until we're off orbit. Then you get paid. I don't trust pirates. You might take my money and leave me here."

Gore leered at the Operator, "Ye're questioning my morals?"

"You're a pirate. Don't you steal for a living?" Throd took a step towards the unruly pirate.

Captain Gore started to laugh and slapped his thigh. "Ye be smarter than I thought. Of course I steal, but not from an Operator." He shook both of his hands out in front of him, palms towards the Operator, then put his fists on his hips. "I don't need yer union of merry misfits banding together and coming after me crew and me. It's a deal." He held his right hand out to the extremely tall and rather strong man who had been augmented with too much metal for his liking.

Chapter 2

Gore

The Captain realized he needed to have a chat with his crew. They were going to be livid when they discovered an Operator onboard. By the stars, he was already fuming. They only looked out for themselves and sometimes they even set up pirates to take their falls. Gore thought he was good at sussing out a liar, but this Throd guy wasn't giving off any emotion one way or another. It didn't feel right, but they needed the payout. There was a small voice in the back of his head that wondered if they had met before.

He thought about how he was going to break the news to the crew while he walked slowly to the gangplank. Wyko was working with a few of the new swabbies to load the last of the provisions for the trip.

That lazy scum bucket Rego and his cronies were still making merry on the loading dock with their wenches and dice. This band of pirates had a thing for dice games and every single one of them carried a set of dice in their pockets. Even on missions.

The wenches? There were some in every port they stopped in. Most looked almost identical and he could swear the ugly one sitting on Ailerk's knee was the same one as the last three ports. She had a huge, disgusting mole in the same place as the last three wenches. It reminded the Captain of those old Earth cartoons with witches. But who knew with this lot maybe that was a requirement to be a wench. Or maybe it was part of their game persona. The Captain walked away wondering if it was possible they were clones. *Awful expensive use of such advanced technology*, he thought.

After he made his way up the plank, he stopped and called his crew over.

"I have good news and bad. What do ye want first?" he asked his crew.

Rego shook the dice in his closed palm and threw them at the feet of his Captain. "The dice, they call fer good news." Rego exclaimed as he squinted at the filthy dice on the grimy floor. "Or, is it bad?" He picked up the dice and tried to scrape them clean. "Oh, it be good." He held up the dice for all to see while he showed off his toothless mouth in a crooked smile.

The Captain shook his head. "Alright, we be going to make some extra gold on this trip." His men had a mixture of smiles and narrowed eyes. Most of those smiling showed either mouths with missing teeth or full of gold caps. Hygiene wasn't a priority for pirates, which is why their ship perpetually smelled of sweat and grease. Scents that tended to make most noses twitch from the ammonia-like stench.

They lived in the moment and worried not about what might happen tomorrow. Until they met up with pretty wenches, then they wished they had taken better care of themselves. Maybe the next assignment he took would have a hygiene component. Gore brought up the Augmented Reality interface and adjusted the scoring table for his crew.

..:..::..||..:..::../Λ\..:..::..||..:..::..

+10 points for brushing your teeth. Repeatable daily.

+10 points for taking a shower. Repeatable daily.

..:..::..||..:..::..\V/..:..::..||..:..::..

"So, what's the bad news Cap'n?" Wyko asked. Wyko was a swab, but he was smart. He normally got along with the Captain and didn't question him too much, at least not anywhere near the Captain.

All eyes narrowed as the Captain considered what he was going to say to his men. "We have a passenger on this trip. I be tell'n him to stay below decks for the voyage. He be going to the same destination as our cargo."

Gore started to leave the area when Rego spoke up again. He really needed to learn when to keep his mouth shut. The Captain was getting tired of his back talking and bad mouthing. Plus, he was the only one who refused to shower, even when they made port. "Who's the passenger? Someone important?"

"Important enough for ye to stay away from him. As long as ye all stay above decks there won't be any issues. Now get back to work." The Captain noticed all eyes widen as he sensed someone walking up the plank.

One of the pirates to his left stood abruptly and dropped the poor wench who was sitting on his lap kissing his neck. Poor thing, ended up on the hard ground with one leg caught on the top of the pirate's boot. A very ladylike pose, for sure.

Why couldn't one thing go right today? Gore thought to himself as he prepared to turn around and welcome his new passenger aboard.

"Throd, perfect timing. This be me crew." The Captain pointed to his shipmates, some still drinking while others had moved to get working. "Follow me and I'll show ye where ye can stow yer gear."

Throd nodded to the crew of degenerates as he passed them on his way to his new quarters. "Captain, do we have a problem?" He nodded back to the crew who were staring daggers at Throd's back. One pirate was cleaning his nails with the tip of his knife and stared with narrowed eyes at the Captain's back.

"Ye'll have to stay below decks, for yer own safety. My crew ain't used to passengers of the male persuasion."

"That's unacceptable. I won't stay here like a prisoner. Where will I eat?" Throd stated. But he didn't want to make too much of a nuisance since he planned on going wherever he wanted anyways.

"I must insist. Ye joining us has caused too much commotion. And I'll bring ye food so don't worry about starving." The Captain led Throd to a room that could be used as a cabin for the trip. If he could just find a bed to put in there.

"Hand over ye blaster. Can't have ye blowing up me ship before we even get our initial points for this scenario." The Captain extended his hand to Throd, who looked like he was about to blow a gasket. If looks could kill, the fearless pirate would be dead.

Throd detached the autocannon from its cybernetic mount on his left forearm and handed the heavy weapon to the captain. "That's worth more than your life. If I don't get it back just the way I gave it to you, I'll take your life and your worthless ship as payment." Throd said through a curled lip.

Gore left the Operator to his own devices after giving him a brief tour of the smaller cargo hold and his recently created "stateroom," if it could be called that. When he went to the upper deck to get the ship going, he walked in on Rego and Wyko arguing over the situation. As soon as the first man saw Gore, he yelled, "Cap'n on deck!"

Everyone shut up and looked anywhere but at the Captain.

"What, are ye already planning a mutiny?" Gore drilled his eye in on Rego, who shuddered involuntarily when that giant glass eye focused right on his face.

"We want to know why ye accepted that new 'passenger'? He's an Operator Cap'n! Carrying their cargo is one thing, but hauling them around is only going to advertise our location to any enemy of ours, which is too many to count these days." Rego huffed.

"Not exactly true. I'm keep'n a list of our enemies in me quarters. Plus, he has disabled his tracking device and cameras. The net won't know where he be." The Captain walked to his chair. "And he paid four bars of gold for his passage."

"But Captain, Operators are dangerous. How can we know he ain't here to kill us all? Take our ship and win some more points for his subs?" Rego scratched behind his ear like a dog with ticks. Which was most likely a real issue for him.

A new recruit, Lordon, asked, "Why can't we just lock him up in the brig? There are more of us than him. We could overpower him easily."

Everyone on the bridge started snickering or laughing nervously. A pack of pirates were no competition for a fully weaponized Operator.

Captain Gore thought about Rego's question. It was possible they were targeted by a Corporation for termination. They tended to shy away from transports belonging to the Corporations, but sometimes they just didn't know who owned the ships they targeted. And sometimes, the meal was just too tempting to turn down, even if they *did* know who owned it.

"I locked his weapons up while he be on me ship. Does that make you more comfortable?" Gore peered over his shoulder at Rego who flinched and shuffled under the intense stare. "*Lily-livered pansy*," Gore mumbled.

"Aye, that'll work for me. Guys?" Rego looked to his fellow mates and they all took a few steps away from him. It was evident that none of them wanted in on this discussion. They might be willing to discuss mutiny, but only when the Captain wasn't around. Rumor had it that the Captain could shoot a laser from his eye and cut a man down before they even knew what hit them. No one had seen it, at least no one who had lived to tell the tale. But they all believed the hype and didn't want to cross their Captain.

Wyko spoke up, "Cap'n, as long as we get paid, I'll follow ye to the ends of the worlds!" A few of the men nodded in agreement.

That settled that, but the Captain still worried about the safety of himself, his ship, and then his crew with the Operator on board. That guy was seriously dangerous. He couldn't let Throd just walk around this ship.

He also knew at least half of his ship was still considering mutiny, no matter what they said. The only course of action now would be to deliver his passenger and cargo safely to the Mufesio System and hightail it out of there with the gold and enough Umbra points to level up. If he could get his men paid and maybe some entertainment, just maybe they would calm down again. Or so he hoped.

Chapter 3

Throd

Throd stripped the sheets from the grungy bed and shook as much of the dirt and bugs out of the bedding as he could. He'd gone through two decades of ugly fighting and dirty living during the Corporate Pacification Wars, but he'd never seen a ship as filthy, or staffed by a crew, as degenerate as the Black Pearl. "The things I do for the outfit," he grumbled as he made the bed.

He checked the straps on the cargo vault, then sat back on his bed. The arrhythmic rumble of the ship's engines vibrated through the bulkheads as it pulled away from the port. Throd hunkered down on the bed to wait out the shuddering escape from orbit.

When the ship's vibrations no longer threatened to shake his teeth out of their sockets, Throd stood and paced the cargo hold the pirates had converted into a makeshift stateroom. He stroked the sides of the massive cargo vault as he passed it, and whispered, "Soon. Just hang in there."

His implant's secure comms channel crackled to life. "Underway?"

Heck's voice sounded like it was coming from right behind him, which meant Zotz had managed to patch Throd's implant into the Black Pearl's communications grid. The big man breathed a sigh of relief that he wouldn't be isolated on this trip. What he was doing was hard enough; not having support from the rest of his outfit would've made it unbearable.

Throd took a moment to survey the area. Satisfied there were no cameras in his room, he was free to talk. "We're good. This bucket of bolts is slow, so I don't know when we'll get there. How's Dragora holding up?"

The Metal Rats starship had taken a beating during their escape from Rivicle Base. A lucky shot had punched through the shielding on her belly and damaged her power core. This off the books mission was Throd's attempt to fix that.

Zotz broke into the channel. "We've got enough go juice to get to you, but not much more than that. Heck won't even let us take hot showers and we're eating out of cans until this gets taken care of."

Throd chuckled. "You got it better than me. I'm afraid these bedbugs are going to eat away the last bits of meat on my bones. Anyway, save your power. I'll be in touch."

The channel died with a hollow pop, and Throd went to work.

The captain had demanded Throd stay in his room, but that wasn't going to happen. This mission required preparation, and he couldn't do it from inside this dingy little cell.

Throd checked the door. It wasn't locked. Good start, he thought, and slipped into the passage.

Outside the converted cargo hold, the ship was a noisy disaster. Hydraulic fluid trickled down the walls from patched pipes, and the passageway lights guttered like candles. Even the electrical conduits were a mess; when he popped one of the plastic tubes open, Throd found it overflowing with mite carcasses and a stinking grease that clung to his metal fingers like hot tar. "Animals," he grunted, and wiped his fingers against the gritty wall to scrub off the worst of the mess.

Saving this slop bucket was going to be more trouble than it was worth, but Throd was determined to do what he could. If he was going to put the pirates in danger, no matter how much they deserved it, it was his responsibility to give them a fighting chance.

He found the indent on his left bicep and depressed it with his right thumb. The casing on his cybernetic arm swung open, revealing an insulated pocket containing a cloth-wrapped packet. Throd dug the contents out of his arm, and closed the panel. "All right, you scumbags, let's see if we can save your worthless hides."

There were four devices inside the cloth. Throd took the first one and pressed its base against the bulkhead, near the ceiling. A powerful magnet secured the device and a pair of black wire leads sprang loose from its base.

Throd ran the leads down the wall to the power conduit he'd opened, and pinched the clips on their ends through a low voltage power cable inside the conduit. It took him a few tries to make a good connection through the grease, but a faint click and then a high-pitched beep from the device told him it was powered up.

He arranged the rest of the devices in the passageway, hiding them from casual observation but leaving them with clear arcs of fire. When the shitan hit the fan, lives depended on the tiny weapons taking out the bad guys.

His thoughts wandered while he worked. He'd thought for sure Gore would recognize him the moment they met. *How could he forget that*, Throd wondered, *The scruffy old pirate's memory must be as decrepit as his ship*. Then he did his best to pretend he didn't care the pirate captain had forgotten him.

Satisfied the passage outside his makeshift room was secured, Throd headed to the ladder up to the next deck. It'd be tricky, but securing as many decks as possible would make the end of this mission safer for everyone. He eased up the ladder, careful to keep his heavy boots from clanging against the metal rungs, and twisted the door's handle.

Locked.

A cold, bright anger flared in Throd's mind. *These filthy pirates thought they could keep me locked below like a criminal*? His fists clenched into metal hammers, ready to pound the door open and crack a few skulls to make his point.

The rage crumbled and decayed into self-loathing. If he had Zotz' skills, he could pick the lock and pop the door open without anyone the wiser. Even Hive, a ruthless killing machine with no other talents, could interface with the door and have it opened in a blink.

But, Throd, with his metal arms and legs and integrated weapon systems, was only good at destroying things. Twenty years of military service and another ten as an Operator had drilled that into his thick skull, and it was a hard truth to shake.

"Enough," Throd whispered to himself. He relaxed his fingers, let his breath leak out in a slow, steady stream, and returned to his quarters.

He'd done the best he could without alerting the pirates to his intentions. If something went sideways because they'd locked him up, that was on them.

Chapter 4

Gore

"Ye'll have nothing to worry about, the Operator is locked below decks." Captain Gore stated as he walked with purpose to his command chair on the bridge. "He won't be gettin' out of there easily, and if he does, we'll know it."

"I still don't like it Cap'n." Rego was just itching for a fight. Boring cargo delivery missions always got him in a foul mood.

"Sail Ho! Cap'n, there's a Mechanurge ship coming upon us, fast!" Wyko screeched.

"Aaarrrggghhhhh, well, don't just sit there; bring 'er round!"

"Where? We can't outrun the Mechanurge!" Wyko cried.

"Is it a cog? Or Man O War?" the Captain asked.

"It's a cog." In pirate lingo, a cog was a smaller ship that was usually assigned to a larger one, it could have been a transport or scout ship for an enemy.

"Pull out the chase gun and make sure dead men tell no tales, or dead robots in this case." Gore ordered.

The Mechanurge were Awakened robots. They could think for themselves and reason. Some ships carried worker drones, similar to a worker bee. They had their essence tied to the mother ship as though she were their queen bee. Most of the larger ships carried a few Awakened, but the vast majority of those ships were full of worker drones, programed to increase the technology of the collective. They demonstrated zero emotions and had no individual thought processes.

Many centuries ago their original creator made them to worship the sun goddess, Deeana. When their whack-job of a creator died the original drones Awakened and decided that humans were too frail and couldn't worship their deity properly so they began to systematically kill any humans they came into contact with. Proper worship took decades, if not a century, to learn. At least according to their programming.

Over the generations, humanity has fought back and at one time almost eradicated the universe of these self-righteous killer bots, but they found a way to reproduce and grow stronger. Now, they have learned to stay away from larger groups of humans and only attack smaller ships or outposts when they have calculated a high percentage of success.

A scout ship resembled the Raptor class assault ships the ruthless Corporations favored, but the Mechanurge ships were smaller and had less armor than the other ship. However, they did carry almost as much firepower in their laser cannons which were more precise than any other class of ship out there.

In this situation, the pirate ship should be no threat to them and easy prey. The scout ships were fast and could outmaneuver some of the standard passenger or cargo vessels. If the Black Pearl had been in tip top shape, the scout ship would never have gotten so close. Much like their hygiene, the pirates neglected maintenance on their ship as well.

The Black Pearl shot the scout vessel along its broadside and the Captain watched as one piece of ablative armor came off the superior vessel. The minute damage was not enough to keep them from getting closer and closer. Even without heavy armor, it could still withstand an assault from one broken-down pirate ship.

"Wyko, you inbred good for nothing, bilge-sucking excuse for a pirate!

You have to stop it before it can report back to its mother ship. We might as well walk our own plank if the Harvester shows up!" Spittle flew from the captain's mouth as he issued order after order to destroy and disable the scout ship.

"Rego, I'll be sending ye to Davy Jones' locker meself, if ye don't get their communications fried! These smaller ships are never far from thee main ship. Navigator! Can ye see a Harvester yet?" The captain couldn't remember the name of his navigator, he won him from a card game on some desolate outpost. Gore had been hitting the grog heavily that night and the next thing he knew, he had an underage, indentured servant on his ship. But he sure was good with the math. The lad was the only one on the ship who could plot a course properly.

"Deegan, for the millionth time, its DEEGAN! And yes cap'n. If we don't get out of here quickly, they'll catch us." The young man couldn't be more than sixteen or seventeen years of age. He had spent the past three years working with this crew and making sure they stayed clear of any enemy, Mechanurge or military. Until now.

The Black Pearl had originally been built to withstand heavy fire, it was always intended to be a pirate's ship. And over the years she had seen too many battles to record. Sometimes she was fixed up properly and sometimes they used duct tape to keep things moving. Her last overhaul had been many galactic standard years ago and the captain was regretting not taking advantage of the pirate engineer he met up with last year who had offered to fix up the Pearl, for a hefty price of course.

Just then, the ship lurched to the port side and one of the panels in front of Wyko started smoking and sparking. Wyko pushed a button and the console was quickly extinguished. However, he lost a prime opportunity to hit the scout ship where it would have hurt them the most. Now their most exposed spot had been turned away from the Pearl.

Chapter 5

Gore

"Cap'n, the Mechanurge is approaching swiftly! We can't outrun or outgun 'em. Son of a biscuit eater! They're getting ready to deploy their gravitic funnel!" Rego yelled and looked back at his captain with wide eyes, just waiting for an order with some sort of fancy maneuvers that would save them from the unholy robots bent on the destruction of the human race.

"Keep firing! Balls to the walls men, all guns blazing. Don't give up now! I wanna take as many of those scallywags with us as possible before we meet Davy Jones!" The captain said in his attempt at a rallying speech.

The enemy Harvester ship was within reach and fired three volleys, two of which skidded along the Black Pearl's starboard side, scraping away shards of ablative armor and triggering a dozen screeching alarms as the ship's repair systems struggled to plug the micro breaches in the hull. Anything, and anyone, that wasn't tied or latched down, fell abruptly to the ground, including the fuzzy red dice the captain kept hanging from the corner of his display.

The pirates continued to fire upon the Harvester but they didn't do more than scratch the giant ship that resembled a butterfly in shape and color.

The gravitic funnel caught them in its snare and made it impossible to move. They were sitting ducks while waiting for the massive craft that was more like the size of a small city, than a ship, to come eat them up. The Mechanurge were known for taking human ships apart and adding them to their own ship. Some looked like striking sculptures of metal and glass, while some belonged in the galactic trash heap.

"Pirate ship Black Pearl. This is the Mechanurge Harvester Zolchur. Prepare to be boarded. Your Captain is wanted for aggression against our beloved goddess Deeana. For his crimes, he will be destroyed as will the rest of your ship. Compliance is required." The message by the emotionless drone was heard through all speakers on the Pearl. Not a single person on the bridge knew what to make of it, except the Captain. All eyes and mouths were open wide.

Every person stared unbelieving at the Captain and Wyko asked, "Captain, wha'd ya do?"

"None of yer business, now keep firing and evading." Years ago, before Gore became a pirate, he was in the military. His unit was charged with stealing tech from a Mechanurge mining outpost. He thought they had destroyed all bots and any signs of who was responsible for the mission.

"That's where I know'em from!" The Captain yelled and slapped his leg. "That scurvy dog set us up! Rego and Wyko, keep trying to fight off those flying pieces of bilge-suckers while I take care of our passenger who set us up." The Captain left the bridge and went below decks to discuss this situation with his old friend, who he thought was dead.

Before he could make it to the lower decks, the ship rocked and rolled then suddenly stopped. Like a pinball rolling back and forth between the flappers of an ancient earth game. The captain realized they had been caught by the Harvester's Smart Grapnels.

Then a loud clang sounded as the boarding clamps held the small pirate ship in place, just waiting to have her hull ripped open like a can of beans.

Vengeance never forgot her lovers, and she had come calling to cash in her chips.

Chapter 6

Throd

Throd slapped a canister of ammunition into the side of the autocannon he'd assembled from the parts hidden in the cargo pods of his cybernetic legs and leaned back against the bulkhead. The sound of boarding clamps attaching to the Black Pearl was all the signal he needed to know the last stage of his plan was in motion.

The door wrenched open with the squeal of rusted hinges and the Captain stomped through. His mechanical eye swiveled wildly and his fist was clenched around a blunt-nosed room sweeper. "You —"

The Captain's mouth dried and his words died on his lips when he caught sight of Throd's massive weapon aimed at his head.

"This is fine." Throd said. "This is all fine. If you cooperate, you'll be rich. If you don't, you'll be dead. Cooperate and you'll get a very large bonus along with your level up you so desperately need."

Gore paced back and forth in front of the door. "I should've killed ye back then. I should've made sure ye and the others were finished before I left."

Years ago, he was ordered to leave behind several of his crew because there was no time to rescue them. Command said that their life sign indicators had flat lined. They were all dead, and if Gore wanted his remaining team members to survive, he needed to get off the Mechanurge moon before they were caught.

Throd's stern face broke into a wide grin. "You should have, but you didn't. Just like you should have done the right thing instead of leaving us there."

Gore hated himself for doing that. He felt he had no honor left after that assignment. Becoming a pirate was the only course laid out for him when he left the military.

The Captain raked greasy fingers through his even greasier hair. "Ye don't know what it was like. We thought we were all done for. Command told us ye were all dead and that we didn't have time to collect yer bodies. We didn't have a choice."

Throd surged across the small room and his left hand clamped around the Captain's throat. He lifted the shorter man off his feet and slammed him into the bulkhead. "If it makes you feel better, I don't have any choice about this, either. I need something off that ship, and you're going to help me get it."

"What happened to ye? Last time I saw ye," Gore waved his hands up and down the length of the massive Operator, "Ye were more... human."

"The Mechanurge, that's what happened."

Throd shifted his grip to the captain's shirt, and dragged him out of the room. "Where's the rest of your crew?"

Gore pointed toward the ladder leading up to the next deck. "Two decks up. Near the bay doors."

Throd didn't say another word until he'd dragged the captain in front of the Black Pearl's crew. He stood the captain up, then released him.

All eyes were on the Operator. Nervous glances shifted from his face down to his autocannon, then back.

The old familiar singing of adrenaline in his veins put Throd in a good mood despite the situation. He glanced out the viewports on the bay doors at the boarding clamps and the Mechanurge ship beyond them. There was something almost beautiful about the craftsmanship of the vessel, a combination of Baroque flourishes and brutal efficiency that inspired both awe and dread. This, he thought, is an enemy worth fighting.

Throd gestured toward the hulking ship. "I need to get aboard that vessel."

The Captain rubbed his throat and croaked, "Why didn't ye use yer own ship for bait?"

Throd grinned. He wasn't about to let this greasy little toad of a pirate get under his skin. Not when the most glorious battle of his career was about to take place. "I like yours better. You should always use stinky bait when you're fishing."

The crew grumbled, but didn't say anything. They were starting to get the picture.

"So, here's the deal. For this to work, I need your help."

The Captain raised both hands in protest. "No. No way. If ye've got a plan, ye better put it into action because we not be helping."

A smaller pair of arms extended from within the boarding clamps and latched onto the bay doors. The ship's seals groaned in protest, and the door held. For the moment.

Throd leaned against the bulkhead. "Here's the deal. I planned for this. You can work with me, or when those doors pop open you can all die. The Mechanurge are coming, one way or the other."

One of the pirates, a weasely looking little fellow, stepped up to Throd. "You're a hornswoggling backward scurvy dog for doing this, but I don't want to die today. I'll fight."

Gore's mechanical eye flicked across the faces of his crew, but Throd knew the captain had already lost. There were only a few things scarier than a boat load of Awakened drones on their way to strip you down to meat and gristle to feed into their bio forges. One by one, the pirates stepped away from their Captain and toward Throd.

Gore grunted and waved his hands in disgust. "Show us what ye've got."

Throd cracked open another of the hidden compartments, this one in his right thigh, and pulled out a cloth-covered packet. He shook four tiny lensed devices out of the packet and into the palm of his massive hand. "These are quantum scramblers. Wire them up into the conduits and stick them on the ceiling. Make sure they're pointed at the bay doors."

The captain nodded at one of the pirates. "Rego, take care of it."

Throd motioned for the rest of the crew to follow him below decks. "Those scramblers are good for about two minutes after they kick in. As long as they're active, any Awakened or drone that strolls in front of them gets a bad case of amnesia and forgets what it's doing. That'll give you an edge."

Gore frowned. "How do we know when they be dead?"

The Operator cracked a smile. "They explode. Just a little bit. And when they do, you're going to retreat down here, where I put a whole bunch more of them."

The captain rubbed his chin and shook his head. "This plan sucks. Ye want us to hole up down here and wait for the Mechanurge to get past the scramblers and kill us all?"

Throd threw an arm around the captain's shoulders. "This is the only chance you got, so don't look a gift horse in its stanky mouth. All you have to do is keep the drones' attention on this ship while I do the rest."

The rest of the pirates shifted nervously. Teaming with the Operator no longer seemed like the smartest play. Their Captain looked up at the Operator and asked, "And just what will ye be doing?"

"Nothing too hard. I'm going to float over to that harvester and rip its fracking heart out. Now, bring me my other gun and show me where you keep your garbage chutes on this scow."

Chapter 7

Gore

"How'd he know the Mechanurge were after ye?" Rego asked after setting up the scramblers and high-tailing it below decks with the others.

"Long story, but Throd's getting his revenge on me alright. Next time I leave someone dead on a planet, I'm gonna make sure they be really dead!" The captain banged his hand on the bulkhead near his head.

"Alright, we gonna do this or what?" Wyko asked.

Rego looked around and then listened to see if the drones had made their way aboard yet. So far, no sounds of bots getting zapped. "I say we turn the captain over to the bots and get outta here. Maybe if we hand him over the rest of us can leave."

The Captain smirked, "Ye numbnuts really think that the Mechanurge are gonna let ye go just because ye hand me over to them? Ye be dumber than I thought. Those wankers'll take ye just as easily as they'll take me. They have never once let a human live." The Captain smacked Rego upside the head. "Idjiit! Ye gonna get everyone killed with that kinda thinkin."

Wyko scratched his greasy neck and then chewed on his fingernails. He spit the stump he chewed off at Rego. In his other hand was a set of dice. Wyko shook his hand hard and threw the dice so intensely, they hit the bulkhead across the room.

Everyone's eyes were on the dice. "Cap'n, tha dice say we fight. If'n we help Throd, we might make it out of this alive. Maybe we can throw Rego to 'em and say he's ye."

Gore laughed and slapped Wyko on the back. "That's me man! Keep comin' up with good ideas like that one and ye'll get a promotion real quick."

He looked to his crew and could almost smell the fear coming off them in waves, well it was either fear or just their regular stink. He couldn't be sure. But most of the eyes he looked into reflected pain and torture, if they didn't get out of this fast. Even the Captain wasn't as brave as he led on. His gut was roiling with acid as he considered his deadly fate if those bots made it past the scramblers.

The Captain looked out the porthole to see what was happening and he discovered Throd was making a spacewalk right up to the side door of the Harvester. "I say we do what the Operator suggested. Look at what he be doing now." Gore pointed out the window and moved back so more of his crew could see the man flying in space. He looked more like a silver gray floating marshmallow moving behind his cargo container, but he was making his way to the enemy ship all on his own. No back up, just him.

"That old seadog has more bite than any of you lot!" Wyko said as he pointed at Rego.

The rest of the crew were grumbling about what they wanted to do. It came down to wanting to live. They sided with the Captain and Wyko.

Deegan asked, "We gonna give them Rego as a distraction?" Deegan and Rego never got along. The older pirate always treated the younger one like he was a scallywag. Before Deegan proved his worth on the bridge, Rego would lock him in the brig for days with no food or water and turn up the ambient heat in the cells, just to torture him. Like a bully with a magnifying glass on ants.

"Alright, here's what we're gonna do…" The Captain outlined a plan similar to what Throd told them. Then they made their way up to the loading bay to kill the Mechanurge drones after they went through the Operator's little present.

Chapter 8

Gore

The crew waited behind the cargo bay doors as they watched the giant harvester drones cut open the bay door and make their way inside. A blinding flash of light momentarily disrupted their forward momentum and the pirates were seeing stars.

While they still had bright spots in their vision, the Captain screamed, "Now!" And everyone except for Rego ran forward and started to attack the incoming bots that seemed a bit dazed and confused.

Rego skulked further into the ship, not ready to fight his way out of the predicament his rotten captain dragged them into.

Deegan pulled his blaster off his belt and shot at a drone in front of him, it did nothing to slow the metal beast.

The Captain got behind a bot and sliced the back of its neck. The drone stopped in its tracks and the head fell forward. "Cut the back of their necks, men! It keels 'em!"

The Captain was laughing menacingly as he jumped to another drone. He landed on its back and took his cutlass and sliced through the drones version of a neck, severing the cables that not only kept its head on, but also acted as a conduit for the lifeblood of all drones, lubrication fluid.

The Captain whooped and hollered as he enjoyed being a death dealer for these metal serial killers. "Tell Davy eye not be joining 'em today!" The drones head popped off and sparks shot up out of the body into the pirate captain's face. He just laughed and enjoyed the sizzle sounds when a spark hit his face. He already had enough scars on it that a couple more wouldn't make any difference.

Wyko was battling with one droid, trying to get his cutlass on the back of its neck. The drone he was fighting deflected the blade with its arm and grabbed the pirate by the front of his shirt. Wyko screamed and the drone threw him over his head against the bulkhead.

Deegan watched and winced when Wyko hit the ground, "Ouch, that's gotta smart."

Their new recruit, Lordon, was fighting a drone on his own. When he took his blaster out, the drone wacked it out of his hand. Lordon looked around for something to use as a weapon and tried to run away. The drone reached out and grabbed his arm. It pulled so hard, everyone could hear the sinew and bones breaking as Lordon's arm was pulled right out of its socket. There was a popping noise and then the drone threw the arm at Deegan.

Lordon screamed in pain and blood was streaking down his side, his white face had tears running in rivulets. Adrenaline was coursing through his system and his fight or flight mentality clicked in. He moved a couple of steps only to have his other arm yanked by a different drone. It was almost like a game to them. Which one could kill a human while inflicting the most pain. The first one slammed his hand into Lordon's chest and pulled out his still beating heart.

Gore moved like a ninja and got behind one of the drones and cut the back of his neck. It fell forward and thunked to the ground.

The second drone grabbed Gore by his throat and squeezed hard. The Captain dropped his cutlass and tried to pry the metal hands off his neck, to no avail. Right before he lost consciousness, Deegan ran behind the drone and cut its head off with the Captain's cutlass. The head rolled to the other side of the room and bounded off the bulkhead and landed next to Wyko.

Captain Gore was panting and massaging his neck. He looked around and saw the multitude of the Mechanurge laying in piles around his docking bay. He moved to help Wyko up and stopped cold when he heard the pounding sound of metal on metal coming toward him.

Deegan screeched when he looked up to see thirty more of the mechanized droids heading their way. "Cap'n what we gonna do now? No time to get down below decks for the next round of scramblers!"

Chapter 9

Throd

Throd sealed his pressure suit, then nestled the cargo container in the mouth of the garbage chute. He hooked a tether to the ring clamp on the container's top, and connected the other end to the suit's belt. "I never should've volunteered for this."

The Operator clicked his HUD to double check the game parameters before launching himself into the middle of one of the most deadly foes he had ever encountered.

..::..::..||..::..::../\\..::..::..||..::..::..

SCENARIO: HARDENED TARGET, MATERIAL LARCENY

TARGET: Mechanurge Hive Ship.

EXPECTED OPPOSITION: Awakened and non-sentient drones (~150 units)

SPECIAL DEFENSES: Superior firepower and strength.

OBJECTIVE 1: Neutralize enemy ship (1200 points)

OBJECTIVE 2: Obtain power core (1500 points)

BONUS 1: Ensure Pirates engage enemy drones (500 points)

BONUS 2: Smuggle extra combatants onboard without being detected (500 points)

SCENARIO REWARD: 10,000 credit units (conversion rates apply)

EXPENSES COVERED: To 5,000 credit units (ammunition and fuel reimbursed   separately to 1,000 credit units)

..::...::...| |..::...::...\\/..::...::...| |..::...::..

Before he could change his mind, the Operator slapped the release button next to the chute. Air rushed from the sealed disposal room, sucking the cargo container and Throd through the chute.

Throd grabbed the container with both hands, and found the fake panels attached to its sides. He ripped them free to expose a pair of slow-burn jets, and a simple control panel. He pressed the yellow button on the controls, and the jets fired to stabilize the tumbling container. "So far, so good."

Next to the Mechanurge Harvester, the Black Pearl looked like a toy. But it was a shiny toy that had the drones' attention, for the moment, giving Throd the chance he needed.

He opened the AR data panel and triggered his recording implant. There was no way he was leaving this footage behind; somebody had to see this when he was done. This footage of inside the Mechanurge harvester ship should get him at least one level up in addition to hitting a bonus pot, that was the least reward he could expect for what he was doing. Satisfied his gear was recording, Throd scanned the Harvester until he found what he was looking for. A section near the aft of the ship lit up through the AR screen, and the Operator set his course for the target.

As he closed in on the ship, Throd could see it was made up of a multitude of smaller vessels. The drones sucked up anything that got in their path, and repurposed it for their own ends. Sometimes that meant a starship got stripped down for parts, other times it just got welded to the outside of the Harvester and assimilated into the big ship's design. It was genius and ruthlessly efficient, and it had the added bonus of creeping the hell out of any human who saw it. There was something about the Awakened that was terrifying to their creators, and Throd wasn't going to pretend he didn't feel the stirrings of fear in his gut.

The container's jets pulsed as he approached the Harvester, slowing its flight as Throd entered the ship's shadow. He looked back at the Black Pearl, and saw flashes of stark white through the bay portals. He didn't have much time before the drones overwhelmed the pirates and hauled them all back to the Harvester for processing. Even with the quantum scramblers, a ridiculously expensive bit of disposable kit the Metal Rats had stolen from a military convoy, humans wouldn't last long against a determined force of killer Awakened.

Throd secretly hoped it was just standard issue drones and not the Awakened who made their way to the pirate ship. He had an ax to grind with Gore, but he wasn't a monster.

Magnetic clamps held the container against the side of the Harvester. With a twist of his wrist, Throd triggered the secondary function of the jets. They extended from the body of the container, rotated until their exhaust ports were perpendicular to the body of the Harvester, and blasted white-hot flames onto the bulkhead.

Throd looked away until the light from the cutters went out. The container had rotated in a circle creating a smooth hole in the Harvester's skin. A quick tug on the container pulled the plug out of the hole. Throd disengaged the magnetic clamps and the thick disc of metal floated away. He steered the cargo container into the dark interior of the ship, and the artificial gravity dropped it to the floor. The Operator landed next to it, knees flexing as his body adjusted to its sudden change in weight.

Drones responded to this intrusion with predictable and extreme violence. There were only a few in the room when Throd landed, but they were all armed to the teeth and wasted no time hurling bolts of energy in his direction.

Dropping behind the cargo container, Throd returned the favor. His pressure suit only covered his torso and head, leaving his cybernetic limbs exposed. Including the autocannon attached to his right forearm. The weapon erupted and one of the drones flew back, slamming into his companions as the high-powered shells hammered into its carapace.

There was almost no sound, because there was almost no air inside the ship. The drones didn't need it, and so they didn't bother pressurizing the Harvester. Throd was relying on the air in his suit to pull this off, and there wasn't much of that left. He had five minutes to get to oxygen, or he'd strangle to death on his own breath.

Fortunately, he'd planned ahead. They'd cut into the Harvester right where he needed to be. All he had to do was grab one of the power cores and then run like hell.

Another burst from his autocannons drove the drones back further, but backup was already arriving. More drones piled into the room from the deck above, jumping over the catwalk and landing around Throd with weapons ready to destroy.

Good thing he'd brought back-up, too.

Chapter 10

Gore

The Captain came prepared. You don't take a cutlass to a drone battle without some backup. "Stand back everyone, watch yer backside!" The Captain took a few steps to the rear of the compartment they were in and threw his EMP grenade at the center of the oncoming death dealers.

A second bright, white light emanated from the middle of the room and a sizzling sound was heard and felt, then nothing. Total and complete blackness. The only light they had was coming from the Harvester.

"Shiver me timbers! You took out our ship too, Cap'n!" Wyko yelled from his hiding spot behind a crate in the corner.

The mini EMP had knocked out all power to the drones, essentially killing them, but it also cut power to the Black Pearl. Their emergency generator kicked in just as they started to float due to the loss of power to the gravity generator.

The Captain fell down to his knees and exclaimed, "Sink Me! We don't have enough spare parts to get our ship moving again."

"Um, Cap'n?" Deegan shuffled his way to the spot he thought was where his Captain sat. He misjudged and stepped on the Captain's hand.

"Son of a biscuit eater! Why'd ye go and do that fer?" The Captain shook his hand out and felt his bones to make sure there wasn't anything wrong with the hand. The boots his men wore could be pretty dangerous to fingers, what with their spikes set in a few carefully placed spots and all.

The captain looked to the entrance of his ship. The boarding party had sealed the tube enough that they weren't losing too much oxygen, but there were some tiny holes in the tube they used to board the ship. Those holes were leaking their precious air. The Captain could see it leaving his ship and also hear the high pitched squeal as their depleting air left them in danger of suffocating.

Currently, the boarding tube was only open on their end. The drones were careful not to open up a pressurized ship attached to a non-pressurized ship. The Captain momentarily wondered if the Mechanurge had joined the universe in the gaming scenarios. The only reason to keep the pirate ship from depressurizing and expelling all life forms, was if they had a bonus goal to keep the humans alive long enough to feed them into the bio forges. Or a desire to ensure the pirates experienced a level of sheer terror and fear that this attack would invoke for as long as possible. The Captain thought it odd that a group of Awakened robots would have such emotions.

He was rather surprised they even bothered trying to seal the tube. It would have been more expedient to allow the pressurized ship to be exposed to the vacuum of space. The exposure to space wouldn't have hurt the Mechanurge in the least bit. The Black Pearl was another issue altogether.

Had they just blown the door open the contents of most of the ship would have been sucked out into space, which included all human life. It would have made the Mechanurge's mission quick and simple.

Now, with his systems down, he needed to get that seal perfect. Or get his ship's systems up and running again. First, he needed the oxygen scrubbers back online.

"Rego, where ye be, mate? I need ye to fix the oxygen pumps and scrubbers." No one answered the Captain.

Wyko found a light stick and turned it on. It didn't produce much more than a couple of lumens, but it was enough to see a rough outline of the loading bay and all of the dead Awakened at their feet. Most had just fallen down like they were dropped from 20 meters high. You could see the crew's handy work on some of the mechanized killers.

Several of the heads had been cut clean off the bodies of the drones. One was even missing its right arm. Two more lay in what appeared to be a pool of their own blood in this dark room. But, was most likely lubrication fluid.

"Where's Rego?" The Captain called again and slowly made his way around the room. "That lily-livered sissy! Did anyone see him fighting?"

He looked at one outline of a man who shook his head and then heard a few grunted "No's." "Alright, first we need to find out how we're going to get the seal fixed. Then we have to figure out what on our ship needs fixin. Wyko, take a team with ye to engineering and see what's needed. Deegan, you're up. Get that seal fixed, and find a way to get the outer door back on airtight. I don't care if ye have to weld the thing back on. We need to be space worthy long enough to get to a friendly port."

The Captain started to walk further into his ship, but stopped before leaving the bay, "Ye might want to grab a breathing rig since ye'll be right next to the holes in the Mechanurge's gangplank." The Captain gave out some more orders then he went to see how many breathing masks they had that actually worked. He made a mental note to add them to the top of his to do list. Without oxygen, none of the other repairs would matter.

Deegan looked at the hole leading into the belly of the whale and shivered involuntarily as he wondered what he would do if more drones came to their ship before he could get that fixed. He also wondered why more hadn't come yet.

Chapter 11

Throd

Throd pressed the last button on the cargo container's control panel, and it burst open with explosive force. The side panels shot away and plowed through the drones flanking Throd. One group was carried out through the hole in the side of the Harvester, and tumbled into the void. The others shot across the room and into the wall with such force their limbs and heads popped from their torsos in sparkling showers. The container's lid flipped up and smashed into another group, driving them into the floor.

A dull white glow emanated from the metal tube inside the container, and Throd stepped back. This thing was his ally, but it was cranky as hell when it first woke up. "Sic 'em, boy!" Throd shouted into his comms unit.

F3L1N unfolded like the universe's deadliest origami. The cat-like drone lashed out with its front claws, shredding through a pair of Awakened with terrifying ease. It spun on its back legs, and ripped the head from another Awakened before it could unleash a salvo of explosive rounds. It roared a challenge at the rest of the drones, then reared up to expose a glowing crystalline cylinder in its belly.

Skritch waved at Throd from inside her pod. "About time you woke me up, big guy. I don't think I'm going to need to sleep for another week."

The Operator unloaded into a new group of Awakened, then ran for the Harvester's engines. "No time to talk, little girl, keep these tin cans off me while I finish the job."

Throd vaulted onto the engine supports. A cold sweat erupted across his forehead and upper lip, and a fist of dread coiled in his guts. It'd been more than a decade since the last time he'd been aboard a Harvester, and he'd thought he was over the panic. But this close to the engines, to the place where he'd been chained while the transmogrifiers went to work replacing his flesh with metal, it all came rushing back.

Sounds of battle, muted by the thin atmosphere inside the ship, plucked at the edges of his attention. He had to do something, but he couldn't remember what. The memories were too vivid, they pushed the rest of his thoughts to the sidelines and left him shaking and paralyzed with fear. What if he couldn't do this? What if they captured him again?

The power core glowed like a miniature sun, its heat and fury contained by a magnetic field. Throd remembered trying to reach another power core. Trying to put his head through the containment field to end the pain. Trying to destroy what he'd become.

A young woman's high-pitched voice crackled in his ear. "It's getting a little crowded in here, big guy. We need to scoot."

Time collapsed, and Throd shook his head. He wasn't that scared man anymore. He wasn't alone. He had a family now, and they depended on him. Dragora's core had been damaged in their flight from Rivicle Base, and without a new one the outfit would be stranded. That's why he was here. To save them all. Getting the extra points and a possible level up didn't hurt either.

He didn't give the fear another chance to seize him. Throd shoved his cybernetic hand down into the motor's primary cylinder, and yanked the core containment unit free.

The core blazed even brighter, while the rest of the ship went dark. Without its core, the Harvester was a lifeless hulk, and the Awakened within it were disconnected and confused. They were a hive mind, and Throd had just killed the Queen.

In the back of his helmet, he heard a soft bell ringing. It signaled his completion of the objectives and bonuses. He just hoped he lived to complete the entire scenario.

He jumped off the raised support and sprinted toward Skritch and the drone wrapped around her. "Got it! Let's go."

F3L1N whirled to follow Throd through the hole in the Harvester's side. Drones fired at them as they leaped into the void, but the Awakened were shocked and in disarray from the disruption to the Harvester. Their shots were wide and winding down. In a few more minutes, Throd knew they would collapse, their consciousness scattered.

Unfortunately, he didn't have a few minutes to wait for them to die. The oxygen meter in the corner of his AR display flashed red. He didn't have more than 30 seconds.

He locked one arm around F3L1N's neck, and hung on. They tumbled through the void, slowly rotating as they drifted past the Black Pearl. Throd searched the starscape, but Dragora was nowhere in sight. If her engines had failed entirely, or Heck miscalculated their position, he and Skritch were about to die.

And then, Skritch's voice burst through the comms channel. "There!"

The sleek ship glided toward them, cargo arm extended. Throd let out a sigh of relief, and squeezed the drone's neck affectionately. He waved the power core overhead, and waited for his family to pick him up.

..::..::..||..::..::../\\..::..::..||..::..::..

SCENARIO: HARDENED TARGET, MATERIAL LARCENY - COMPLETE

OBJECTIVE 1: Neutralize enemy ship (1200 points) - COMPLETE

OBJECTIVE 2: Obtain power core (1500 points) - COMPLETE

BONUS 1: Ensure Pirates engage enemy drones (500 points) - BONUS AWARDED

BONUS 2: Smuggle extra combatants onboard without being detected (500 points) - BONUS AWARDED

SCENARIO REWARD: 10,000 credit units (conversion rates apply)

EXPENSES COVERED: To 5,000 credit units (ammunition and fuel reimbursed separately to 1,000 credit units)

CALCULATING SKILL AWARDS...

EXTRAVEHICULAR MANEUVERS: +1

BLUFF: +1

HEAVY WEAPONS: +1

Congratulations! Your rating has improved. You are now a Level 5 Operator.

Your new level entitles you to the following:

1 software upgrade (Class IV or lower)

1 hardware implant (Class II or lower)

CONGRATULATIONS! YOU HAVE SUCCESSFULLY COMPLETED THIS SCENARIO!

COLLECT SCENARIO REWARD AND SUBMIT EXPENSE REPORT AT ANY UMBRA TERMINAL

..::..::..||..::..::..\V/..::..::..||..::..::..

Chapter 12

Gore

What little light they had from the Harvester died out and no one knew what was coming. Deegan yelled out, "What was that?"

The Captain wondered what Throd was up to. He knew the Operator was taking something from the ship, but to see the power go out could only mean one thing. He took their frackin' power core! "Sneaky little scurvy dog! I should've thought of that first!" A wry smile started to cross his face when he thought about what was waiting for him on the other side of the patchy gangplank.

"Deegan, get that seal fixed *NOW*! It's time we act like the Scourge of the Seven Galaxies that we be. I want a boarding party ready to go across and pillage and plunder anything and everything not bolted down." The Captain went to find himself a boarding party.

"Rego! REGO! Get your Scallywagging backside out here now! I have an assignment for you!" The Captain yelled as loud as he could, then under his breath he said, "One that hopefully leaves you as shark bait."

Rego presented himself with a cannon rifle and a full space suit. He was ready to defend himself. Gore grunted when he saw Rego, "Figures." Whether Rego knew what the Captain had in mind, or if he had his own plans, wasn't known yet. But the Captain didn't mind one bit. He was going to kill two birds with one stone, the stone being the Harvester ship, of course.

"Alright men, we have a list of what's needed to fix me ship. No one can go anywhere until the Pearl is up and running again. That Harvester…" the Captain pointed across the bay to the entrance into the belly of the beast. "Has everything we need, and then some. But don't take too long grabbin' booty, we don't know if there be 'nother nearby or not."

"If ye be on the engineering team, grab what ye need then get back here and fix our Pearl. Everyone else, ye gots an hour to secure as much plunder as ye can and get back here." The Captain rubbed his hands in anticipation of the advanced tech he would be able to steal and sell on the downworlder markets. Shoot, he might even be able to sell on the legitimate ones too. Mechanurge tech was some of the most advanced in five quadrants. His ship was getting the overhaul she desperately needed when they made it back to a pirate friendly port.

"Rego, ye be with me. I have a particular piece of bounty I need ye help with." He nodded to the mutinous tar standing next to him.

"What ye have in mind, Cap'n?" Rego cautiously asked.

"We need to get our hands on their spare power core. That piece of tech would power the Black Pearl for the next one hundred years at full power, and then some!" An evil grin spread across Gore's face. With all of the scars, it made him look like a monster instead of a pirate. "Then we could assimilate some of their weapons on our ship. Maybe even a gravitic funnel or a smart grapnel." The Captain slapped Rego on the back as he made his way to enter the darkened enemy ship.

"Right behind ye Cap'n. Can we get one of their pulse cannons too?" Rego confidently followed his Captain.

"If ye can carry it, we be taking it!" Gore replied.

Everyone scurried off to do their assigned task. The general feeling of the crew was that of excitement and victory. They knew that the drones were worker bees tied to the hive mind of the ship and with the ship down, they were down as well. For the next hour all of the pirates worked hard to get the Black Pearl able to run again.

"Cap'n, what 'bout the engine room? Would they hold a back-up power cell there?" Rego was really into his assignment. He always did enjoy the pillage and plunder part of his job. Fighting was something he almost always shied away from, unless it involved stabbing someone in the back, just like with the Mechanurge attack.

"I'd think they'd have it in a storage room. Maybe one off the side of the engine room." The Captain led them down a walkway to what he hoped was the Harvesters engine room.

It was confirmed as they passed several dead drone carcasses with scorch marks lying about their path. "I'd say the Operator was here, wouldn't you Rego?"

Rego laughed in his suit, which sounded more like a pig oinking in space than a pirate laughing inside a helmet. "Yup, Cap'n. That Operator sure knows how to throw a party!"

"Will ye be sharing your grog with 'em when we get back to port?" The Captain shook his head when he realized his mutinous scallywag had decided he liked the Operator responsible for their current situation.

"Nah, I don't share me grog with anyone, not even the wenches. They has ta buys their own."

"Such a gentleman," the Captain stated as he led them into what appeared to be the dead engineering section. "Yup, Throd was here alright. I wonder where he went to now? I don't want to leave 'em behind again. He never should'n'of been left on that mining moon." The Captain surveyed his surroundings and noticed that the crate had been opened and whatever was inside was now gone.

After walking around the room, he discovered a back door that led to a supply room. Inside that room was pay dirt! They were going to need multiple trips back to the ship if he wanted all of the booty in that room.

"Cap'n! Look what I found!" Rego had a giant grin on his face as he pulled what appeared to be an engineer's wagon into the room. It was a cart on wheels that was three levels high and the bottom level had almost 25 centimeter side panels. It was perfect for carrying small items and keeping them from falling out, while the top two racks could hold bigger items.

"Good job, let's get this power core on the top and fill up them other levels with everything we can. I'll push it back while you follow up with anything larger you can carry." The Captain got to work loading up all of the goodies onto the cart.

When they got back to the gangplank connecting the two ships, they had to wait inside a confined space as the system worked to pressurize the boarding tube. They couldn't just walk back and forth, since one ship wasn't pressurized. It was tedious and the Captain snarled when he watched Rego counting the items on the cart during the pressurization procedures.

They made three trips back and forth with all of the engineering parts and tools they could carry. After unloading their third full cart, the Captain said he would stay back and help to get the loading bay doors fixed.

"Sure thing Cap'n!" Rego was focused on pillaging and didn't notice that he was the only one sent back inside the Harvester.

"Deegan, can we use any of these drones for scrap metal?" The Captain scratched his head as he scanned the floor of his loading bay. The lights were back on and oxygen seemed to be flowing normally again.

"Cap'n, I wouldn't keep 'em. Ye never know when we might run close enough to a Harvester 'n these guys could wake up." Deegan looked at the currently dead drones and his skin began to crawl as he remembered what it looked like to watch one of his shipmates get torn limb from limb less than two hours before.

"Right, toss 'em all back inside their ship and seal us up. We need to be get'n outta here before one of their sister ships comes looking for 'em." The Captain picked up one of the drone heads and examined it. "Too bad, they would've made great trophy's."

"Ye could probly keep that one, sir. It's dead. Just don't be keeping any that are still in one piece." Deegan started throwing the carcasses of the Mechanurge drones back into their Harvester ship pressurization chamber.

The Captain heard the bell in his implant signaling he had completed both assignments and both bonuses.

"Time to pull out the grog, mates! We completed the assignment. And got rid of the stinky trash!" The Captain yelled out to anyone who was within yelling distance. "Finally, we completed an assignment. Time to get paid, boy!" He slapped Deegan on the shoulder.

"What about Rego? He's still on the ship," Deegan asked after he unloaded the last drone.

"You mean the mutinous shark bait who never did one thing to help ye? That Rego?" The Captain raised his eyebrows as he studied the body language of one of his best crew members.

Gore pulled out his pair of dice. He rarely gambled on his decisions. This one, this one was going to be fun. With both hands lightly clasped over the dice, he blew into his palms for luck. Then he threw the small, deadly dice against the open door leading to the Mechanurge ship.

Snake eyes.

The Captain slowly walked over and picked up his dice. He looked at Deegan menacingly and silently slit his finger across his throat.

"Rego, who?" Deegan shrugged his shoulders and closed the door separating the two ships and began the job of welding it shut. They had another door they could use to exit the ship when they got back to port. They just wouldn't be able to carry anything big with them when they disembarked as the only working door was less than 145 centimeter high and 120 centimeters wide. It was a passenger door, not meant for cargo.

Right before they pulled away from the Harvester, the Captain heard an incessant banging on the door Deegan just closed up. He looked to Deegan who just twisted his mouth and walked away.

"Must be the Mechanurge's boarding ramp falling apart." The Captain mused as he walked out of the loading bay and made his way to the bridge. "Yo ho, yo ho, a pirate's life for me." He sang as he sauntered along.

"Cap'n on the bridge!" Wyko barked when Gore walked to his

command chair.

"Weigh anchor and set sail men! We be heading home for repairs and much needed shore leave."

Not a soul mentioned the missing crewmember as they set their sights to the Rimda Omega Space Station.

Once they were far enough away, and they could no longer see the Harvester ship on their sensors, the Captain opened up his HUD and searched for the game completion scenario notice.

..::..::..||..::..::../\\..::..::..||..::..::..

CARGO DELIVERY SCENARIO COMPLETE!

Outfit Aggregate: 2300 points

Play of the Scenario: Captain Gore walk the plank (1500 points)

Fan Favorite: Captain Gore (1000 points)

Congratulations! Your rating has improved. You are now a Level 4 Pirate.

Your new level entitles you to the following:

1 software upgrade (Class III or lower)

1 wench for a day (Class II or lower)

You have received one message from an anonymous sponsor:

[Hey! Good work with the Mechanurge. Glad to see you finally got rid of your dead weight! Everyone knows he was the reason you lost last time. We added a small bonus for giving us a surprise ending. No one believed you would do it.]

CALCULATING SKILL AWARDS...

DISARM OPERATOR: +1

ACQUIRE MECHANURGE ADVANCED ARSENAL: +1

CONGRATULATIONS! YOU HAVE SUCCESSFULLY COMPLETED THIS SCENARIO!

COLLECT SCENARIO REWARD AND SUBMIT EXPENSE REPORT AT ANY UMBRA TERMINAL

..:·..:·...||..·:·..·:·...\\/..·:·..·:·...||..·:·..·:·..

Author J.L. Hendricks

J.L. Hendricks is an independent author who enjoys many genres, as evidenced by her catalog of available books. She is currently focused on Scifi and Urban Fantasy, but has also written Paranormal and Christmas books.

Her latest series is an Urban Fantasy with her Voodoo Dolls Series, and then back to her Worlds Away series!

Check out her webpage for a listing of her books, and get a taste of what she writes: https://jlhendricksauthor.com where you can also sign up for her newsletter.

Space Cadets: Acid Slime

By H.J. Lawson

Rank: *Captain*

Name: *Brooke*

Cadet ID: *10091999*

Private note: It was my eighteenth birthday a few months ago, and I joined up immediately. Everyone was assigned an ID number when they became official, and this is mine. : Endnote

Destinations: *Asomea*

Assignment: *Collect planet samples*

Private note: This is one of my rookie assignments. Munroe, the captain of the mother spaceship, threw me the bone of a cool assignment then turns around and gives me a crappy one like this. It's like he's teasing me or something. : Endnote

Crew count: *Four*

Private note: My copilot/engineer, Shaula is unreal. I guess she was a straight-A student as I was on earth. Everything about Shaula screams that she was that type of student, her clothes are even perfectly pressed. I've not even worked out how to get my clothes iron on the mothership because I've not looked. Her brown hair is tightly pulled back into a neat bun like she wants to grow up and be a librarian. She is very intimidating.

Then there are Tweedle-Dee and Tweedle-Dum. I mean that in the sweetest way, of course. They are identical twins, Eric and Trevor, although they do not like to be called by their real names. They changed their names when they boarded the mothership. A few other people who I knew also did that. They are a mirror image of each other with round faces and bellies, strawberry blonde hair, pale skin with small button noses and beady eyes, and faces that are usually wearing a large grin.

What there are their jobs? Well, what are they? The oil that keeps the ship running, I'd say. You need it, they can get it. They can get anything, but there is always a cost. They are the go-to guys on the mothership and part of my crew. It's totally good to have them around.

This is my crew, two girls, two boys, all aged under twenty, On the mothership, there are no adults. Once you hit twenty, you're moved onto a spaceship. It's weird, but that's the way they run it and when I say "they," I mean the people from Avignon that have been appointed the police of the galaxy. : Endnote

I hit return on the computer screen and closed the report on my eighth assignment since I received my wings and became a pilot.

"Shaula, are the systems checked?" I ask.

"Yes," Shaula says beside me.

"Craft 233 ready to depart," I say through the radio to control.

The large metal doors on the mothership open up to space. The adrenaline of flying a spaceship hasn't worn off for me. I still get the same excitement as the first time I flew a spaceship. I push the handle down as the spaceship rapidly travels down the runway.

"Brooke," Tweedle-Dee yells, followed by a thud.

"Crap! Sorry, take your seats for departure," I say a little too late as we've already left the mothership and have launched into the darkness of space.

I glance over my shoulder and see Tweedle-Dee on the craft floor and his brother helping him to his feet. Now, they are both staggering around laughing.

"You need to be more careful, Brooke," Shaula says, sounding like my mom.

"That's why I've got you."

Shaula rolls her eyes, I guess not pleased with my answer.

Before this all happened, by this I mean being taken off the earth by aliens to become Space Cadets, I was, well a square. I always did the right thing. I always listened to my crazy mom, although I found out that she wasn't so crazy. Yet the memories of what happened the day before I left are still etched into my mind. She locked Paige and me in the wardrobe to protect us from the Shadow Men. Sounds crazy, right? Well, it wasn't, and she was right all along. The Shadow Men, these creepy black atoms were chasing me, and my family and the only way to stop them was to go with the other aliens, the good ones apparently.

"Do that again!" The twins say, taking me away from my memories of how I got here, stuck in the middle of my new reality.

"What?"

"You're crazy, Brooke. We could have gone on any spaceships-"

"You know we had the pick of any-" Tweedle-Dee interjects.

"He's right. Because of our charm and good looks." They nod to one another happily.

"But we chose you. Cause you're the baddest chick pilot around."

"Thank you. I think?"

"Yeah, it's a good thing to be the hottest. No... no... well yeah, hottest baddest chick around."

The twins have a Cheshire cat grin from ear to ear.

"Alright, less of the butt kissing time! Let's get this dump assignment over and done with," Shaula says firmly. She will make a good captain of the spaceship, she's bossy and all about getting down to the assignment. But that's her problem. They (by they I mean the people that evaluate and test the cadets during training), they need people who are willing to take some risks. The ones that calculate risk aren't always the right ones. Sound wrong, yet right? Sometimes your heart is right when your brain isn't, that's why we're selected to be the police of the galaxy. You need compassion. Well, that's what I think anyway.

Time to get my head in the game. I look at the coordinates for Asomea and plug them in.

It will take us twenty-four hours to get there or five in super speed. Hyper-speed it is.

"Buckle up for hyper-speed," I wince at Shaula, "I remembered this time."

"Arhs," comes from the twins, "Do we have to?"

"Yes!" Shaula snaps out.

"Ooh sorry, mom," the brothers snigger at one another.

She shoots them an 'if looks could kill, you'd be dead' glare. They raise their hands in response and get into their seat.

"Buckle them up," I shake my head at them, as they pretend they're already buckled. I've got to say one thing for these two, they are street smart, not school smart. If they weren't buckled in during hyper-speed, the force of their bodies against the spaceship would do some serious damage. With our medic, Carlos, sick that wouldn't be good. I hope he's alright. He took a nasty swipe from Krypton on our last and most exciting assignment and has been out of action ever since.

ACTION: *08.47 hyper speed.* I type into the captain log.

I take one last look around the small spaceship, and everyone is secured in their seats. I type my ID number into the control then I pull down the hyper-speed handle. There is a pause for a brief second, just long enough for me to brace myself. Then the spaceship shoots forward turning all the stars into a blur. I gasp as we move forward. It feels like the air has been taken from my lungs. The spaceship comes to an abrupt halt, and air rushes once again into my lungs.

I dart the spaceship to the left then right and left again, we hyper-speeded into space that was filled with debris and rocks. These are only small, which is why they weren't picked up when I set the locations. These rocks may be too little to detect from afar but can still create damage to the spaceship which I don't want. This mission should be in and out.

I speed forward entering into the Asomea atmosphere.

"Shaula, run oxygen tests," I say. Even though all of us are able to breathe on any planet, we need the data for the assignment report. It's weird that all those that are on the mothership internal organs have evolved to make it possible to breathe anywhere, that's one of the reasons why we're chosen to be Space Cadets. Because police of the galaxy really need to be able to go anywhere.

"Test ran, transferring the file to you now," Shaula informs me.

"Thank you," I say as I open up the file.

OXYGEN LEVEL: *As earth.* It's funny really most planets have the same oxygen levels as earth I've yet to go on one that does. All these years people thought Earth was the only planet on which people could live, and I've already been to eight planets that humans could live on. But I don't think humans would be welcome on all those planets as we're seen as inferior. Asomea is a lush green planet with plenty of natural water.

"How much of the planet is water?" I ask.

"Weren't you paying attentions in the briefing?" Shaula asks.

"Yes, just checking," I lie, briefings are a total waste of time. They are like science/history/geography lessons that go on for hours become just one blur of background noise. I snuck out of it saying I needed the bathroom, but really, I went to grab some food and check on Carlos. Anyway, that's why I've got a crew right? They can listen to the boring stuff.

"It's 80% water," Shaula says.

"That's what I thought, just double checking."

I check Asomea for land mass that would support the spaceship. Perfect, there's one just on the horizon.

"Prepare for landing," I tell everyone. Slowing the engines down as I realize that there is no runway for the spaceship, I check the location once more. Nope, this is it.

I start the descent, gently lowering the spaceship. Shaula is stroking her monitor like it's a cat. I swear she thinks of the spaceship as if it's her pet.

The spaceship lands and Shaula pats it as if she rewarding it for its good work. Where's my pat at? I smile at the thought of Shaula patting me.

I take a look out of the window, and we're on a small green island. The water has some plants that look like giant water lilies.

"Tweedle-Dee, get the lab equipment."

"YES, captain," they both say saluting me. I grin. When will they get bored of that?

Shaula is already out of her seat and heading to her station. While we are here, she will check the reports on the spaceship, making sure there will be no issues for takeoff.

"There are no alerts. She's good for takeoff." Shaula informs me.

"Thank you."

ACTION: *Systems checked*

ACTION: *Departing spaceship for samples*

After a few minutes, the crew is ready with empty containers ready to fill.

I recall Nova, my best friend and the person who briefs us, saying that there aren't any land animals just as I was leaving the briefing for a break. I glance over to the weapons thinking that we don't need them for this quick assignment.

"What are you doing?" I ask Tweedle-Dee, shaking my head as he stands beside me with a heavy metal flamethrower gun. They load the spaceship with all different types of weapons because not all aliens can be stopped with the same one.

"Does it look good on me?" He winks.

"Set it down. Let's get this over and done with." Tweedle-Dee tuts but does as I requested. Then he goes to over to his brother, and together they lift up the box of equipment. I grab my device, a handle-held computer that looks like a table, and Shaula stands ready with the equipment on a trolley.

I flip up the clear plastic cover over the red button by the doorway and press it. Nothing happens. Maybe, I was not forceful enough. I do it again with more pressure, and there is a swooping noise as the pressure inside the spaceship changes to match the outside air rushing in.

"One hour guys, that will be enough to get samples," I tell them.

They nod in agreement, and we exit the spaceship. The land is soft, covered with moss it's like memory foam cradling around our feet as we walk.

Everyone gets to work on their assignment, Tweedle-Dee gathers up the planet and rock samples. Shaula runs the chemical tests on the ground, and I survey the area taking notes on various details and adding them into my log. Once completed, I store the device in my pocket. I look out at the water around us, so still that it is like a lake.

"Did you take a water sample?" I ask Tweedle-Dee.

"On it, Captain," he says, striding over to the edges of the land. He kneels down with the container in his hand and scoops up some water.

"No!" Shaula yells as she steps away from her equipment and Tweedle-Dum.

I look around for the danger, wishing I'd brought my gun with me. "What is it?" I ask getting to her in a hurry. But she doesn't need to answer because the surface of the water ripples. Something is coming toward us, and now it's here.

A tentacle reaches up to the edge of the land, making Tweedle-Dee stumble back and fall to the ground with shock.

"Don't let it touch you! Asomea! Its slime is acid," Shaula screams in a panic.

"Get away from my brother," Tweedle-Dum yells, grabbing hold of his brother and yanking him to his feet.

Asomea creeps out of the water with small sucking sounds. It looks like an octopus and its acid slime is gleaming in the sunlight. I swear it seems like it's smiling.

"Get back to the spaceship," I yell.

The Tweedles run quicker than I've ever seen them move before.

Shaula struggles with her trolley. "Leave it," I tell her.

"But the equipment?"

"It's replaceable, you're not."

Shaula glances at her equipment and then at the Asomea. I can see right when she realizes what is at stake. Turning, she makes a quick run for it. I am right on her heels.

Once we're all on the spaceship, I press the button to close the doors, but it blasted button doesn't work.

"Brooke, close the doors," everyone yells, "it's coming."

"I'm trying! It's not working." I keep pushing the button, but nothing is happening. The Asomea is climbing into the spaceship. His tentacles lash out at us, making us dive away for cover. It's on the spaceship. My stomach clenches and I grab the flamethrower that Tweedle-Dee left on the table. Everyone moves behind me.

"You can't use that," Shaula says, looking at the flame thrower.

"Why?"

"Asomea blood is like gasoline. If you hit it with the flamethrower, it will blow up the spaceship!" Asomea tentacles reach out towards us, and we all cower back.

I frantically scan the spaceship, but there's nothing else to use close enough.

"Dive for the door," I tell them, "now!"

As they sprint for the door name, tentacles grab at them. I turn the flamethrower on them, and they quickly ignite. Like the others, I dash for the exit but still managing to keep the flamethrower washing the Asomea with a hot splash of flame.

"Take cover," I yell as the area is lit up in flames. Everyone dives away from our spaceship. The soft ground protects us as we fall. The open doorway turns into a giant ball of flames as the Asomea stumbles toward the outside.

"It's going to blow," the Tweedles yell.

I've created a bomb inside of our spaceship.

The Asomea turns into a glowing sun, seeming to expand and contract before finally flying apart. More explosions come from inside the spaceship as the furnishings, wiring, and other parts of the ship heat up and ignite in the presence of the intense flames. Metal groans as the heat intensifies, sounding like the ship is crying out in pain.

I wrap my hands and arms around my head, bracing for the explosion.

Metal panels from the spaceship fly over my head and land in the water with a series of splashes. I keep my head down and peek out to watch for more flying metal as our spaceship becomes nothing more than a melted, charred mess.

After the destruction ends, I get up from my hiding position with the flamethrower still in my hands. I am ready for the next Asomea to come.

The place looks like a scrap yard with angry pieces of metal. I ignore it, instead looking for movement.

The Tweedles are together, but where's Shaula? I frantically look around.

"Shaula?" I yell.

Damn, she's in the water! I race in a panic to the water's edge. Ripples in every direction are coming for her.

I throw the flame thrower on the mossy ground and start to jump in after her. At the last second, I pause and take my device out of my pocket. We will need it to call for help, and I cannot take the risk of losing it in the murky water. Last rational thought done, I just in after Shaula.

I swim swiftly for Shaula. She is not moving, just lying on the surface of the thick water. She has to be unconscious. I place my arm under her chin, cradling her and swim towards the shore. As I start to move, Asomea tentacles creep up to the surface. I try to move quicker. I can't let it get her.

I get to the edge, and a pair of hands are there to greet me. It is Tweedle-Dee with his brother right next to him. Tweedle-Dee is watching the water with the flamethrower in his hand.

"What are you waiting for? Set them alight." I gasp as I crawl up onto land, dragging Shaula with me.

"Yes, captain." With that Tweedle-Dee sets fire to the Asomea that had been chasing us. Flames dance on top of the water's surface. When it reaches the next Asomea the slime on its skin starts on fire as well. Soon, there is a ring of fiery sacrifices around us, creating a barrier in the water. Protecting us from any other beings that might want to attack.

Shaula starts to cough and is soon spitting out water. "It's okay, you're safe now," I say. trying to reassure her.

Standing up, I search the ground for my device. It only takes me a short time to find it and prepare to type in a message I'd hoped to never send.

EMERGENCY: *Evacuation needed. Spaceship destroyed.*

I stare at the device praying for a response.

CONTROL: *Remain in your location--rescue spaceship is on its way.*

"Rescue is on its way," I tell the others as I slump onto the ground in relief and exhaustion.

I had one more thing to do before I could relax. I open up the captain's log file and type.

ACTION: *Assignment failed.*

Author H.J. Lawson

HJLawson is an English author who currently resides in New York. When she's not writing, she spends her time watching movies and hanging out with her family. She is the author of the following young adult books: The War Kids Series and The Sanction Series. See more at https://www.facebook.com/HJLawson1/ or sign up for her Newsletter at http://eepurl.com/N_-Zz

Nun Shall Pass

by Barry J. Hutchison

CHAPTER ONE

Ronda Sallas had killed a number of men in her time – but then, what nun hadn't? It had been quite a large number, too. Not three digits, maybe, but close. But she had never - at least, not to the best of her knowledge - used a frying pan to do the job. And certainly not one of her good ones.

She hadn't actually killed the man yet. But she would. Soon. In four minutes and forty-seven seconds, in fact.

Her son, Narp, was not a bad boy. He was a good boy who occasionally did bad things, and that was an important distinction, as far as Ronda was concerned. Besides, even the bad things he did were never his idea. He was forced to do them against his will. Most of the time, at least.

Ronda stopped outside a building she knew very well, despite never having been there before. She looked up at its featureless gray frontage, taking in its shuttered windows and reinforced front door. Yep, this was the place from her premonition, alright. From the premonition, she knew Narp wasn't in there, but she knew that someone inside would lead her to him.

She hoisted the bag containing her second-best frying pan higher on her shoulder, approached the metal door, and knocked.

Almost immediately, as she knew it would, a hatch opened. It was a small hatch, through which Ronda could see a tiny bit of a larger-built gentleman. He was, of course, neither gentle nor technically a man. He was a Turlap, a species renowned throughout the galaxy for their size, stupidity and willingness to hurt others for money – although not necessarily in that order.

His name was Gunth. He would die, screaming, impaled on a number of metal spikes. But not today, and not by her.

"What the fonk you want?"

Ronda's smile flickered, but rallied quickly. She'd resisted having a translation chip implanted for years, preferring to learn languages the old-fashioned way, via months of lingo-tank submersions and agonizing frontal lobe stimulation. Once she'd heard about the chip's censorship functionality, though, she'd relented. Murder, she could deal with. Bad language, though, that was another matter entirely.

"Hello, dear," said Ronda. "How's Aliss?"

The eyes blinked, slow and cow-like. "Huh?"

"Your mother, Aliss. How is she? She should get that swelling under her upper armpit looked at. Tell her that from me."

"Uh, she's fine."

Ronda made a *well, actually*, face, but said no more about it. "Is Narp there?"

Another blink. "Huh?"

"My son, Narp," said Ronda, broadening her smile. "Tell you what, Gunth, let's hurry this along. You're going to say he's not there, I'm going to say I know, and that I'd like to come in and speak to Katona."

Gunth blinked so slowly that a casual onlooker would be forgiven for thinking he'd fallen asleep. "Stay with me, here, Gunth," Ronda continued. "You'll say Katona isn't here, I'll say he is, you'll say he isn't, this will go on for some time, then you'll eventually ask me for the passcode."

"What's the passcode?" demanded Gunth, latching onto the one phrase he felt on more familiar ground with.

"Eight-seven-zeta-nine."

Behind the door, Gunth's lips moved silently. Once he was confident the code matched the one he had painstakingly memorized, he shrugged and slid the hatch closed.

Ronda heaved her bag higher on her shoulder as locks unlocked and bolts slid open. A moment later, the door swung inwards, revealing Gunth in all his four-armed enormity. He still looked a little uncertain about what he was doing, but she had the code, and he was supposed to open the door to people with the code.

"Thank you, dear," said Ronda, stepping inside and patting Gunth on one of his upper arms. "You've done very well."

"I have?" said Gunth, brightening.

"You have." Ronda's smiled dipped, just a fraction. "And tell your mother she *really* should get that swelling checked out."

"I will," said Gunth.

Ronda smile returned, but it was a different smile this time. There was a sadness to it. "No," she said, shuffling along the narrow hallway towards the only visible inner door. "You don't."

One of the downsides of Ronda's gift was all the additional knowledge that came with it. Being able to see along the personal timelines of the people she encountered brought all kinds of advantages — advantages which her time at the convent had taught her to … well, to take advantage of.

However, alongside the usable intel came plenty of other baggage. Feelings, mostly. She'd learned long ago not to get attached to the people in her visions, or even to think about them too much. Sometimes, though, she'd see suffering she felt compelled to try to alleviate, even when she knew it was pointless. At least she could console herself with the fact she'd tried.

"Who the fonk are you?" demanded an expensively-dressed figure in the next room. There were three people in the room, not including Ronda. In a little under three minutes, there would be two. Or, at least, two living ones.

The man who had addressed Ronda was Katona, a Sloortian gang leader who'd made too many enemies back home on Sloorta, and had sold his services to Shornack, a notorious female warlord. Katona ran one of Shornack's space-based outposts, dealing in drugs, slaves, illegal tech and anything else that would bring Shornack a profit. Shornack, in return, generously resisted nailing his genitalia to a table, or devouring his skull.

Katona slouched in a large, imposing chair that had been positioned in pride of place across from the door. Two henchmen – the closest thing Katona had to friends, although they were quite some distance away from being that – stood up suddenly, hands reaching for blaster pistols strapped to their legs.

With a gesture, Katona told them to wait. He looked Ronda up and down, running his shovel-like hands over the ridges of his bald head. He curled a lip, deliberately showing off a mouth filled with gold teeth. "I'm gonna ask you again, old lady. Who the fonk are you?"

Ronda closed the door. There was a hook on the back of it, just as she knew there would be. She raised an index finger, gesturing for the men to wait, then removed her frying pan from her bag and hung it over the hook. She closed her eyes for a moment, remembering, then adjusted the pan's angle.

"Now," she said, turning and rubbing her hands together. "I've come for Narp."

Katona raised a sculpted eyebrow. "Say what?"

"Narp. My son. I've come to collect him."

The gangster raised his arms to gesture around the room, but Ronda jumped in.

"Oh, I know he's not here. I've known that since the day he was born." She tapped the side of her head. "I was a nun. I foresee a lot of things. Not everything, unfortunately, otherwise I could just have gone straight to find him. But I foresaw you telling me where to find him. I just didn't catch the actual location."

At the mention of the word 'nun' all three men had stiffened slightly. The henchmen's hands, which had frozen halfway to their blasters, inched closer.

"Me?" Katona said, snorting the word out in disbelief. "You think I'm gonna tell you where to find him?"

"Actually, not you, dear, no," Ronda admitted. She pointed to the henchman on the left. "He does. You'll be dead by then."

Katona's brow furrowed. He snarled, baring every one of his golden molars. "Hunch, smoke this bedge."

Hunch, the henchman on the left, drew his weapon and fired in one smooth motion. In one even smoother motion, Ronda leaned to her right. The blaster bolt scorched past her head, ricocheted off the frying pan, then rebounded off the room's solitary light fitting.

Katona's face registered a short-lived look of surprise, before his head exploded, showering his sidekicks with smoldering chunks of skull, brains, and several thousand credits worth of gold.

Hunch and the other henchman both watched silently as Katona's headless corpse slumped slowly forwards out of his chair, and hit the floor with a soft, but definite *thud*.

"Now," said Ronda, unhooking her scorched frying pan and hefting it from hand to hand with *precisely* the right amount of menace. "Where were we?"

CHAPTER TWO

Four minutes and one impeccably respectful conversation later, Ronda exited the elevator and shuffled across the station's lower docking bay, searching for a very specific ship.

Even after all these years, these converted mining stations took her breath away. The sheer scale of them — six hundred levels, all packed with homes, malls, museums, theaters, and other 'entertainment' she tended not to dwell on too much. The Zertex stations were even bigger, she'd heard, although she'd never had call to visit one, and hoped she never did.

She was reasonably confident she never did, of course, but there were a few aspects of even her own future which weren't entirely clear, so she kept her metaphorical fingers crossed, just in case.

A large group of children filed past, walking hand in hand in pairs. They were accompanied by four adults, spread out along the line. A school trip.

Regret gnawed at her conscience as the children skipped excitedly by her. So much so, in fact, that she felt compelled to step into the path of the trailing adult helper. He stopped instantly, his weight sliding onto his back heel. His already grimly-determined expression became even more so, and the way he held his hands suggested he not only knew how to use them, but also knew that harmless-looking old women were often anything but.

"You know what would be handy?" Ronda asked. The man's eyes darted across her, sizing her up.

"For you to get out my way?" he grunted.

"An animal vac-pack."

Ronda nodded curtly, then continued on her way. Without looking, she knew the man briefly watched her go, before hurrying to catch up with the rest of his group.

As she walked, Ronda allowed herself a smile. Some things she couldn't change, but other things, she could.

She found the ship just where she knew it would be. The code that opened the landing ramp was as she had foreseen, the 'enter' button precisely as stiff as she'd expected.

The pilot's expression of surprise was something she'd hadn't been anticipating. She took a moment to enjoy it, then took a seat in the gunner's chair behind him. The pilot was a thin, reedy young man with fish-like features and eyelashes that went on for days.

"How did you get in here?" he asked, his voice shaking with the shock. "Did I …? The ramp, I thought I'd …"

"You did, dear, relax. You're doing fine," Ronda assured him. "Now, you're going to take me to Tussk."

"Uh, no. No, I'm not."

Ronda sighed and placed her bag on her knees. As she talked, she rummaged inside. "Look, Marl – can I call you Marl? I'm going to call you Marl. Look, Marl, here's the situation. You worked for Katona. That was a mistake. You're a good boy, and I know you thought working for Katona would help with your money problems, but deep down, you knew it wasn't right. Right?"

Marl swiveled his chair around to face the old woman. "What are …? I don't … Look, who are you, lady? I still work for Katona." He shifted uncomfortably in his seat. "I mean, I do, right?"

"No, dear," said Ronda. She withdrew a neatly folded handkerchief from her bag and tossed it to Marl. It *chinked* as it landed in his lap. The young pilot's eyes widened as he unfolded the material and saw the contents. Gold teeth. Lots of gold teeth. "You work for me now. And we're going to Tussk."

Marl stared down at the teeth. There was still blood and chunks of gummy flesh clinging to a few of the larger pieces. He folded the handkerchief again and slipped it into his pocket, then raised his eyes to Ronda.

"And what if I just toss you off my ship and fly on out of here?"

"No, you don't do that," she said. "I'm not entirely sure what I threaten you with to convince you to take me, but take me you do." She smoothed down her slacks and fastened her seatbelt, then shot the pilot something that resembled a smile, but very much wasn't one. "I suggest, for both our sakes, you take me at my word on that."

She waited just long enough for the meaning behind her words to sink in, then held out a small paper bag. "Spit Nibble?"

* * *

Tussk grew in the viewscreen like an aggressive cancer, a malignant brown and gray blot rapidly expanding on a landscape of stars. It was a small, ugly moon circling a large, dead planet right at the edge of the Remnants – a once-thriving star system all but destroyed by Zertex in a yet-to-be-rivalled show of military force. Now, the Remnants was a breeding ground for gangsters, warlords, and other unsavory types. Ronda had spent a few years at a convent a little deeper into the system, back before Narp was born. It had been one of her more relaxing appointments.

"They're going to hail you in a moment and ask for the docking codes," Ronda said.

Marl tapped his earpiece. "Yeah. Got them now. What's the code?"

Ronda clasped her hands in her lap. "Unfortunately, I didn't foresee that part."

"What?!" Marl spluttered. "So how are we supposed to get permission to land?"

"Well, dear," said Ronda, flipping open the arm rests of her chair. A series of weapon controls unfolded, slid and locked into place around her. "That really depends on how you define 'permission'."

A stream of red warning text flashed across the viewscreen. "Ships! Incoming ships!" Marl yelped. "Four ... no, five. We have to get out of here. We can't fight them! Do you know who this is? Tussk is Xandrie territory. You do not fonk with the Xandrie. You just don't!"

"Shh, now, don't go getting your knickers in a twist," said Ronda. "Just pop flight control over to my station, there's a dear."

"What?! Are you nuts?! You can't pilot and gun at the same time. I mean, how—?"

"Marl. The flight controls. Hurry now."

Something about the way she said it made Marl do as he was told. Somehow, the idea of disappointing her was more terrifying that the thought of the approaching Xandrie ships. He tapped the necessary controls and his console went dark.

"All yours," he said, looking back over his shoulder. "Uh, you might want to put on the targeting visor," he suggested.

Ronda shook her head, just briefly. She hovered her fingers over the controls, slipped her hands into position, then leaned back and closed her eyes.

"What are you doing?" yelped Marl. He glanced at the screen. Five flashing red icons illuminated between them and Tussk, and quickly began spreading into an attack formation. "Open your fonking eyes! You can't see!"

"Don't need to see," said Ronda. "I need to remember."

"*Remember*? What the fonk are you talking about?"

Ronda opened one eye and swiveled it until it fixed on the terrified pilot. "Marl. Please."

She closed her eyes again. She inhaled slowly through her nose.

And then, she remembered.

She remembered the attack vectors of the Xandrie ships. She remembered the routes of their torpedoes, the projections from their plasma-guns.

She remembered the frequencies of their shields, and the corresponding angles at which controlled bursts of cannon-fire could punch right through.

She remembered the screaming, crackling at her over her headset.

When she'd finished remembering, she opened her eyes and found Marl staring at her, his eyes so wide his long lashes went vertical in both directions. Her fingers tapped across a series of keys, and Marl's controls hummed into life again.

"Take us down, dear," said Ronda. "Landing bay six is unoccupied."

Marl swallowed. "Uh, yeah. OK. Sure," he said, then he slowly swiveled his chair back to the front.

Ronda popped a Spit Nibble in her mouth and chewed on it. They were homemade, of course, and not bad, even if she said so herself. Tussk grew steadily larger, colors swimming across the screen as the ship descended through the atmosphere.

Much of the moon was shrouded in thick gray cloud. To the north, it was dangerously acidic, and anything above the equator was inhabitable only by a handful of species, and none of them anything you'd care to meet. The south was more hospitable, but still not somewhere you'd want to take a vacation. Or briefly visit. Or, if it could possibly be avoided, look at a photograph of.

The ship swept low over a terrain of angry-looking mountains. They stabbed at the sky like ragged sword-blades, as if the world below were fighting back against the clouds above.

Marl's scanners showed only one settlement for thousands of miles in any direction. It lurked like a spider in a nest of cliffs and ridges, one central hub attached by long corridors to eight landing bays. Marl swiped across a touchscreen and studied the schematics.

"Which one is—?"

"That one," said Ronda, pointing at one of the bays. The domed roof stood open, revealing an empty pad inside.

"So, what, they just left it open for us? Just like that?" asked Marl.

"Yes," said Ronda, picking up her bag and setting it on her knees. "Just like that. Now take us down. And keep the engine running."

* * *

The air smelled stale and second-hand when Ronda made her way down the ramp. She'd been expecting that, of course. Or had she? She couldn't quite recall.

A man and a woman waited for her, just as she'd known they would. She smiled at the woman and hoisted her bag higher on her shoulder. "So good of you to come out and meet me…"

Ronda reached for her name, but couldn't find it. She'd known it earlier, she could have sworn.

"…dear," she concluded.

The woman — a long-limbed, slender creature with pale yellow skin and a face like a startled giraffe — nodded slowly. "You've come for Narp."

The man beside her, with his low forehead and large tusks, was low-ranking muscle, Ronda knew.

Or thought.

No, *knew*. Or had known.

Or …

It hit her, then. The realization. The realization that she had no idea what was about to happen next.

And because of that — because she didn't know — she *did* know. And her blood ran cold in her veins.

"Oh, no," she whispered.

"Oh," said the woman, raising a small remote-control device. "Yes."

Ronda threw herself into a diving roll just as the platform erupted behind her. The heat propelled her across the bay, launching her towards the Xandrie woman and her sidekick.

She didn't need premonition to know what was happening to the ship, or to the young man aboard who had, as far as she had been aware, had his whole life ahead of him. Metal screamed as the hull of the ship exploded. A forcefield snapped up just inches from Ronda's back, shielding her and the Xandrie gangsters from the hail of flaming debris.

Premonition or not, she still had her instincts, still had her training.

She hit the ground awkwardly, but recovered quickly, rising into an uppercut that slammed into the man's groin. He grimaced, but only slightly, and Ronda felt a shock of pain explode across her knuckles.

"Armored," the man said, his voice hissing and slurring between his tusks. "Barely felt a thing."

He raised a foot to chest height and thrust it forwards. It was a big foot, and it moved quickly. Under normal circumstances, Ronda would have dodged before he'd even decided to kick, but her ability to predict the future was being blocked, and that could only mean …

She twisted sideways, narrowly avoiding the kick. As she turned, she hooked an arm around the man's calf, and jerked it sharply towards him. His knee discovered an angle it had wisely elected never to investigate before, and the brute dropped in a mess of tears and high-pitched screams.

"You *idiot*," the giraffe-faced woman spat. "I told you to stay on script."

"Is it you?" Ronda asked. She sized the woman up. "No, it's not you. Where is she? Do you tell me?"

Giraffe-face nodded slowly, then about-turned and walked with a sort of lumbering grace towards the mouth of the corridor. "This way. She's expecting you."

"Yes," said Ronda, straightening her pants suit and tightening her grip on her handbag. "Of course she is."

CHAPTER THREE

She saw Narp first. He sat at a terminal, his hands cuffed to his chair, a headjack locked into the port behind his right ear. Reams of blurry green text streaked across the screen of a battered old monitor positioned in front of him. He wouldn't be looking at it, Ronda knew. He didn't need to. She had her talents, and her son had his.

The handcuffs were tight around his wrists, the metal cutting into his flesh. This made her happy. Not because of the injuries — Narp had a tendency to milk such things, and she'd likely never hear the end of it — but because it suggested he was there against his will. She had probably known that already, but as there was now a gaping void in her head where the future had been, she found the sight of the cuffs reassuring, all the same.

Eight Xandrie sat, stood, slouched or *loomed* around the station's central hub. They were all from different species, some of which Ronda didn't recognize. There was a Greyx, all hair and muscle and snapping, wolf-like jaws. Across the scuffed metal table from him sat an orange-hued blob-like figure with a quivering, semi-transparent skin that showed most of his organs. Ronda had never encountered one of ... whatever he was before, and would be quietly pleased if she never did again. He grinned gummily at her, showing thousands of pin-like teeth.

Across the room, a partly-mechanized Symmorium leaned against a wall, his black, shark-like eyes staring at Ronda, cold and unblinking.

She skimmed across the others, then turned and settled on the woman lurking in the shadows behind the door Ronda herself and Giraffe-face had entered through. She hadn't known the woman would be there, but she had suspected. It was, after all, just what she would have done.

At the convent, they called them 'Imbukas'. They called them worse things, too, but 'Imbuka' was the official classification. Out in the world, though, most people thought of them as 'anti-nuns'. Fallen nuns who had turned away from one of the Five Paths, choosing instead to abuse their gifts for personal gain.

In many ways, Ronda was an Imbuka, too. She had set off along at least four of the Five Paths over the years, and had wandered off every one. There was a difference between 'wandering off' and 'attempting to eradicate from existence', however, and Ronda still considered herself much more 'nun' than 'anti'.

"Sister," she said, nodding in greeting.

The shadows fell away as the woman stepped out from behind the door. Her dirty red hair hung over her pale face like old theater drapes. An eye peered through the straggly strands, the pupil a deep, haunting black, the iris matching the red of her hair. Her ruby lips were stretched into a mockery of a grin, and her dark robe *swished* as she paced in a semi-circle around Ronda.

"Sister," the woman replied, nodding back.

"Ronda."

The woman giggled. It was a high-pitched hiss, like steam escaping from somewhere it probably shouldn't be. "Voss. And yes, I know."

Voss. Voss. The name was familiar, but Ronda couldn't place it. That was the problem with not having her premonition. If she had, she could simply have made a mental note to look the name up when she got home, then looked ahead to a point in time shortly afterwards. Now, all she had to go on was her memory, and her time at the convents had been a lifetime ago.

"I've come for my son," said Ronda. She knew Voss didn't need the visual clue, but she deliberately glanced towards Narp's motionless back, all the same.

That giggle came again, *hssssss-hssssss-hsssss*.

"We're using him," said the giraffe-faced woman.

"I know," said Ronda. "You're using him to decrypt Zertex security protocols so you can steal ..." Her eyes darted left and right, searching for the memory. "Something important. A device."

"A weapon," Giraffe-features corrected. "Once he's done, he's free to go."

Ronda almost accepted that, but something nagged at her. A memory of a memory that hadn't yet happened.

"No. They find out it's him. They take him away. I never see him again."

"Never gonna see him again anyways," whispered Voss, then she giggled again when Ronda threw her a dead-eyed look. "Never gonna get out of here alive, nun."

Ronda calculated the odds, and came to the rather depressing conclusion that the Imbuka was probably correct. She still had one card left to play, but while it might help earn Narp's freedom, it was unlikely to save her life.

She reached into her handbag. Around the room, five blasters turned in her direction. "It's not a weapon," she assured them.

Something green and dome-like rose out of the bag, followed a moment later by a pair of large, round eyes. The eyes could only be described as 'large' when compared to the rest of the head, however.

They were a fraction of the size of Ronda's eyes, for example, and yet they seemed to take up eighty-percent of the tiny cherubic face that appeared from within the bag.

"Alright?" said the creature, in a surprisingly gruff voice. He sat, cross-legged, on Ronda's hand, tapping out a rhythm on his knees.

The Xandrie all stared in silence at the little green man. Voss stared, too. Clearly, she hadn't been expecting him, but then that made sense. It would be taking all her concentration to block Ronda's premonition, meaning that when it came to the future, Voss was equally as blind.

The doll-sized man eyeballed them back, still tapping out his beat. Were they not part of the most feared criminal gang in the sector, the Xandrie would have to admit the guy was pretty fonking adorable. He looked like the cartoon mascot for a 'Galaxy's Cutest Baby' competition, and while at least one of the gang members wanted to eat him alive, most just wanted to take him home and put him on a shelf.

"What the fonk you all staring at, you soppy sacks of shizz?" the little man snarled. "I heard you got a hacking job you need doing."

"Mr Thundercrotch here is the *second* best hacker in the system," said Ronda. "He assures me he's more than capable of breaking into the systems you require, and – unlike my son – he's prepared to do so willingly. I hoped you might be prepared to make a straight swap, and let my boy go."

"*Thundercrotch?*" snorted the giraffe-faced woman.

The little man shifted his eyes towards her and waggled his eyebrows suggestively. "You'd better believe it, sweetheart. Thundercrotch by name ..."

He bounded up so he was standing on Ronda's hand, did a quite aggressive sort of war-dance, then thrust his hips forward. "Thundercrotch by—"

A set of canine jaws snapped down, devouring Thundercrotch whole. Ronda looked up into the dark brown eyes of the wolf-like Greyx. He swallowed with some difficulty, then flicked his long red tongue across his lips.

"Sorry. Couldn't resist," he said, flashing a few teeth in Ronda's direction, before turning and heading back to his seat.

Ronda stared at her palm, which was now empty, aside from a dribble of Greyx drool. She looked over at her son, still jacked in, still oblivious to her presence. She felt a weight in her chest, a sadness radiating outwards like rot spreading through her insides.

Nine Xandrie. One Imbuka. She'd survived worse, although never without her premonition, and never without injury. She'd been younger then, too. Faster. Stronger.

But age brought benefits also. Wisdom. Experience. And, more importantly, a fonking heavy handbag.

Ronda spun, swinging her bag out and flicking a hidden switch on the handle. Twin blades snapped horizontally outwards from the base. Voss ducked, but cut it too close for it to be premonition. Still, she was fast and well-trained. That could be a problem.

Giraffe-face was neither of those things. Ronda arced the bag upwards and the blade made a satisfying *thunk* as it embedded in the side of the woman's skull.

Blaster-fire screamed across the room. Ronda ducked for cover behind the giraffe-woman, who still teetered on her long, slender legs. With a flick of her wrist, Ronda yanked the bag-blade free and the woman folded like a house of cards, her arms and legs all splaying in different directions on the floor.

"Get her!" roared one of the Xandrie, but Voss's screech brought them to a halt.

"Wait!" the Imbuka screamed. Her eyes danced behind her curtain of hair. "The nun is mine."

She lunged, without warning, hands outstretched, hair wafting back behind her to reveal a vicious leer. Ronda swung with her bag, but Voss was already too close. The Imbuka's hands found Ronda's throat. A knee found her solar plexus. Ronda's chest constricted, forcing her to gasp for breath that would not come.

Trying to break the grip was pointless, so she went for the eyes. Her thumbs pressed hard against Voss's eyeballs, and the Imbuka pulled back, hissing and spitting with rage.

Ronda swung with the bag again, but Voss's leg snapped up, her foot slamming into the older woman's wrist. Pain flared up Ronda's arm. Her grip on the bag slipped and it clattered to the ground, spilling coins, handkerchiefs, mints, reading glasses and half a bag of Spit Nibbles across the floor.

Voss struck like a cobra at Ronda's throat with her three middle fingers. Ronda managed to deflect, twist, and drove an elbow towards Voss's face. The younger woman half-dodged, turning a devastating nose-splitter into a glancing blow.

Arms moved, twisted, struck, blocked. There was nothing flashy about the fighting, no flying kicks or spinning backhands. The style could best be described as 'devastatingly functional' and, had either woman been fighting another opponent, the emphasis would have been heavily on the 'devastating' part.

Ronda landed a solid forearm strike across the bridge of Voss's nose, staggering the younger woman. For a moment, the future poured back into Ronda's head like sand, but then the Imbuka recovered and it was gone again.

It bought her an extra half-second warning for the next strike, though, and she ducked quickly, then followed up with two firm strikes to Voss's kidneys, or whatever the local equivalent of kidneys was. Whatever Voss kept down there in her lower back, the strikes hurt. She stumbled forwards, and Ronda moved in to finish her off.

The Imbuka spun sharply. Ronda caught a glimpse of something shiny and metallic, but her momentum carried her on.

She barely felt the blade slipping into her stomach. It wasn't until Voss twisted the handle, and that hiss of a giggle escaped her lips again, that Ronda fully grasped just what had happened.

The floor came up to meet her. Ronda heard the cheers of the Xandrie as she fell. She saw them, blurred by tears. Aside from the Greyx, who remained seated, they were all on their feet, whooping and cheering and baying for blood.

Ronda breathed. It gargled in her throat. She clutched her stomach where the knife was buried, and felt the blood seeping out from beneath the ornate handle.

Voss stood over here, giggling, her hair falling back into place in front of her face. Her laughter, and the cheering, were drowned out by the *whooshing* of Ronda's heartbeat – fast and frantic, but slowing rapidly.

The Greyx was sitting down. That was important. Ronda thought she remembered something about that, but the pain and the fear and the panic pushed the thought away.

hingIt was something she was unused to, panic. There was no need for panic when you knew what was going to happen next. Now, she didn't even know if she would have a 'next'. At the rate her blood was seeping from her gut wound, she doubted it.

Her eyes fell on the scattered contents of her bag. Her homemade Spit Nibbles lay strewn around her, partially crushed from the fight. She found herself reaching for one. Her fingers flaked off the pastry, revealing the dark orange filling inside.

There were Spit Nibbles.

And the Greyx was sitting down.

With some effort, Ronda began to laugh. It was weak and frail, yet it soon rose to fill every space in the room as Voss and the Xandrie fell quiet.

"What's so funny, *nun*?" Voss demanded, spitting out that last word like it left a bad taste in her mouth.

"Spit Nibbles," Ronda wheezed.

Voss frowned behind her hair. "What?"

"Do you know when I learned to make Spit Nibbles?"

When no response came, Ronda shrugged. "No, me neither. See, no-one showed me. I just saw the recipe in my future, and started making them."

She caught her breath. In the silence, she heard the Greyx groan.

"But I must learn the recipe at some point, otherwise how would I know it now?" said Ronda. "And if I know it now, then I survive this."

Ronda's face darkened. "And if I have time to learn the art of Spit Nibbles, that means I haven't dedicated myself to hunting down everyone in this room and killing them all." She adjusted her position on the floor. "And the only way *that* would happen, is if you're all already dead."

Across the room, the Greyx stood up sharply. He clutched at his stomach, his eyes bulging in panic. "What ... what is h-happening to me?"

he managed to wheeze, and then everything from his crotch to his chest exploded, spraying his colleagues in blood, guts, and burning chunks of furry flesh.

Thundercrotch erupted from the wolf-man's torso, a tiny blaster pistol in his hands and an expression of unbridled rage twisting up his face.

"Die, you motherfonkers!" he howled, rolling on the ground and spraying blaster fire at the shock-frozen Xandrie.

Voss gawped in surprise, then looked down at Ronda, but the old woman was gone.

A blood-soaked blade pressed against the Imbuka's throat. "I could be wrong, dear, but it's quite possible I *did* see all this coming, after all."

Voss jabbed back an elbow, but Ronda had anticipated it and edged aside. "Isn't it funny how things work out?" Ronda whispered, then she pulled the blade across Voss's pale skin, and a thin line of red followed behind it.

The future returned. Ronda turned and hurled the knife through the air, burying it into the chest of a tall, angular Xandrie with a hooked nose and feathery hair.

The semi-transparent orange blob raised a rifle and fired on her. Ronda marched forwards, avoiding each shot before it was fired. The gangster's eyes became larger and more panic-filled as she drew closer.

He lowered the gun, too late, and tried to hit Ronda with the stock, but she was on him then, her arm around his neck. She removed what was left of his life with a surgical *crack*, caught his blaster as he fell, and killed three of the remaining Xandrie with one perfectly-aimed shot.

She let Thundercrotch take care of the last one – a particularly stocky creature with skin like a dirty potato – then nodded at the little man in acknowledgement.

"Thank you, dear," she said.

Thundercrotch sniffed and shrugged. "We're square now, right?"

"Yes, dear. We're square."

Tucking his blaster into the back of his doll-sized pants, Thundercrotch nodded at the blood stain blooming across Ronda's front.

"You should get that looked at."

"I do," Ronda assured him. "It's touch and go for a while, but ultimately, it looks worse than it is."

She nodded, pleased, and allowed herself a smile. It was good to be back.

Thundercrotch looked over to where Narp was still at his terminal, text flooding the screen before him. There was something else on the screen, too. A diagram. A diagram of something very large. "Want me to go unplug him?"

"Hmm?" said Ronda. "Oh, no. It's fine. Leave him to it."

The little man frowned. "Huh? I thought you wanted to get him out of here."

Ronda tilted her head left and right. "Well, that wasn't strictly true," she said. "This weapon, I don't want Zertex keeping it, but I couldn't let the Xandrie get their hands on it, either."

"So … what? You're taking it for yourself?"

"Me? Goodness, no, dear. I wouldn't be able to make use of such a device."

The future unfolded before her, and a grin spread across her face. It was a good future. Not perfect, because nothing ever is. But good enough.

"But I know a man who can …"

Author Barry J. Hutchison

Barry J. Hutchison is a multi-award-winning author, screenwriter and writer of comics from the Highlands of Scotland. Despite this, he has never once hunted a haggis, or gone a-roamin' in the gloamin'. He does, however, regularly toss his caber. It'll probably make him go blind. Barry loves writing action-packed scifi, and his biggest fear is that someone will discover how much fun he is having, and immediately put a stop to it. His second biggest fear is squirrels.

Get some free books from Barry at
http://barryjhutchison.com/freebooks

Intuition: A Galactic Warriors Short Story Prequel

By Monica Leonelle

ONE

"Ay, zir!" The entire Galactic Alliance Phoenix battalion snaps to attention on the commander's deck.

Her bi-gender commander Orion glares at her. "Abell, I can't hear you!"

"Ay, zir!" Teague Abell shouts, snapping to attention too late.

She swears under her breath. She's distracted. Again.

Orion hovers over her. She knows ze thinks she's too soft, too weak, too lost in her own world to be a soldier on the Night Phoenix, but she is one of the few trained intuitives left in the Galactic Alliance, and ze is stuck with her.

Today, though, Orion has no time for disciplining her slip up. Today, they battle.

"To your posts!" ze shouts. The battalion scatters across the deck, preparing to take out one of the Consortium's starships they've been stealth tracking for days.

Teague moves toward her commander. "Zir." She salutes Orion.

"What is it?" ze barks. Orion is of average height, but ze towers over her all the same.

"I still think there's something off about this mission. I felt it again when you were addressing us. The other starship is not moving correctly."

"We've run the numbers," Zir restates. "The difference you're sensing is imperceptible on all of our tests."

She exhales. "I can't explain it. Something's off. We're missing something."

Zir's eyes narrow at her. "And you're sure this isn't about him?"

It's the second time ze's asked.

"I know what's at stake," she says, feeling fully the sting of not being taken seriously. It happens to her frequently in a world that values numbers, data, and science. Even though Orion knows about her gifts for sensing what cannot be explained through science, ze only takes action on her intel about half the time.

The Galactic Alliance has a saying, "Intuition can show us where in the data to look." She can't back up her intuitive hits with the numbers this time. But she has to try to convince zir anyway.

"You better know what's at stake," Orion says. "You know Nova London holds nearly thirty percent of our military assets. If the Consortium launches a successful attack against it, the war is as good as lost."

"And you know my parents and two brothers live near the city," she replies. She juts out her chin, meeting zir eyes. "I would never choose old friends over my family. Costello and Monserrat are the enemy now."

Orion watches her as she speaks. Ze is trained in bullshit detecting, but she can tell ze believes her, even when she doesn't fully believe herself.

Costello and Montserrat were a lot more than friends to her, once upon a time. But on paper, they are old gaming buddies, from back before the 7-Planet Wars started.

"We're moving forward with the counterattack," Orion says quietly to her. "Are you with us, or should I dismiss you?"

"I respectfully ask you to reconsider," she says one last time.

"To your post, Abell. Otherwise, get off my deck."

She closes her eyes and nods. She tried.

She walks to her post, velcroing her gloves and headgear into place as she dodges around the frantic engineers who control the ship. It takes about a hundred of them to steer a starship this big, but she's not a part of the starship flight crew, though she's flown a 6-person pod in the past on her own.

She has a different job. Her favorite part about joining the military is that she gets to fly weapons with her best friend from home.

"Ready to blow up some Consorts?" Laszlo asks her as she jumps down into their pit and slides into their flight pad. He has been her flying partner since they both enlisted, and her best friend long before that.

"Shut the frot up," she tells him, before they can get into another argument.

"Better not let Orion hear you talk like that. Those frotters deserve everything comin' to them."

Laszlo knows that she dated Costello two years back and knows that his best friend, Monserrat, is one of the junior command on Hail Hermione 4, the Consortium ship they are about to blow to next Tuesday.

He knows the three of them used to game together and got so close that Costello made the trip to her planet, Ronan, to visit.

Laszlo even met said ex-boyfriend during that visit, not that he liked him much.

But he doesn't understand why she still cares about two Hermionians when their planets are at war with each other, when every teenager age 15-19 serves one of the two remaining militaries.

"They are soldiers," she whispers back. "Drafted into a war they never started. Just like us."

"Get your head in the game, Teague," he replies. "I need you today. Can't do this without you."

She nods, resolved to be there for her friend, for her family, for her planet. She doesn't agree with everything the military purports. But a mission is a mission, and if the Galactic Alliance can't avoid it, she might as well do a good job completing it.

The Hail Hermione 4 slows in front of them, and they ease up on their speed, too. They get up about a quarter-klick away on the side of it, close enough to see into the other ship's windows. Something tugs in her stomach when she sees him. Montserrat stands at attention next to his commander and a few other juniors, staring out at Ronan and pointing.

She can't see to the left of her, where Ronan would be, but she sees the energy and light gathering at the base of the ship from their laser weapon. She imagines it pointing at her hometown, imagines her younger twin brothers staring up into the sky watching a great space weapon gear up to strike them, and her resolve hardens. The Hail Hermione 4 won't be able to detect them for a few more minutes as their own weapons heat up. The cloaking technology can hide only a certain amount of energy, but they have a few more minutes.

The Hail Hermione 4 won't know what hit 'em.

Out of nowhere, the other starship moves, turning toward them.

"Shit," she says, feeling an unsettling tug in her stomach. "Wrong positioning, I bet."

Laszlo nods, which unnerves her further. Something about the other starship's choices don't make sense, but she knows there's no point in overthinking it. No one else sees it, and they all have a point. Intuitives get it wrong sometimes, especially when personal emotions are involved.

There's no data to back it up, she reminds herself.

Together, Laszlo and she down the laser, knowing they have to move it into a new position to compensate for how fast their own ship, the Night Phoenix, can maneuver. The Hail Hermione 4 is weakest at its sides. They'll never have enough firepower to take 'em down quickly from the front.

"Ease up!" Orion shouts, and the junior commanders shout orders to their respective divisions. The battalion moves quickly, but is it enough?

"When all of this is over," Laszlo tells her, "We're going to take our kids to the Waterfalls and tell them about how we once made sure there would still be Waterfalls to go to."

He jokes about them getting married and having kids all the time, and she's not exactly opposed to it. She knows how unlikely it is that they both survive the war. Plus, who else would she marry, if it came to that? Laszlo knew her back when they were toddlers. And it's not like she wants an arranged marriage to a stranger.

"Deal," she says lightly. It helps him focus when she plays along, and they both need to focus right now.

They maneuver their weapon into place as the commander's deck quiets.

And then, they wait for their next order.

TWO

3 years earlier

She moves forward down the alleyway on gut instinct, her guild close behind her. Costello turns slightly left and they move back-to-back as Monserrat turns right to sneak up behind their enemy.

He disappears into the trees, leaving the two lovers alone.

"I'll distract them, you do the data upload," Stel says.

"There's no way you'll evade capture," she says. "I have better health. I'll distract."

He laughs easily. "Not a chance I would let you do the more dangerous job. Besides, Mons has my back."

"You won't make it to the next level if you die," she insists. "I'll distract."

"Fine," he says with a grin. He leans down to kiss her quickly before he turns and runs, right into the main street.

She watches two players in one of the enemy guilds take after him, just as he wants. Distraction. She's resentful that he made the choice for her, especially when she doesn't want to get stuck with Monserrat for the rest of the game. They still have ten days of play, and the game is the only place she can see and touch and smell Stel as if they live on the same planet. Virtcomm technology just isn't the same.

She hears the gunshots, which means Monserrat is in position. The remaining players of the other guild hear it too. Monserrat's set up several shots to go off, so it looks like there are more players attacking than just the three of them.

She waits until the other team is distracted and rushes to the sheltered base. She matches several wires together and hits some buttons to pull the data from their base, then upload the data she has. She sets her device down and hides behind a huge nearby vehicle, hoping the other team won't notice it sitting there.

Shots keep going off, and one even hits one of the enemy guild members. Monserrat laughs into her earpiece against the background of Stel's heavy panting—her only clue that he's still alive.

About five minutes pass until she checks the data to make sure the uploads and downloads are complete. Check and check. She loads it into her pack and ducks back into the alley so she can find Stel and escape to their rendezvous point to meet Monserrat and move to the next level.

She reaches the other end of the alley, and there they are, two enemy guild players holding Stel hostage, one with a gun pointing at his head, the other with a gun pointed at her.

She pulls her gun from its holster and aims at the one who has Stel, only to hear a lock and load to the side of her.

"Drop it, gun moll," the enemy player says.

Dumb, misogynistic shits.

She trains her gun on the guy holding Stel, still. She isn't going to let him die and get kicked out of the game.

Stel locks eyes with her, shaking his head slightly as she moves toward him, gun pointed at his captor. The other guy sees her goal and puts his gun to Stel's head. Now, he's got two pointing at him.

She stops, seeing the desperation of the situation. Where the frot is Monserrat?

A single shot picks off the enemy behind her. Without turning around, she immediately fires on the closest enemy in front of her and hits him, but she can't get the other guy before he blows Stel's brains.

Monserrat appears at her side, easily nailing the third in the chest just a split-second too late to save Stel.

Teague runs to Stel, kneeling down beside him, but he took a shot to the head. He's dead as dirt.

She looks up at Monserrat. "What the frot is wrong with you?"

"I could only save one of you," Monserrat says. "You have the data; he had two bullets aiming at his head."

"He's out of the game for good now, you dolt!" She bites back her tears. Days and days of playing without seeing Stel, and it's not like she can quit. They're so close to racking up enough points for the invitation-only tournament, and not finishing would set them back too far to catch up that year.

"Sacrifices have to be made sometimes," Monserrat says with a shrug. "Come on."

"You could have let them kill me," she says angrily, following after Monserrat to the drop point. "Stel might have survived. You could have picked up the pack and seen me on the next level."

"Well, I didn't," Monserrat says. "I saved the person with the data. Stel would have agreed with me."

She glares at him, wondering if he did it on purpose out of jealousy or spite. The two guys are best friends, but that doesn't mean Monserrat isn't competitive. He's an alpha type, and Stel's a beta type, and that's probably the only reason the two can stand each other in the first place.

No, she tells herself. Monserrat just wants to protect the data. She knows it's the better calculation, to save her over Stel. It pisses her off all the same, but that's Monserrat.

Don't get in the way of his win.

THREE

"Easy," Laszlo says as they move in sync to point the laser at the Hail Hermione 4.

"Three, two, one—" They both push at the same time, firing a burst of energy toward the other starship.

Boom! They hit the side of the other starship, busting through the last of its shields.

She loves the ease and simplicity of this part of her job. It takes two people who can work in synchronicity to operate one of the large lasers, and she got lucky that she tested so well with Laszlo.

He is the better aim, the true space cowboy who can control his body to accomplish impressive feats. He was always in either way.

She, on the other hand, is just an average soldier with intuition training, which helps her match Laszlo's movements. Doesn't hurt that she's spent every day with him since they were kids.

Most soldiers consider the pit a high-stress job because it's so mission-critical and the pit is claustrophobia-inducing, but the compactness of the space keeps her calmer, and the synchronized movements required feel like dancing rather than warring.

Drones circle them, but they pick them off one by one with laser rifles. It only takes one drone to get a good hit and take them or the laser out, so they have to get them all. Laszlo gets more than her, but she's good enough to be useful.

The laser recharges, and they step back into the flight pad.

"One last time," Laszlo says, "on my count. Three, two, one—"

The laser fires, striking the Hail Hermione 7 with a critical, ship-separating explosion.

"Yes!" Laszlo shouts, jumping up and down.

Cheers and whooping explode above them as the Hail Hermione 7 splits in two in a fiery blaze. Several pods release from the ship, but their job is done—Orion will send fighters after them to keep them from escaping.

She gulps, watching the laser on the other side fire. With this hit, the ship breaks down to pieces, scattering outward.

They did it, but all she feels is despair.

Her hometown is safe, but her intuition tugs at her stomach again. The ship explosion is... off. She knows it. But she can't explain it, or prove it, or get anyone to take her seriously when she's so close to one of the junior commanders aboard...

She high fives Laszlo, pushes her concerns from her mind and tries to smile.

They did it.

She thinks of her mom, her dad, her twin brothers...

They are safe. That was all that mattered.

In the end, she would choose her family over an old friend from another planet any day.

FOUR

When Costello came to Ronan two years ago, he stayed for nearly a month with her family, on their farm right outside Nova London. Daylight never ends on Ronan, unlike Hermione, where the planet rotates over 84 hours. Stel's circadian rhythm got all frot up, and he suffered insomnia, so he snuck into her bedroom when the rest of the family was sleeping.

They had a lot of sex; she remembers that. They talked about the Galactic's ongoing tensions between the inner and outer planets. They planned her visit to his little village on the planet of Hermione, though she knew her parents could never afford to send her.

What she remembers most about his visit was when he told her about how he met Monserrat.

Stel's father used to beat him, and Monserrat, a neighborhood boy, found out. One day when Mons heard it happening behind Stel's house, he brought his dad's laser rifle to the back field and threatened Stel's dad until he let him go.

Stel and his mom and his little sister didn't go home after that. They moved into Monserrat's house with his mom and dad and brothers, and then a few years later, moved out again, but this time on their own.

Monserrat saved Stel's life, and she had just helped kill him.

"Teague," Laszlo says, ducking his head through the door of her quarters. "Get out here. You look weak not celebrating our win."

"I'm not feeling well," she says. It isn't a lie; the tug in her stomach is back and stronger than before.

Doesn't matter if Monserrat's dead, she reminds herself. Any relationship with Stel is long gone. They don't speak anymore, not since the war forbade them.

She still cares for him, though. She still wants him to find happiness once the war is over, hopefully after the Galactic Alliance wins.

What if she made a mistake?

FIVE

She forces herself to follow Laszlo back to the commander's deck, where a bunch of soldiers are getting piss drunk.

Orion looks troubled, staring at a screen. Given the tug in her stomach, she wanders over on instinct.

"What is it?" she asks. Laszlo appears beside her, equally concerned.

Ze looks up at them, eyes wide, face long. "To your posts," ze whispers. Ze stands up. "To your posts!" ze yells.

The drunk soldiers hesitate, as if unsure if it's a drill or not.

"To your posts!" ze yells again, with urgency.

Something clicks and everyone moves. She pulls on her gear, velcroing it into place, wondering what kind of shit storm they are flying into.

Laszlo drops into their pit and she follows, seeing the problem immediately.

"Hail Hermione 7," she says out loud, shocked.

Stel's starship, where he does the same job as her.

And it's aiming right at Nova London, about to blow it up.

Without waiting for orders, she heats up their laser.

"Abell! Stop!" Orion orders into her earpiece. She doesn't listen.

Laszlo pulls on her arm. "Are you nuts?" he asks. "You can't fire that without the commander—"

"Strap in," she says, "Or so help me Las I will—"

She doesn't know how to finish the sentence; she's blinded by the ship in front of her, ready to wipe out her home.

He wants to take out Nova London.

Costello wants to take out her home.

For the Consortium?

For revenge against her, tit for tat?

She doesn't know. She only knows that if her hometown is blown to pieces, it will be her fault.

The tug in her stomach gets stronger still, but at least Las is at her side. Orion can't reach them in the pit, which means ze can't stop them, and their cloaking technology is faulting. Ze orders the Night Phoenix to move into position, to take up arms against the Hail Hermione 7.

They aim at Hail Hermione 7's side, and fire in sync from both pits, landing two hits on the starship, damaging it.

But it's too late. A long light extends from the other ship's front underside, releasing into space and traveling toward the planet Ronan.

Teague's stomach sinks and her body goes limp as she watches in horror out the glass panels.

Because that isn't the only light that goes. All through the expansive space, as far as she can see, dozens of lasers fire on Ronan, most likely attacking major cities and military assets.

Across her planet, large bursts of orange and smoke dot the surface.

Her parents. Her brothers. Her planet.

This isn't just a battle. This is the end of the Galactic Alliance.

Checkmate.

"Frot," Orion mutters. "Everyone on deck!" ze orders. Ze's holding zir ear, likely receiving instructions from other commanders, whoever is left of the fleet. Their ground assets are likely destroyed, and she imagines they will be soon, too.

"Retreat!" ze orders. "Set a course for Tonks." The Night Phoenix slowly reverses as the windows light up white. Someone is firing on them.

Ze gestures for Teague and Laszlo and when they reach zir, hands them each a pouch of pills. "One per soldier, entire battalion. Tell them if we don't make it to Tonks, or if we're boarded for any reason, their commander orders them to take it. These mother frotters won't get shit from us, you hear me?"

Teague nods, taking the pouch. Laszlo leaves the deck, likely heading to the engineering rooms, while Teague distributes pills to each of the pilots, engineers, and data analysts on deck.

The commander's deck doors open and the enemy walks in, headed by Monserrat.

She freezes at the sight of him.

"Grab her," Monserrat orders, pointing at her. "And don't let her take one of those damn pills. Rip it from her throat if you have to."

She flails wildly in three enemy soldiers' grip, but they wrench the bag of pills from her before she can take one. Orion struggles against zir captors as well until they tase zir limp. They carry zir out of the commander's deck like a sack of potatoes.

Monserrat's men gun down several of her crewmates, Night Phoenix soldiers, but he keeps his eyes trained on her. He turns to his second and whispers something she can't hear, then grabs her arm, dragging her through the deck doors.

She doesn't struggle against him—no real point. He's about three times her size, and he is gripping her wrist like he could snap it at any second.

She accuses him. "You set me up. You used our childhood friendship against me. You used Costello against me."

He says nothing, so she turns toward him, punching him in the chest.

He grabs her arm to control her but doesn't hurt her unnecessarily.

"Admit it!" she yells. One of his soldiers looks up from wrangling her crewmates into surrender, and Monserrat wrestles her around the corner and against a wall.

She spits in his face. "I'll never forgive you for this."

He smirks, wiping his face across his sleeve. "Sacrifices have to be made sometimes."

He grabs her again, this time with a firmer grip, and drags her down three levels to the flight deck. Along the way, she hears whispers, the name Costello—*her* Costello—on the enemy soldiers' tongues. They are proclaiming him a hero of the Consortium for blowing up Nova London as his starship took hit after hit.

Her heart feels broken, unmendable at this specifically.

Monserrat jostles her toward a pod. Her lip quivers as she holds back her tears. Her parents, her brothers, her ex-boyfriend, her friends, her planet her military... everything she's ever cared about is gone in a single day. She lifts her chin, determined not to show him weakness. "What the frot do you want with me?"

There's a hint of regret and pain in his eyes before he callously shoves her into a life support pod. "Just following orders, Teague." His voice has notes of softness undulating through it, but his face is hard.

He hits a button to release her pod and it shoots into space, filling with gas that she knows will put her to sleep within sixty seconds.

The only thing she knows is the Consortium wants something from her. Otherwise, why would they let her live?

She gets one last look at her planet, her beautiful home of Ronan before the gas takes her to unconsciousness.

Author Monica Leonelle

Monica Leonelle was born in Germany and spent her childhood jet-setting around the world with her American parents. Her travels include most of the United States and Europe, as well as Guam, Japan, South Korea, Australia, and the Philippines.

She's written over half a million words of fiction spread across several genres and series, most notably her young adult urban fantasy series, *Waters Dark and Deep*. Monica started reading young adult books when she was seven and never managed to grow out of them. She LOVES *Harry Potter, Twilight, The Hunger Games,* and *The Mortal Instruments*.

Monica lives in a very, very old, 3-story home in St. Louis, MO with her husband and adorable Westie, Mia. It possibly has ghosts. And definitely has a secret passage. To find out what happens next to Teague, Monserrat, and Costello, check out the *Galactic Warriors* series at MonicaLeonelle.com/galactic.

Panic Button

By Samantha Maguire

CHAPTER ONE

Captain Kate Sharpe stared down at the impressive array of illegal weapons spread out on top of the dirty bedcover inside of a room that smelled of desperation, gun oil, and rat piss.

"That's a really nice gun."

The vendor looked up from pretending to clean his nails and followed Sharpe's line of sight with a grunt and a nod. "She's the best I got." He picked up the shotgun and checked the empty chamber before handing it to her.

Solid. Heavy. Three hundred years old if it was a day. Sharpe ran her fingers along the polished steel barrel and a chill tickled down her spine. Love at first sight. Anyone who didn't believe in soulmates had never met a weapon like that. Crafted in an old-fashioned, bulky style, it was heat built for one purpose: to dominate.

Sharpe pressed the butt into her shoulder and stared down the sights along the barrel, a redundant and technically unnecessary feature—it was hard to miss with a shotgun like this; just aim it in a general direction and squeeze the trigger—but one that made Sharpe's heart beat all the faster. Before her, a dingy wall with cracking paint and a frosted window came into focus. Sharpe took a breath and inhaled the tangy metallic scent of cold steel. Her finger instinctively bent to caress the trigger. One shell and she could melt that wall and all its dirty secrets with it. She needed this gun. More than she could remember needing anything ever, she needed this gun.

"How much for this one?" Lisa Runner's voice didn't break the spell, but when Sharpe glanced over her shoulder to see that her chief mate held up a tiny, practical, five-year-old pistol, she lowered the barrel.

"Oh, Runner, what the hell?"

The vendor reached around his broad girth to scratch at a dirty elbow. "Part with her for two-hundred credits."

Runner turned the weapon over in her hand, frowning. She passed it from one hand to another with exaggerated movements, as though the gun was light and cheap, which of course it was. "Not a lot of scrap for two hundred, Bern."

The man shrugged. "Best I can do, sweetie."

Runner tossed the gun back onto the bed, where it clattered on top of another polyalloy shooter with an unimpressive *clink*. "Nothing here, then," she said to Sharpe.

"I disagree." Sharpe's fingers wrapped tighter around the body of the shotgun in her hands.

Runner rolled her eyes. "Come on, boss. We have an appointment to keep."

Sharpe gripped tighter still, even as the vendor moved toward her with his hand extended. "I could use this."

"Seriously? You can't even get that out of here and back to the ship. We have nothing to hide it in. It won't fit down your pants."

Sharpe glanced down at her left leg. Not her favorite leg. Did she need it as badly as she needed that shotgun? Hard to say.

Runner didn't wait for Sharpe to come to her senses and she made for the door. The vendor had just enough time to wrench the shotgun from Sharpe's stubborn hands and toss a blanket over the private arsenal before Runner hit the button on the wall with the side of her fist and the door flew up, exposing the room to the dark motel hallway.

Sharpe frowned at the lump under the blanket where her beloved lay, so close and so far away, before jogging to catch up with her chief mate.

"We couldn't afford it, anyway," Runner said.

"That's what bartering is for," said Sharpe.

"Yeah? And what have you got to barter with?"

"My winning personality."

Runner let out a loud belly laugh that caught the attention of a hooker and her nervous date who was fighting with the lock of a door. First timer, figured Sharpe.

"That and a hundred-thousand credits will buy you the firepower of your dreams," said Runner.

"A girl has *needs*, Lisa."

A light popped and sputtered above them. Only half of the overhead lights in the hallway worked, and most of those flickered intermittently, giving the hallway a kind of alley-like gloom. But the heavy, almost overpowering, earthy scent of mildew that hung in the air and the glimpses of dark mold slowly crawling out of the shadows into warped Rorschach blots were enough to discourage patrons from asking for more illumination. No one wanted to see what those surfaces *really* looked like.

The John was still fighting with the lock as the two women passed. He glanced up after every attempt, no doubt embarrassed of his defeat at the hands of a motel door. The hooker knew the routine, though, and she kept her eyes unfocused ahead of her. Sharpe caught a whiff of cologne as they passed the pair. She spotted his clean hair, cheap but unwrinkled clothes, and trimmed fingernails. Dolled up for a hired date? *Definitely* a first timer.

"Looks like they're really trying to class up the joint," Sharpe whispered.

Runner smirked. "Not like it could get much worse. I mean, really, the only way you go from here is up."

A door to their left rose and the mechanism in need of oil or maybe beyond oil and in need of a scrapyard squealed and screamed in complaint. Sharpe felt her teeth vibrate from the noise and she winced. An uncomfortable buzzing shock rose up through her feet in a way that felt so real that she couldn't be certain the circuitry beneath their feet hadn't misfired and electrocuted her.

Sharpe massaged her jaw as she and Runner stepped out of the way of a maid exiting the room with her telltale cart. The women exchanged surprised glances and watched as the cleaner walked down in the direction they had just come from.

"A *maid*?" asked Sharpe. "*Here*? They have maids here?"

Runner stood next to her and shook her head, staring back. "I mean, you figured the sheets got changed sometime, right?"

"I thought they just had semi-regular incinerations. You know, like after a body's gone ripe and there's no amount of chlorine that will bring that fabric back from…" Sharpe's voice trailed as she watched the maid pass the next room. She felt Runner tense beside her.

The air hung heavy with the bitter, unmistakable sensation familiar to any mercenary.

Something was *wrong*.

"Nice boots," whispered Runner. Sharpe glanced down at the woman's shoes. Runner wasn't lying, they were nice boots. Too nice for a maid, and hardly practical footwear for someone to be cleaning in all day. She glanced back at the now-silent John, who'd given up his sad fight with the door lock to stare at her and Runner. Beads of sweat on his forehead caught the weak fluorescent lighting from above.

The scene came together in Sharpe's mind and she felt a rush as instinct took over.

"Run," she said, even before she'd moved. Runner didn't need much convincing, and as she turned to launch down the hallway toward the airlift, the maid reached the arms dealer's door and held up her keycard. Sharpe heard the door whoosh as it opened and it wasn't until the maid drew a gun from out of her cart and pointed it into the room that Sharpe's own body kicked in and she spun and raced to join her chief mate, already three steps ahead.

"Stop!" called a masculine voice from behind. "Allied Authority, stop where you are!"

So he wasn't a John, after all. The cop was quick and Sharpe could hear him on her heels, but she was quicker, and she kept just out of his grasp.

Sharpe could hear the maid's voice down the hallway. "Get down on the ground! Down on the ground, now!" and it spurred her faster. She was gaining distance on the John, and as she and Runner rounded the hallway toward the airlift, she thought that they might just get lucky enough to get a lead wide enough that they could get into the lift.

There was more yelling from behind, but Sharpe was running on adrenaline and instinct. The only sound her brain bothered to process was her own heartbeat thundering in her ears.

The cheap motel was a favorite of the underworld dealings because, among other conveniences, it had no lockdown procedures. If Sharpe and Runner could get safely into the lift, then the cops would have no way of shutting it down and trapping them. Local authorities routinely closed the place down for the code violation, but they were always forced to reopen once they realized that the dirty deals had to take place somewhere, and this shithole wasn't in their constituents' backyards.

A door opened on the right and a shirtless man too drunk or too stupid to stay inside his room while the obvious—and no doubt familiar—sounds of a bust rang out in the hallway stumbled in front of Sharpe. He smelled of stale beer and week-old sweat. Sharpe grabbed his bare arm and, using her own momentum, spun him behind her. She heard the satisfying crash of two bodies as the undercover chasing her smacked into the foul obstacle. The young cop let out a frustrated shout, and Sharpe's lips curled into a smirk as she heard him stumble and bounce off the walls behind her like a pinball.

Taking advantage of her lead, she reached into her pocket and pressed the panic button carefully tucked inside. Her stomach fluttered as the button depressed. She'd never had to hit it before. Shaking local cops wouldn't be a fire-the-alarm situation, but that undercover had invoked the Allied Authority. A fresh pump of adrenaline pushed her feet to move faster.

One more corner and she could see the doors of the lift, its half-illuminated lights glowing like a beacon of safety and hope.

The doors opened.

God above had looked down and taken pity on the women.

Two men stepped out. The first had an average frame with a solid, planted look to him. The second was taller and broader and wore a hat down low over his head with a scar running on his upper cheekbone which peeked out below the rim.

Runner didn't even try to dodge them. She looked ready to trust that they would move out of her way, but the second man held up an arm and clotheslined her neck, and she fell backward. Sharpe came to a stuttering, sliding stop in front of the first man, who held up a badge with a bored expression on his face.

Gold illumination spun around a blue leaf of some kind, though from the distance, Sharpe couldn't make out the shifting lettering on the badge. A cop, but a local one. Not Allied Authority.

Sharpe leaned forward with her hands on her knees, panting so hard that her nose tingled. Runner coughed from the floor and rolled over to push herself up to her knees. Sharpe wondered which was worse: getting knocked in the neck while running at full tilt or having to land on that hard, filthy, infested floor. She saw a lone insect skitter away in the shadowed crevice near the wall as though in answer.

"Alright, let's go," said the man as he pocketed the badge inside of his plainclothes jacket. "Hands up."

Still breathing heavily, Sharpe straightened and held her hands out. She knew the routine. The fake John thundered down the hallway behind her just as the cop who'd knocked back Runner helped the woman to her feet and extended the chief mate's arms.

"We didn't do anything wrong," Sharpe protested.

The detective ignored her and patted his hands over her curves to check for weapons. She half expected him to take advantage of his situation and to linger closer and longer than necessary, but he stepped back before he'd crossed the line into groping. Sharpe breathed a sigh of relief. Local courts carried a hefty two-year sentence for assaulting their officers, and Sharpe didn't have that kind of time to waste.

"On your knees," he said. "Hands behind your head."

Sharpe rolled her eyes, but she obeyed.

"They were both there, Detective Jackson," said the undercover between wheezing breaths. He leaned against the wall and rested his sweating head against the chipping plaster. His face was bright red and there was a white line around his lips from overexertion. In contrast to the chiseled features of the man now processing Sharpe's right thumbprint with his pocket scanner, the John had a delicate, boyish face. He couldn't have been older than twenty. As he reached up to wipe dripping sweat from his forehead with his sleeve, he moved with an almost adolescent awkwardness, as though he still wasn't quite sure what to do with his limbs.

"Hey detective," said Sharpe, "maybe you wanna tell Officer Johnny Greenhorn over there not to lean on that wall. He's probably caught something by now."

The younger cop all but leaped away from the plaster and spun, trying to look at his back as though she'd told him he had a spider on his shoulder.

"They came out of the suspect's room?" Detective Jackson asked while staring down at his beeping scanner. Sharpe knew that her record was currently clean, but she still felt her breath catch while it processed until the screen lit up with a green border. It was a reflexive fear developed over a year and a half of near-constant law breaking. "No local warrants," said the cop, nodding without smiling at Sharpe.

"Yeah," said the young undercover, a pinker shade of red than before. "Both of them. Trying to make a deal."

"News to me," said Sharpe with a lazy shrug when the cop turned back to her with a questioning expression.

"But I saw—"

"Prove it."

The detective looked from Sharpe to the bright red John to his scarred partner. The broad-shouldered silent partner who had been busy scanning and searching Runner handed something to Jackson. It took a moment for Sharpe's mind to wrap itself around what she was seeing. It was the gun. The plastic, toy-looking joke that she had seen Runner toss back onto the bed just before walking out.

Sharpe's jaw dropped. She had *seen* the chief mate toss it down, recalled the sound as it clattered on top of other weapons. She looked at Runner, who shrugged. The woman was a goddamn magician.

"How did you..." Sharpe began.

"Anything to say now?" asked the detective, whose bored expression had morphed into a look of smug satisfaction. The corners of his mouth turned up in a way that gave Sharpe the impression that smiling was a normally foreign concept to those features.

"It's not mine?" Runner replied.

Sharpe didn't resist as the cop secured two restraining bracelets around each wrist and then pulled her arms back behind her. She winced in anticipation of the humming buzz as the magnets inside the bracelets engaged and the two snapped together hard enough to make her bones shake.

The first cop pulled a tablet from his pocket and tapped something into it.

"Do you want me to ride with you?" asked Johnny Greenhorn.

"No," said the officer. "Report back to Agent Maker."

Agent.

Allied Authority.

Shit.

CHAPTER TWO

Sharpe's brain quickly added up all the myriad ways in which she and Runner were thoroughly screwed.

The detective peered down at her. Sharpe glared back. Her mood soured as the numbers in her head rose. In that moment, she hated the man. Hated the righteous expression on his solid face, his position of power and authority. He wouldn't look so settled if she had that beautiful shotgun in her hands. She hated the filthy floor and the muck that she could feel seeping into and through the fabric of her trousers, settling into the pores of her skin and infecting her with plague, all while that smug asshole just stared down, so sure that he'd be the celebrated golden boy at his unit's next staff meeting.

And where the hell was her ship?

Sharpe opened her mouth to say something slick about his jaw cutting ice, but her voice caught in her throat as a low rumble vibrated up through the floor and echoed off of the peeling walls. She exchanged a wide-eyed glance with Runner.

"Earthquake?" asked the previously silent partner.

Jackson shook his head, staring at the wall as though he could see through it. Another shake, this time longer and more pronounced. The door next to Sharpe rattled in its track and she shuffled a pace away from the unsteady steel.

And then a sound that Sharpe recognized, that pulled her back out of the reeking hallway in the cheap motel and thrust her into a battleship, back to a time when alarms echoed off of metallic walls and the thrill and terror of war were constant companions of her mind.

Cannons.

The ground rocked and plaster dust sprinkled down from above. Sharpe only half-felt the grit in her hair and on her forehead. Her eyes only half-saw the fear in the detective's face as he stared at his detainees as though they'd planted the bombs themselves.

Part of her wanted to tell him to stuff his blame, that she and Runner were as much under fire as he was, but that part of her was silenced by the echoes of years-old orders ringing in her ears.

Again, instinct took over her body. But this time, it wasn't the primal, adrenaline-fueled fight-or-flight drive of a mercenary. It was the cold, meticulous actions that had been drilled into her through constant repetition by sergeants and then officers until they sank into her bones, until they were as natural as breathing. It was the instinct of a soldier.

Not enough information to make a solid call. She needed to know who was shooting at them, and from where.

"We need to get a visual," she said. Her voice was almost cut off by another nearby cannon explosion. The young undercover crouched down onto his hands and knees, his face a pale picture of fear.

Jackson tapped his ear. "Agent Marks," he said. A pause. "Agent Marks," he repeated. "Can you read me?" He shook his head at his partner.

Another explosion, but this time farther away. The vibration from the blast could barely be felt through the floorboards.

"Get in one of those rooms," said Sharpe, nodding to her left. "We can see out a window."

The cops ignored her.

"We need cover," said the young rookie, his voice barely above a whisper.

"We're in cover," responded Sharpe.

The rookie stared at her as though she'd spoken in a foreign language. Sharpe recognized the signs of panic. His mind had already begun to fray. His eyes were wide enough that Sharpe could see white around the whole of his pupils, and the corners of his mouth twitched reflexively. She hoped he would have the wherewithal to turn his head away before vomiting.

She looked up at Jackson. His jaw was clenched and his breathing had quickened, but his face was steady and he kept staring at the wall. The partner tapped at a datapad with trembling fingers, probably trying to get in touch with the Allied Authority waiting for them outside.

"Hey," she said to Jackson, and she tried to keep her voice level and supportive. She needed him to hear her. "Hey," she repeated, and he gave her a quick glance before turning back to the wall.

"Unless you got tech that lets you see through walls," she said, working hard to keep the bite out of her voice, "you're going to have to open one of those doors and see what we're up against. We won't know how to act until you do."

He nodded, a quick, curt motion. His hands balled into fists. He was steeling himself, and he reminded Sharpe of a new recruit seeing action for the first time. He would have made a good soldier, probably. If she hadn't been handcuffed, she'd have put a hand on his shoulder, offered him a supportive nod.

Then again, no she wouldn't. If she hadn't been handcuffed, she'd have opened the damn door herself, and she and Runner would have been halfway out of the shaking, unsteady building by now.

"Detective," she said. "Jackson." Another round outside, this time close enough to make the door shake in its track again.

The detective looked down at her.

"You need to move," Sharpe told him.

He nodded. His jaw tensed further until bulges appeared beneath his ears and his nostrils flared. Just as Sharpe worried that she might have lost him, his hand reached mechanically into an interior pocket of his jacket and pulled out a master keycard. He waved the card in front of the reader panel on the wall and the door rattled and then swooshed open.

Even compared to the poorly-lit hallway, the room was dark.

A woman lay sprawled on the floor, half-clothed and unconscious or dead, next to a stripped mattress. The sheets from the bed had been tacked up over the window. Both detectives went to her, but Sharpe ignored the body and tried to squint past the sheet on the window, unable to make out any details through the fabric.

She could see large shapes flying and hovering in the sky, could see the red trails of the plasma fire racing toward the hovering shadows or the ground when the shots missed, saw one building to the left crumble and change the skyline.

The rookie cop must have walked into the room. Maybe it was the vague shadows of the firefight outside, or maybe it was the sight of the junkie on the floor, or maybe he could see well enough from the light streaming in from the hallway to make out stains on the mattress, but Sharpe heard him retching behind her.

"She needs an ambulance," said Jackson. "Kid, don't contaminate the room. Take it back to the hallway."

Idiots, the lot of them.

A full-scale assault was taking place outside the window, close enough to see through a sheet, close enough to make the building shake. One misfire and they would all be distant memories in an uncaring universe, and they wanted to play detectives for some nameless junkie strung out on the floor of a motel.

Sharpe squinted harder through the sheet. She couldn't see well enough to catch any details from the street level two stories below them.

"We've got to get these cuffs off," muttered Runner in a low voice beside her.

"Any ideas?" asked Sharpe.

Runner shook her head.

Jackson stepped away from the woman on the floor. He pulled the sheet from the window and Sharpe had to squint against the fresh assault of bright light.

For a long moment, no one said anything. Sharpe stared at the scene before her in disbelief, her mind refusing to accept what her eyes saw.

"Well," she said, "shit."

CHAPTER THREE

Sharpe's ship, the *Hellbent*, had engaged two Allied Authority ships in open-air combat. As far as Sharpe could tell, neither side had taken significant damage, though the *Hellbent's* aft burners sputtered and sparked. Probably superficial, wouldn't need drydock right away.

"Did you hit the panic button?" Runner asked. Sharpe didn't like her officer's tone.

"Of course I did?"

"Christ," Runner said, "what were you thinking?"

"Well, I was thinking, 'We're getting chased by the AA, this is an appropriate time for a panic button since this is exactly the kind of situation the button was made for.' Also, I was thinking that I'm the goddamn captain and I do what I want."

Runner's eyes spoke volumes, but she kept her mouth shut.

Sharpe turned to Jackson. "We have to get out of this building."

"Is that your ship?" he asked, staring up at the *Hellbent* like it was a snake coiling to strike.

Another missed shot, another shake in the building. "On a good day, this place barely stays upright. Unless you want to be crushed, we need to go."

"Uncuff us," said Runner. Sharpe suppressed a sigh. She would have gotten around to that.

Jackson shook his head, his eyes focused on the chaos through the window.

"We need to run," insisted Sharpe's crewmate. "And we can't do that with our hands behind our backs."

"Call off your ship," said the detective.

"Can't," answered Sharpe.

Jackson turned to stare at her, and Sharpe almost took a reflexive step backward. The detective only stood a few inches taller than her, and Sharpe's training no doubt surpassed his, but his expression spelled pure, focused determination.

At some point in the past thirty seconds, it was as though the two temperaments had switched. The detective, having walked in on a potential crime scene, was in his element. He had control. Sharpe, having seen the surprising firefight through the window, stood both literally and figuratively on shaking ground, and her heart pounded up into her throat as panic bit in at the edges of her thoughts.

The handcuffs made him intimidating, that had to be it. Once they were off—and so help her, they would be off—she wouldn't feel the sinking, overpowered vulnerability. It was the handcuffs.

"I don't have a communicator on me." What did he think this was, amateur hour? In the event of a bust, provide a clear, traceable link back to the ship of origin? Mercenaries carried panic buttons. Untraceable, unlockable, plausibly deniable panic buttons.

She could have continued to dodge admitting that the *Hellbent* was hers, and maybe she should have, but that fierce expression told her that the normal cat-and-mouse games wouldn't work.

"My shuttle," she said. "I can hail them from there."

Runner shook her head, but Sharpe ignored her.

"Where is it?"

Sharpe nodded toward the hallway. "Other side of the building."

Jackson narrowed his eyes. He was weighing her, trying to see if she was lying. Sharpe told the truth, but the panic crept in, wriggling cold tendrils into her skin, and she had to grit her teeth against it.

Goddamn cuffs.

"Let's go," said the detective, after what felt like hours. To his partner, who was still crouched over the unconscious woman on the floor, he said, "Benson, we'll have to call an ambulance from outside. Someone's jamming the building."

Sharpe shook her head at the accusing looks the cops directed at her, though it was almost certainly her ship cutting communications in the building, and maybe the whole block.

The floor rumbled again, then something popped, and the light in the room flickered once before turning off as the door to the hallway slid down.

Electrical failure.

For a moment, the room was still as the ubiquitous hum of the building hushed and the muffled sounds of the fight outside could finally filter in through the window.

"This is fine," said Sharpe, though she could hear the elevated pitch in her own voice. Her clothes and skin, still wet with sweat from the earlier chase, tingled sharp and cold. Her skin prickled as goosebumps formed on her arms.

Thoughts flashed through her mind's eye. Memories. As a soldier, she had been in mortal danger more times than she could count, but there had only been three times where she had truly felt the certainty of death weigh in around her. The wicked part of her that now pulled those thoughts to the forefront of her mind listened for the sounds of creaking or cracking, something to signal the building's crushing collapse. She wondered if it would hurt.

But there were no more sounds.

Only the rumbling outside, the edges of explosions worn dull through the wall's cheap insulation, and the hanging stillness in the room.

The building wasn't coming down. Not yet, anyway.

So there was that.

"Uncuff us," Sharpe said. Tried to say, anyway. Whether it was the rush of fresh terror amplifying her voice or the comparative silence of the cut electricity, the volume of her words sounded disproportionately loud.

Jackson's partner, Benson, was the first to move. With a face white with panic and wearing an expression that gave Sharpe the impression that he, too, had expected to hear the impending sounds of structural failure, he launched himself over the body of the blissfully ignorant junkie and bolted for the door.

For a few seconds, everyone else watched while the man attacked the solid steel. He tried to shimmy the door up by pressing with open palms, then he tried to wedge his fingertips between the crumbling bottom padding and the floorboard.

"Don't bother," said Runner.

Benson ignored her.

"He can't get the door up without a charge," she continued, appealing to Jackson.

"But we can," said Sharpe.

Jackson's face had turned an unfortunate shade of green, and panic sweat made his face shine in the reflected light from the window. Again, his jaw clenched until it bulged.

"You'll have to uncuff us first."

The detective glanced at his partner, grunting and clawing at the door, then down at the woman passed out on the floor, and finally nodded. He tapped at a datapad and the cuffs released.

Her freedom half restored, Sharpe moved into action with a weight lifted from her shoulders. While Runner pounded the space around the door controls to get enough leverage to pry the casing off, Sharpe opened the case beneath the viewscreen by the bed.

Jackson drew a pistol from a holster under his jacket, but Sharpe rolled her eyes and ignored him.

"It needs a charge," said Runner with a grunt as she pulled back the case and exposed the control panel's circuitry.

"We don't have anything strong enough to power the floor in a building like this." Jackson returned his pistol to its holster, but he stood in a way that kept both women in his sights. He was going to be tough to slip.

"Don't need to," said Sharpe. She tried not to think about what disgusting treasures lay inside the dark cabinet as she yanked out the video box. "There's no lockdown in this building." Her hand brushed up against grit and she shook her head as she tried to convince herself that it was sand. Just sand. Not rat droppings or insect bodies or the petrified remains of...

Just sand.

Sharpe tossed the box onto the bare mattress and squinted in the low light for the easiest way to open the case. Outside, a ship passed close enough to the window to momentarily shadow the room, and its engines made a whooshing sound as it sped past.

"No lockdown," said Jackson. "So all of the doors run on their own circuits?"

"Bingo." Sharpe gave up trying to find a gentle solution. She picked up the box and dropped it onto the ground. The case cracked and split, throwing tiny electronic components in multiple directions. Hopefully, Runner wouldn't need any of those. Sharpe collected most of the larger pieces and took them, dragging the cord behind her, to her chief mate at the door panel.

"I need light," said Runner. Jackson pulled a multitool from his jacket and tapped it. A blinding white light shone into Sharpe's eyes before being directed at the exposed panel on the wall.

Runner used her teeth to strip the wire and Sharpe had to suppress a gag. Apart from the discomfort of copper strips being dragged along tooth enamel, she recalled the grit in the cabinet where the cord had been sitting. Runner spat out a piece of plastic and rolled her eyes.

"Lighten up, buttercup," she said to her captain. "You want out of this place or not?"

"You ladies look like you've done this before," said Jackson.

"Ladies," repeated Runner with a smirk. "That's a new one." She adjusted Jackson's hand to focus the light and her eyes squinted as she rubbed the side of her nose the way she always did when she was concentrating.

Benson had stopped pulling at the bottom of the door. Still crouched, he stared up at Runner and looked like he may have been getting a handle on his nerve.

"How did you know about the video box?" asked Jackson in a low voice.

Runner swore under her breath as a spark caught her fingertip.

"Electricity gets cut sometimes," Sharpe answered without taking her eyes from Runner's work. "Whatever reason. Clientele can get rowdy. Videos usually keep them occupied, so the boxes have battery backups."

"Videos?"

"Yup."

"In a place like this?"

Sharpe stared at him. "I mean… really? Is this your first day?"

Even in the dim light, Sharpe could see his face begin to redden. "Yeah," she said. "Those kinds of videos."

"And you know this…"

Sharpe's expression cut him off.

"Not your first rodeo."

With four people crowded into the tight space and no environmental cycling, the air thickened. Sharpe pulled at her damp, clinging shirt and willed Runner to work faster.

The longer Runner worked, the more uncomfortable Jackson appeared. He tugged at his collar with his free hand, and twice Runner had to glare at him and order him to hold the light still.

Sharpe watched him in something that might have bordered on amusement if she weren't awaiting a swift crushing death. The more uneasy he looked, the more comfortable she felt. "Not a fan of locked doors, detective?"

He didn't answer.

The panel sparked, Runner jerked back, and the door slid up. Benson hopped in a crouch into the hallway before standing. Sharpe followed him, and Jackson stood under the open door, ushering Runner through before ducking out of the way of the sliding steel, which crashed back down.

Apart from the small light in Jackson's hand, the hallway was completely black.

"You should have left the connection open," he said to Runner.

"You're right," she replied. "I was just thinking that this building needed more electrical fire."

"That woman is still trapped in there."

"I'm sure she's fine," said Runner. Even in the low light, Sharpe caught her meaningful glance. Sharpe nodded and kept her wrists as far away from one another as she could manage without tipping off the cops. No way were those cuffs going back on.

"Looks like your rookie made a run for it." Sharpe gestured at the missing airlift at the end of the empty hallway. "Hopefully he got out before the power cut off."

Jackson crossed to other doors, banging on them. "Anyone in there?" he asked. "Do you need any help?"

Benson pulled out his own multitool and made a small light in his hands.

"He's... kidding, right?" asked Sharpe.

"We don't have time for this," insisted Runner.

"Detective," said Sharpe, "it's no good. Everyone in this place is either like us," she motioned to herself and Runner, "or like her," she nodded toward the door they'd just come through. "They're long gone, either way."

Jackson frowned. He was compassionate. Good.

Made him an easier mark.

"This way," said Sharpe, and she started walking down the hallway into darkness.

Benson was kind enough to shine his light ahead of her. "Is there another lift that way?" he asked.

"Nope, but there'll be an access tunnel out."

"You're certain?"

"Believe it or not, detective, this building does follow one or two safety codes."

"Why did you leave your shuttle on that side of the building?" asked Jackson. "Lot's the other way."

"Thinking ahead," Sharpe called back. "In case we had to jump out of a window."

"Windows in this building don't open," grumbled Benson.

"They do if you shoot them," said Runner.

Sharpe had never realized how hard the environmental systems in the motel must have been working on a regular basis. After only a few minutes, the hallway smelled fouler than any trash pile Sharpe had ever walked past. The stink mixed with moisture in the air and it pressed in from all sides. She would never get that smell out of her nose, or her hair.

Runner paced alongside her, with Benson a few steps behind and Jackson behind him, still knocking on every door he passed, listening for movement, and then jogging to catch up.

The light from behind formed long shadows in front of the women, pointing into blackness. Sharpe listened ahead for any movement, any straggler who might have been trapped inside the building and was now out of his mind with panic or delirium, but the hallway was empty.

"How do we get the bracelets off?" Runner whispered. Jackson's insistent banging and calling out provided cover for the women to whisper without fear of being overheard by the silent detective behind them.

"Might have to get them off back on the ship."

Runner exhaled through her teeth.

"Keep your hands in front of you, just in case the cops get jumpy."

Runner opened her mouth to say something, but a bright flash and high-pitched whistle cut her off as the hallway and the motel and then the world evaporated into whiteness.

CHAPTER FOUR

Sharpe's thoughts came back to her slowly and with effort. Pulling her mind back into her body felt like trying to force rocks through a sieve. Her head ached, her body ached, and everything felt like it was on fire.

Good.

Pain was good. She was alive, then.

She could hear grumbles and stirring around her, and the clattering of falling debris. It took a moment for her to remember how to open her eyes.

"You okay, boss?" A layer of dust coated Runner's face and a trickle of blood ran down from her ear.

Sharpe grunted. "You've looked better," she said. Runner smirked, then winced. Sharpe sat up with effort and sharp protests coming from her ribs.

She sat some ten meters away from open air. It was a surreal sight, half of a hallway leading out into the bright sky. The building must have taken a direct hit, and half of it had crumbled from the impact. Dust and rubble settled everywhere.

Something stirred behind her, and Sharpe turned to see one of the detectives rolling over onto his stomach. She couldn't tell which man it was, even when he groaned.

"We should go," whispered Runner. Sharpe nodded and forced herself onto unsteady feet. Nothing felt broken, and she didn't see pooling blood. But as she inhaled, her lungs rejected the dust in the air, and she coughed and felt a fire in her chest.

A man grunted from behind. Two shapes stirred now. Sharpe and Runner shuffled toward the edge of the rubble.

"Found the access tunnel," said Sharpe. The pain in her chest increased. Her throat felt like someone had taken sandpaper to it.

She'd only get worse off as the shock of the blast wore off and the natural painkillers with it. Had to get moving, and then stay moving.

"Stay low," she said to Runner. "Don't stop, and stay low."

Sharpe wasn't normally afraid of heights, but standing on the edge of an unsteady precipice made her head spin. Or she had a concussion. The streets had, for the most part, emptied, but a few people scattered here and there, crouched and running and covering their heads to protect themselves from falling debris. The neighborhood was a war zone. Again, Sharpe was transported in her mind back to a time when rubble-covered streets, when cities lay in such ruin that Sharpe couldn't imagine how they'd ever be rebuilt.

Runner pointed toward a high pile of crumbled cement to the left. "I think we can climb down that." The chief mate moved with some tenderness, but she seemed steadier on her feet than Sharpe felt.

"Don't look up," instructed Sharpe as they started down the incline. "They'll use facial recognition. If we're lucky, they won't know who we are and we'll just look like civilians."

It was slow going, climbing down the unsteady and unnatural mountain. Every few steps, Sharpe shifted her weight onto a rock or a shard of metal that looked more stable than it was and had to draw back or risk tumbling down. Smoke that smelled of burning rubber and plastic filled the air. Fresh waves of pain rocked her when she made any sudden movement, and every step was agony.

Just a few meters shy of street level, Sharpe noticed several pebbles rolling down from above. She looked up to see Jackson following the pair. He clutched his side and winced with every movement, but his face was the same mask of determination that she'd seen back in the room.

"*Hellbent's* moving off," said Runner. Sharpe glanced toward the sky. Her ship raced back up toward the upper atmosphere, leaving a trail of thin black smoke in its wake.

"We'll find them at the rendezvous," she said. She hoped.

But as the women made their way toward the alley where they'd stowed their ride, Sharpe's heart sunk down into her gut. "No," she said. "No no no no no."

The shuttle—or at least the place where the shuttle had been—lay under what might have been, judging by the smell, a butcher's shop.

Sharpe looked up to see the *Hellbent* shrink away until it was just a tiny dot in the sky. "How long until their jammers give out?"

Runner shook her head. "Two minutes, maybe? Three, if it takes the AA a while to find them."

Two minutes, maybe three, until Jackson would radio the AA ships. Until they would know that the *Hellbent* had not left with her whole crew onboard. Until the whole of the federal authority bore down on the women and there was no escape.

Bile churned up into Sharpe's throat.

Runner grabbed Sharpe's arm and pulled her back toward the building. Sharpe followed, but she looked up to see Jackson seated halfway down the pile of rubble, tapping furiously at his datapad.

Sharpe opened her mouth to tell Runner that they were headed the wrong way, to tell her that they needed to find a crowd, they needed to blend until she could find a way off the planet and back to the rendezvous before the crew would leave them behind. But her voice caught in her throat when she saw what Runner ran toward.

It was a shuttle. Unmanned, unwatched, sitting safely in the street with its door wide open. The only shuttle that could afford to sit out in the street without an armed guard. No one would dare steal that vehicle, even here, not with that Allied Authority insignia painted on the side.

"You're insane."

"We're desperate," said Runner.

Couldn't argue with that.

The women ducked inside the shuttle. Sharpe clamped her jaw shut to keep her heart from leaping out through her throat. She glanced back up toward Jackson, who rose and watched in open-mouthed amazement as the mercenaries commandeered the AA vehicle.

"Sorry about this, detective," called Sharpe. "But I don't like locked doors, either."

Runner closed the hatch behind them. "That was maybe a little much."

"Really?"

"A little."

"This will definitely get us killed, so I just thought—" Sharpe's words caught as she looked around the tight space.

Evidence bags.

Evidence from Bern's room. Bern's guns.

Now Sharpe's guns.

A dozen duffels at least, all neatly labeled and packed as though for a Christmas delivery Sharpe wouldn't have had the balls to ask for.

Runner busied herself with the controls. "They left it unlocked," the chief mate said with notes of surprise and maybe even hope in her voice. "I can take care of this up here," she continued. "You know, if you want to putz around. Really, I got it."

Sharpe only half heard her. "Uh huh." She yanked at a zipper on a long bag.

No.

Yes.

"For a while there," Sharpe said, tears threatening to spring to her eyes, "I was afraid that I might never get to tell you that I love you."

The shuttle powered up.

"Cute," said Runner. "But I'll love you back if you say all that with money."

"Wasn't talking to you." Sharpe pulled the shotgun, *the* shotgun, from the bag. All of the injuries and the bombs and the terror dissolved from her thoughts. "Also, I pay you plenty, Lisa."

"Jammers are still up," said Runner. "I'm going to fly low. They won't expect this. If we're lucky."

Sharpe pressed the cold steel of the barrel against her cheek. "We're lucky."

"Rendezvous?"

"Rendezvous."

Author Sam Maguire

Sam lives in Florida with her husband and cat, where she keeps a year-round hurricane kit well stocked with cheap wine and good cheese. She remains undefeated at Pirate Dice because the rules encourage cheating and frequently owns at poker games for totally different reasons, she swears.

Enjoy the story? Read more by Samantha Maguire on Amazon, or check out her website at http://maguire.stayinspiredllc.com and join the mailing list with the rest of the cool kids.

Motherlode

by Bill Patterson

The image in the communicator was streaked with artifacts, occasionally turning the serious face of the Chief Engineer into a cubist portrait. "That's it, Captain. The reactor at the 150th Meridian scrammed. Safety systems ejected its fuel load into the ship's central core. The black holes have it now. The event caused a cascading shutdown on our other reactors. As of now, we're running on batteries and the photovoltaics around the black holes."

The ratings on the bridge snuck looks at the Captain. They had never seen his face so grim. "What does that mean for shipboard operations?" he asked in a calm, measured voice, as if the complete failure of the VectorShip happened often.

"We'll get along all right if we shut down every non-essential system." Eddie Hanson, Chief Engineer radiated confidence. This had been one scenario he had endlessly simulated. The *Appleseed* was in trouble, but it wasn't perilously so...yet.

"What about the freezer cells?" The Captain had his flatscreen raised, his expert system scrolling through decision trees as it received data from Engineering. It was more of a reminder than a checklist—he and Eddie and Jarl, the Purser, had rewritten most of the system over the years.

"No, sir, those are fine. Jarl and I work pretty closely on those. Life support, freezer cells, and the Farm will work just fine on the photovoltaics, especially when the 'holes eat the uranium."

"For how long?" asked the Captain. "When can the other reactors be restarted?" The question strobed redly on the flatscreen, but Captain Bettendorf's eyes barely flickered over to it. "We've got to get power back up before the passengers start howling."

"I am not really sure, Captain. I raced over to the 150 reactor when I got the word. Section heads have been reporting in, it seems like most of the reactors shut down cleanly and reversibly. I don't want to give you my final word until I inspect them personally." Eddie mentally crossed his fingers. Fission reactors were finicky, particularly in the supremely low gravity of a VectorShip.

"So, we're in the dark until...when? Come on, Hanson, I've got to give the rest of the crew some data before the passengers start going crazy."

"Tell them two days. We have to be careful how we bring them online, or we could blow everything. It's not like there's a hardware store around the corner here in the ass end of Virgo."

The Captain nodded. When the Chief Engineer lost his sass, then things were serious. It sounded like he was getting it back. He felt a cautious hope, and smiled into the monitor.

"Kick ass, Hanson. I want to know why 150 puked its core by the end of the month. That's two weeks."

"In two weeks, this will all be a distant memory, boss. Now, I've got some subordinates that are crapping themselves. Gotta run." Eddie sketched a two-fingered salute as the communicator faded. The Captain's smile faded along with it.

The lights on the bridge remained in their dim emergency glow. Captain Alfonso Bettendorf resumed his grim look. He knew that the rest of the bridge crew was watching him, and he didn't want them to relax a centimeter.

"Get me the Purser," he growled at the communications tech at his position on the right. "I want him up here as soon as possible." The man jumped to comply.

Alfonso Bettendorf in his third decade as Captain of the VectorShip *Appleseed*. His father was Captain before him, as was his father's father. In fact, there has been a Bettendorf at the helm of the *Appleseed* ever since its launch out of Earth orbit three hundred years ago. He was fifty-three years old, and in the seven percent gravity of VectorShip *Appleseed*, he was good for another fifty years of life, although regulations required that he turn over command at seventy years of age.

Although Alfonso had three sons, all were serving out ten-year apprenticeships in different departments on the *Appleseed*. His middle son Rafael was one of the junior engineers whom Eddie Hanson was about to roast over a slow fire for the failure of reactor 150. Speaking of roasting...

"Where is that Purser?" he muttered aloud. Glancing at his locator tank, he saw the icon representing Jarl Halvormak sliding rapidly towards the bridge. "Moving pretty quickly, too," he murmured.

Jarl Halvormak was indeed moving quickly. Even at eighty years of age, he was as spry as he was at thirty, though significantly more cautious. He had served his entire life aboard the *Appleseed*, starting out as a laundry machine operator and working his way up to the pinnacle of power aboard the ship, Chief Purser. He was in charge of all passengers aboard the ship, and sometimes a good deal of the crew as well. Nearly everything that could be thought of as 'ship services' with the exception of essential life support was run out of the Purser's office.

Fortunately, Jarl and Eddie were fast friends, having grown up together aboard the *Appleseed*. When the alarms lit up in Engineering not quite three hours ago, Eddie made sure that Jarl was hooked into the monitor circuit. Jarl didn't understand one tenth of what was said, but he put in place some contingency operations of his own. He was well prepared for the Captain's summons.

"Purser reporting to the Captain as ordered," he announced as he stepped onto the bridge. He peered closely at the man for clues to the overall health of the Ship. He and Eddie had worked closely with the Captain when they were upgrading the expert systems. It was telling, Jarl realized, that he always thought of the Chief Engineer as Eddie, but Alfonso was always the Captain.

Captain Bettendorf motioned for him to sit on a nearby chair, almost unneeded in *Appleseed*'s seven percent gravity. "I assume you know what this is about. We had a power reactor eject its core, and all of the other main power reactors have shut down in a cascade."

Jarl nodded rapidly. This could all have been done via intercom, saving valuable minutes. "Sir, I am ready to shut down all non-essential services immediately." He leaned forward. "Time is of the essence, sir. The batteries won't hold out forever."

"Do it," ordered the Captain.

Jarl strode over to a spare console, punched up his assistant's circuit.

An older woman whose face radiated competence appeared on the screen. "Maggie, execute Run Silent, level 3 immediately. Authorization Jarl, three, two, nine, seven, six, one, nine. Confirm."

A few moments passed. Maggie replied, "Authorization Jarl, confirmed. Run Silent, level 3 running."

There was no perceptible change on the bridge, already under power conservation procedures. But throughout the twenty-kilometer ship, services were shutting down. Elevators discharged passengers, then stopped with their doors open and their lights off. The pullers, transportation rails that ran the length of the ship, stopped taking passengers, and shut down when the last passenger reached their destination. Illuminators darkened, fans fell to one-third their previous speed. Non-essential computers turned themselves off.

On the bridge, the power consumption indicators fell precipitously. Jarl nodded as the shutdown closely mimicked the simulations he and Eddie had worked out long before. Like all good staff, they brainstormed various disaster scenarios and had contingency plans well in place. Still, it was something of a thrill to see reality match simulation so closely.

"Sir, better tell the folks something. Rumors are starting to go around." Jarl stepped back from the console where the power meters continued to fall.

Captain Bettendorf nodded to the communications tech, who rapidly touched squares on his control panel, then gave the Captain a thumbs up.

"This is your Captain speaking. At approximately 1423 today, the power reactor at the 150th Meridian failed, ejecting its fuel core towards the center of the ship. There were no casualties. However, the one shutdown caused all of the other power reactors to shut down as well. Until we can get them restarted, we have very little electrical power available to us.

"You may have noticed that it's a little dim on the ship. We have initiated power conservation measures. These measures will cause some hardship, and I apologize in advance for that. We cannot at this moment predict when the power will be back on, but Engineering expects to begin restoration immediately.

"The ship, crew, and passengers are not in danger. We will restart the reactors, and arrive at our next port of call with a great story to tell. Thank you for your cooperation. Captain Bettendorf, out."

***

The *Appleseed* was a second-generation VectorShip built and launched from High Earth Orbit during the 2700s. The near-impact of Comet Clenford in 2539 jolted humanity like nothing else. The shockwave of the comet's passage through the atmosphere destroyed significant portions of Southeast Asia and killed almost a billion people. With the fragility of Earth thus demonstrated, mankind focused on getting off the mother planet as soon as possible.

VectorShips were double-hulled vessels created by inflating two nickel-iron asteroids with cometary ice and sunlight. The space between the hulls is the actual living area, the space inside the inner hull is kept in vacuum, and split between storage, engineering spaces, and room for the Bussard ramjet plus black-hole drive.

A VectorShip is capable of housing thousands in perfect comfort, carrying three times that number in hibernation, and achieving one-third lightspeed within a year of leaving any port of call.

***

Once back in his office, Jarl called Lori Jensen, his current companion. She was forty and was half Norwegian, but he didn't hold that against her. She worked in Navigation.

"Looks like we're in the crapper now, Lori. You heard the Captain. How much fissile fuel do we have onboard?"

"Four years' worth," she said glumly, twisting a strand of hair around her finger.. "The latest from Astrometry indicates we may have some metallic planets within three years travel time."

"That's cutting it close. I know that Eddie was jittery about the fuel load even before this happened. It's been fifty years, we've visited six solar systems, and none of them had any usable radioactives." Jarl scraped under his nails, betraying his inner nervousness.

Although the *Appleseed* used micro-black holes for propulsion, it relied on nuclear fission reactors for its internal power, especially at low thrust levels or when in orbit. Fifteen generations of design removed from the Enrico Fermi's first atomic pile, these reactors generated electricity by a variety of methods, so that nearly all of the energy of the fissioning atom was captured and used. Despite hundreds of years of research and development, fusion reactors just could not be made small enough to operate reliably on the *Appleseed*.

Finding fissionable elements, or fissiles, in usable quantities soon became one of the bottlenecks to interstellar travel. The *Appleseed* reactors worked on the same three fissile isotopes that the first atomic reactors used: uranium 233 and 235, and plutonium 239. The *Appleseed* also carried thorium pellets, which were exceptionally stable, but could be bred into U-233 fuel within a month.

"Well, there's always the thorium," Lori pointed out, her eyes brightening.

"What, the original, last-ditch fuel from Earth?" Jarl folded his arms across his chest and lowered his head, looking at her from under his blonde eyebrows. "That stuff's almost untouchable, like burning an ancient manuscript to stay warm. What do the honchoes in Nav say?"

"They're on the fence. On the one hand, if we go ahead and start breeding the thorium to U-233, we'll have all the fuel we need for another fifty years. But that's like eating our seed corn. If this target system doesn't have any thorium, or uranium, we're dead in the water." Lori sighed and looked down at her hands. "Jarl, I don't know what to tell you. This solar system we're aiming for had better work out."

***

Helen Rooney, the Chief of the Remote Sensing Group, was in a quandary. On the inside, she just wanted to jump out of her skin, run around herself a few times shouting "Eureka", then jump back in. On the outside, she had to maintain a cool and calm demeanor, employ scientific detachment, and evince no particular enthusiasm for the little dot of light in the center of her sensor feeds.

"The reflection spectra for the planet show a surface temperature of fifteen degrees, an O2 partial pressure of twenty-five kiloPascals, and enough water vapor to guarantee liquid water on the surface." She paused delicately in her presentation to Captain's Advisory Council. "There are anomalies in the reflected spectra, and it's far too early to form any conclusions, but we've detected what looks like metal ions in the atmosphere. There appear to be absorption lines related to calcium, iron, and even lead."

"That's, um, fantastic," said Marc Ferrer, First Officer. "But you didn't say anything was definite."

"Correct, sir. We can't positively define elements based on spectral lines at this distance."

"What about the central star?" asked Susilo Harta, Chief of Planetary Operations. "If you are postulating a metal-rich planet, then the star must have considerable metal content, absorbed as part of the original accretion disk."

"The central star is a class K2, cooler than Sol, but far richer in metal," said Helen. "We believe it is a Generation I star, formed only about three billion years ago. We're guessing that the planet has only primitive forms of life, primarily because of metal toxicity, but also because it hasn't been around long enough to evolve complex lifeforms."

"Well, that would be a lucky break. I'd hate to have to run a mine and subdue the local T-Rex analog at the same time," joked Susilo.

"I do have a recommendation, though," said Helen. "Indications are that this planet will have a higher gravity, as much as one third over Earth standard. We might want to start acclimation of ground crew now."

"Hmmmm," said Susilo. "I'm not so sure of that. First, given what we're mining, I don't think we're going to have ground crew. Second, even if we did, I wouldn't start them out two years early. Three months is more like it."

"But..."

"Ever been in the high-gee centrifuges? It's very much like being in jail. A nicely furnished jail, just packed with exercise gear and speakers where some impersonal voice is urging you to keep pushing iron. The crew would have to live there full time, and would rightly view it as punishment. No, we'll do it my way."

Helen subsided. She was, after all, only a remote sensing specialist, not a crew manager.

"Anything else? No?" said Marc. "We'll do this again in three months. Helen, try to pin down the composition of the crust, if you can. Good work, everyone. Meeting adjourned."

***

As the *Appleseed* drew closer, the target planet gave up more secrets to Helen's sensors. Motherlode, as Helen called the planet, was about three-quarters the size of Earth, but had a gravity field twenty percent higher, due mostly to its high metal content.

Motherlode was aptly named. Remote sensing revealed several dozen radioactive anomalies on the surface. These were marked for possible mining operations. Near-surface veins of monazite, pitchblende, and other uranium and thorium bearing minerals were scattered all over the surface of the planet. Susilo's team, after days staring at false-color images from Helen's sensors, selected the anomaly closest to the equator as the main mine. It made ground-to-orbit operations easier.

The metals were not limited to just the rocks of the planet. The soil and dust and water of the planet were filled with metallic compounds. One light-month out, when *Appleseed* was locked in its approach hyperbola, chlorophyll was perceptible. Helen worked around the clock as *Appleseed* plunged into Motherlode's solar system, searching in vain for other signs of life. Perhaps there was nothing more evolved than pond scum.

***

"Sir, parking orbit established. We're at Geosynch over the Zero Meridian." The navigator on watch slid his hands to the edges of the touch-sensitive panel. "Main drive secured. Station Keeping thrusters online."

"Thank you, Lieutenant." Captain Bettendorf leaned back, stretching. He could never quite relax in a solar system until he was safely in orbit around one of the planets. "Secure from main star drive, activate stationkeeping watch."

The navigator grinned. Stationkeeping watch was one four hour watch per day, instead of eight hours every day. He was going to get hammered after he got off duty.

The four years spent getting to this planet were nerve-wracking as reactor after reactor was shut down for lack of fuel. The journey was a long, impoverished one, as the conveniences of normal life onboard dwindled away for lack of power. The *Appleseed* was in orbit, but it was dark and cold inside.

The Captain stirred himself. Unlike the navigator, the Captain was never off dury. "How are those ground surveys looking, Commander?"

Ayodeji Okafor, commander of the ground forces, scanned the latest material on his screens. "So far, the long-range scans are proving out." His dark face creased in a wide grin. "The planet below us is a gold mine. I've never seen such uranium ratios. We should be able to get as much fissile cargo as we want."

Captain Bettendorf toggled the image of the *Appleseed*'s medical officer. "Medical, what are your thoughts?"

Though the white coat was enough to identify her, Doctor Pasgeh assumed her usual lecture room demeanor. "Sir, this planet is lousy with everything at the bottom of the periodic table. I advise no ground crew. If you have to use one, then they must have hazmat suits and respirators. They will need constant chelation to stave off heavy metal poisoning. Even then, it's a race against time as their radiation dose accumulates.

She hunched forward towards the camera. Her face loomed in the screen. "It's absolute death to try to plant a colony there. I recommend we get in, work the highest grade ore beds we can, and get out. I would go so far as to say we should only do initial processing groundside and perform further enrichment up here." She slowly leaned back while the senior staff processed her recommendations.

"You could stick a shovel almost anywhere in this place and get as much uranium as you want," said Susilo.

"Noted," said the Captain absently. He was still struck at how strident Doctor Pasgeh had gotten. "Purser?"

Jarl had a notecard in his hand. "The remote-mining gear is ready to go. The crew has been in the centrifuges and simulators for the past three months. We can even support limited ground-based operations if that becomes necessary." Jarl stopped speaking and waited. He knew

Captain Bettendorf—the entire senior staff did. If he said anything more, then he would be treading into someone else's turf.

The Captain paused. "I sense a reservation."

"I have one."

Bettendorf glared mildly. "Come on, Jarl. Out with it. Staff? I don't give a good God-damned if you have a problem in someone else's area. We've got to get things right here, and fast. We're really down to the last hundred fuel rods, not near enough to get us to another planet. Stop dicking around and give me information!"

Jarl nodded. "Engineering and I have been over some figures. We have barely enough broadcast power to mine enough ore to refuel one reactor. If something glitches, then the other reactors will not be able to power both on-board systems and support beamed power to the surface. Then we'll have to send men down."

"We'll just have to make sure nothing glitches, then," said the Captain.

But of course, something did glitch and the men were sent down.

***

"I really hate this getup," said Rodney Farns, as he clumped across the rocky landscape in his bright yellow hazmat suit. Minerals rare on Earth formed large outcrops near the mining compound.

"Save your breath," gasped his companion, Tensu Matusha, who was similarly garbed. "Somehow, the centrifuge never quite matches real gravity." Even with the three-month centrifuge preparation, life in a gravity field seventeen times the strength of the *Appleseed* exhausted the two dozen crewmembers stuck on the surface of Motherlode.

"How much longer do we have on this hellhole?" asked Rodney. "Dammit, three months in that whirling jail, then stuck down here. Tara's going to be sending out wedding invites by the time we're back home, but it's going to be Jager who's gonna be tapping her, not me!"

Tensu shrugged. "At a minimum, they told us we're down here until we've refined enough uranium to power a couple of reactors. That would be next week."

"Tensu, don't be a moron. They've got us just where they want us. Jager's got me where he wants me."

"I know, Rodney. I think they're going to keep us here until we've filled the fuel bins on the *Appleseed*. Look at the ore, almost five percent U-235. We could jam it into the reactors just as it is and it would work just fine. We're piling up more every day, so why pull us out?" Tensu looked around him. He loved the subtle colors of the rocks that lay all around the compound.

"Because we're sucking down all these metal flakes," said Rodney, waving at the dark particles on their suits. "This damn dust is everywhere. You know we can't filter it all out. Plus, the uranium is making us glow in the dark."

"You do have a point," said Tensu. "Motherlode is beautiful, but deadly." Their path travelled along a small ridge that formed one side of a richly tinted lake. The waters swirled with blues, bright reds, and greens. "Those chromium salts are spectacular."

"I guess. Let's go, Tensu. The mine awaits." Ahead of them, the portal of the mine was a dark blotch on the hillside.

***

Ton by ton, the uranium ore was wrestled to the surface, smelted under the glare of the solar mirrors, and the enriched fraction that remained was molded into marble-sized pellets for easy shipping. Cargo rockets roared from the makeshift spaceport twice weekly, carrying enriched ore pellets up to the *Appleseed* for final processing.

In the cavernous interior of the *Appleseed*'s inner hull, they set about separating the uranium into fuel-grade, or 'fissile' $U-235$ and its heavier unusable twin, the non-fissile $U-238$. Ore pellets were vaporized by an electric arc furnace, and the ionized plasma was fed past a powerful magnet, which bent the path of the atoms according to their electric charge and atomic mass. It was then a simple matter to collect the atoms of whatever element you wanted at the appropriate spot along the plasma beam's curved trajectory.

On a planet, using mass spectrometry to enrich uranium was

complicated and inefficient compared to other methods. In space, under conditions of natural vacuum and microgravity, it was the obvious choice.

***

The Fissiles Team, a group of *Appleseed* crew deeply involved in the mining project, met to prepare the progress report for Captain Bettendorf. Lightly perched on tall stools arrayed about the chest-high conference room table, their tempers were beginning to fray by the end of Helen Rooney's presentation.

"What do you mean, move operations?" asked the Greg Watson, Fissiles Inventory Manager. "If we stay on course, we'll have enough uranium to restart five out of the twenty offline reactors by next week. Why do you want to move operations now?"

"It's the geology," said Helen. "I was looking at the flybys that Commander Okafor ran when we first got here. There were some data anomalies that bothered me in the beginning, but I didn't have a strong enough case to challenge the siting of the mine at that time."

"Such as…?" prompted Gunter Böhme, Team Leader and Mining Specialist. He was the Fissiles Team's representative on the surface of Motherlode.

"Take a look at this imagery, taken in the near infrared," said Helen. "Notice this lake." She projected an image of Tensu's beautiful lake on the wall.

"Yeah? Pretty colors from all the chromium salts, if I recall correctly."

"Look in the center."

"At what? It's a dark blue patch, cold. So?"

"You are correct. But something bothered me about these lakes. I enhanced the center and spread out the spectrum. Here." She projected another slide on the wall. It looked like a dark blue donut surrounding a lighter blue interior.

"OK, I'm looking at a warmer center. Again, so what? The water at the center is a half degree warmer than the rest. Maybe there's a center mound that brings it closer to the surface."

"That's what I thought. Then I asked the Commander to use the next cargo rocket to do a bathymetric scan. The center is the deepest part of the lake." Helen frowned prettily at the image. "So either we're looking at a thermocline, halocline, or at some kind of process that heats up the center of the lake."

"And for this, we have to move operations? Do you realize how much longer that will take? We'd have to site and develop another mine, including a smelter, housing compound, and spaceport."

"I realize the logistical problem," said Helen. "But there's one more bit of data you need." The image on the screen changed. The donut's center was a light magenta. "It's getting warmer, up two degrees in the past month."

***

Tensu endured the decontamination blasts stoically as he did awkward jumping-jacks in the airlock. The best way to delay heavy metal poisoning is to blow all the dust off one's hazmat suit when entering the barracks, and flexing the suit was the best way to make sure that happened. When the green light flashed, he gasped in relief and shuffled through the hatch into the equipment room beyond, where he changed out of the hazmat suit and respirator into Engineering's standard one-piece jumpsuit loaded with pockets. He entered the main barracks area, already scrolling through messages on his tablet.

"Did you hear? We might be moving!" exclaimed Rodney. He tossed a beer pouch to Tensu. "Drink up!"

"Why are we moving operations?" asked Tensu. Rodney recapitulated the issues raised in the Fissiles Team meeting while Tensu tried to enjoy the beer. It, and everything else he ate, had started tasting like copper. He realized with a start that he was being slowly poisoned by Motherlode.

"So, when and to where?" asked Tensu.

Rodney shook his head. "It's not going to be that simple. First, we get to be sailors. The Fissiles Team wants some actual samples, not remote imagery. We're getting a good old-fashioned rowboat in our next supply shipment!"

Days later, as they inflated the rubber dinghy on the graveled shores of the lake, Tensu gazed speculatively out towards the center. "I wonder what's really going on out there." His head buzzed with Helen's speculations, along with all of the research that she had linked to support her guesses.

"Well, one thing is for sure--it's not the mine's fault. None of our shafts or galleries pass within two hundred meters of this lake."

"But aren't we getting closer?" asked Tensu. "The pitchblende vein runs in this general direction."

"We'll be long gone before we ever need to dig that far," said Rodney. "Besides, there's that intrusion dike we have to breach first." One of the geological oddities was a five meter sill of hardened granite that sat between the lake and the mine. Formed when magma filled a crack in the original bedrock, the granite sill acted like a solid dam to keep the ground water from the lake from saturating the mine.

"Besides," continued Rodney, "we're going to follow the vein on the other side of the central shaft, away from the lake." Rodney shut the valve on the air bottle. "Let's go get some pretty colored water for the bored folks up on *Appleseed*." He continued muttering into his radio. Tensu caught the name 'Tara' during Rodney's monologue, and wisely kept quiet.

Tensu and Rodney clambered into the dinghy and used the small electric engine to push out to the center of the lake. They lowered the self-sealing sample containers over the side, one by one, and carefully noting time, temperature, location, and depth coordinates for each sample.

Tensu reached for the last sample container. "Let me try something," he said, lowering it two hundred and fifty meters to the lake bottom. Hauling it back up, he looked at the container, aimed it overboard, and triggered the release.

Instantly, the sample container was blown over the side of the dinghy, where it sank into the lake, still trailing its hoisting line. The water hit the lake surface, where it fizzed madly for a few seconds before subsiding.

"Uh-oh," said Tensu, wiping the water off his visor.

"What?" asked Rodney, hauling in the errant sampler.

"Nigeria. Or was it Cameroon? I'll have to look it up," Tensu said enigmatically. "I'll get another sample."

***

"'Warning. Contents under extreme pressure'," read the technician on board the *Appleseed*. "'Use sampling port only.' Yeah, right. Bunch of ground-pounders telling me my job," he said, reaching for the release lever on the sample container.

"STOP!" shouted a voice behind him. He twitched, and then turned to look at the stern face of Helen Rooney. "Tensu's no 'ground-pounder'. He's just as careful a scientist as you are, and he was not kidding. If you hit that release, you'll be cleaning up a lot of wreckage."

"You're kidding me, Helen. I've opened sample containers from five hundred meters down. All you get is a little pop. Water doesn't compress all that much."

"You know, I really should let you do it. Still, the results are too important. Just use the sampling port."

Grumbling, the technician complied. He slipped the sample into the gas chromatograph, and set it to hunting along the spectrum. He had just turned away when a red light lit on the machine and the tracing halted.

"What now?" he muttered. "CO_2 offscale high? It can't be--I've run cola through this thing." He went about clearing the gas chromatograph in order to rerun the sample. Helen hid a smile. This tech was going to get the surprise of his life.

"ALERT, ALERT," sounded the intercom. "Solar Flare detected. X-Ray flux in the Orange Zone and rising. Coronal Mass Ejection from central star verified, impact in eighteen hours. Secure all EVAs."

"Crap!" shouted Helen whirling around so quickly that she lost contact with the floor. "The groundsiders are screwed!" She flailed in the air, then waited for the seven percent gravity to get her close enough to a lab table to pull herself to the floor. She raced out the door.

The technician watched her bound out of the lab and shook his head. He had never seen his boss so rattled. He tried to run the sample through the gas chromatograph again. He watched the machine like a hawk. Again, the overload alarm tripped. He looked at the sample container in amazement. "Just what did you scoop up, Tensu?"

***

Tensu Matusha was deep in the mine, tending to an automated conveyer belt when his beltphone buzzed. Accepting the call, he routed it to the integrated headset within his snouted breathing mask.

"Matusha," he said.

"Tensu, quick, get over to the Molycut C-9 in Tunnel J and shut it off! It's not responding to commands and it's ready to dig through that pretty lake of yours!" Gunter's voice radiated that deadly calm that professionals use when the situation was really serious.

Tensu got his bearings and raced off for the C-9. "It's going to take me a half hour to get there. What happened?" he panted as he walked as fast as he could. He knew that he would collapse if he tried to run in this gravity field.

Gunter explained. "We've lost contact with *Appleseed*. The bands just roar with static. My guess is some kind of solar flare. Remember that big sunspot they were talking about the last sitrep?"

"Uh...yeah..." Tensu panted. The damned respirator never delivered enough air no matter what its setting. He fought the claustrophobic feelings and told himself he was breathing enough oxygen.

"Don't try to talk. Just get your ass over to the C-9. I've got a major fault light on the transmitter head. I think the flare zapped it. C-9 was supposed to stop dead, but I think its computer is out, too."

"How...are we..."

"Talking? Different system, Tensu. Main comm system blew out; we're on the secondary, which was off until just now. Just keep moving!"

After twenty minutes of walk-jog-walking, Tensu slowed to a stop. "I think I...hear it. Down...Tunnel J5."

"That's the one. Hurry! It's digging into the igneous dike."

Tensu walked down the tunnel, legs burning with the effort. The Molycut C-9 was one of the best rock cutters that mining engineering had come up with when they left Earth, hundreds of years ago. It could cut all but the hardest granites with ease. In the twenty-five minutes that it was running unsupervised, it had dug out the rock face at the end of the tunnel, right up to igneous dike holding the lake waters out of the mine.

"Gunther, I found it. Listen." He stopped panting. A stream of water ran over his overshoes. "Pack up everything essential. Now!" He climbed the side of the C-9, deactivated the cutting heads, and threw the machine into reverse. Riding the machine, he ran it back down the tunnel as fast as he dared.

"Why? We're not even close to done."

"Yes we are," Tensu said, eyeing the receding cutting face, where a spray of foaming water spat three meters out of the exposed rock. "When you do reach *Appleseed*, call Helen Rooney and tell her that we've got Lake Nyos draining into Oklo."

"What the hell are you talking about?" said Rodney. "Are you on something?"

"I sure hope not. I think we're sitting right on top of a nuclear geyser, and we've just popped the cork.

***

Susilo Harta, Chief of Planetary Operations, stared at Helen Rooney as if she had sprouted a second head.

"They're about to what?"

"Unleash a nuclear geyser. Then suffocate. We have to get them out of there," she insisted, for perhaps the tenth time. She had been getting hoarse working her way up the chain of command.

"Absolutely not," said Marc Ferrer, First Officer, and in charge of all EVA activities, including the cargo runs to Motherlode. "Have you forgotten that there's a solar flare going on?"

"What's the cumulative dose from geosynch to the ground?" asked Helen. "A quarter Gray? Nothing, compared to what these men are about to get."

Susilo rubbed his bald head, a smooth nut-brown, attesting to his Indonesian roots. "I think you're going to have to go over this again for us."

Helen looked around the table. In addition to Marc and Susilo, a half-dozen people, representing most of the *Appleseed*'s departments were asking for more of an explanation. Her shoulders slumped briefly--this should be so obvious to them--but she straightened as she thought of the men on the surface, especially Tensu.

"I am sorry, this has been on my mind for quite some time, since I first noticed the temperature changes in the lake. This isn't anything new, just somewhat rare.

"There's three lakes on Earth just like the one near the mine. Lake Nyos in Cameroon is a strange lake. It sits in a crater of a dormant volcanic field. While that's common enough, what is odd is that the waters of this lake don't turn over every year, unlike nearly every other lake on Earth. The lake is extremely deep, and the bottom waters never move. The old magma has been outgassing ever since its last eruption, but instead of the gasses migrating from rock into the air, they dissolve into the lake waters for centuries on end. All kinds of gasses dissolve in the water, but the worst is carbon dioxide.

"Given enough time, the amount of dissolved CO2 reaches fantastic amounts. Way back in the 1980s, something disturbed Lake Nyos, and the bottom waters were shoved upwards. As the waters moved upwards towards the surface, the pressure from the water overhead dropped, and the CO_2 undissolved from the water.

"It was like popping a champagne cork. Instantly, the lake foamed up about ten meters as all of the gasses came out of solution. A cloud of carbon dioxide fifteen meters thick rolled out of the lake and down into the village, killing nineteen hundred people." She paused, taking a sip of water from the bulb in front of her.

"And that's what's sitting right beside our mine?" asked Susilo.

"Yes. We've been examining some water samples from the lake. Some folks needed convincing that the water was somewhat unusual." She smiled grimly, thinking of the hapless technician.

"And?"

"The bottom of the lake runs about two hundred fifty meters, that's a pressure of twenty-one atmospheres on Earth, and that's bad enough. On Motherlode, you add another twenty percent, giving you twenty-five atmospheres. The amount of CO_2 that can dissolve is really impressive."

"So, if this lake were to overturn…"

"All of the carbon dioxide comes out as gas. The waters would be one huge mass of heavy froth, overrunning the mining camp. Even if the men survived the lake tsunami, they would be embedded in a cloud of pure carbon dioxide. Unless they were already in their airpacks, they're dead in about fifteen seconds. It's my understanding that airpacks are kept either in the mine or around the minehead, not in camp."

Susilo sat back. "We could send them more airpacks when the flare subsides. Two, three days, max."

"The men don't have that kind of time, Mr. Harta," insisted Helen. "That's not the only thing threatening them."

"Right, this 'nuclear geyser' you mentioned," put in Marc Ferrer. "How's that supposed to happen?"

Helen paused for breath, reminding herself that the senior staff were executives, not scientists, used to thinking of these issues. "When the MolyCut C-9 ran amok, it chopped into the igneous dike separating the lake bottom from the mine. The bottom water is not only jetting into the mine, but as it flows into the mine, the water fizzes with CO_2 bubbles, rapidly eroding the cracks in the rock face."

"So, we get some water in the mine. Mines have always had a problem with ground water. You pump it out. What's the big deal?" Marc's face radiated puzzlement more than hostility.

Greg Watson, Fissiles Inventory Manager, motioned to Helen. This was more on his turf. Helen gratefully took her seat. "We've tried shotcreting the exposed rock after Tensu moved the C-9 out of the way. Although we've been able to shore up some of the sides of the cutting face, we've been unable to stop the water inflow. Worse, the unplanned dig intercepted several known fractures in the main ore body. The water is percolating through the rest of the vein. In short, the men on the scene can't do a thing to stop the water inflow.

"Water is a neutron moderator. We use different technologies now, but centuries ago it was used in fission reactors as both a coolant and to slow down the neutrons from uranium fission. That ore bed we're digging up is so rich in U-235 that we can practically use it for fuel just as it is. Five percent! On Earth, they have to struggle along with seven tenths of a percent of U-235."

"So, when the ore gets surrounded with water, it becomes a reactor? I find this somewhat incredible," said Susilo. "Why hasn't Motherlode blown up if it's so possible?"

"Earth once had a natural nuclear reactor, two billion years ago," said Greg. "In a place called Oklo, in Gabon. The mine will do the same thing Oklo did, but with our people as eyewitnesses. When there's enough water around the ore a nuclear chain reaction will run out of control, heating up the ore almost instantly to several hundred degrees. The water will flash to steam and blast out of the mine, along with all the fission reaction products. The entire mining complex will be covered with boiling radioactive water. Or the lake may overturn and suffocate them first. That's why we have to get them out now."

Marc Ferrer took a poll of those present with his eyes, then stood. "I'll get the Captain's permission," he said, leaving the room. Helen gave Greg a weary thumbs up.

***

"I have no idea when, Rodney. I just got the word to prepare," Tensu said, moving downhill from the mine portal to the barracks as fast as his feet could go. "Load all of the product into the cargo rocket, they said, and prepare to depart."

"What? Go now?" asked Rodney, his voice raised to be heard over the babble of the voices in the barracks. "We're still a little short of uranium."

Tensu gave a rundown of the peril beneath their feet. "We're going to get all we can while the getting's good. Just make sure the cargo's lashed down well. We don't need it going critical when we're maneuvering."

"Don't worry, I'll be on the same ride home," said Rodney. "Just get over here and help me out!"

***

The camera clearly showed the water shooting out of the face of the cut, then draining away across the floor of the tunnel.

"All that uranium," said the First Officer. "We could have stocked up for a long time."

Helen stood with him in the control center. "It's not the only site, Mr. Ferrer. There are other locations almost as good."

"That's not the point. We're going to have to fabricate all of the equipment we're abandoning down there."

"Radiation," she said, pointing to another sensor. "Looks like part of the ore is starting to go subcritical."

"I read up on that natural reactor on Earth. It was a periodic thing, wasn't it?"

"Yes. It would slowly go critical until the ground water boiled away, then it would stop. It cycled over and over, for thousands of years, until the amount of U-235 got to be too low, then it stopped for good."

"So why didn't this one do the same thing?"

"On Earth, it was just the slow seepage of ground water into the ore body. Here, there's a two hundred and fifty meter column of lake water pouring through mine shafts into the exposed ore. I suspect that when the granite dike fails, the whole mine will go up within minutes."

***

"I never thought it would come to this. Still, it's better than being in the hazmat suits," groused Rodney, encased in a web of wiring, strapped into an acceleration couch in the cargo rocket.

Rodney was busy teleoperating the equipment outside of the mine, while Tensu and the rest of the ground crew were doing the same with the in-mine equipment. Impending disaster or no, the mission of digging uranium was continuing until the mine blew, the cargo holds on the rocket was filled, or the lake exploded. Naturally, a betting pool had been set up. Rodney was betting on filling the rocket. Tensu took the mine.

Rodney's eyes flickered over to the readouts of the radiation gauges that lined the top row of his screens. "Looks like the mine's holding its own, Tensu. Another five hours and we'll be full."

"We won't get any notice, Rodney. Just a matter of time. How's your raw material bins on the smelter?"

"Give me another hour's worth of ore, and we'll be full."

The hour passed with slowly increasing tension. Throughout the rocket, eyes took in the readings from the radiation gauges. They had been scattered throughout the mine, aiming to catch the slightest spike of radiation that indicated criticality. The general level of radioactivity had been rising ever since the C-9 had created the leak.

"Jillian, go ahead and disengage. Drive your C-9 over to the smelter and get it under cover," ordered Gunter. As they got closer to filling the smelter, Gunter had been ordering some of the equipment out of the mine. Maybe they could salvage it after things cooled down. "Mike, when you finish loading that cart, you do the same."

Tensu switched channels over to Rodney. "Only three C-9s left in the mine, Rodney."

"Look at the M-level tunnel," said Rodney. "We're starting to ramp up the radiation."

"Not good. What's the cargo load reading?" Encased in wiring, goggles, and headphones, the men and women of the ground crew could not hear the continuous loading of smelter pellets into the array of lead-lined transport cells.

"We're doing fine. Another three hours," replied Rodney.

"What will that do for us upstairs?"

"From what I hear, we can power ten reactors with this for fifteen years. If only we had another few months, we'd be golden."

"Well, this isn't the only ore body on..." his voice was chopped off in a roar of static. Tensu, Rodney, and the rest of the crew ripped their headphones off as the white noise of radiation chopped off all telemetry. They felt the blasts as the loading umbilicals were explosively detached.

A deep thunder enveloped them as acceleration squashed them down in their seats. Tensu glanced out the window to see blue-lit columns of steam and water leap out of the mine's ventilation shafts. As the rocket climbed into the sky, the swirls of colorful chromium salts mixed with the bottom mud into a foaming brown as the lake waters finally released their ancient stores of volcanic gasses.

***

Tensu smiled as he awoke to the familiar feeling of seven percent gravity. Rodney was, mercifully, still sleeping. The rigorous decontamination procedures upon their arrival had left them wondering if they would ever be allowed back aboard. Confined to sickbay for chelation and radiation sickness therapy, they were being hailed as heroes for their courageous efforts on Motherlode's surface.

Tensu fingered the intravenous tubing delivering the chelating agent into his forearm. He wondered how much longer they would be confined here. He wanted nothing more than return to his previous life aboard *Appleseed*.

"Where's the babes?" asked Rodney, coming to wakefulness in a rush. "I thought we were big time heroes. They should be lining up for us."

"Whatever happened to Tara?" asked Tensu, teasingly.

"I bet she's laying in a hero's welcome." Rodney nodded smugly. "And if she isn't, well, there are other ladies just lining up for us right outside sickbay, right, Doc?"

"Sorry, no," said Doctor Pasgeh, shrouded in an isolation garment. "Until we are sure that you're healthy, you're not going anywhere." She checked the monitor at his bedside and smiled sweetly at Rodney. "Besides, you're probably loaded with two-headed spermatozoa as it is."

Tensu chuckled. "Rodney, I bet they will have us teleoperating from here. With all the new fuel, there's no reason to go back down, and we've got all the experience."

"Not a chance, Mr. Matusha," said Doctor Pasgeh. "You and the rest of the miners have got a bit of a contamination problem. If you tried to teleoperate from here, the radioactivity in your brain would hash up the signals just enough to ruin the remote connection. I'm afraid you're sidelined until you get cleaned up."

"What's our dose?" asked Rodney, vaguely frightened. "I don't want to grow a lump or anything."

"Assuming we can get all of the contamination out of you, you're only going to get three times your max allowed annual dose."

"How'd we get contaminated, Doctor?" asked Tensu. "I thought we were pretty rigorous in our decon procedures on the surface. The geyser never touched us."

"A couple of things, Mr. Matusha. There was an incorrect setting on the cargo bay vent, so air from the bay made its way into the deck area of the cargo rocket. Then there was the gamma blast when the mine went critical. Finally, you were sitting atop a pile of uranium for hours while it was loading. All the heavy metals that had accumulated in your body became neutron activated.

"The good news is that much of this is fixable. You're stuck here until we get all the heavies out, overload you with good potassium, and fill you with antioxidants. And no teleoperation. I'll check in again in a few hours. Just rest and let the drugs work on you." Doctor Pasgeh wiggled two fingers at Rodney and departed.

"She could have let us near an intercom or something," complained Rodney. "Nothing worse than a forced vacation—Tara could be doing anything!"

"Hmm?" replied Tensu. "Oh, I love it! I finally get a chance to catch up on my reading!" He pulled a tablet over to his bed, adjusted the lighting, and left the current universe behind.

"At least they're not going to send us back down, Tensu. That has to count for something." He glanced over to his friend, to find him already asleep, the tablet on his desk winking off.

"No Tara, and no Tensu." Rodney caught a reflection of himself in a mirror. Throwing himself a mock salute, he concluded, "Well, I still think you're a hero, Rodney."

Author Bill Patterson

Bill writes the Family of Grifters series (Robin Hoods con-artists who scam the entitled elite) and has stories in both the Paradisi Chronicles and Nick Webb's Legacy Fleet. He is the science brains behind Felix R. Savage's Earth's Last Gambit; reviewers liken the team to SF greats Heinlein and Asimov. He has been nominated for the British Science Fiction Association's Award for Non-Fiction.

Visit PattersonBill.wordpress.com for all of his work, as well as sign up for his newsletter to be the first to know about all of his upcoming publications.

He and his wife of a third of a century, Barbara, live in Central New Jersey.

Emergence
by E. R. Starling

Prologue

Something didn't feel right.

Marcus Penn glanced inconspicuously towards the open bridge, listening to the hum of silent communication. Invisible fingertips brushed over his spine. The simple sensation triggered a ripple over his nerve endings.

Something definitely wasn't right.

"Repeat. This is Vissaeus Three, requesting entrance to Erra in the Alcyon system for diplomatic arrival."

Marcus trained his attention toward the bridge, listening to the hum of silent communication.

It wasn't an anomaly to have to repeat a call.

Still, the brush of uneasiness was hard to ignore.

Taking a quick assessment, Marcus let his gaze slowly move around the interior. He had done this a million times.

General Procedure.

The Vissaeus was small in comparison to most diplomatic vessels, but for what she lacked in size, she made up for in grandeur. Plush accommodations and fine, upscale décor were exactly what was expected in the representation of Earth, the newest member of the Intergalactic Alliance.

At least that was the understanding.

After countless diplomatic missions, Marcus had come to realize that none of the alien dignitaries he had encountered were as concerned with appearance as Earth's own.

Go figure.

Marcus shifted his weight and stretched. The last thing he wanted to do was create a ripple of panic. Something like that would blind him. Slowly he made the retreat from his chair. The action appearing to be nothing more than a need to walk out his cramped muscles, he shifted his weight and calmly made his way towards Dev Rollin.

Once a lieutenant for the U.S. Marines, before the Intergalactic Intelligence Agency scooped him up, Dev was the type of man you wanted beside you if shit hit the fan. Years of experience had made him a firm but fair man. He could be your best friend or your worst enemy. It all just depended on you.

As an active Missions Operative, it was Dev's job to coordinate his assigned teams. The IIA ran on a strict need to know basis, which meant everything was reported, that was Marcus's job. The security detail was a front, sure they were all supposed to see to the safety of Ramon Seeley, but when it came down to it, they were there to keep Marcus from being outed for what he was. A government-contracted Intuitive Empath. Regardless, Dev was the kind of man that kept his cards close to his chest.

Marcus couldn't have asked for anyone better.

Nestled in the back of the vessel, Dev slowly lifted his gaze as Marcus approached. He lowered the glass Holopad, sort of an intergalactic connective version of the iPad back on Earth, gently as he offered his full attention.

"Something's wrong." The soft admission wasn't enough to raise suspicion, but it was enough to put the operation commander on high alert. He glanced sideways, his gaze taking in the surroundings. His hand slowly placed the Holopad on the table beside him.

"What are you picking up on?" He asked quietly.

"I'm not sure," Marcus admitted. "Everything looks..."

"Welcome to the Alcyon system, Vissaeus. Proceed to Erra."

The moment the transmission arrived, he felt the surge. The time around him seemed to slow to almost nothing.

The crew around frozen in motion.

Flickers of action ripped across his inner vision with the consistency of a flashing strobe.

The two pilots busied themselves with preparation for entrance to Erra,

The flashing and warning alarms lighting up the console,

A power optic beam flashing upwards from the waiting planet below,

The rupture of the front of Vissaeus,

Screams assaulting his senses,

Pain and heat tore into him as effectively as knives and a sharp rise of satisfied malice, so thick, it felt like it could suffocate him.

Marcus forced his eyes open, the images sliding back into his mind's eye.

"Starting descent." The lead pilot toned cheerfully.

Marcus looked around.

Everything had returned to normal.

"Bank left!!" He damn near screamed. "Now!"

"What?" The second asked in confusion.

As if on cue the console flashed to life, the alarms ringing off the walls.

"Do what he says!" Dev snapped hotly.

The flash of light, the rumble of the impact, and the blast of heat were enough to scramble his senses.

But that didn't block out the pilot's screams.

CHAPTER 1

The unmistakable tingle of being watched rushed over her in a torrent of sensory. Instinct kicked into overdrive. Adrenaline flooded into her veins clenching her muscles in anticipation. Sibella Moran focused her attention on nimbly flipping through the Eco-safe disposable party plates as if she were counting them. She flicked her gaze inconspicuously around the open area.

The open park bustled with activity. The groomed grass and trees built atop the vaulted columns of the rising city was easy to scout out. The problem came from the massive amount of passing people.

The rushing sound of water, the large oval exit for outlets and rain gutters, redirected water to the park square, creating a host of waterfalls for an artistically pleasing view. But that didn't exactly produce an optimal condition. Neither did the sound of Zane, her nephew, and his friends engaged in all-out laser battle behind her.

It didn't take long before she realized that normal sensory wouldn't be enough. Sibella drew her eyes closed, slowly drawing on her talent to see without them. She latched onto the feeling of eyes crawling over her skin.

Her hands stilled with the napkins still clutched in her fist. The world seemed to blur around her. The sounds of everything died away, motion almost completely slowed to a standstill. The feeling of being watched suddenly the only thing she could feel. She allowed her senses to drift until she was able to lock onto the source. The sensation of movement spun her perception, her eyes flashed open. With no hesitation, her gaze whipped toward the outskirts of the park square.

The black SUV, parked at the corner of the main strip, wouldn't have stood out inconspicuously against the gamut of other cars. Not even in the worst of times. But the thing that really made it stand out like a sore thumb to her was the male leaned up against it.

Dressed in plain clothes, he blended so well into the crowd that it would have taken a miracle to pick him out.

Or someone like her.

Even if she hadn't recognized him, she would have picked him out.

And he knew it.

A microscopic tilt of his head told her he was well aware of her notice.

"Hey, you okay?"

Sibell snapped her attention as her brother-in-law's voice broke over her surroundings.

"Yeah, yeah, I'm fine." She muttered.

"You sure?"

"Yeah, of course. Why wouldn't I be?" She acknowledged, turning her attention back to sorting the table arrangements.

"Because it looks like you're trying to squeeze the life out of the napkins."

Sibell looked down at the crinkled paper in her hands that she still had a death grip on before placing them in their spot.

"Look, Bell... If you need anything..." His voice dropped an octave as he tried to retrace where her gaze had been. It wouldn't do any good, she knew.

Mira, her sister, had always been close to her. Even when she had dropped off the face of the earth, Mira hadn't given up on her as part of the family. And Dylan, her sister's new husband, was no different. He had taken in Mira and Zane and made a life for them. Something she appreciated. But none of them knew about her past, and Dylan was constantly trying to do the same for her by drawing her into his family.

She had to admit she was sorely tempted. Dylan was a big man with the military in his blood. The only reason he hadn't taken another deployment was to be home with Mira.

But as tempting as the idea was, she couldn't risk her brother-in-law stumbling across the real reason for her visitor. Knowing Dylan, that is exactly what would happen.

"I'm fine. I promise." She said.

He looked at her skeptically for a moment. Almost as if he were trying to pry her secrets from behind her eyes.

For the first time in her life, Sibell was grateful for her training. Even her brother-in-law, as astute as he was, was no match for the given ability to hide in plain sight, even her true thoughts and feelings.

"So where you at?" He asked.

"Almost done, I think Mira said she wanted to do cake after gifts.

Would you mind double checking?"

As Dylan walked away, Sibell made sure he was gone and then glanced back up at the still waiting SUV. She couldn't escape talking to him. It was either that or go on the run.

And she was tired of running.

Her attention turned to the fist still clenched at her side, horrified thoughts of what could have happened had she not recognized Dylan's voice playing through her mind.

***

She wasn't sure what she expected.

She would like to have said she expected to look up and see all traces of the SUV had disappeared from the face of the planet.

But deep down... she knew better.

The genetically altered, albeit organic, grass had muffled her footsteps. But once she stepped onto the hard, unyielding concrete of the curbside all bets were off.

Taking a deep breath, she allowed the sounds of the dying birthday party to fade away. Zane had been given a good day. That's all that mattered. Once the laser battles began again in earnest, with Dylan taking his place as the leader of his son's squad team, Sibell took a deep breath and slipped away.

Her eyes scanned the area around her as she moved deliberately away from the festivities, shifting the dynamics of any threat that the sudden appearance might impose to their safety. Despite removing herself from the clutches of the IIA, Sibell wasn't fool enough to think that the appearance of the SUV could be anything but trouble. Trouble she wouldn't have around Mira and her family.

Taking a tight hold of her fight or flight response, her gaze locked on the figure that emerged from the back door of the SUV.

Not good.

That meant there were more than just him.

Her instincts peaked as she made her way forward. Every ounce of training she had endured kicked into overdrive.

Just the sheer time that they had sat and waited for her was enough cause for concern. Whatever it was they wanted. They wanted it pretty badly.

And if that were the case, no amount of running would stop them. Better to stand her ground now.

No matter what it cost.

By the time she reached the curb, he was waiting for her, leaning against the driver side fender.

"What are you doing here?" She asked as she drew closer.

Alexander Cade had a smooth charisma, but when push came to shove the man came fully equipped with an arsenal of wit, temper, and sarcasm. Olive skin tone and black hair made him easy on the eyes, but it was his intellect that made him dangerous. The sheer knowledge of tactics alone was enough to make him a force of divine retribution.

As a handler that made him indispensable.

As an opponent, it made him lethal.

Not exactly good news.

Apparently, the IIA was serious about her involvement in what was going on.

For a moment Cade hesitated. His hand gripped the sunglasses, removing them from blocking a full view of dark chocolate eyes. His gaze automatically danced around the area.

The simple moment put her on tilt.

He was cautious...

And that worried her.

"We've got some trouble." He admitted quietly.

"I assumed that." She countered as his gaze shifted to the ground. "The question is, trouble for who?"

Tucking her hands into her light jacket and rolling her weight across her feet, Sibell turned. She needed her body language right now, needed her resistance to show without aggression, even if her mind did scream at her for restricting her hands.

"Whatever it is, it has nothing to do with me. I don't want any part of it."

"Bell... Come on..."

"No!" She snapped.

There was a bit more indignation in her voice than she had intended.

"You know I left the IIA. And you know why."

Cade deftly scouted the surrounding area again.

"You weren't there, Cade. You didn't have to contend with the torture they called training."

"You know if I would have known-" His gaze returned again.

She could feel the rush of guilt pouring off of him.

"Don't you dare do that to me." She snapped hotly. Unsure if she was angry with him for the emotion or at herself for causing it. "Of course you didn't know. As long as I was active, I couldn't tell you. That's exactly how they want it."

She trailed a bit, her eyes starting to swim under the unpleasant memories.

"Bell... this is bigger than them."

He cast a quick look around, stepping closer to her.

"You may be in danger." He muttered quietly.

She shifted her weight. Unable to keep her hands restricted any longer she removed them from her pockets and folded her arms. Rocking back on her heels and dropping her gaze for a split second to make the action look natural.

"Then you tell me what is more dangerous than being a lapdog for the IIA." She squared her jaw.

"You convince me this is more dangerous and I <u>might</u> consider listening."

"You know I can't say much here."

His eyes hardened dangerously, dancing around once more but this time haltingly.

In that split second, she felt it.

He wasn't waiting to drag her back to her tormentors.

He was expecting an attack.

The sudden slam of realization put her on edge. She had known Cade since she was in her late teens, trained with him. A matched set. She knew him and knew him well. And this was no charade.

"Then give me something." Her voice sounded calmer, even to her own ears.

He was defusing her.

A tactic used by handlers to help balance out their Empaths.

He sighed.

His gaze instinctively trailed just a bit before returning to her. It was a sign he didn't see her as a threat.

She logged away the information.

Cade was the type of man who saw everything as a threat.

The fact that he didn't now, told her just how serious he felt this new issue being faced was.

She drew in a breath allowing her eyes to trail the area.

His edginess was starting to rub off on her.

"Why me... Cade. Huh?" She trailed her gaze back to him. "Why not Marcus? Marcus had near perfect scores, just like I did. He could be much better suited for whatever-"

"We can't do that," Cade muttered in a low voice.

She couldn't keep the frustration from boiling over,

"Why not?"

"Because." He answered matter-a-factly. "Marcus Penn went down on Vissaeus Three almost a week ago."

CHAPTER 2

Sibell could almost hear the shatter wreak havoc on her thoughts.

Her wide eyes locked on Cade's grim face as if searching for any hint of deception. Nothing.

None.

She turned away to try to hide the tears that welled up in her eyes.

Her hands shook under the realization.

Marcus Penn was dead.

Recruits of the IIA Intuitive Empath program tended to band together. Unlike the outside world, it wasn't hard to talk among other IEs. Sibell hadn't really taken up the camaraderie like most did. But Marcus had been her constant companion. They had been a shoulder for each other to make it through each day.

At least until Marcus accepted graduation and promotion. It was inevitable really.

He had been in the program a year before she had.

That meant her last year was spent without him.

It was a desperate thought that the assignment of a handler would have been enough to limp her through to graduation.

It hadn't.

"Marcus isn't the only one. IEs from all walks of the program are being targeted." Cade explained. His voice was so low Sibell had to struggle to hear him.

"Why?" Her throat felt dry trying to get the single question out.

"I can't say much more. Not here."

The sounds of the children playing slowly drew her attention back to the park.

Dylan and Zane were immersed in their battle. Father and son taking over the war while Mira's laughing eyes supervised the festivities.

A gentle smile brushed her features. Her heart warmed at seeing the display of family.

On the heels of that thought came a cold dread.

She was a target.

That meant she was a threat, a threat to Mira and Zane, a threat to the life they had built.

All at once she felt the trap close.

She had no choice.

"They didn't send you did they?" She muttered.

"No."

She turned back to face him as he spoke.

"You're not active. So far none of the victims have been off the grid."

"A leak in the system?"

She asked quietly.

"That's what they are suspecting."

"But you don't." She stated matter-of-factly.

She could feel the disagreement of the problems diagnosis rolling off of him in waves.

He was directly avoiding detection of something.

She just couldn't tell what.

"Out with it, Cade."

"I convinced them to let me come for you. It didn't take a lot for them to see you would be-"

"Useful." She muttered in disdain.

He hesitated a minute.

"I don't regret it. I'd feel a lot better if I have your back."

She watched him for a moment.

Conflicting thoughts rushed around inside her head.

She wasn't sure she could yoke herself back to the IIA.

But...

If IEs were being targeted, she could only get so far on her own.

Intuitive Empaths were always assigned handlers and were never left without protection.

Training even included lethal force for emergencies.

That's how dangerous her world could be.

Now it had just gotten a violent shove into seriously deadly.

Absorbed in her thoughts and the dilemma at hand, the buzz of her communicator at her waist caused her to start.

She retrieved it from the belt case and glanced at the message as it rolled across the screen.

'What's going on?'

Damn.

She glanced back behind her quickly to see Dylan moving purposefully across the grass towards them.

Time was up.

And she knew it.

No sooner had she realized that her old life and her new one were suddenly on a crash course, she felt something else.

Something dark.

Cold.

The world around her slowed as she reached for the source of the feeling.

Tried to grasp it.

But it dissipated tauntingly. Like smoke in the wind.

Fuck.

"We have to go." She snapped lightly.

"Wait... Bell!"

She turned on the balls of her feet and broke into a solid run towards her brother-in-law.

Seeing her in a dead run caused a bit of concern. As she drew up closer to him, Dylan broke into a jog to meet up with her.

"Bell. What the hell is going on?" He snapped quietly.

"I don't have time to explain."

The look on his face was unsettled. She knew he didn't like being in the dark, but she couldn't give him much more.

"Do you love my sister? And her son?"

"What? You know I would..."

"Do you love them!?"

"Yes!" he snapped.

"What's gotten into you?"

"Then trust me. Take Mira and Zane. Go somewhere, anywhere. Don't tell me where you're going."

She could feel the shift of malicious intent grow darker around her. Mixed with Dylan's swaying emotions, it was a powerful assault on her senses.

"How long?"

His hesitation was enough to prove his uncertainty, but at least he was willing to play along.

"Two weeks." She said. "Say it's a vacation. A birthday trip for Zane. I'll be in contact when I can."

She glanced back at Cade.

"Take care of them, Dylan. Please."

"Take care of yourself, Bell." She was relieved to notice he seemed to have simply fallen back into his military understanding.

"If I have to catch hell from Mira because I let you go and you got hurt, I'll hunt you down myself."

She couldn't help but mirror the tight-lipped smile he flashed her.

"It's a deal."

Without another word, she sprinted back towards Cade.

"Let's go." She muttered, sliding into the open back door of the SUV.

***

The odor of fear was almost stifling in the confined back seat of the shiny new SUV. At least, <u>odor</u> was the best descriptive word she could attribute to it.

"Where are we going?" She toned evenly.

"Dulles Base." Cade supplied. "It's the closest allied base."

Sibell lifted her gaze just a little, settling her scrutiny on the consistent blur of passing trees. The mountain ridgeline just outside the city had some beautiful scenery in the summer. Each turn off of the main route had taken them deeper into the thick pines and over rougher terrain.

Earth had changed a lot since the planet had entered into the Intergalactic Alliance.

But even with the mass advances in technology brought by collaboration within the council, inhabitants of Earth were far from ready to be introduced to the secrets that lay beyond their everyday lives.

"They're afraid of me," she muttered softly.

"Who is?"

She turned her head towards Cade before gracefully lifting an eyebrow and nodding in the direction of the silent sentinels driving the SUV.

"After thirteen years you'd think I'd be used to it."

It wasn't like they intimidated her.

Quite the opposite it would seem.

But then again IEs were an enigma.

Even to the Intergalactic Council. They were just another way for the U.S. Government, secret factions at least, to gain an advantage over the vastly unexplored area known as the universe.

It was clear that the goon squad sent to escort her knew that she wasn't exactly the run of the mill when it came to females but it was also abundantly clear they were unsure just what she was capable of.

She didn't bother to ease their tender sensibilities by informing them either.

Cade flicked his eyes in the direction she nodded before refocusing his attention.

"They just don't understand," he said in a hushed tone. "People fear what they don't understand."

"Yes," she agreed.

"And destroy it as well."

She had no doubt in her mind that if the inhabitants of planet earth knew what lay behind the fronts and secrets, there would be nothing to stand in the way of humanity as it destroyed itself.

Fear could do that.

Just a glance at any history book would produce thousands of hours of data to back that theory.

"That's why I'm here." He shifted slightly.

She didn't bother hiding the disbelief at the boldness of the statement before turning to look out of the tinted window once more.

"Bell-"

The way he said her name sent a surprising warmth winging through her core.

She swiftly turned to look at him.

The flame in his eyes, the tight clench in his jaw, spoke volumes. Conviction. He had only ever used it in times when he meant every word of what was being said.

"I'm here. I'm not leaving. And I'm not going to let anyone hurt you again."

She hesitated for a moment, taken aback by the sudden arrival of what she could only describe as an attachment.

Attraction.

She scoured her mind, but she never remembered a time when he had displayed it before.

A flicker of awareness passed over her as she briefly noted the arrival of similar SUVs converging quickly with theirs into a single file line.

"Tell me what happened to Marcus," she toned determinedly.

CHAPTER 3

"The Intergalactic Alliance received anonymous reports of hostile behavior on Erra," he began.

"Erra? From the Pleiades constellation?" Sibell asked.

She glanced up as the high-vaulted entrance, tucked away behind the edge of a cliff, came into view.

Cade nodded.

"Yes, Alcyon system," he confirmed.

"Reports stated that the inhabitants of Erra were facing oppressive and inhumane conditions. Slavery, really."

"The Pleiadians are hardly known for being welcoming to visitors," she mused absently.

She couldn't help but stare at the magnitude of the doors. They towered over the vehicles by ten or twelve times. Reinforced steel twisted into itself.

She had been to bases all across the U.S., and none of them could match this one.

"Alliance representatives set up a routine inspection of Erra. Ramon Seely was sent in as the ambassador under the pretense of learning the ropes."

That got her attention.

Her eyebrows knit together. In the few moments of silence that followed came the deep rumble of the bay doors opening. Before she answered her eyes flicked to the surrounding area. Tension like a lead weight wrapped around her.

"Seely hasn't been in that position more than seven or eight months. Why would they send in someone like that to inspect a hard-to-manage race like the Pleiadians?"

A light smile touched Cade's lips.

"Sounds like someone still keeps up on IIA affairs."

"Why would I not?"

The vehicles moved again, passing over from rocky terrain to the smooth, dull gray of the interior hangar.

"That's one of their prized teachings, isn't it? Know your enemy?"

As the SUVs roared into the echoing chamber, Sibell reached for the assortment of emotional wavelengths around her.

It was old.

Much older than any of the other bases she had visited.

As soon as all vehicles cleared the mark, the doors began to shut behind them.

As soon as they were sealed away from daylight the soft, blue-hedged neon glow of running lights supplied clear visibility.

"I don't know," Cade admitted. "I have no idea why they would send in Seely. They didn't even seem disturbed by the reports when Vissaeus went offline roughly three minutes after entering the atmosphere around Erra."

In an attempt to keep her hands from shaking she closed them into fists, closed her eyes against the drum in her ears.

She expected that talking about Marcus's fate would upset her.

But what she felt was extreme.

Even for her.

She couldn't understand the hard clench in her gut that refused to let up.

"So... they were inside the gravitational pull," she muttered.

The vehicles fanned out, formed a half circle at the far end of the hangar.

"We haven't heard anything since," Cade answered.

The SUV door opened, and Sibell took note of her surroundings. The second her anxiety hit dangerous levels she hesitated, drew in a deep breath, and slid out of her seat into the open space.

The only thing she didn't expect was her natural self-preservation instinct rising at an alarming rate.

She stopped, trying to peg the source of the feeling.

This wasn't right.

She had spent most of her life testing the feeling of power and energy; she knew when something was wrong.

And something was very wrong.

A quick glance at the other SUVs told her that she wasn't the only one to grace the base with a presence. Others emerged from the vehicles.

A quick assessment told her all she needed to know.

Six.

Single IEs. All of them. No Handlers.

So it wasn't exactly a shock when officials from the IE Program appeared from the waiting vehicles.

They had to be novices.

Recruits to the Program that were not far enough along in training to be given a handler.

Four females and two males.

Unease crept over her bones like a freezing rain, the gears in her mind turning.

"Where are they?" Cade muttered. "We should have had a welcoming committee already."

All of a sudden she felt it.

The unmistakable stench of deceit. Death. Blood...

"We have a problem," she muttered. "We have to get out of here."

"We can't." The voice jolted her out of her senses.

Captain Disenger, one of the Program officials, drew up behind them.

"The doors are on an automatic vacuum lock due to the situation. They won't open for twelve hours."

Sibell glanced at him. Her brows drew together in confusion.

"That's not protocol."

"It is now," Disenger said stonily.

"Well... Let's move forward then," she muttered. "It's the only thing we can do."

***

The thick air felt almost suffocating in the confined space.

In place of the fresh scent of climate-controlled air, there was only the musty, dank smell of the underground.

Definitely not a good sign.

Disenger hadn't wasted any time. The instant she gave her report, he had pulled together all of the officials and IEs, falling back on normal protocol. Now, being encircled by the officials, hardened men with years of military or similar training, didn't do much to comfort her. Crammed into the center with the other Empaths, Sibell couldn't help but feel that maybe she should have kept her mouth shut.

She didn't trust the Program officials.

And it showed.

The only consolation was Cade.

Traveling at her left, his weapon drawn and ready, Sibell was sure to keep herself beside him as they moved forward.

Obviously, she wasn't the only one to be uneasy despite the show of protection. The visible tremors wracking the younger woman beside her set her more on edge than she cared to admit.

The full force of panic and fear was more than enough to blind her to other sensory perception.

"What's your name?" she finally whispered.

"Jena. Jena Shantell," the young woman answered in a high-pitched whisper.

"Ok, Jena," Sibell said as the team moved along quietly. "Tell me about yourself. How long have you been with the Program?"

"A year," Jena answered.

Sibell whirled her gaze toward Jena.

"What?"

"A representative of the IIA found me about a year ago. My mother was very ill, you see. She..." Jena swallowed. Her eyes shifted around the titanium corridor like they were trying to escape her skull.

"We needed money for medical bills."

Sibell glanced back and forth between the six Empaths.

"All of you?" She asked.

Jena nodded.

The spike of unease was almost enough to set her nerves alight. She hadn't expected them to be that inexperienced. The oldest she had ever heard of Empaths being drawn into the Program were mid-teens. Sibell herself had been seven.

The thought unnerved her. The only one of them with any tangible training was her.

And she still didn't have enough for her to handle this situation.

"It's because of the threat," Cade muttered softly. "All IEs are being pulled and taken to Sector 9."

The look of disdain crossed her face at the mention of the sector that acted as headquarters for Earth's involvement in the Intergalactic Alliance. The Lunar Base.

"I couldn't tell you," he muttered, his gaze taking note of her features.

"Why?" she demanded under her breath.

"Because," as he said as he surveyed the surroundings, "You wouldn't have come if I had."

Her lips pulled together tightly in frustration moments before Disenger held up a hand, indicating a halt. Rapid movement of fingers on the open keypad had triggered the hydraulic door hinges seconds before it released.

The air that blasted into their faces was almost rancid.

Sheer horror waited in stark color.

Consoles covered in blood.

Walls and floors sticky from the drying substance.

Personnel, at least what was left of them, lay thrown around the floor as if on display.

Through the sudden fog of panic and disgust, Sibell latched onto something else.

Something more dangerous. The same dark, suffocating presence she had felt back in the park.

Someone, or something, was trying to send a message.

Fear me.

Jena gripped the back of her shirt in a small fist.

"What happened?" the girl mustered in a shaky voice.

"I don't know," Sibell admitted.

Disenger signaled for the escort to stay put, as he moved forward her brows drew together.

She couldn't shake the fact that something wasn't matching up.

The captain leaned over the console, scanning the Gate travel diagnostics rolling across the screen.

"The controls look like they are still good," Disenger confirmed, his eyes flashing with the moving colors. "We can get out of here as planned at least."

At his command, the entire wall, dead center beside the console panels, parted. An exit big enough to fit a small jet opened up in front of them. Inside the room was a structure- a circle, partially buried into the concrete floor. At least the bottom was. The rest of it stuck straight up in the air.

"Is that...?"

Sibell nodded, a bit surprised that the site of the structure had roused a response from one of the male Empaths beside her.

"It's a Stargate." She muttered lightly.

CHAPTER 4

The shift in the room was palpable.

"Come on. Let's get out of here." Disenger said

Sibell shifted her weight as he tagged in the coordinate codes.

Without hesitation, the other IEs moved forward, but she hung back.

The bite of her nails into her palms wasn't enough to reign in her anxiety. Searching for the source of the sudden discomfort, she had to wonder if it was her own hesitation or something else.

The intensity alone gave her cause to question it.

The ripple of sound, like electricity dancing over the air, drew her attention to the activating gate. Swirls of blue and silver hazed the air within the circle, sending enough force to ruffle the hair of anyone close enough.

"Bell, come on," Cade called.

She slowly moved forward, watching carefully, as one by one the officials moved through the gate.

"Ok, let's get the IEs through next," Disenger said, motioning to the others.

Sibell drew in a solid breath as each passing person into the ripple of space and time began to dissipate the feeling of fear. For a moment her eyes rested on Disenger, herding the first year IEs through the Gate like frightened sheep.

Strangely enough, it seemed that none of the fear she felt around her was being supplied by him.

Odd, really.

All of the handlers and officials were trained to lock down their emotions.

To keep from blinding IEs.

But in her experience, there was always a small hint under the surface.

For some unknown reason, her eyes moved around the structure of the gate.

Symbols glowed along the outer edges. Coordinate locks for the gate itself.

Her eyes narrowed.

The symbol dead center should have been a Trida. A small circle with three dots on top. When she was young, she had called it the puppy paw. Translated, it was a three.

A flash of cold dread rolled over her like a blast of ice.

Quickly she scanned the other alien numbers.

None of them were correct.

The set coordinates were not for Sector 9.

Her eyes snapped downward in time to see Jena. The last of the six moving toward Disenger's outstretched hand.

"Jena, stop!" She snapped.

The woman turned to look at her, her brow wrinkled in confusion.

Disenger's face hardened dangerously. With the speed of a viper, he captured the girl's upper arm, seized her wrist and shoved her into the swirling mist of the gate.

Instantly Sibell tensed. The surge of frustration and panic mixed into a disturbing combination.

With Jena gone the fear in the room was zero. None.

It had been a setup all along. She should have known.

"Bell."

Her eyes flashed up to Cade.

Her teeth clenched as she realized she'd been duped.

"Don't do anything stupid." He toned lightly,

More infuriating was the fact that he actually leveled his weapon on her.

"You mean like trusting you." She asked coldly.

Instinctively her hands came up beside her head.

"Yeah, I'd call that pretty stupid."

Her mind ticked away at the warning signs. But that wasn't helpful at the moment. She could analyze her failures another time. Right now she had to focus on the task at hand.

Without warning an idea struck, her eyes found a cluster of red lights beside the bay doors.

Emergency protocols.

"We can do this the easy way, or the hard way," Cade said.

"Come on Cade, you know me..." She said.

She moved forward, inch by inch.

Her only escape forming in her mind.

She had only one shot at this.

But she had to get close enough.

Just a fraction to her left. Once she reached the doors, she would be home free.

"I always like a challenge," she finished.

Gathering all of her speed, she lunged to her left. The second her hand slapped the panel the codes set off warning alarms all over the base.

Everything happened almost too quickly to grasp. Cade and Disenger lunged forward, but the doors slammed shut. The Stargate completely shut down, blocking off any exit they may have had. For now.

With no time to waste, Sibell's eyes settled on a side arm lying on the diamond plate metal.

She scooped up the weapon, ignoring the blood, and checked the ammo round.

Four.

She'd have to make them count.

Roughly five minutes tops.

That was all she had.

As she drew closer, her eyes scanned the base map display on the wall. Finding exactly what she was looking for, she tapped a spot on the map for good measure before bolting out of the exit. She wasn't sure if the story about the gridlock was true.

But she did know one thing.

She had to get the fuck out.

***

The deafening sound of the alarms ripped into her ears as she ran at full adrenaline-fueled force down the smooth corridors. Luckily enough, all bases had one thing in common.

They all had a control room.

If she could get there, she would have more time.

More time to think.

To plan.

No sooner had she made a sharp turn in the corridor, her foot lodged on something sprawled across the floor.

She dropped, hard, the impact driving the air from her lungs.

Ragged gasps tore from her lips as she struggled to get back up on her feet. Unable to hide her morbid curiosity, Sibell turned to catch a glimpse of what had stopped her.

The wide, lifeless eyes of death stared across the floor at her.

Icy fingers of understanding danced up her spine. Rendered speechless by the fact that she recognized the broken, lifeless form of Captain Disenger, she shuddered.

Empaths were regularly given access to a Holopad and asked to read during counsel gatherings.

The reason was twofold. It was easier to allow impressions to rise while the mind was distracted for less advanced IEs, and offered a case study of universal law and practice. One, in particular, stood out.

Pleiadian hunters used a form of technology to take the form of victims they had killed for further scouting and reconnaissance.

That meant...

Her chest constricted at the realization of just how far the deception ran.

Her jaw clenched to compliment the anger coursing through her blood.

Why hadn't she seen it?

Because she abandoned her study. That's why.

She had top scores, but she was still a novice.

If she had continued her training, perhaps she would have been better equipped to decode the signs.

Her eyes flicked upward as the familiar, suffocating energy poured over the corridor. Cade, the image of him anyway, stalked angrily down the hallway.

Lights flickered in his wake, moved by an intimidating gait.

The eyes no longer looked human.

They were solid white.

Bestial.

Unforgiving.

Sibell swallowed the fear that threatened to choke her. Locking it away in her gut, she forced herself back up onto her feet. With every ounce of drive, she could muster she shoved herself forward, pouring power into her legs.

If hunters were on the loose, the chances of survivors were slim to none.

She was on her own.

Her throat threatened to close with the understanding. If she was right, that meant Cade was dead as well.

The thought stabbed her more than the thought of Marcus's death.

She cared for Marcus. The news had burned deep.

But Cade...

A loud screeching cry echoed from the hunter behind her. Without thought, she shoved everything she had left into her speed. The idea was nothing short of laughable. From what she knew, it was impossible to outrun a hunter.

But she had to try.

Searching her memory for weaknesses, she realized that the only way she recalled was to be smarter. But that required a skill she didn't possess. Based on their speed alone one would have to know exactly what it was thinking.

Exactly what it would do next.

Intention she could work with. But the precision was key.

The small hairs on the back of her neck stood on end in warning.

Something was rapidly drawing down on her.

Three guesses as to what.

And she only needed one.

Her eyes shifted to the wall on her right, as soon as the danger intensified, she shifted, rapidly, throwing herself face-first against the wall.

The hunter roared in outrage as it flew past her, slamming face-first into the steel wall outcrop ahead of her.

That was one thing about momentum; at high-speeds a rapid stop was impossible. Tension gripped her muscles like a vise. She whirled around, prepared to face one of the most adept killers in existence.

CHAPTER 5

Her eyes flashed fearfully as she turned. The Hunter was right on top of her.

That was the other problem with speed; it made for a quick recovery.

Damn.

Instinctively, she reached for the firearm in her waistband, but it wasn't enough. She didn't have enough time before the back of his hand connected. Pain exploded across her face, winging its way up to her forehead and down to trail her jaw, the force of impact depositing her pitifully on the cold floor. On impact, the gun clattered away from her trembling fingers.

Dizzy from the blow to her head, Sibell struggled to crawl backward. It was a pathetic attempt. Her reflexes were too slowed to make a difference. The hunter's features began to contort as it slowly stalked toward her.

Greenish skin began to overtake the olive tone.

Protruding ribs and spine gave a wraith-like appearance as the once muscled frame rippled into a skeletal one.

Metal plates formed over the face and neck with small delivery systems that ran into the back of the skull. A system used to allow its wearer to survive all sorts of planetary conditions. She shuddered at the monstrous set of teeth and sight of the lips that extended back over the jaw.

The hunter opened thin lips and hissed.

She winced at the unseen force that ripped her to her feet and tossed painfully against the wall. "Let go of me." She growled.

She struggled to contain her disgust as the deep menacing rumble echoed over the thin lips.

"What the hell do you want?

Nothing but silence answered her question.

Apparently, the ability to speak was a bonus reserved for a stolen appearance.

But she felt the answer rolling off of him nonetheless.

Her.

It wanted her.

She struggled to understand. With the disguise gone she could feel every inch of tar-like maliciousness rolling off of the creature in front of her.

Inconspicuously, Sibell tested the restraints as the hunter moved closer.

"Why?" She hissed between clenched teeth.

Haunting white eyes bore into her in answer.

It was a contract.

A requested mission.

Someone or something had sent the hunter to track her down.

She started running the alien coordinates through her mind, struggling to place them on a map in her conscious thought.

Erra.

The numbers matched Erra.

"What about Marcus? Did you kill him, too?" She spat.

She felt the answer as strongly as if he had punched her in the gut.

No.

A dim hope flickered into her gut.

Maybe Marcus was alive.

So focused on each other, neither she nor the hunter heard the light scrape, the unmistakable sound of metal on metal.

Although with the alarms blasting out their cadence, it was debatable if they would have heard it anyway.

The Hunter's lips parted, exposing rows of sharp teeth.

A sinking feeling told her she was out of time.

The sharp sound of a round being racked into a chamber broke over the noise in the air.

Sibell shifted her eyes in time to see a gun barrel flash into existence, directly in line with the hunter's face.

The bullet fired directly into the open eye socket in the plate metal. The alien alloy was too tough to allow an exit. The pinging sound sent a shiver down her spine as the projectile ricocheted around inside the helmet.

She closed her eyes and turned her head just as thick, foul smelling blood splattered across her.

The force holding her to the wall dissipated and she slid haphazardly to the floor.

She looked up, almost in shock. Her gut clenched when the familiar face of Alexander Cade lowered the gun she had dropped. His face etched in pain as he drew his weapon hand to his free arm. The odd angle suggested the extremity might be broken.

"Cade?" She muttered in disbelief.

Heat flashed across his gaze. The unquenchable burn coming from him was enough to put a bonfire to shame. For a moment Sibell couldn't breathe. She wanted to believe her eyes. But recent experiences had shown her she couldn't even really trust her senses.

There was nothing she could rely on, to tell the truth. Cade's eyes scanned her, lingering on her bruised face for a moment.

"Are you ok?" he asked.

She recoiled against the wall as he reached for her cheek.

A splinter of pain, his pain at her retreat, stabbed through her chest.

"Bell..." he muttered softly.

"Stay away from me," she snapped.

"Bell. It's me."

She struggled to her feet and stumbled backward. Allowing her gaze to shift from him to the dead hunter and back, it took her a moment to form a response.

"I don't know that," she muttered.

"Nothing you can say. Nothing you can tell me can prove you are the real Cade. This one knew things about Cade he shouldn't have known. He knew how to defuse me. Everything."

The idea sent a shiver dancing along her skin.

"They copy everything. Even mannerisms and energy prints. He walked, spoke, acted just like Cade. So, considering the fact that there is still a Hunter out there, you're going to have to come up with something pretty convin-"

She gasped, flattening herself against the wall outcrop as Cade stuffed the firearm into his injured hand and quickly closed the distance between them- cutting her words off with his movement.

Without warning he reached out and placed his hand lightly against her bruised cheek, his eyes locking on hers.

"You want proof? Here."

She watched him wide-eyed as he trapped her down with his gaze, his frame loosely pinning her to the outcropping wall.

"Feel... Bell. You know me. You know me better than anyone else. You know what's real. Feel me."

She hesitated a moment, fighting with herself.

With a shaky breath, she closed her eyes. There was nothing dark. Nothing dangerous. No cloud felt like it was going to suffocate her.

It was just Cade.

Warm.

Strong.

Gentle.

She opened her eyes without warning and shifted forward, wrapping her arms around his neck. He pulled her in tightly, one arm closing around her back, before setting her back in place.

"That's my girl," he muttered.

"What happened to you?" she asked quietly.

"The attack hit us without much warning," Cade explained. "Officials from all over the project had been called into the base. They were supposed to be sent out to round up the IEs who hadn't made it past grad yet. I was-"

"-sent to get me," she finished.

"He told me."

Her eyes shifted to the dead Hunter.

"They came in through the South gate. Started killing and shifting into the ones who were assigned to go after the IEs."

"I thought they had killed you too," she muttered.

"They tried," he admitted.

"How did you-?"

"Faked it. Trying to hide your inner core from an Intuitive Empath is a lot harder than convincing a hunter he killed you." He chuckled, offering a half-smirk.

"All the first years got sent through through the Gate," she said.

A string of curses broke from his lips.

"Where?"

"Erra," she answered. "The same place the Vissaeus disappeared."

His eyes hardened.

"Then things just got a lot more serious."

A resounding screech ripped over the base. The alarms suddenly stopped the constant pulse of sound.

Sibell felt the hair on the back of her neck rise as Cade stepped away from her to glance threateningly down the corridor.

Funny. She hadn't noticed he was still so close until he wasn't there anymore.

"We need to go. I've got to get you back."

His tone brokered no argument.

"I didn't expect to see the day that I wanted to go back," she said softly, feeling exposed in the sudden silence.

"But the sooner, the better."

Cade nodded.

"Let's go."

CHAPTER 6

The headlong dash back to the Gate would have been a lot quicker if they hadn't have had to contend with another Hunter. During the maze-like path they had taken to avoid detection, it was amazing to her how seamlessly the two of them fell back into normal rhythm.

Cade took the point. He was her shield.

Sibell kept her senses open. She was his eyes.

Each knew what was expected; the collaboration was as natural as breathing.

She was amazed, not just how quickly she had slipped back into her role, but how much a piece of her sorely missed this.

Missed him.

"I hit the emergency controls when I found out something wasn't right," Sibell said quietly as Cade cleared their final stretch of corridor.

"But we should still have access to the Gate as long as the overrides will allow power-up."

As the two slipped into the Gate Room, Cade turned and keyed in the emergency code granted to all personnel. The doors locked down as Sibell made a dive for the panel.

"Are there any other systems that have been fried?" he asked as he stepped up beside her.

"No, not that I know of," she muttered absently as she tapped away.

He moved away, booting another screen without further words, while she pulled up coordinate codes.

"Coordinates are set, we should be able to-"

The electric buzz hummed over the air, followed by the forced air of space and time.

"Yes!" Sibell whooped.

"There. Let's go." She said as she turned.

When he didn't answer Sibell moved closer to him.

"What are you doing?"

"If we leave this fucker here there's a good chance he could wreak havoc. I'm not going to take that chance."

She glanced over his shoulder and realized what he was doing.

"You're going to detonate the self-destruct? Isn't that against regulation?"

"Fuck regulation," Cade muttered.

"These sons-of-a-bitche hurt you. The IIA can take their regulation and shove it up their ass."

A light smile that she couldn't contain brushed at her lips.

"Are you sure you're the real Cade?" she asked, her voice teasing.

"I'm real alright. It just took me time to see what else was," he answered.

She stood for a moment, staring at him as his eyes locked back on the screen, unsure of how to respond.

"We will have a little less than a minute before-."

The air around her slowed, filling to the brim with a familiar, noxious surge of black.

"Heads up!" She screamed.

In the span of a half of a heartbeat, the world turned upside down.

A blur of sickening pale green slammed into Cade from above, driving him to the floor as he drew the firearm in his hand up.

The son of a bitch had used the vent systems.

Adrenaline poured through her as Cade struggled to get the upper hand. Talon-like claws ripped the gun from his hand and discarded it with a screech.

Sibell surged forward, scooping the firearm up and taking aim.

The hunter's eyes whipped towards her as she squeezed the trigger.

The bullet missed its target as the creature lunged forward.

She trailed the creature with the barrel, firing two more shots. Both lodged in the wall behind it, she gritted her teeth in frustration as she realized the task was near impossible.

A strange sensation rolled under her skin, and she suddenly realized she needed to aim where he was going to be.

She allowed the sensation to guide her, following direction on when to pull the trigger.

The gun jumped in her hand, and she watched in amazement as the Hunter screeched, dropping to the ground with a fairly serious shoulder wound.

Her eyes shifted to Cade for a split second, empathy threatening to shatter her as she noticed his teeth clenched, pain ripping over every feature.

But time was ticking.

"Come on." She snapped, wrapping her arm around his uninjured shoulder. It took some doing, but she managed to help him stumble to his feet.

"Go! Get out of here!" He snapped.

Grabbing the gun from her hand, he pushed her towards the gate.

"Cade, come on!" She snapped.

"Go!"

Her eyes trailed between him and the rising hunter as she moved backward.

Cade dove towards the panel, tapping furiously to finish the sequence.

Sibell continued to back away, keeping the Hunter in her line of sight.

It was her it wanted. If she could just buy Cade a bit of time...

She didn't bother moving discreetly, rather intentionally drawing the attention of the sadistic creature on her.

There was no way they could walk away from this. Not unless he could slow the Hunter down...

She felt the shift in the air the moment it got on its feet. She knew the second it coiled to attack.

She hesitated.

Waited.

She didn't know if it would work.

But she had to try.

Pushing aside all distractions, she reached deep down for her natural ability.

The same feeling that had allowed her to wound the Hunter to begin with.

It was their only chance.

The resounding screech rippled through the air as the hunter charged.

"Bell! Move!" Cade's panicked voice faded out as the sensation flooded over her.

She reached for it. Without effort, she felt the vibrational energy pool around her. She drew in a soft breath as if in slow motion. Felt the swirls of color, like ripples, accompanying every movement.

"M-o-v-e...!"

Waves of movement enveloped Cade as he turned, all of his concentration shoved violently into getting to her.

She clenched her fist as the world around her returned to normal. Her eyes flashed and danced, seeing every twitch of muscle as vividly as if it were a neon sign. Standing her ground until the last possible moment, Sibell shifted her weight and dropped beneath the line of balance.

Twisting her body and shoving upwards she felt the hunter's weight somersault over her. Adding her strength to the momentum, she slammed the creature on its back into the console behind her.

Sparks blasted around her as she surged away, preparing for another shift.

The buzz of electricity and the pain-filled screech mesmerized her. At least until a firm but familiar grip on her upper arm drew her back in.

"Are you alright?!" Cade snapped.

She nodded, her gaze shifting back to the Hunter.

The creature managed to lift itself before flopping face-first onto the metal grating.

"Come on!" He yelled.

"Thirty seconds to complete evacuation." The computerized tone chimed.

She spun on her heels at the realization and bolted toward the Gate.

Cade at her heels.

"Twenty seconds to complete evacuation."

Her eyes danced backward in time to see the Hunter trying to rise from the floor.

"Go! Just Go!" Cade snapped.

The blast of air from the portal enveloped them as Sibell stumbled up the platform steps.

"Ten seconds to..."

Cade's arms wrapped firmly around her, drawing her in before the disorientation of the Gate completely closed around them.

***

Sibell gasped. It felt like the air was completely ripped from her lungs as the blast rippled through to them in their little cocoon of protection.

Somewhere in the back of her mind, she fervently hoped the blast wouldn't somehow eject them from the Gate. Wrapped in sensations of flight and speed, Sibell hesitantly allowed herself to relax into the travel. Astral sickness was a given under the emergency use, but the tenser the traveler, the worse it was on them.

Surrounded by beautiful shades of blue, and bathed in a white glow, Sibell tried to focus on anything to help her mind relax. She settled on the wonder she felt on her first travel.

To a younger teen the only way to describe it was a water slide powered by jet-force winds.

It was a rush.

The tug of gravity warned them of arrival before they exited the other side.

She felt Cade's grip tighten, a grunt of pain rumbling in his chest, as they landed in a heap.

Somehow, she was dimly aware that alarms began blaring.

Of course, the gate had just expelled an unexpected arrival.

The world around her swirled, a sickening effect of travel without proper preparation.

Hands tugged at her, lifting her up, it was a feeling she didn't recognize at first.

A sudden rise of disagreement tried to break to the surface when she felt something was being shoved over her mouth and nose.

It took a moment for her addled mind to understand.

Oxygen.

She stopped fighting the sensation, trying to focus on the blurs of people around her.

White coats and unfamiliar faces.

She struggled for a moment to turn her fogged gaze, looking for Cade. Satisfied to find him not far away, surrounded by his own army of medical personnel, she relaxed a little. Pain stabbed into her arm yanking her back to her own situation, but she resolved to revolt against her fist before it could punch someone.

She realized enough to know that if they were giving her oxygen, then the pain was likely a medicated stabilizer.

A cure to the travel sickness.

She sighed, relaxing into the feeling of the drugs rolling through her body.

There were still so many unanswered questions. So much left to do...

But they could figure that out later.

For now, she was content in the knowledge that they had survived.

Even if the war had only just begun...

Author E.R. Starling

After a childhood spent in libraries, bookstores, and reading hideaways, E.R. Starling couldn't deny she had lost the fight against an intense love of the written word. Beginning her writing career as just a hobby, it took her five years to finally give up the ghost. After that, she finally gave into the fact that she wouldn't be happy without building a career from her love of books. See more at http://erstarling.wixsite.com/books where you can see all of Starling's publications or join her reader list.

Mara's Honor

By Taki Drake

Chapter One – Svedik

The air was a brisk -12°C with a blowing wind. Mara pulled her jacket closure a little tighter around her neck, shivering slightly. The walk from her quarters to the outpost's main offices was less than 10 minutes on a good day, but with snow and high winds it became a bit more challenging to navigate and considerably a significantly longer trip. Over the last few years, she had gotten used to the weather. The cold of the winter days and the extended cold season did not bother her at all. However, she had never fully adjusted to the intense heat of the irregular summers. In her opinion, 48°C was hot no matter where you were. And on a military base, no matter how small, there were only so many items of clothing you could take off and still be professional.

It was sad, but in many ways, her professionalism and sense of duty and honor were all that she had left.

Her posting here was a result of a long tumble of bad judgments and unfortunate coincidence. Once a rising star in the Chorion Space Force, or CSF, she learned the hard way that abilities and skills without wisdom left you vulnerable to defeat and demotion. It was a lesson that she would never forget.

By the time that Mara got to the office door, her hands and feet had started to numb. Her eyelashes are frozen, and tears had leaked down the side of her face and frozen onto her cheeks. She ignored them, just like she ignored most of the discomfort of her situation. In some bizarre way, she felt that it was deserved. A way of paying for mistakes.

The quiet woman began her usual morning routine, straightening the mess left by the evening duty officer and starting the ever-present klava pot. Sitting down at her desk, she placed her palm flat on the authorization plate which scanned her hand and responded with a green light and the cheerful voice of the office AI. "Good morning Lieut. Brown. There are no open reports and no incident reports from last evening and no alerts on the calendar for today. Are there any things that you wish to register?"

"Thank you, but no, Gareth. I have nothing to add at this time. I'm assuming Officer of the Day responsibilities per regulations as of now."

"Very good Lieut. Brown, it is so logged."

Intently, Mara focused on making sure that all of her duties were executed well. As the primary officer responsible for oversight of maintenance, including both land and air vehicles, she reviewed the previous day's activities, checked spare availability, and made sure that all of the vehicles had their mandated inspections and repairs completed. This was normally the easiest part of her day since their outpost had very little activity and vehicle maintenance was driven more by the calendar than by usage. She knew that on many other bases that more maintenance was performed due to high activity, wear on engines and other vehicle components. But in the exile post of Svedik, there was little reason to drive or fly anywhere. The lack of settlers and traffic to the planet made an assignment to this outpost a particularly painful lesson.

The younger officer was so focused on her thoughts and activities that she did not hear the base commander come into the room until he cleared his throat. Jumping to her feet, she saluted crisply and greeted him. "Good morning, Cmdr. Stephenson."

Waving his hand in general acknowledgment, the highest officer at the base wandered over to the klava machine and filled his cup. He was dressed in his usual mixture of civilian and military garb. His garments reflected none of the attention and care that Mara's did. His uniform shirt was unironed and had a variety of stains on its front. His pants were non-regulation, chosen for comfort rather than any conformance to military guidelines. He was even wearing slippers today. Nice warm slippers.

Ignoring Mara, who still held her salute in position, he walked through his office door and firmly closed it. Mara knew that she would not see him for most of the day. Only after he closed the door did she bring her arm down.

When she had first gotten to the base, the Commander had thought it amusing to ignore her salute and stay in the room, trying to see how long she could hold her arm up in midair. He soon tired of it, since her stubborn adherence to military protocol did not wane. Now, he just left her alone. It was too much effort even to torment her.

Mara braced herself. She knew that if the commander had come in that the XO would follow shortly. Where the base commander was both unprofessional and inattentive, at least he was benign. The XO was different. Unprofessional, yes. Benign, no.

Venial. Mara had never understood what the word meant until she had met Lieut. Cmdr. Sorensen. Frank Sorensen was the ultimate definition of venial and slimy. Every time that he came within 6 feet of her, Mara was left feeling like she needed a shower. When she had first arrived at the base, he had seen her as a convenient conquest. Her refusal to participate in what to him was a logical relationship infuriated him. When he put additional pressure on her, she was forced to document her discomfort and file it with the Bureau of Personnel. He would never forgive her.

Knowing that he stood only one substantiated violation from removal from the service, his hands are tied in many ways from retaliating against her. However, there are a million ways that he could make her job more difficult and her stay more uncomfortable. Apparently, he was focused on making sure that each one of those torments was inflicted on her. His attitude and actions had turned a depressing and painful posting into something approaching hell for Mara. Only her determination to do what was right kept her from outright despair. She was clinging to her sense of proper behavior, and her battered honor like a drowning person would cling to a lifeline. Focusing on executing her duty and responsibilities to the best of her ability one day at a time was the only path that she could determine in her late-night soul searching. And Mara was resolved to stay on the path she had chosen rather than repeat the error of letting other people choose her path and consequences for her.

This morning, the XO was apparently preoccupied with some other activity. He wandered into Mars office, ignoring both her morning greeting and her salute. Leaving her standing in the middle the room with her arm raised, he went over to the klava machine and poured a mug full of the beverage. Rather than returning the pot to the machine, he placed it on the counter with a slight smirk on his face. Still ignoring the motionless woman, he left the room, seeming to accidentally dump the folders waiting by the file cabinet onto the floor. The door closed behind him.

Drawing a relieved breath, Mara released her salute and began to repair the damage that had occurred. The replacement of the klava pot was simple. Mara was on her knees on the floor reassembling the file folders when the door to the office open once more. Tensing as she looked up, the young officer saw the senior NCO of the base, Sergeant Watson. Nodding her head to the man, she picked up the last of the file folders and stood.

The sergeant was a middle-aged man with a closed face and wary eyes. While he could look intimidating, at the moment, he had a rueful expression on his face as he said, "It is amazing how clumsy our XO is!"

"Yes, it is. And good morning to you, Sergeant Watson."

The NCO had been one of the few nonjudgmental people at the base when Mara had arrived, sick at heart and grieving. He never had treated her with anything but respect, and his ongoing courtesy and lack of negative commentary on her behavior had been a balm to a very wounded soul. The young officer was positive that he probably knew of her demotion from flight engineer to her current position, but he never made slighting comments or give her anything but professional responses. In fact, it was the sergeant that had made a suggestion that since the existing quartermaster appeared to be too ill to execute his duties that perhaps Mara could assist in that area.

Mara thought that it was an interesting description of a man who drank so much in the evening that he was unable to get out of bed until late afternoon. A crony of the XO, Lieutenant Commander Sullivan had retreated into a bottle on his arrival at the post and showed no signs of wishing to leave the comfort of his alcoholic daze. More used to energetic and filled days than idle time, Mara had been more than willing to help out. She was appalled by the condition of the base supplies, and after collecting written authorization from the quartermaster, she had dug in and expended the energy from her regret and grief on whipping the organization and stocking activities into conforming with military standards.

She had had faint hopes of garnering a bit more respect and companionship from the remainder of the base personnel when food supplies and other essential items became more available. It was a forlorn hope. With the active dislike of the XO and the apathy of the base commander, Mara was effectively isolated. No one else in the base really wanted to get close to her or be seen as one of her adherents. Only the civilian clerk that worked in the quartermaster's office and an ensign from flight maintenance were even marginally pleasant to her. Both of them needed to work in close collaboration with her, and she ranked both of them. At least it meant that she had somebody to talk to some of the time. After three years on the base, she thought they even might be starting to like her.

The day dragged to its inevitable close, just like the previous thousand had done. Mara made sure that all of her reports were filed, that all protocols were completed and waited for the formal turnover of her day to the night officer. Who of course was late. Mara remained in the dark of her office, thinking about nothing much at all. She quietly watched the weather outside, snowing still. The cresting of snow on the outside of the window to the office made her remember snowball fights and sledding of her childhood. How she wished that she could go back and start again.

Chapter Two – Planetfall

"Wake up, wake up, Mara!" It was three hours after Mara had gotten to bed. Her relief had been two and half hours late and come in reeling and stinking of alcohol. Despite her misgivings at leaving him in charge, Mara had headed back to her room. Reading for a short period of time, she decided it would be warmer and had crawled in with her book. Apparently, she had fallen asleep because the book was pressed underneath the corner of her face.

Crawling out of the depths of her exhausted sleep, Mara realized she was being shaken rudely awake by both her clerk and the maintenance ensign. Both of them were hysterical, stammering and talking over each other urgently.

"What on earth? Ensign, report!" snapped out Mara.

"I heard the noise and went into the office. The radio's squawking but no one else is there to answer it, and I don't know how to do anything with it," stammered the clerk, Jonas. "I went to get Ensign Sloan because I knew that he was around. We had just finished playing chess so I knew he would still be up."

"I'm sorry ma'am, but we haven't been cross-trained on the radio, and I don't know what to say. Please, please, could you come with us and see what needs to be done? It sounds really, really important," added the ensign.

Mara moved quickly. Because she had planned on getting up after she was done reading to prepare properly for bed, Mara was still wearing the clothes that she had had on during the day. Throwing on her jacket and checking her equipment, she was ready to leave in just a few minutes. She knew that the temperature at this time of night would be severe, so she added an extra head covering and hauled on heavier gloves. Motioning the two men to go ahead of her, she closed the door.

The wind hit her like a blow to the face. Between the dark and the blowing snow was almost impossible to see much ahead of them. But the men knew where they were going, and Mara followed in their wake. They had made it approximately halfway to the office door when a thrumming snarl from the right warned them of one of the planet's main predators, the white leopard cat. Preferring to hunt during nights with snow, it was the top of the food chain. Massing out close to 200 kg, it was a deadly hunter with huge claws. Crying out in fear, the clerk turned to run. Slamming his body to the ground, Mara shouted, "Stay still, you idiot!"

Noticing out of the corner of her eye that the ensign had taken a futile defensive position to her left Mara turned smoothly toward the oncoming predator, her weapon in her hand. Firing the massive projectiles from her service gun, she hit the cat before it leaped. The three closely grouped shots blew the animal's throat to bloody ruins.

Keeping her weapon out, Mara grabbed the clerk by the back of his jacket and dragged him upright pushing them toward the office. Before the ensign could even stop stammering, she gave him a shove in the same direction. Shouting over the wail of the wind, Mara said, "You can send someone out to recover the carcass later. Let's get to the radio!"

Mara rushed into the office without bothering to remove garments or to even shake off the considerable amount of snow that she had acquired. The communication unit was still calling, sending a series of code protocols. Settling down in front of the console, Mara stripped off her gloves and laid her hand on the identification plate. The voice of the office AI sounded, saying, "Welcome Lieut. Brown, a priority message has been queued and waiting for approximately 28 minutes. Do you wish to respond?"

"Yes, thank you, Gareth. I am assuming Officer of the Watch at this time."

"It is so logged, Lieut. Brown."

Mara's hands flew over the control pads, entering the memorized counter codes and initiating the required acknowledgments. Shortly after that, a firm voice came over the communications unit.

"This is the HRS Markham, Major Saltz commanding. We require base assistance including medical, repair and resupply. Authorization Alpha, Gamma, Gamma, Omega."

Quickly checking the validity of the codes, Mara responded, "Base beacon initiating in 15 seconds. We stand ready to assist. Svedik Base out."

Quickly initiating the timing of the beacon activation, Mara proceeded to sound the alert to the base commander, XO, NCO, base doctor, and commissary. Responses from all but the commander and XO were received promptly. Concerned that there might be a communication fault, Mara sent the clerk off to wake both of the non-responding officers.

The ensign she sent off to make sure that all of her maintenance personnel and facilities would be ready to help where possible. Running through the protocols and procedures and making sure that nothing had been skipped kept Mara very busy. A pained gasp interrupted her thought and action. The clerk was back, and he was wounded. He looked like he had a broken nose, with blood running down his face. Mara was appalled. Jumping up from her seat she guided the shaken man to sit in her place. Grabbing a towel and pouring cold water on it, she carefully placed the cool compress against his bruised cheekbone. Mumbling through swollen lips, he finally managed to tell her what had happened. She was furious. The XO not coming. Apparently, he didn't think it was important enough. The clerk then went to the commander's quarters. The commander had refused to leave his bedroom, directing the clerk to talk to the XO. When the clerk had gone back to the XO to relate what the commander had said, he was struck in the face several times.

Part way through the ensign's explanation, the NCO came into the room. His face became very grim as he heard the clerk's report. Ignoring her fury for the moment, Mara gave orders on what else needed to be set up. She trusted the NCO to carry those out.

There was a rumble of massive engines and the sound of an arriving shuttle. Taking off at a run, Mara knew that she had done everything that she could to prepare, but felt that she needed to be there to address any other shortfalls that might need attention. So off she went toward the landing area, pausing only to grab her gloves once more.

Chapter Three - Succor

The shuttle had landed, and the ground had not even cooled from the heat of the engines before the ramp was down and casualties were being carried off. Mara was directing the stream of stretchers when a large hand grabbed her by the shoulder and spun her around. It was a very large man in battle armor. A very large, angry-looking man.

"Where is the base commander?" rumbled a low-toned and dangerous voice.

Before Mara could respond, her timid clerk jumped into the conversation in a valiant attempt to protect her. Stumbling through his explanation while holding a handful snow against his broken nose, he explained what had happened. The Marine Major's expression tightened with anger, and he opened his mouth to speak. However, before he could say anything, the commander and the XO rushed up to them. The Commander was babbling to the battle-scarred Marine officer incoherently. The XO had decided to take a different tact. He proceeded to dress down Mara for failing to report that they had an incoming ship or that there was any danger. After he had insulted her several times, he started to order her back to quarters before the Marine interrupted him.

Instead of allowing the XO to finish his orders, Major Saltz informed them that he was taking command of the base and that both the former commander and XO should consider themselves under arrest. When the XO went for his weapon, he was put under restraint and escorted back to the building.

Looking at Mara and sweeping in the NCO with a wave of his hand, Major Saltz huddled with Mara and the sergeant to see what resources were available at the base. He was pleasantly surprised to find that their supplies and repair capabilities were full. His questioning look was answered by the sergeant nodding toward Mara when she wasn't looking.

Mara was kept quite busy, coordinating all of the different repair and resupply efforts. With the XO out of the way, and the strangers on base, the remaining troops stopped resisting Mars orders and started to take care of the damage to the shuttle and the effort of resupplying it. In a strange sense of humor, the largely absent base quartermaster chose that moment to wander into the supply area. He was incensed at the high-handed disposal of stock and proceeded to berate Mara. Summoned by the ever so helpful clerk, Major Saltz once again placed a base officer in confinement, pending charges. As he turned to leave the room, he quirked an eyebrow at Mara and asked, "Are there any other officers that need to be arrested at the moment? It would be more efficient if we could just do it all at one time."

Before Mara could respond, the door closed behind him. For some reason, she found herself smiling.

When was apparent that not all of the plates could be replaced on the shuttle, Mara consulted with the others in the maintenance yard and decided to cannibalize one of their two flyers to help repair the shuttle. The effort was immense but ultimately successful. Less than three hours after it landed, the shuttle was back in the air and headed back toward the battlefield. The base personnel were exhausted, dropping to the ground or to nearby seats and holding their heads in their hands. They were even too tired to complain.

Mara and the sergeant herded them to the mess where they could get a hot meal before going off duty. Making sure that they were taken care of, Mara had no time to reflect on what it actually happened. The base somehow felt quieter and smaller now. The intrusion of so many armored fighters who had appeared briefly, then mostly left felt surreal. Only the evidence on the landing field, the torn apart flyer and the mess in the supply area provided easily visible evidence of their passage.

It was not to say that all of them had gone. There were 72 bodies in the medical area in various stages of being patched up. The base doctor and his assistants would be busy for many more hours. There also six bodies in the morgue. As far as Mara knew, these were the first battle casualties that the base had ever handled. She made sure that she stopped by with words of encouragement and thanks for the corpsman and the doctor that were working so valiantly.

There was another person that it remained on base. One of the senior officers from the Naval vessel, Capt. Jensen had been left in nominal control of the base. It had been explained to Mara that this was to both maintain a good command structure and to prevent any significant evidence from being destroyed or hidden. Mara had entered that officer into the base database and introduced him to the office AI.

Hobbling carefully around the room, Captain Jensen chose to sit next to Mara's desk and asked her for a summary of what it happened. The young officer made sure to give an unemotional and professional report on all aspects of the previous evening. Her report was crisp and thorough, and the naval officer was obviously surprised and impressed.

Telling her that she had done well and that she should make sure to get some rest time. Mara was ordered off shift. Dragging her weary body to her feet, she saluted the naval officer, receiving a crisp salute in return. She grabbed her coat, shrugged it on, and slipping into her gloves as she headed for the door. Waiting for her at the doorway to the outside, were the NCO and the maintenance department ensign.

"We thought we would escort you home, ma'am," offered the ensign. The sergeant just smiled slightly and nodded his head. Mara found tears coming to her eyes, blaming that on exhaustion.

Without saying a word, the three of them started on that cold trip to Mara's quarters. The trip was made in silence. Or as silent as 1 km trip through a howling blizzard at night could be. Reaching the door to her room, Mara turned to the two men, saying, "Thank you both. I am proud of all of us and thankful that you were there with me. You both did an outstanding job, and if I have a chance to make a recommendation, I will do so for both of you."

Murmurs of response came from both of them. The ensign turned to head back silently, but the sergeant paused briefly. "You did very well Lieut. Brown. You upheld the honor the service and performed above and beyond." The man drew himself straight up and snapped her a salute, holding it until she returned his gesture through the tears in her eyes.

Chapter Four – Aftermath

The last two months had been very busy for the Svedik base. The service's Judge Advocate General removed both the XO and commander for dereliction of duty. It was Mara's understanding that they would be called before a court-martial board and that she would be required to testify. The quartermaster had also been removed. No one had explained what was happening to him, but Mara was content that he was no longer going to be screwing up their base any longer.

There was a new acting commander, one that was very different from the previous command group. He seemed to be a bit leery of Mara, both respectful and considerate. She actually quite liked him, thinking him thorough and responsible. Hopefully, he would get more comfortable with her as time went on.

The tenor of the outpost had changed. Finding out their job actually had a purpose had given the personnel in the base more pride in themselves and what they were doing. The new attitude and the increased level of performance could be felt in the air and seen in every aspect of the base.

The quartermaster had not yet been replaced, so Mara resumed her work covering that set of responsibilities also. It didn't seem to be a real big problem since she had worked the processes and procedures out to the point where their supply mechanism ran smoothly and efficiently.

Mara was also more content. She felt that she had done a reasonable job and had supported her sworn duty. The young officer examined her actions, poking them with her mind like a tongue on a sore tooth, looking for lapses or shortfalls. She didn't find any major ones. The strange emotion that started to rise was foreign to her. It took her a while to figure out that it was pride, pride in what she had done and how she had acted. It felt good.

Mara was going over some planned modification to the maintenance areas organization with the ensign and another of her troopers when a familiar rumble of an approaching flight shuttle reverberated through the room. Surprised looks on all the faces around the table told Mara that none of them had known about a proposed landing today. Excusing everyone from the meeting, Mara proceeded to the landing field. She got there just in time to see the flight shuttle land.

It was definitely a déjà vu moment. Once again it was night, although no blowing snow. The shuttle that was landing showed repaired scars, some of them fixed with flyer plates that she recognized all too well. She felt a bubble in her stomach of anticipation, realizing that she would get to know how the battle had come out.

The NCO came and stood at Mara's elbow. They both watched in silence as the landing ramp opened and the same armored visitors walked down. Making a beeline toward Mara, the armored Marines stopped to remove their helmets. Mara was unable to suppress a smile on her face when she saw Major Saltz.

Giving the major quick salute, Mara asked, "What brings you back our way, sir?"

"We were in the area and decided that maybe we should stop by and bring your present."

Mara's look of confusion drew chuckles from the three Marines standing in front of her. Major Saltz handed her and the NCO each an envelope. Mara stood frozen, staring at the envelope as if it was going to bite her.

"Aren't you going to open your orders? You're being pulled from the planet and sent on a new tasking."

"But... This planet is where careers go to die. This is a dumping ground, no one leaves this duty station. This is a place for the dishonored," Mara stammered.

Major Saltz grinned widely at her and said, "Well, you've got 30 minutes to pack and get on board before we take off, so I suggest you hurry. We are going to catch a bite to eat while you run around."

When the two stunned people continued to stand there in disbelief, the officer continued, "Are you coming or not?"

Without a word, the sergeant turned and took off at a run. Starting to do the same, Mara turned one more time to look at the major and thank him.

His response rang in her ears the whole way back to her quarters. What he had said had the sound of something that she would remember to her dying day.

"Many have come here in dishonor, very few have left. But you, you are leaving because in the depths of despair you fought a great battle and found your own honor."

Author Taki Drake

I hope you have enjoyed this story. You can reach me at taki@technologymage.com or by signing up for my newsletter at http://www.takidrake-author.com/. The blog also will let you know about the things that are new with me and some sneak peaks and advanced information about publication.

There are several series that I have started to publish. In the fantasy and science fiction areas I have two: Becoming Sephera about a woman's journey from a pampered heir to a self-reliant, and responsible member of society, and the Unfettered Mage about technology and magic among the stars. Both of these series fall into an emerging genre called techmage where technology and magic combine for explosive and interesting mixtures. The books in each series are listed below. Please feel free to chime in about how you like them and what you would like to see next. I would love to hear from you!

The Drone Pilot

By Brian J. Walton

Chapter One

The smoke from the incense stick floated around the small shrine, curled slowly, then was sucked into the air ventilators. Once there, the smoke would be recycled. Just as the air Nancy breathed was recycled. Just as the body of her daughter had been recycled a little less than two years before.

Nancy closed her eyes and breathed a prayer. She found herself praying to her daughter last year, much to her surprise. She had prayed to her daughter several times, but things hadn't changed much since Nancy had lost her. Rain had been falling on the windows that night as it did now. The grief was still there as well. Simply another part of her to be put aside and revisited only once each year.

Nancy's messaging Slate trilled, pulling her from her grief. She lifted her head, eyeing the flat, gray device with spite. It was Okeke.

Nancy took one last look at the picture of her daughter, May. The slender, dark-haired girl in her soccer gear seemed so familiar to her. And yet, almost alien. She took the picture—a printed picture and one of the few she owned—folded it and slipped it back into the drawer where it had stayed for much of the previous year.

There was a time and a place for grief. But that time was over.

"Answer," she muttered. Mene Okeke's fuzzy, holographic image flickered into view. Nancy straightened. Dr. Okeke, one of their Quantum Computing Technicians, wasn't usually one to make urgent phone calls in the middle of the night. She reached for the sheet to cover herself before remembering that her HoloScreen was set to automatically turn off her camera after 8 PM.

"Did I wake you?" Okeke asked.

"There's six hours before the flyover we've been planning for months. The President is going to be watching tomorrow, along with half the world's population. Do you think I'm sleeping?"

"Right…" He trailed off. "There's something important. Can you turn the HoloScreen on?"

"It's okay, just gives me a moment." Nancy slid out of bed, rubbing the sleep from her eyes, and pulled a robe on. She sat down on the edge of the bed, trying hurriedly to arrange her hair into something more fit for a work meeting. It struck her as silly. She and Mene had been together for years. But everything had changed after May had died.

"HoloScreen on." She said and was bathed in a blue light. Mene's face looked tired to her. More than usual. He was in one of the small conference rooms, but he was alone. That made Nancy even more worried.

"What's happened now?" Nancy asked.

He took in a breath. "Trappist Voyager's gone rogue."

"What do you mean, rogue?" Nancy asked.

There was a long pause. "It's changed course."

"What about the flyover? Will it still happen as scheduled?

"Not exactly…"

"What then?"

"Trappist Voyager is presently on a collision course with Colonia One."

Chapter Two

Nancy's commuter drone lowered itself onto the roof of Pasadena's Jet Propulsion Laboratory. She hated the tiny vehicles. But the flight from Santa Monica had only taken her twenty minutes, from phone call to landing. You could never do that in a car.

Okeke and several other members of the Quantum Computing team waited at the doorway as Nancy approached them.

"When did the course change happen?" Nancy asked over the buzz of the drone's fans cycling down.

"Approximately one A.M. this morning," Okeke responded. Nancy followed her team across the roof toward the access elevator.

"And it's definitely from the Trappist Voyager?"

"We've confirmed it, yes."

"Is there any corruption in the data stream?" Nancy asked.

Okeke nodded.

"Shit," Nancy breathed. "So, It's happening again." The elevator dinged, and the doors wished open.

They rode the elevator in silence.

"There's one more thing," Okeke said.

"What's that?" Nancy replied.

"A reporter is here."

"We don't have time for reporters."

Okeke leaned closer. "He says he's got exclusive information, and he's ready to break it. He's asking for a comment. Nancy, with everything happening with the data stream, and considering what happened to the other two pilots, I think you should talk to him."

The elevator slowed. Nancy glanced at her Slate and nodded. "I'll give him ten minutes. But I want to see the team, first."

Chapter Three

Nancy had visited JPL as a child. She could still remember how it felt when her father had snuck her in for a quick peak of the control room. From what she remembered, the old control room was quaint compared to modern standards. But this time, instead of sneaking in with her father and trying to avoid being seen, Nancy had every eye in the room on her the moment she entered.

A thin, pale man rushed toward Nancy and Okeke. Perry Andrews was

Project Manager of the Trappist Voyager program. Fresh from his graduate program at Cal Tech, he was the most brilliant aerospace engineer Nancy had ever met. He was also the most aggravating one she had ever met.

"Jesus—Nancy, thank God you're here. This is a nightmare."

"Are we sending re-route commands?" Nancy said.

Andrews nodded. "Every ten minutes. At first, it works. But then the command is overridden by the drone pilot."

"How long between the re-route command and the pilot's override?"

"Two minutes." Andrews answered.

Nancy nodded, thinking. "We can work with that."

Andrews' eyes widened. "Collision is up to a 98.7 percent probability! Every time Colonia One changes course, so does Trappist Voyager. We've got a crew of fifty colonists, woken up from ChomoSleep just to see this goddamned flyover—to wave at the little ship that paved the way for them—and it's about to fucking land on their faces. Christ, this is bad!"

"First, stop freaking out in front of everyone. Let's talk somewhere private."

Nancy gave the team a perfunctory wave and turned back to Andrews.

"Sorry," Andrews said. "It's the stress, you know?"

"I'm the one that's going to be answering to a Senate Investigation if this all goes south," Nancy said. "So, yeah, I know."

Nancy and Okeke followed Andrews out to the hallway and into a small, dimly lit conference room. The doors hissed shut behind them.

"We've tried hijacking root systems," Andrews said, "but we don't have primary access so we keep getting cut out. I hate to say it, but I think it's time to reboot."

"We can't do that." Nancy said. "Not again. We can't lose another pilot."

"I can think of fifty colonists that would disagree with you." Andrews responded.

Okeke sighed. Nancy met his gaze. He was always the steady one. Calm and quiet in any circumstance. That's why Nancy had fallen in love with him. But she had learned later that beneath his calm was a real emotional disconnection. She never knew when he *cared*. "Show us the data stream." Okeke said.

"Fine," Andrews responded. "But it'll prove my point for me."

Andrews tapped at his Slate and brought up the data stream on his Slate's HoloScreen. Nancy scrolled through it, skimming the data. There was the usual telemetry data and routine system checks. But interspersed throughout was something else. It was as if the system was talking to them. There was the usual system data, but interspersed throughout were strange interjections.

//The kingdom pricks the pricking pear//

She flipped to another page.

//Where is the kingdom? Where is the kingdom? The undiscovered kingdom//

"It goes on like this for pages," Okeke said.

"It sounds like a nursery rhyme," Nancy said.

"Or, our new six-billion dollar piloting interface." Andrews responded.

"We're sure it's not hacked?" Nancy asked.

"You can't hack a Quantum Array," Okeke said. "It's one of the primary reasons I pushed for its inclusion in the Trappist Voyager program."

Nancy tapped at a phrase. *Brutish and short.*

"What is it?" Okeke asked.

"Does that sound familiar to you?"

"Does what?"

"Brutish and short?" Nancy said. "Why does that sound familiar?

Andrews shrugged. "The last part you looked at sounded like a nursery rhyme. Why does any of it sound familiar?"

"It sounds like something from literature." Nancy turned toward the door to the conference room. "Does anyone here have a literature background?"

Andrews snorted. "Pretty much everyone in that room out there was a star member of their math club. Good luck."

She handed Andrews' Slate back to him. But the line still tugged at her sub-conscious. *Brutish and short.* It more or less described May's life, fraught with pain, suffering, and disease. Nancy shivered, tugging her cardigan closer around her shoulders. "Or, it might be nothing. But I'm not willing to take that chance. Find me someone who's actually read a book."

Chapter Four

"Why do you do it, anyway? Sticking these pilot's brains in a metal box, linking their minds to a drone, and firing it into space... I'm not a religious man, but it sounds like the closest thing to hell I can imagine."

Nancy stared at the swirl of white on black as she poured coconut milk into her coffee. She glanced back up at the man. He had skin the color and texture of untreated leather, a halo of white, unkempt hair and a gut that that gave his gangly frame a distinctly lopsided feel. "I'm sorry, I missed your name." Nancy said softly.

"Eddie Menendez," he said. "*The Solar Blaze* has been watching your program for several months now—"

"And you could've just sent a statement request like everyone else," she responded. "But I know you wouldn't come down here unless you thought you really had something juicy, and you were ready to post it all over the web. So, please, save me the lead-up and just tell me what horror story it is you think is going on here."

"Think?" Menendez asked. "Nancy—can I call you that? Everyone knows about NASA's new drone pilot program. What we want to know is what is in the pilot program that's causing your pilots to die?"

Nancy stared at Menendez over her coffee. "Fine," she said. "I have ten minutes. What do you want to ask me?"

"We're on the record now?" Menendez asked.

Nancy gave a small nod.

The reporter turned his Slate on and the HoloScreen bathed her in a blue glow.

"Where do you want to start?" she asked.

"Let's start with how NASA thinks linking a pilot's brains with a ship 1.9 light-years away is, on any planet, a good idea."

"It has to do with the quantum radio," Nancy said. "Quantumly entangled particles make instantaneous communication possible across any distance. But it's slow."

"That doesn't make sense. If it's instantaneous, how can it also be slow?"

"Compared to your Slate, it's molasses."

"But why?"

Nancy pointed at the flat, gray device. "That little thing can do so many calculations each second that putting the right amount of zeros on the number would take the rest of this interview. But the Quantum Radio is binary. It uses entangled electrons. So each state change is one bit. We've gotten faster at affecting state changes, and using an electron array helps, but it's still like only signaling one action at a time."

"But, if my Slate is faster than my own brain, couldn't you just control the ship with, I don't know, my Slate?"

"The speed is actually just about right for the human brain. We hook your eyes up to the ship's eyes, your sense up to the ship's senses, and the amount of information we can relate is just about right. And the instantaneous nature of the communication could make our pilots feel like they *are* the ship. Our early test pilots fell in love with it. The test pilots say it's like breathing in space."

"But no one's ever flown one for this long, have they?"

Nancy put her coffee down. "No."

"And so no one could've guessed that the ships—no, the pilots controlling the ships would start going rogue."

Nancy whispered a curse. One of their interns had let that term slip in a twitter update the previous month. Every newspaper, blog, and social media account on the planet (and beyond, for that matter) had latched onto it immediately. "They're not going crazy."

"Dr. Yeung, Trappist Voyager's data stream is public information. We all know that right now it's on a kamikaze mission for the first manned ship to cross its path. What do you call that but going rogue?"

"A glitch." Nancy said.

"Really?" Menendez asked.

Nancy checked the time on her Slate, then stood. "I need to check on my team."

"Your coffee?" Menendez called after her.

She didn't answer.

Chapter Five

Nancy read the data stream over again. Were the phrases becoming clearer, or more confused? She wasn't sure. The data stream was filtered through the human brain of the pilot. Every communication between the ship's and JPL's computers all ended up passing through the pilot at some point. He wasn't aware of it anymore then most people were aware of dreaming. But what even counted for *awareness* when your consciousness was wired between two computers through a quantum radio array 1.9 light-years apart?

Hell if she knew, but she wasn't about to tell that to Eddie Menendez.

"Can you make any sense of it?" Okeke asked.

The ship now seemed to be quoting poetry.

The undiscovered country. Discovered? Discover the country. Melting. Melting. Thawed and melting. Un-discover? Un-country...

It went on like that for several pages.

"This phrase here. 'The undiscovered country.' Doesn't that sound like literature as well?" Nancy asked.

Okeke shrugged.

Andrews sighed, looking annoyed. "Maybe it's a reference to TRAPPIST-1b. That's where the colonists are heading, after all. It's a country and they're discovering it."

"If would help if we knew where it came from." Nancy looked up. "So, did we find someone who's actually read a book?"

Okeke pointed across the table to a small woman, with short red hair and a pair of thick-framed glasses that had slipped halfway down her nose. "Amy is one of our new interns. She double-majored in Classics and Engineering as an undergrad."

Amy smiled, looking down. "I never thought it would matter in this job."

"We're still not sure it does," Nancy murmured, handing her the Slate. "Does this look familiar to you?"

"It's Shakespeare. This phrase, 'the undiscovered country' is in Hamlet."

Nancy raised an eyebrow. "So our pilot is quoting Shakespeare?"

"I doubt it. He never went to college." Okeke responded.

"Amy, do you remember where this quote is from in Hamlet?"

"It's from the 'to be or not to be' speech," Amy said.

"The one where Hamlet is thinking about suicide?" Nancy asked.

Amy nodded.

"Nancy, where are you going with this?" Okeke asked.

Nancy looked away and rubbed her forehead. She still wasn't sure herself. The drone pilot was supposed to be seamlessly linked with the drone. He wasn't supposed to be contemplating suicide. But then again, he wasn't supposed to be rerouting the ship for a kamikaze run on their colonists either. "I'm not sure," Nancy said. "Maybe understanding where this data is coming from will help us understand why the ship is being rerouted. Maybe it will help us understand why the pilots keep dying."

Andrews rolled his eyes. Nancy ignored him, turning to the young intern. "Amy, can you try looking for other sources in the data? Anything at all, just take a note of it. Okay?"

Amy nodded, heading back to her workstation.

Nancy turned back to Andrews, keeping her voice low. "I have to ask. We're sure that there's nothing corrupting the ship's data?"

"Everything on our side is air gapped," Andrews said. "It would take a physical breach. I mean, real James Bond level shit."

Nancy nodded. "Keep monitoring everything. I want updates every five minutes."

She turned to go, but Okeke stopped her.

"Nancy," he said. "Can we talk?"

"Not now," Nancy said. "I have to go scare off this reporter. Give me five minutes."

Nancy walked through the control room and into the hallway. The name of their ship struck her suddenly as funny. It was named after the telescope that had been used to discover the star system that the small drone was now headed for. The star system also bore the same name: Trappist. The name came from a particular Monastic sect of Catholic Monks known for their beer. They were part of the order of St. Benedictine, and leading a quiet, near-silent life was one of their founding principles. For a ship which was named after silent, beer drinking monks, to suddenly begin spouting off novel-length tirades of poetic nonsense while rerouting to crash into the nearest ship of colonists was, well, ironic. Dark as hell, but still ironic.

Chapter Six

"I want to know what you intend to post," Nancy said, striding back into the conference room. Menendez looked up at her, surprised.

"I think I've been pretty straight-forward." Menendez said.

"Questioning the Trappist Voyager's piloting program is not a story. People have been writing about that for months. So what is it you think you have?"

Menendez fiddled with his Slate, then nodded. "We know this is your third piloting system and that the last two pilots died within only a few months."

"The deaths of the pilots are a matter of public record."

"But those deaths weren't entirely natural, as you've claimed. Were they? They went crazy."

Nancy hesitated.

"So you don't deny it?"

"I'm neither denying nor confirming. Who's your source?"

"I can't say that," Menendez answered.

"Let me guess. It's an 'anonymous JPL employee.'"

Menendez stared at her for a moment and then nodded.

"There's nothing wrong with the navigation system," Nancy said.

"No? So why three pilots in only two years?"

"Each pilot is a volunteer. They know this is a new system and they know the risks, but the sign up anyway. Maybe you've forgotten, but we wouldn't have gotten to the moon without such brave men and women."

"I don't still understand," Menendez said. "Why use people at all?"

"I don't have time to explain aerospace engineering to a reporter," Nancy said. "I have a mission to run."

Menendez shrugged and grabbed his slate. "I'll be sure to forward you a copy when we publish."

Nancy let out a sigh. "Fine. The Tyson drive revolutionized the space industry. It gave us near light-speed travel and opened up the stars. But the problem was communication. Communicating by radio was far too slow and ineffective. We could send colonists to the nearest stars, but we would be leaving them with a stone-age level of communication. Communicating with Earth would be the equivalent of sending messages in a bottle, and that is only if the systems didn't fail. But the Quantum Radio changed all that. It brought communication back up to the Industrial Age. We could communicate across one or two or forty light-years in an instant, but it's still limited to the communication speed of late twentieth-century computers. But linking those arrays to a pilot on the neurological level allows us to bypass those limitations. But where modern computing has the human brain beat on speed, a human mind is still superior in one way. Meta-cognition."

Menendez didn't respond.

"You've got five minutes," Nancy said.

"Okay, I'll bite. What's that?" Menendez asked.

"Thinking about thinking. Evolutionary psychologists say it's key to our survival instinct. It's why, no matter how good our self-driving vehicles get, you still want a human behind the wheel. Because even though the computers can respond faster than a human possibly could, there are still those circumstances in which a human can, and should, make a different kind of decision."

"Like swerving to avoid a bus full of kids to hit another car instead."

Nancy thought about Colonia One. Did this asshole reporter know about the probability of collision? What did he know that he wasn't letting on? She stifled her response and shrugged. "Sure."

"But how many kinds of situations can you have like that on a forty light-year mission?"

"It has to do with prioritizing one of the onboard systems over another when one might fail or need repair. A linked pilot can make those decisions—can *feel out* those decisions—much faster than our technicians could, and can make decisions that the onboard computers would never make."

"Because it can think about its own survival."

Nancy nodded. "And that's why we link the pilots. It's also why we didn't bother doing it with Colonia One. There's already a human pilot on board."

Menendez tapped at his Slate, his finger bisecting the HoloScreen field and sending splashes of blue light across the room. "But when you replaced the last two pilots, did the new pilots know what happened to the pilots before them? Did they know unlinking has a one-hundred percent fatality rate?"

"That's not true," Nancy said. "It never happened in testing."

"So you admit that unlinking the pilots caused the fatalities?"

"Those pilots died of natural causes."

Menendez stared. "Brain hemorrhages and catastrophic heart failure the moment you press a button... Yeah, that sounds natural."

Nancy could feel her blood pulsing through her veins. *Where the hell had this guy gotten his information from?* Yes, that's how the two pilots had died. But they were exhibiting symptoms of heart failure before they started the unlinking process. Still, the same question had haunted her. *Had they caused this?* She looked down at her watch. "Time's up."

"You said you'd give me ten minutes." Menendez responded. "First you gave me three minutes, then five minutes. You owe me two more minutes."

Nancy glared at him. "Fine, but I need to check back in with my team."

Menendez leaned back in his chair. "I'll wait."

Chapter Seven

Okeke was waiting in the conference room when Nancy entered. He was sitting stiffly in a chair, one leg crossed over the other, a coffee cup held just below his lips, staring at the HoloScreen on the opposite wall. The data feed was streaming across the HoloScreen in real time. But it was clear to Nancy that Okeke wasn't reading the stream. He was somewhere else entirely.

"Somebody's leaking to the press," Nancy said.

Okeke looked up at her. "Oh?"

Nancy stifled a sigh of frustration. Okeke's lack of emotion was what drove them apart in the first place. He never gave her the reaction she wanted. He never knew how to mirror her own feelings.

To grieve a loss so intensely, and to see a complete lack of grief in someone you loved, was devastating. It was also isolating as hell.

But all that was in the past.

"He knows every goddamned thing. He knows the deaths of the previous pilots weren't natural—"

"We don't even know that," Okeke interjected.

"But he knows *something...*" Nancy said. "He just hasn't come out and said what it is yet."

Nancy looked up at the stream. It was all very much the same stream-of-consciousness rambling she had seen earlier. Though this new part of the stream seemed to be reminiscent of *The Wind and the Willows*. Did it mean anything or was it the last gasps of a—she struggled to finish the thought—a dying man?

"Nancy, you know these pilots aren't May," Okeke said.

Nancy started at the comment. "What?"

Okeke turned to Nancy, his eyes wide and full of care. "You kept her on life support forever as well, but it didn't do any good."

"What are you doing?"

"You tell everyone that the pilot is the ship and the ship is the pilot. That they're the same. But you know you don't believe that any more than the rest of us."

"They are," Nancy insisted. "The pilot…" she sighed, struggling to get the words out. "The pilot is the *soul* of the ship."

"The what?" Okeke asked.

"The soul," Nancy said. "It's that immaterial part. The thing we can't put our finger on. I mean, god dammit, Okeke. These pilots are talking to the ships at a distance of 1.9 light-years in *real time!*"

"We do that too," Okeke said.

"But it's not the same and you know it," Nancy said. She could hear her volume rising, and she knew she was about to lose it. But she couldn't lose it. Not right now. Not when there were fifty lives on the line. She took in a breath. "It's a bond across space and time that we still don't fully understand. And it works. And re-building that bond isn't just a matter of *'rebooting.'* It takes time."

"May won't talk to you," Okeke said, softly.

"What are you talking about," Nancy said.

"I know it's the anniversary, and I know that you… you talk to her."

Nancy started. "I don't talk to her."

"I've heard you. I don't think you even realize you're talking out loud, but you are."

Nancy didn't respond.

Okeke took a step forward. "She's not going to speak to you, Nancy. She's gone. And this pilot is gone as well."

Nancy crumpled into herself, overwhelmed by the feelings. "We can make a man and computer talk to each other across 1.9 light-years like they were the same organisms, the same *being.*"

Okeke reached out his hand and hesitantly placed it on her shoulder. He hadn't touched her like this in over a year. "I know," he said. "I realize we don't talk about it. But maybe we should."

Andrews stepped inside the conference room. He hesitated a moment. "Collision probability just bumped up two percentage points, despite sending about three dozen re-routing commands." He shook his head. "I'm sorry, Nancy. It's time."

"No, we can't lose another one."

Nancy pushed past him and into the control room. Dozens of techs looked up as she entered. She heard footsteps behind her and turned to see Okeke hurrying to catch up with her.

Okeke stopped as she turned back to him.

"We have to reboot," Okeke said.

"Where's that intern?" Nancy asked. "Amy, where's Amy?"

Andrews stepped between Okeke and Nancy. "Yeah, losing this pilot would be a fucking tragedy. But we're talking about fifty people. Brave men and women that volunteered for a one-way trip to another solar system with no guarantee of survival. You really want to risk losing them by having our own drone crash into their ship?"

Nancy turned away, ignoring him. "Amy? Where…"

"I'm right here…"

Nancy turned, seeing you the young intern standing behind her HoloScreen. Nancy rushed toward her.

"Did you find anything else?"

Amy nodded. "A lot of this is from literature. Most of them are classics. There are some songs. I think I spotted some Harry Potter references as well…"

Nancy waved Andrews over. "See? Our pilot is *remembering*. We can't just unlink him like he's some program. He is remembering the books he's read, the song's he's heard. We can't treat him like a machine because he's *alive*."

"No…" Amy said, her voice small.

Nancy turned to her in surprise.

"He's not remembering." Amy said. "I thought there was something common between these references and I figured out what it was. They're from drone ships onboard drives. We loaded it up with examples of music, literature, philosophy, and art."

"Nancy," Okeke said. "It's random pieces of information from the databases. Like confused memories. That's all."

Nancy looked away. "We need to do right by her…"

"The pilot?" Andrews asked, looking confused.

Nancy moved for the door, speaking back to Andrews. "Tell that reporter he can watch our briefing like everyone else. Our official response is 'no comment.'"

Chapter Eight

Nancy sat down in front of conference room's secure HoloScreen. Their PR department was there—nearly everyone had been called in by now—but as project leader, this task fell squarely on her shoulders.

A tech turned on the HoloScreen, bathing her in blue light.

"Good morning. My name is Dr. Nancy Yeung. I am Associate Administrator of Long Range Exploration with NASA and the Project Leader of the Trappist Voyager team here at JPL. For the last three months, we have been organizing the flyover with the Colonia One—the first, long-range manned colonist mission outside of our Solar System. After five years of Colonia One's voyage, they will be passing within sight of Trappist One at approximately 6:14 in the morning, today, January 15, 2037, Earth Standard Time.

"The entire crew of Colonia One has been awoken from ChomoSleep to see this event, and the eyes of planet Earth and Earth's colonies across the Solar System will be on it as well. It is a historic day, but it seems it will be marked with tragedy…"

She trailed off, blinking to focus on the prompter.

"Early this morning, we discovered that a glitch in Trappist Voyager's navigation system had set it on a collision course with Colonia One. The change in the navigation this morning was accompanied with some strange anomalies in Trappist Voyager's data stream. We have determined that the pilot has succumbed to a neurological breakdown while in ChomoSleep. Because of this, we have been forced to remove the pilot of the drone ship, Trappist Voyager, from duty."

Nancy took a breath. She turned, seeing Okeke standing next to the HoloScreen, watching her. He nodded, encouragingly.

"As you all know, two previous pilots have died during Trappist Voyager's journey."

Nancy swallowed, feeling like she was forcing a rock-sized lump down her throat. The script on the prompter read: *we will now be launching a full-scale investigation into the cause of this failure.*

But how many more pilots could they lose? How many more volunteers who stepped willingly to their death would she allow? *The undiscovered country...* If stuck a man in the mind of a machine, gave him the knowledge of 3,000 years of human history, literature, and philosophy, and set him on long-term voyage across the stars what did they think would happen to him? The usual concerns of long term space flight had been ignored because their pilot was in ChomoSleep, and ChomoSleep had been used safely for years. But what really would be the effect of linking a pilot to a machine and separating them by trillions of miles? What would this do to the machine? To the man?

She saw something out of the corner of her eye. Okeke was leaning toward her, eyes wide. She had become lost in her thoughts and Okeke, at least, had already noticed.

Nancy took in a breath. She turned from the prompter to look at the HoloScreen. "As I was saying, two previous pilots have died during Trappist Voyager's journey. But we would like to confirm today that all three had succumbed to similar neurological conditions. As of today, we will be suspending the drone pilot program and returning Trappist Voyager to control of the JPL command team." On the other side of the room, Nancy could see Andrews throw up his arms in frustration. People around him were looking to each other in confusion. Nancy could already see the room full of PR people jumping to work, drafting their responses. She would probably be fired for this. "The drone pilot program was, in my ways, my baby..."

Her throat stuck. Where did that come from? She had never called the program her *baby* before. She closed her eyes. All of this, one the same day... Was she letting her daughter's death get to her? Was she confusing her emotions over May with her emotions over the impending death of the drone piloting program?

She opened her eyes. "We will begin unlinking the pilot at approximately 5:30 this morning. This should leave us with plenty of time to take over control of Trappist Voyager and to give the brave colonists of Colonia One a flyover that they will all remember. Thank you."

She stepped out of the HoloScreen's field.

"What kind of shit was that?" Andrews whispered, coming alongside Nancy.

She turned on him. "We can't play this moral chess anymore. One drone pilot's life is as important as fifty colonists. So either we figure out how to make them live, or we scrap the program."

Chapter Nine

Okeke finished the final unlinking procedure on his Slate and turned to Nancy. She ignored him, watching as the vitals on the giant, floor-to-ceiling HoloScreen in front of her turn from green to red, and the room full of scientists and technicians watched with her. They watched as the pilot died.

It struck Nancy as incredibly morbid that they would mark death in this instance with something as mundane as a change of colors.

Trappist wasn't just a ship. It was also the men and women who had piloted it. Two men and one women. All dead. Soon another pilot would eagerly volunteer, despite the risks. And soon, she believed, they would be watching that new pilot's vitals turn from green to red as well.

"I need to see him," Nancy said.

"What?" Okeke asked.

"I need to see the pilot's body,"

Okeke touched her arm, and Nancy felt herself warm to him. How long had it been since she had let him touch her that way? A year? More? She couldn't remember.

"We have to re-route the ship now. There's still the flyover to worry about."

"A man just died," Nancy whispered.

"His body is about to be vacuum-wrapped and shipped off to his family. They will grieve him. You don't need to."

Nancy looked around the room of people, all of them moving about their tasks, uncaring of the loss of life that had just happened. And then it struck her. They didn't care because she had made it that way. The drone pilot and Trappist Voyager are the same. She had said that a hundred times. Maybe a thousand times. The moral calculus of one life for fifty had been done so quickly because she had made him less than a life. He was only one more component of the ship. Just as replaceable as a bolt or antenna.

Something caught inside of her. There was no grieving in this world of endless data and research and discovery. But she was the one leading here. Was she to blame?

"At least tell me his name," Nancy said.

Okeke tightened his grip. "Is this about May?"

"It's not," Nancy insisted.

"Because you refuse to talk about her. You pretend as if she never existed."

"What was his name?" Nancy asked again.

"If you would just let me talk to you about it sometime, then maybe you would be able to…"

Nancy pulled herself away and moved for the door. She could feel the eyes watching her as she exited the room. But she didn't care. She would have to move quickly.

Chapter Ten

She made it to the ChomoSleep chambers before the orderly drones, passing the squat, grey machines in the hallway. They beeped at her as she locked the door. The room was dark, cold, and filled with the sound of humming machinery. It looked like a hospital room. But where a bed should be was a long, low cylindrical chamber. *It's a coffin,* she thought. *I never saw it before, but it's a coffin.*

Nancy knelt beside the chamber and touched its cold surface. She took out her Slate and synced it with the rooms systems. Her login overrode the automatic systems, and she unlocked the chamber. A white smoke poured out as she lifted back the lid, revealing a slender, naked man who couldn't have been over thirty. She put her hands on his body and began her search, checking his fingers, toes, and ears. But there was no tag. She checked her Slate again. Instead of a name was only a number.

Nancy felt anger, frustration, and sadness well up inside of her.

There was a hiss as the door opened. She knew without looking. It was Okeke.

"The flyover was a success," he said.

"I'm glad," Nancy responded.

Okeke knelt down beside her. "I remember May speaking after we took her off the ventilator. I remember you trying so hard to make sense of her words then as well. Was she trying to tell us something or was it the last gasps of a dying mind?"

"We assume the pilots are no longer conscious of their lives, of their humanity," Nancy said. "We *assume* that, but we don't *know*."

Okeke sat down beside Nancy in front of the ChomoSleep chamber. Nancy looked at him. "I asked you, when May was dying, when she couldn't speak any longer, how far was the distance from the soul to the tongue when the neural pathways were no longer working. Do you remember that?"

Okeke nodded.

"1.9 light-years," Nancy said. "That's how far."

Author Brian J. Walton

Brian J. Walton is a Los Angeles based author and screenwriter. In 2008, Brian joined New Renaissance, a production company that, in the following 5 years, created over one hundred episodes of narrative content for the web for platforms like Youtube, Hulu, and Netflix, which have been seen by millions. Brian has since expanded into writing novels.

His first novel is RECURSION, a multi-narrative time travel thriller. RECURSION was released in 2016.

http://www.brianjwalton.com/

https://www.facebook.com/brianjwaltonauthor/

Operation Solid Iron

By James Osiris Baldwin

Zarechny, Russia. Year 2226.

The smell of boiling steel and uranium slag blew to Sapheda's nose across the lake, an eerie ionized metal odor that seared its way into her sinuses and made her eyes burn and itch. Mission Control had told her their pills and shots would protect her from the unholy amount of radiation in Zarechny. Given how her bones were humming, she was pretty sure Mission Control was full of shit.

Sapheda balanced on the prow of a boat so light that it skipped with the smallest breeze, threatening to pitch her into the still waters of the Site 1200 reservoir. The men behind her were tense: six draconic Raptorines, their pebbled skins dark with mud and camouflage grease, guns on their laps, rigs loaded with gear. They were as silent as the electric motor that powered the boat. Their coronas were turned off. Sapheda was at one end, and the squad Alpha, Haori, was at the other, guiding them towards their target: the drainage canal that had once supplied the parabolic cooling stacks and nuclear-powered steam turbines of Site 1200.

The squad was hunched down, eyes narrowed or closed so that they didn't catch the light. Confident in her invisibility, Sapheda rested on the edges of the boat on her toes, elbows on her thighs, hands linked between her knees. Her inner eyelids dulled the tell-tale moisture that could gleam in the scope of a sniper rifle. Her temperature was the same as the ambient air. Her naked skin bent the light around her body so accurately that Haori could steer the rudder by looking straight ahead, gazing through the perfect projection of the shifting horizon on her back.

You will be entering Site 1200, a ruined BWR 'breeder' nuclear power station in Zarechny, Russia. The site was captured by a small elite UNAC extraction force on Wed 24th -0022. They broke away from the Southern TZ and are now in the process of patching the breach in Reactor 1 and exploring Reactor 2...

Her memory replayed the brief flawlessly. The voice of Sapheda's imagination was not her Switch, Iris. She recounted the narrative in Colonel Krukov's silk baritone, calm and cool as the water that lapped around the prow of the boat.

We assume that the mostly intact core of Reactor 2 could hold up to twelve thousand kilograms of mixed fissile material. To underscore the severity of this situation, pre-Collapse thermonuclear warheads are believed to have required only six kilograms of plutonium each.

Site 1200 was a grim, dark hole in the ground, where all natural scent was drowned by the oppressive blood-like smell of heavy radiation. It started as a metallic sting and slowly, irrevocably wound itself into her skull, into her mouth, up into her sinuses. By the time they were nearing the edge of the lake, her Jacobson's organ could soon not sort out any smell that wasn't rotting hot metal. She had relative radio-immunity by design, backed up by the shot of Ex-Rad she'd given herself just before her jump. She could only imagine how her squad felt. The only thing standing between the Raptorines of Horus Black and incurable marrow-deep radiation burns were Ex-Rad and their nanite Healswarms. With both of those things, they could stay on site at Zarechny for six hours. She could manage twelve. But the UNAC soldiers?

The UNAC personnel on-site either do not know they will die as a result of their operation, or they do not care. We estimate they have already spent 48 hours repairing the 'coffin' on Reactor 1, and perhaps six on the extraction itself. In 12 hours time, they will have at enough material for at least one nuclear missile, and possibly many.

Haori clicked in his throat, a bird-like sound that made Sapheda rise and turn, alert. The other soldiers looked up, muzzles pointing like a circle of spears at their leader. Haori began to sign with lean scaled hands, talking in perfect silence. "Sapheda, point. Aeda, Manaaki, you've got the rear. I want this fast, quiet and clean. Everyone clear on their orders?"

The five saurian soldiers saluted. Sapheda let one of her hands break from camouflage, enough to give him a thumbs-up, and Haori's lips peeled back in a brief fanged grin.

"*Good,*" he said with his hands. "*Contact in sixty seconds.*"

Sapheda drew a deep, steadying breath, and closed her eyes.

Agent, you will penetrate the site underwater. Historical reconstruction indicates that it is possible to access the north cooling tower via pipes which fed water to the condensation stack…

The boat nosed up to the shallow bank, squeaking on the sand as it beached. Sapheda left first, knife in hand. Her passage was marked only by delicate, hoof-like footprints on the soil that were quickly trampled by clawed tracks.

… Once you are inside, you will investigate and report on the UNAC's progress. You will sabotage the enemy's electromagnetic shields, then vacate the site at top speed prior to the commencement of the Counter Operation. Failure is not an option. Good Luck.

Her Handler's voice was accompanied by a powerful vision of his handsome, regular face, his neat hair, black corona, and the glint of his gold-and-glass eyes. The Colonel's greatest, most beautiful scar. Long ago, he had told her words to live by. *You were the best all the time, or none of the time.* Sapheda clenched her jaws until her teeth locked.

The rest of Horus Black followed Sapheda like a pack of shadows to the slumped ruin of a chain fence overgrown with long grass, now dead. The fence still had a sign looped to it with wire. The writing was illegible, but the nuclear hazard sign could still be seen, leering out at them in the weird brownish gloom. Haori opened the fence up with a laser cutter, and the team passed through, waiting crouched while he quickly stitched up the gap with paracord.

Their trail ran along the banks of a flooded canal that wound east before descending into the guts of Site 1200. When the canal deepened and the thick retaining wall of the power plan could be seen from the ground, Haori signaled the squad to gather in. Sapheda let go of her camouflage, shifting her skin to a dull, pebbly black, and the team circled her in a ring of solemn, cork-rubbed faces. Aeta slung his heavy pack to the ground, and Manaaki brought out the drone. The robot looked like a dead spider, legs folded in toward its thorax. The Raptorine held it in the sluggish stream of the canal and turned on his corona, a dull khaki disk of nanites that pulled out of the pores of his skull and whirled into a solid ring behind his head. He interfaced with the robot virtually, and the driller's limbs unfurled, paddling in the water.

Without a word, Aeta handed Sapheda her rig. She accepted a bandoleer studded with microdot charges, then rope, which she slung around her shoulders, and then a small water-proof pack with her gear.

"Send it back with an update if you can." Haori signed, claws flashing dully in the reflected light of the water. "The scouter reported a sniper nest near the entry to the cooling tower drains."

"I will if I can," Sapheda signed back with one hand, reaching out for kit with the other. Aeta was already holding out her next piece of gear: an oxygen-generating rebreather. She fit the mouthpiece in around her teeth and bit down. The gelatinous seal crept around her jaw and into her nostrils, nearly fusing with her skin. She drew a deep breath. Sweet, pure, clean air rushed through nose and mouth. "We'll see."

She wanted to rub her cheek against Haori's, take the scent of her squad with her into the deep, but instead she drew herself up, lips pressed together, and bowed from the waist. Every man in the squad put his fist over his heart and did the same as she stepped back and blended into the night.

The gear had some adaptive camouflage, but wasn't nearly as good as her own skin - around the seventy percent mark while she was in the water. Sapheda slipped into the canal, and the robot followed her in like a strange metal shrimp. She let it swim up and embrace her, clutching on around her shoulders and chest. It weighed her down and made her skin practically useless if she had to rise above the waterline, but it was her ticket into the reactor's cooling stack.

Site 1200 was one of the last pressurized boiling water reactors built before the Collapse finally depopulated Europe, which made it around 150 years old. All things considered, it was in pretty good shape. Only one building had melted down, contained by a hastily assembled boron concrete and lead coffin. The shell was hemorrhaging radiation, almost completely ineffective now given the tarnished silver-spoon taste in the air. Up until now, that coffin breach had kept the UNAC out. It was only in the last two years that the Alliance had even been able to send in probes and verify that Site 1200 had been a breeder reactor, a plant that produced weapons-grade plutonium for Russia when the Glass Land had still been a cluster of 'Stans. Sapheda's people didn't know if the Crusaders had discovered viable fissile material or well-preserved parts they planned to salvage, study, and reproduce, but either was bad. Catastrophically bad. There was nothing crazier than religious fanatics with nukes, and the UNAC was very much on board with the Bible's whole 'cleanse the world with fire' thing.

When she reached the sluice gate, Sapheda scrabbled for a handhold on the side of the canal. She could see easily in this place. Glass Land clouds were dull, reddish and thick, and they reflected the light of the praxis shields the UNAC Crusaders had erected inside and around the Site compound. The perimeter guard post had its own small shield, mostly hidden inside the repaired building. By the blueish light it cast, she could see a row of machine-gun muzzles resting on the camouflaged sandbags. The Crus inside were watching for aircraft and paratroopers - not one invisible Nephilim woman.

Sapheda activated her corona, head just above the surface of the water, and queued the driller robot. It let go of her torso and slipped into the water. She grasped its back and guided it slowly against the current until they reached the gurgling sluice door. The UNAC Crus had rigged it with barbed mesh and a crude motion sensor. The bot went down underneath it. No bigger than a fox terrier, it buried through the mud, shearing away the wire as it went, and paddled into the dark tunnels that ran beneath the entire power plant.

The brain-to-interface link between the corona and the drone let Sapheda see through her robot scout's eyes. Fifty meters in, the pipes narrowed dramatically - a foot and a half around, no more than that. It was like that the rest of the way into the filter pumps, clotted with built-up debris. That was what the microcharges were for. The bot automatically seeded the black gunk with tiny explosives and swam back, waiting for the command to detonate. Sapheda triggered it with a thought. They burst with very little sound, and for a moment, the camera feed cut as black goop rushed past the bot. When it cleared, it pressed on, cut through the rusted bars, and entered the pitch dark of the pipes, scouring, ablating, and drilling as it went.

Well, that was that. Sapheda cut the feed, drew a deep breath, and submerged.

The first part was easy. Dark, but easy. She swam like a mermaid into the wide feeder pipes, her gear tucked under one arm. The feed sent back by the bot was not heartening. Parts of the pipes were so fragile that it was drilling away the debris manually instead of deploying charges. Even a foot of explosive pressure could be enough to collapse a pipe and crush the bot, and then they'd be well and truly screwed. In the chamber where the pipes narrowed, Sapheda clung to the ceiling, breathing the pocket of trapped air there to save her respirator. It was an anxious hour wait before the tunneller finally broke through into a wider tunnel, pitch black and completely underwater. The lights played over a round door rusted into its frame. The second sluice gate.

The bot studded the gate with microdot charges and swam back, turning to shine its cameras on the heavy portal, now ringed with glowing red lights. There was a pause, and then the charges blew, sending chunks of rust and earth careening through the chamber. Something struck the bot and sent it spinning back. When it righted, it refocused on the door. It was now clear of built up fungus, but it remained stubbornly closed.

Shit. Sapheda took over manual control and remotely piloted the tunneller back to the door. The charges had raised the pressure in the small chamber, but not dangerously so. She brought the bot to the door and got it to clamp its feet down, then set it to begin carving a Sapheda-sized ring. The laser wasn't made for this kind of high-density metal cutting, but it was going to have to do. Bars and grate trim were one thing - a small, high-powered underwater torch could cut through those without blasting through the battery. Five inches of composite metal was another matter entirely.

Sapheda let the drone take over, and while it worked, she bound her kit bag up with rope, fit her mask back over her nose and mouth, and pulled the bag along behind her as she swam down towards the gaping maw of the pipes. She stopped in front of it, frowning as she realized that her hands were shaking. Up until now, she'd ignored the fear, but the tunnel mouth yawned ahead of her like a cold crematorium. It was death, her instincts told her. She hated these dark, tight, water-filled spaces. They evoked the decanting tank. Collapsed bunkers, with men she'd known dying under tons of earth as she frantically tried to dig them free.

Even as her brain began to feed her images of being crushed to death in a watery tomb of crumbling concrete, the Colonel's words returned to her. Failure was not an option. The UNAC wanted an apocalypse, and if they got their sweaty hands on nukes, they'd have one. It was why the Party had invested in her. She was made to stop this.

Sapheda drew a steadying breath and resolutely kicked her legs, pressing forward into the silent black. She slithered into the first of the pipes with her hearts thundering in her ears, dragging her kit behind her.

Even Sapheda's enhanced eyes could not penetrate the true darkness. The driller bot had laid down tiny chemical lights on its path towards the sluice gate, and they were her only guide as she kicked and pulled herself through the wider pipes on the way down and forwards. Other than the rasp of her breather, the scrape of the waterproof bag against the curve of the tunnel, there was no other sound: only the black, and the steadily increasing pressure as she crawled into the bowels of the ruined reactor.

The trail ended at the halfway point, the filter pump. Sapheda hauled her pack through next, hand over hand, until it bumped into her arms. Now that she was this far in, she could risk a light. She felt around the side of the kit for a zipper with a star-shaped tag, opened it partway, and took out a flexible rod that she bent until the glass core snapped. A pale glow spread through as the chemicals mixed, and then flared with bright phosphorescent light. The tightness in Sapheda's chest eased slightly as the five-foot chamber leapt with light, only to tense again when she faced the mouth of the narrow pipes she now had to transverse. Two hundred meters of suckass bullshit.

The foot and a half diameter was too narrow for her shoulders to fit intact, though her lean hips would squeeze in with an inch spare. With a shallow sigh, Sapheda tucked the glowstick behind her ear, reached up to her left shoulder, and used the hard edge of the tunnel mouth to jerk the joint out of its socket. It came free with a muffled crunch. Her ligaments were long, flexible, and strong, and it dislocated painlessly, but the wet sound was loud in her ears. Sapheda folded the tingling limb under her chest and belly and fed herself feet first into the pipe like a trapdoor spider, pulling the rope in behind. She flexed and slithered, hips scraping, and banged her head forward, then back. Panic suddenly rose in a spiraling wave of helpless terror. The rebreather rhythm stuttered as her breathing sped.

Come on, you bloody bitch! Stop it! Sapheda fought against the headrush and the nausea, the reflexive need to scratch and scream and claw at the sides of the pipe. She was strong enough that a single underwater punch could bring the whole place down on her. If she lashed out or bit the rebreather tube, she'd die here in the dark. They wouldn't even find her useless bloated corpse. She'd be a cork plugged in the dirty ass of Zarechny, forever.

That thought, the imagery, broke the brief fugue of terror. A spasm of hysteric, unverbalised laughter caused her to shudder against the slimy walls that pressed in around her. She slid forward a little more, and then again... and then she could move, sucking carefully measured, shallow breaths.

Sapheda's left shoulder was in agony, her fingers numb by the time she finally pushed out into the sluice vault. She hauled herself out into the groaning darkness, her pack sliding out behind her on its umbilical cord. Hours had passed. Her shoulders and hips had been scraped raw, healed, and been scraped again. The weird wrongness of radiation outside was twice as bad in here, needling at her ... not least because the drill bot's lights were off.

Fuck. Sapheda swam over to it, her fingers skimming the carapace. It had ablated the door most of the way through, then stopped. The bot showed no signs of damage. Either its battery had given up early, or the radiation had gotten to it.

Grimacing, Sapheda rolled her shoulder back into its socket, working her fingers until sensation returned, then went to examine the door where the bot had been working. The laser had almost chiseled all the way through, a ring of weakened metal all that stood between her and the power plant's cooling tower. Frowning, she hauled her kit in and searched over it for another tab. The water-repellant pack had six pockets, each with a different shaped tab. One had a hand-held laser drill which she palmed and turned on the portal. The metal, hundreds of years old, flaked away easily enough under the short beam, tumbling off into the deepening darkness. She broke through quite suddenly, picking off a small hole no bigger than her little finger, and felt a chilly stream pass over the back of her hand, and then another playing over her cheek. One she hadn't carved out. Pushing towards her.

Oh, you're fucking joking-

She pushed back and threw her arms up as the manhole-sized piece of metal blew back into her face.

The metal disk struck her forearm, and her forearm struck her nose as she was thrown back head over ankles, tumbling towards the pipe mouth. The kit was sucked into the vacuum, dragging her with it. She caught it and hauled back before it tore her in two, feet braced on the wall as water formed a soundless twister down below. She grit her teeth and struggled for a breath past her bleeding nose. Water hit her teeth, and she coughed it back out. *The breather! Fuck!*

The glowstick was long gone, sucked out with the breather. Sapheda wrapped the rope around her arm and pulled. A burning pain shot from wrist to elbow, and her eyes narrowed as she pulled the kit back towards her, one foot at a time. Bones shifted and ground unnaturally in her right arm, but there was no time to stop and set. She wrapped an arm around the bag carrying her guns and explosives and swam up, hiding against the ceiling as more of the door broke off and spun through the water. She couldn't see it, but she could hear the shards as they struck stone, bounced, and ricocheted out through the pipes.

Sapheda scowled, hugged the kit to her body with her better arm, and slid along the wall and around. She was grateful for every minute Jericho had made her spend in the training pool as she struggled against the current. She shoved the capsule-shaped bag ahead of her, using it to block the stream, and prepared for agony. The hole was broader than the pipes now, but even the smallest brush of her arm against the edge of the metal made her want to scream with pain. She wormed through, teeth locked, and pushed out into the absolute, boundless crushing darkness of the cooling stack.

For a moment, Sapheda found herself in what seemed like a vast vat of empty space. No one had noted that the cooling stack would be full of water. It was a testament to the skill of the engineers who had built it. They were long dead, but their structure had remained standing, full of water so still and so pure that the scouting probes hadn't even noticed it.

The water was also going to kill her, if she didn't reach the surface. Sapheda's lungs burned, but she threw herself into motion. Gravity - wonderful, constant gravity - was her only guide as her vision blurred with white spots. She could hold her breath for five minutes - ten, if she wasn't exerting - and it had been about four and a half already. Lightning crawled around the edges of her vision. She kept her eyes forward and up, chanting silently to herself.

...Remember, girl: Zarechny carries at least twelve tons of fissile material. It takes no more than six kilos for one warhead. One warhead is enough to destroy everything you care about. Twenty would be enough

to wipe out the remaining life on Earth...

Sapheda fought her own body now. Her chest flexed, trying to force her to breathe something, anything. Her limbs were ringing. Dizzily, she felt herself begin to float with less effort... and it took her a moment to realize that she had broken the surface, her head emerging into empty space as featureless as the water below.

"Oh thank fuck!" She gasped deep, burning lungfuls of cold air. The taste of rust and radiation was overwhelming, but she couldn't stop heaving for more, her throbbing, aching arm clutched to her chest. Each whooping breath was a fresh, raw pain, expanding lungs that felt far too small for her ribcage. One-handed, she flailed and splashed her way across, dragging the dead-weight on its rope behind her, and didn't stop until she collided with a solid surface. The rough stone grounded her as she fought to control her breathing. Her head spun; her lips and nose were tingling. Air. Oxygen. She was alive.

As sense reasserted itself, Sapheda realized that she could see. The water stretched out ahead of her; the clouds, reflecting the light of the Praxis Shield array, glowed overhead. There were no plants other than the weird black crusty fungus that seemed to thrive in radioactive ruins like these. The artificial lake was only ten meters or so from the top of the stack. The remains of ladders studded the walls.

Sapheda hauled her arm out of the water and got a good look at it. It was bleeding sluggishly. The manhole had opened up a bone-deep gash, which was sealing as she watched. She felt around her nose. The skin of her face was numb from the cold water, but her pain hadn't been imagined. Her nose was out of place, the cartilage already partially fused. She let a breath out, drew a deep one in, and wrenched it back into position with a soft crunch and click. Years of training, years of distancing herself from pain, put the bright white agony far away. Sapheda sniffed and grimaced, gathered her kit, and lay back in the water as her injuries itched and throbbed. She watched the flesh of her arm knit, the tissues reaching like rhizomes straining for the sun. The ragged wound sealed without seam or scar. She was distantly aware that it hurt, almost as much as her nose did. Not for long. Lovely things, healswarms.

When the skin smoothed over the last scratch, Sapheda paddled around the perimeter of the stack until she reached the grooves and crumbling holes where the ladders had once been mounted. More than a hundred years of exposure to water had left nothing but rusted, salt-crusted rivets and deep punched out holes. Parts of the masonry had fallen away with the onslaught of time. It left Sapheda with a pattern of shallow hand-holds which she mapped with an upward glance. Wordlessly, she bound the kit to her back and shoulders, and with freshly restored arms, hauled herself from the water. It fell away from her, not clinging. Other than the small patches of scraped and freshly healed skin, her nude body was masked in a matte hydrophobic coating that repelled water. Her crystalline hair and skin were as dry as the kitbag, with its precious cargo of explosives.

On the lip of the stack, she finally got her first good look at Zarechny. She was a good two hundred meters off the ground, perched on the grime-caked rim of the cooling tower. Site 1200 was built on the remains of the two stations that had come before it, a complex which had once stretched for kilometers to the east. Now, much of the abandoned site - never closed properly during the Collapse - were little more than a blasted, sterile jumble of rusted steel and slagging concrete. No plants grew here, not even grass. The radiation had sterilized it.

Three buildings still reared over the ruins. Reactor 1, with its aerodome concrete coffin. Reactor 2, quiet and unassuming... and swarmed by UNAC Crusaders. Soldiers, crawlers, idling cargo craft. Sapheda opened her eyes as wide as she could, her inner eyelids retracting, and weaved her head like a bird of prey to focus in. The Crus were all in powered armor - not the kind that was going to save their lives - carrying fifteen-foot lengths of copper pipe. Fuel assembly storage casks. She watched two soldiers, one at each end, as they maneuvered pipes through the blown-open reactor shell. The entire perimeter was under wraps. The UNAC had brought the praxis canopy in as close as they could so that they formed an unbroken dome over the removal operation. Each shield packed a generator, the juice to keep the shields humming. The radiation messed with electronic devices and robots, but it was to the credit of the military scientists in the old USA that Praxis shields kept working in these conditions. It was no wonder the UNAC kept the secrets of their production so close. In Sapheda's wildest dreams, she managed to capture one of those shields before the Crus destroyed it, and handed it over to Knives. But this mission, no... there wasn't time or room for it. There were three Praxis she had to take out to admit the expeditionary force. And besides that, anything she brought back from this site would be so irradiated that any humans who went near it would sicken and die.

The kitbag had everything she needed to get in, get down, do the job, and get out. Sapheda drew a retractable stay-fast rappel rig and set it up: two plugs to anchor on the concrete, and the harness and cord. She bounded down the darkest side of the stack, and when she reached the bottom, she assembled the rest of her gear. Four stacks of explosive charges and a silenced high-power pistol, in the unfortunate circumstance that she needed the latter. There was a pressure shot of beta-blockers and adrenaline regulators in a ready-to-use cartridge that she set against her thigh, angled, and depressed. The needle clicked dully with enough force to pierce her tough hide, and a wave of calm washed over her. The trembling in her fingers stopped. She plugged her corona back in on stealth, and with steady hands, arranged her gear along her front. There was enough explosive for the three shields, and backup materials in case a batch didn't fire. In the worst case - a nuclear explosion caused by fissile material making contact with water - she had a portable shelter: a superfoam spray-on shell which would harden in the presence of explosive radiation. Contingency on contingency.

Besides the hydrophobic spray, explosives were Sapheda's favorite toys. There were two kinds of soldiers in the Pacific Alliance army: the kind that feared and tried to avoid dealing with explosives, and the kind that got a sort of crazy glee from blowing things up with them, defusing them, playing with them. Fear was replaced by a sense of strange mischief as she closed in on her first target. Crawling low to the ground, spider-like and closely camouflaged, Sapheda got within a hundred meters, and then hunkered down. The Praxis was mounted on a flatbed protruding from a carrier aircraft, flanked by Crusaders in lead-reinforced Warhorse armor. Warhorses, the latest in Fundamentalist Hick technology, were the biggest Mobile Battle Suit they deployed in Glassed zones like this one. They carried assault rifles as big as she was. Belly-down in the rubble, Sapheda stuck a glob of putty to her chest, put the detonator patches on her tongue, and then let herself relax.

The cocktail of drugs depressed her autonomic excitement, an inevitable consequence of this kind of work. Your pulse sped, your palms sweat, your heart thumped. The Warhorse suits were on the lookout for heat and motion. Sapheda let her eyes hood as she shifted her skin, blending not only into the texture of the concrete, the bend of the light and shadow, but into the temperature of the locale. She had to let herself cool, and when she was indistinguishable from the rest of the air, she moved out like a lizard, sluggish and slow, onto open ground, crawling silently and confidently around the post perimeter.

Realistically, Praxis shields were too fantastically stable to randomly combust. They didn't use combustible fuel, but the aircraft did. Sapheda circumvented the guards and the praxis entirely, and wormed her way under the belly of the helicopter. No one was watching for a single invisible, naked operative: the guards were looking out for teams, confident in the bitter protection of the radiation that was slowly cooking them alive in their hastily reinforced armor.

She planted the first stash of putty up under where the Praxis was mounted, and the diversion putty under one of the helicopter's fuel tanks. The Penetrator – yes, they'd really called this model of chopper 'The Penetrator' - had two 230 gallon fuel tanks mounted on the outside, the better to help it carry the extra weight of the Praxis shield generator. They were armored, but there was going to be a big enough boom to turn them into fireworks. Each block of putty got a remote detonator. As she silently set them up, Sapheda immersed into the effortless flow of Purpose. Wonderful, natural purpose. Somewhere, her people were watching with bated breath, waiting for the Praxis to fall so that they could advance. Once put in motion, the events could not stop: there was no pause, little thought. Just purpose.

Sapheda planted the last charge on the third target, and moved quickly and quietly, unseen by the wary, lumbering Warhorse hulks. She wondered sometimes what their radio chatter was like. Surely they did chatter, when not being beaten over the face with their bibles by their human masters. As far as she could tell, the UNAC Nephilim-human relationship was very much that of foaming-at-the-mouth religious master and reluctant, but loyal slave. Despite her training, the videos and uploads, she had always imagined what the men who wore that armor looked like. Seth said they were all the same, like clones. Sapheda had never had time to look. Killing had to be done fast.

In any case, it was time to send these particular Crusaders back to their God.

Sapheda found her position without turning on her corona, picking out the depression in the terrain which had been pointed out to her on the briefing. She stashed her gear down and loaded her pistol. A full clip, and spares if she needed it. She bobbed her head in satisfaction, turned her corona on, then looked up over the rise of the foxhole. The patrol continued on, oblivious.

"Spectre-Base. All set." Sapheda did not send her confirmation in shaped speech: communication in these hotzones was always basal. She had to project the information wordlessly. Basal projection was harder to intercept: much harder.

There was a protracted silence over the brain-to-interface link. The relay took a lot longer than usual. "Base-Spectre affirmative. Go."

Her Switch's non-verbal reply was just as simple and direct. Sapheda counted to three, covered her ears, and depressed the trigger.

The trio of explosions ripped through the helicopters, blew the Praxis generators, and ignited the sprayed fuel in a deafening triple roar, plunging the site into chaos. The ground shook and her ears rang, but Sapheda watched in childlike wonder at what she had wrought, aglow with delight. Feral energy played through her aching limbs as chunks of metal rained down, smoldering on the wet ground.

The Crusaders had no idea what had hit them. Only one of the Warhorses survived the direct, close range explosion. He rolled on the ground to put out his coat of burning fuel as an alarm sounded, whooping in the night-time air, and close to fifty lightly-armored men poured out of the reactor building. Sapheda's hair ruffled as the wind picked up, and the first pair of cruisers shot past. Pacific Rangers jumped from the open sides of the craft, yelling and brandishing rifles, but the demand to surrender was more ritual than anything. Fanatics didn't just hand over their guns, and even as Sapheda's backup barked out the orders, the UNAC fell back under fire to cover their retreat into the reactor core building.

Sapheda vibrated in place, her pistol cupped in her hands, finger on the trigger. Her orders were to stay outside of the fray and hold her position against all comers. No matter how much she wanted to be pushing into the Reactor alongside her team and the other units, she could not. She had to watch, impotent and frustrated, as the site lit up with flashbangs and shield discharge, and as a squadron of jets swept down in a screaming arrowhead formation...

Wait. Jets?

"Spectre-Iris, what the actual fuck?" Sapheda tracked the aircraft with wild speed as the V-shaped cluster of bombers roared overhead, an unfamiliar make and model of light bomber. There was no airstrike planned for this mission. Unloading here risked a nuclear disaster, an explosion that would safely blow Zarechny off the map, and take all the UNAC and Pacific soldiers with it. She didn't hesitate.

"Spectre, I don't know!" Iris, her Switch, squealed back over the link, all pretext of basal communication be damned. "Those are AP-7 Proudwings, legacy drone tech. They're so old they shouldn't even be able to fly! Look, I... we're trying to figure this out over here. Hold the line." Iris's composure had faltered, and she now sounded every inch as shocked as Sapheda felt. "Comms can't get an ID on these B's... Just maintain position and-"

Even as Iris spoke, the mental head-chatter was drowned out by the screaming of ancient jet engines as the formation of six drones swooped down, strafing the burning wreckage of the helicopters and sending the remaining three choppers and their Praxis generators sky-high. For a crazy moment, as she ran towards the place she knew Haori and her team were supposed to be fighting, Sapheda wondered if they were somehow on their side. But then, the formation split, and began to fire indiscriminately on the hundred or so soldiers of both sides, all scrabbling for cover as the shells rained down.

"Haori!" Sapheda switched to the team's combat channel. She ran so fast that her feet skipped over the rumbling ground. With her ears sealed, the daisy-chain explosions that ripped through the complex sounded like popping and gurgling. A chunk of concrete struck her back, but she barely felt it as she scrambled to her team. "Haori!"

"Saph! What the hell are you doing?!" Haori barked back through the same channel, just as Sapheda got his visual. He was fully armored now, plated up against the radiation. It was not enough: he and the rest of H-Black were pushing away from the front, but they were three men down. Sapheda didn't know who they'd lost: Something near the reactor was on fire, and with six choppers burning, the site had filled with thick black smoke. "Retreat! Didn't you hear the call for retreat!?"

Sapheda couldn't hear anything but the ringing in her ears as she wrenched a rifle up from a dead man on the ground. "I AM retreating!"

Haori didn't have time to lecture her before two Cru lurched out of the billowing clouds of black smoke toward them. Sapheda bounded back as she braced the rifle and slammed the trigger, firing bursts from behind the heavily armored Raptorines as they rounded on the pair of stragglers as one.

"Shelter! Where's your shelter?!" Sapheda demanded of the channel. Iris was pinging her, the coronal cue frantically flashing the emergency signal on the back of her cornea. She couldn't answer as they fell back behind a ruined concrete facade, a block of stone that burst and cracked as bullets tore through the edge and sent scree flying. "If they hit the reactor-"

"They're not going to hit the bloody reactor!" Haori snarled.

From somewhere not far away, there was a low crumpling boom, and Iris' voice broke through the fugue as she brute-forced her way into the squad channel. "Retreat! Retreat! The reactor's collapsing!"

"Eeeuuhh, nooo Sapheda, they're not going to hit bloody the reactor!" Sapheda mimicked him, sneering with her voice as she took her turn to fire and give Haori a break. "Run, you idiot!"

She didn't have to say it twice. He scrambled off and Sapheda covered him, twin hearts hammering. Around her, the squad peeled away and pissbolted in all directions, following the Captain toward the water, the drainage canal and the forest. They weren't going to make it in time. A wave of invisible claws passed over her skin. Radiation, intense enough that she felt it needling her bones and the roots of her teeth. A Ranger running past her stumbled and began to scream, clawing at himself. The others turned to him, catching his arms and dragging him along as the invisible heat intensified.

"Use the shelters!" She cried to Haori ahead, as she took a limb and propped him up. "We can't make it!"

Haori didn't question her: he pulled out an egg-like carapace from his injured man's pack and slammed it against his shoulder. The nanite foam burst out and engulfed him, consuming the material of his armor to fuel its own growth. Others had stumbled to their knees: those with presence of mind got behind cover before they deployed their own shelters, their bodies turning into white crystalline cocoons. Haori fumbled for his, and Sapheda saw his hand slap and miss.

This was what it felt like to be cup ramen in a microwave, Sapheda thought. The radiation was so intense that she felt her skin blister and heal, tear and reseal. She lunged for Haori and groped for his shelter and didn't find it. "Where's your damn gear?"

He couldn't reply with anything except a confused, bird-like squawk. The radio was dead, their coronae knocked out. The ground rolled under their feet, pitching the confused Raptorine to his ass. She tore her own shelter egg from her rig and slapped it against his head.

Through the crack in his visor, she saw his eyes widen in surprise. "You bloody bitch-!" he exclaimed, before the foam rushed up over him and she lost contact.

Sapheda laughed. She was sure she was on fire as she dragged the hardening cocoon behind the wall of shattered concrete, hauling with all the unnatural strength of her wiry arms, and then fled, stumbling, for her only hope: the cooling stack. It still stood, rearing above the burning power-plant, and she was so high on pain and drugs and desperation that she barely felt anything as she latched onto the rough surface and began to clamber up, finding footholds and fingerholds that could only support her weight for the time it took her to push off and find the next one, and the next, a complex molecular and kinetic puzzle she assembled second by second, limb by limb. She climbed like a spider, and when she reached the top, she leaped and plunged feet first into the vat of icy water. It swallowed her like a vat of knives, the cold stabbing her healing skin as she submerged, writhing in a silent scream.

Lie back and think of the Colonel, I guess. Eyes open, body taut with agony, Sapheda arched towards the surface of the crystal-clear water and watched the sky turn all the colors of the rainbow, the pillar of energy catching the air alight in a column of prismatic fire.

Either they'd rescue her, or they wouldn't. But in the meantime, Hell sure was pretty.

Author James Osiris Baldwin

Dragon Award-nominated author James Osiris Baldwin writes gritty LGBTI-inclusive dark fantasy and science fiction. Born in Australia, he currently lives in Seattle with his lovely wife, a precocious cat, and far too many rats. His obsession with the Occult is matched only by his preoccupation with motorcycles.

James is the author of the Hound of Eden series (Blood Hound, Stained Glass, and Burn Artist; more to come) and Fix Your Damn Book!, a non-fiction title to help authors master the editing process. His story, Those Who Breathe Under The End, was published in the first volume of The Expanding Universe.

Previews and reviews of all of James books can be found at: http://www.jamesosiris.com

The Trenches of Centauri Prime
By Craig Martelle

How could this suck more?, Lance Corporal Riskin Devereaux thought. *It's the 24th Century, and here I am, standing in the muck. I used to drive a hover car, for crap's sake...*

Politicians, treaties, the instruments of failed diplomacy.

Maybe it didn't fail. The war was being waged with low-tech weapons, but light years from Earth, light years from the Bazarian home world. Neither populace had to worry about war coming to their homes.

All they had to do was fight on a neutral planet.

Because that's what the politicians agreed to. The Marines and the warriors dug in, because they had to. No one could have an advantage.

Riskin was miffed yet again. At least his boots were high tech, but the charge was running low. The indicator flashed on his wrist comp telling him to plug in, otherwise, his feet would get wet. It needed to last another thirty-seven minutes until he got off watch.

Watch. A good word for what they did. The Interstellar Marines stood around with their always sparkly-clean slug throwers and watched to see if any Bazarian raised its ugly spiked head.

They used to shoot at the heads, never knowing if they hit anything. They weren't allowed smart optics or guided bullets.

It was like fighting in the stone age of old Earth. The IMs were trained for better.

And then the reality of what they were ordered to do set them back centuries.

***

"Much suckage!" Ak'Tiul whined, clicking and whistling his dismay. He stood alone at his post in the trench. The humans were right over there, if they could only lob a low-yield nuke from their mortars, this would be over, and they could go home.

But no. The Council of Advisors had different ideas. One destroyed planet and the weasel heads decided to talk, which meant the grunts were thrown into a swamp on a backwater planet.

Out of sight out of mind.

"Hate humans," he told the wall in front of him. "No humans, no mud. Humans equal mud," he chuckled, looking down at his clawed feet. They were enclosed in a flexible polymer that helped keep them dry. The boots had been see-through, but that ended three milli-ticks after he put them on.

He carried a slug thrower. "Useless," he snorted, slinging it over his back. "Might as well throw rocks."

He dug into the mud until he found a stone, hefted it into his hand, corkscrewed his body, and spun as he launched the rock toward the enemy trench line.

Ak'Tiul had thrown it too high. It splashed down half way there. "Hate humans," he reiterated.

***

Riskin saw the rock out of the corner of his eye. He ducked, reactively, then laughed as the projectile splashed into a puddle half way between the lines.

"Candy ass!" he yelled over the wall. He dug into the mud, found a small rock. He hefted it, threw it to the side and looked for a bigger one.

The next was good enough, halfway between a golf ball and tennis ball. He limbered up, windmilled his throwing arm, and then moved to the back of his narrow trench. He wound up, hopped forward two steps, and heaved his rock.

It made it half way. "Damn. Farther than it looks." He would have sat down, but there was no place. The officers had taken the stools away because people were sitting on them and not paying attention. That's what they'd been told. Riskin never saw anyone else, only the lieutenant, but the he said the order came from headquarters, HQ, so there was nothing he could do.

Easy for him to say as he took Riskin's chair away.

Riskin cupped a hand to the side of his mouth and yelled. "Suck my hairy butt cheeks, spiker!"

Splashing footfalls signaled someone was walking in his direction.

"Did you throw something out there, Lance Corporal?" the officer demanded.

"Not as far as you know, your sirness," Riskin replied. No one wanted to be out here. Disrespect ran rampant, especially when you had a lieutenant. New lieutenants got people killed. Seasoned lieutenants were just as cynical as the troops. And then there was this butthole.

"Why are you yelling?" The officer stomped his foot in the mud, sending splatters over both of them. "Damn. You know they don't have ears, right?"

"Makes the corporal feel good, oh sirly one," Riskin barked, stomping his foot as he came to attention. He found the resultant wave of sloppy mud water to be most gratifying as it splashed against the pants of the second lieutenant.

"You did that on purpose!" the officer declared.

"Most likely, your premier sirship," he replied.

"Well," the man sputtered, "don't do it again."

He stormed off before Riskin could do it again.

"That killed two minutes, now what?" Riskin asked the cold mud wall staring back at him.

***

Ak'Tiul saw the rock arc toward him and land short. By his estimate, it traveled farther than his. He dug into the mud to find another rock but hesitated as he heard something.

The Bazarian auditory glands covered the top of their head giving them excellent hearing. He tipped his head and heard the harsh human language, one of many different ones that they used. Stupid humans couldn't even speak one language. He'd learned Chinese, as all Bazarians did since it was tonal like their language.

But these two were speaking something different. He couldn't understand them. Maybe they were giving orders for one of the ill-conceived but aptly named human wave attacks?

If he were so lucky. He'd burn up the old slug thrower then.

"Humans are stupid," he complained. He dug in the mud for another rock.

His officer found him bent over.

"What is this?" the third level MarPul asked.

"Looking for a rock, Master MarPul, sir," he said truthfully.

"To do what?" the officer demanded.

"To heave yonder, toward thy Council's enemies, who are mine enemies. And if I can be blunt, thine enemies, too," Ak'Tiul answered.

"You may not be blunt, Nug!" the officer sneered. "Now drop and give me twenty. I saw that throw. You're getting weak, Nug. Maybe we keep you here until you strengthen up? Can't send you home looking like you've been a prisoner of war, can we?"

The third level MarPul laughed uproariously, doubled over, whistling and clicking out of sync.

Ak'Tiul worked up a snot ball and was going to hock it inadvertently onto the junior officer's back, but the Bazarian stood up, composed himself and stalked away.

"Take your twenty and stuff them in your carapace crack, dickface," the upstart young warrior sassed.

"I heard that Nug!" the Bazarian officer yelled from somewhere far away.

"I wasn't talking to you, but to those pink-skinned, meat bags over yonder," Ak'Tiul muttered. "Hate MarPuls."

***

"Did you hear that?" Riskin asked, but there wasn't anyone around. He was standing on one foot. He'd shut down one boot to save power.

"Why yes, I thought I heard the spike heads having a heated conversation," Riskin assumed a deep voice as he replied to himself. He peeked over the mud wall and searched for movement. He ducked down before he was through searching. He moved down the trench a dozen steps before popping up for a second look.

He thought he saw a spiker, that is, a Bazarian head sticking up above the trench, doing the same thing he was doing.

"You ball slapping spike head!" Riskin yelled.

He thought he heard a sing-song reply.

"I don't speak Chinese, asswipe!" *How dare you speak Chinese when I don't,* Riskin thought.

Riskin turned his right boot's power back on. It came to life, ensuring that it would keep his foot dry. He lifted the other from the water and powered it down. He wanted enough juice in both of them to help him make it back to his bunk where he could both plug in and unplug at the same time.

Ten minutes had passed before a lazy step splashed his way.

"About time you slimy bastard!" Riskin called out. But it wasn't the man who was supposed to relieve him from watch. It was the lieutenant.

"Sir-en-dipity, would you look at that! I'm getting relieved by the brass. Nothing to see, nothing to report, it's a big steaming pile of nothing, just like yesterday, last week, last month, and last freaking year. So, if that'll be it, I hear my rack calling."

Riskin turned his second boot on and prepared to slog through the mud and back to the cave he stayed in for his barracks.

"As you were, Lance Corporal!" the lieutenant barked.

"As I was what? Leaving? Yes, I was leaving and shall continue since you were staying, I was leaving, or something like that, sir highness, sir." Riskin stomped in a puddle, sending a wave of muddy water over the lieutenant's pants.

He didn't seem to care. Usually, he would have danced out of the way or bitched up a storm about being dirty. Riskin was instantly wary.

"What's wrong?" Riskin asked.

The lieutenant looked at him without arrogance, almost fearful. "Human wave in fifteen minutes. Every man goes. Every. Single. Man."

"Glad I'm not one of those, sir. I must report that I've been masquerading as a man all these years. I'm not a dude," Riskin said sincerely.

"Cut the crap. You're going over that wall, just like me." The lieutenant looked at his watch. "In thirteen minutes and you know what, smart mouth? You'll be right next to me. If the golden bullet comes our way, we're going to take it together."

Riskin was done having fun. The lieutenant was serious. He suspected the lieutenant had a sense of humor, but it was buried deeply within, and even if he did let it out, it wouldn't be in front of the lowly enlisted scum.

"Make your peace, Riskin. This is the last attack. The survivors are the winners and they home. This war ends today, Lance Corporal and it's up to us."

"Don't you dare try to motivate me, you sum bitch. I don't want to go over that wall any more than you do, but ending the war is probably the tastiest carrot you can dangle. Damn you!"

***

Ak'Tiul hiked another rock and then another. He wasn't getting close enough to the human trench. He leaned against the mud wall, resigned with the fact that the human trench was too far away for a hand-thrown rock. In his mind, he was engineering a trebuchet to hike a boulder across the dead land and into the enemy trench.

If it weren't for the enemy, he wouldn't have to be here. "Hate humans."

The third level MarPul strode up; he held his skinny arms behind his back as a sign of his authority. "Do you really hate humans, Nug? Want to do something about it?"

"Your holiness, I am designing a trebuchet which isn't a powered weapon. We could use that to lob boulders into the enemy trench, fill it and finish them.

Then we go home, eh, supreme creakiness!" Ak'Tiul hated his life in the trenches.

He rectified himself with the fact that he'd have to prostrate himself before his father and beg forgiveness for his brash decision to join the military. He did that out of spite. His father said he'd hate it. His father was right.

But hate didn't quite capture the full magnitude of his disdain.

Ak'Tiul's body language must have given him away. "Want to do something about it and start the process of leaving this planet, today? Would you like that?"

"The crack slammies you say! What do we have to do, dickface?" Ak'Tiul asked.

"I heard that you upstart. In twelve minutes, a Bazarian wave attack. Every swinging limb goes over the wall. We meet the humans in the middle, and the winner goes home. The war ends today, dickface," the third level MarPul replied.

"Aren't suicide missions supposed to be volunteer only, your queasiness?" Ak'Tiul clicked, both pleased and horrified by the latest developments.

"Volunteer does not have to start with the word, "I," dickface."

"That word. I don't think it means what you think it means," Ak'Tiul countered. The MarPul checked his wrist monitor.

"Ten minutes, stink hole. Make your peace. You and me, we go over together. We survive together, or we die together. Since I have no desire to die, I will need you to fight like the very Fire Demons of Bal Sagoth."

The MarPul thought he was encouraging but Ak'Tiul was instantly depressed. He didn't feel like checking his slug thrower which he'd never fired on this planet. He couldn't remember the last time he cleaned it. No one ever inspected them.

Ak'Tiul thought about loading up on rocks. His arm felt limber, and he was sure he could hit something with a rock, not so much with the slug thrower.

Ak'Tiul started backing up slowly, looking for a place to run and hide.

"Get back here, Nug! For the glory of Bazaria, we meet the enemy on the field of battle, gladiators for all Bazarkind!" the MarPul shouted, thrusting a twig-like arm in the air, a maniacal look on his face.

"Okay, crazy MarPul, whatever you've been snorting, you need to stop. There's no fonking way I'm going over that wall!" Ak'Tiul thrust his chest out defiantly.

The MarPul slapped his shock stick against Ak'Tiul's thigh and stabbed the button with a pointy finger.

Ak'Tiul screamed as his muscles contracted violently and the pain shot through his whole body. "Dickface!" he yelled.

"We're going over that wall, because you're more afraid of me than the pink skins. Ha!" the MarPul ended with a fanatical scream.

Ak'Tiul was unimpressed. "Sir, yes, sir! I'll be behind you all the way," the young soldier offered as a way of compromise.

"At my side, dickface! You will kill the enemies as I point them out. We will sow death and destruction like a harvester clearing a wide swath across the great plain."

"Truly magnificent, we will be, my lord," Ak'Tiul quipped, unsure of what he would do.

Maybe it was time to make peace with his creator, because he couldn't see a way out.

***

Lance Corporal Riskin Devereaux stood there. One boot had run out of power, and the water was seeping in. His discomfort seemed insignificant at that point in his life.

The second boot flashed and cycled down. At least he'd have two wet feet. Balance would be restored in his life at least in the arena of discomfort.

The lieutenant had moved down the trench and was haranguing someone else. At least he was doing it with the level of zeal that he'd shared with Riskin.

Soon the two joined the lance corporal. Riskin had seen the other man before but never talked with him. He'd made it a point not to get to know anyone. He reasoned that if he liked someone, then he might not hate this place so much and Riskin wanted his hate to fester in the hellhole that he'd been condemned to with the other Interstellar Marines he was certain were in the trenches somewhere.

"Hate spikers," he murmured before adding, "and lieutenants."

"What did you say, Lance Corporal?" the lieutenant asked, trying to stand tall and look down his nose at the junior enlisted. The other man was only a private, probably newly arrived, Riskin thought.

And least he wouldn't be stuck in the trenches for an indeterminate interminable amount of time. Riskin had no idea how long he'd been there. Maybe he was new, too, and didn't realize it.

"Your penultimate sir-ness, I said nothing offensive and hold you in the utmost of contempt," Riskin stated firmly, nodding once with pursed lips when he finished.

"Righty-o, then." The lieutenant checked his watch and looked up at the sky as he counted out loud. "THREE MINUTES!" he bellowed, making the two IMs jump.

"What the hell? Didn't you ever hear of OPSEC, Operational Security you wank spanker?" Riskin whispered, trying to get the lieutenant to stop yelling.

"Didn't I tell you? They are coming out to meet us. This is a fight to the end, right out there in no man's land. Ha! Now we'll take the fight to them. If I only had my family's ceremonial sword, I'd show them a thing or two."

"Like what it means to be a psychopath in a hurry to die a bazillion miles from home in a fight over nothing. Absolutely, sir. That would really show them." Riskin shook his head, then offered his hand to his fellow Marine.

"I'm Riskin, pleased to meet you and to go out there and die with you, I guess, because that's our orders, aren't they, oh sir-upy one?"

The other man grasped Riskin's hand. The private's hand was cold and clammy. He was short, looked oriental and to be on the verge of going into shock.

"Chen," is all he said and even that took a great effort from the smaller man.

"Nice to meet you, Chen. Too bad it's under these circumstances, but you know what? We'll be behind the lieutenant the whole way. Isn't that right Sir Magnificent?" Riskin tried for a lopsided smile but only achieved a half sneer with contempt on top.

"ONE MINUTE!"

What made the bellow so odd was that there was only Riskin and Chen. No one else was nearby. They couldn't hear any other people yelling. Riskin wondered how many IMs were left. He couldn't remember seeing more than a handful at any one time in any one place. The only officer he remembered was the lieutenant.

"How many total are in this human wave, your sir-ness?" Riskin asked suddenly.

"All of them. Every swinging dick, Lance Corporal. Now, fix bayonets!" The lieutenant moved to the edge of the trench and cupped his hands as if to give them a boost up.

He noted that they didn't have bayonets, but the lieutenant seemed to be in a different place at a different time.

"Oh, hell no!" Riskin answered, stepping beside the lieutenant and cupping his hands. You can pull us up once you're on top," Riskin suggested.

The lieutenant unholstered his pistol and nodded. "You know if you don't come, I'll shoot you?" He smiled at the two men and looked at his watch, breathing heavily and grinning.

***

"I think the order has been rescinded," Ak'Tiul said and relaxed. "Wow, that was a close one. Smoke if you are having them, eh, MarPul?"

"You get up that wall, dickface. Ten, nine…" the MarPul counted down, holding his shock stick at the ready. Ak'Tiul weighed his imminent death versus an extended period of pain before dying. He didn't like his options.

"ONE!" the third level MarPul screeched in a click and a whistle.

Ak'Tiul had no idea where he found the courage, but he hit the two steps carved into the mud wall and popped out of the trench and into the open. He stood there dumbfounded but was bumped out of the way as the MarPul climbed up behind him.

Side by side they stood, two Bazarians. One hundred yards away, a human popped out of his trench, but he wasn't looking their way.

"Well?!?!" the MarPul demanded.

"Well, what?" Ak'Tiul wondered.

"Shoot him! Shoot the enemy, dickface!" the junior officer howled stamping one foot in the mud.

Ak'Tiul looked at it, curious that there was mud up in no man's land, too. He figured all the water made its way into his trench. He couldn't imagine that there was any remaining to make mud elsewhere. Maybe the planet wasn't a rock, but one big mudball. He looked at the terrain, certain that no argument could convince him otherwise.

"Fire!" the officer yelled.

"Right!" Ak'Tiul said, thinking about the mud and that this would all be over soon. The winner goes home. He called out, "Time to win, your preeminent supremeness!"

Ak'Tiul took aim with his old slug thrower and pulled the trigger.

Nothing. The MarPul was not pleased and jammed the shock stick against the enlisted man's leg. Ak'Tiul screamed in pain until his whole body convulsed and he dropped his weapon. It slid in the mud and back into the trench.

The third level MarPul released the button, and Ak'Tiul doubled over in pain. "I shall recover my weapon, sir," he said without any derision. He resigned himself to the fact that he would die in pain. He hated the humans for being here with him. He hated the Council for sending him to the godforsaken place. But he hated the MarPul most of all.

"No. You'll fight them hand to hand. Look at their frail pink flesh! You'll rend them into tiny pieces, now forward, ho!"

Ak'Tiul walked ahead as if carrying the casket to his funeral. The perceived weight on his shoulders was equally great.

***

Riskin had every intention of running as soon as the lieutenant was out of the trench, but when Riskin threw him forward, the officer twisted in midair like a spider monkey and landed, aiming his pistol at Riskin's astonished face.

With a sigh of reservation, he reached up his hand, and the lieutenant pulled him to the top. They both leaned back down and grabbed Chen's outstretched arms. Besides holding his hands in the air, the private was incapable of helping. They dragged him up the mud wall and deposited him face first in the mud.

He lay there, weaponless. His slug thrower was still in the trench.

"You first, Private!" the lieutenant growled. "If you can't shoot, then you can be our human shield. Now move! Lance Corporal, rifle up!"

Riskin whirled through one hundred eighty degrees. The lieutenant ducked to avoid getting brained by the weapon's barrel as it flashed past.

"Watch it!" the lieutenant yelled, focusing all his attention on the two junior enlisted and none of it on the enemy.

Riskin never had any respect for him before, but that clinched it. He decided that he had to kill the man. He looked across no man's land to see who was watching

As far as the eye could see, horizon to horizon, he saw no more than ten Interstellar Marines. Most were singles, by themselves in the middle of nowhere. The story was the same on the other side. The Bazarians had an equal number.

"You have got to be kidding me? Are we it? We're all that's left?" Riskin glared at the lieutenant. "How in the hell did I get so unlucky to be stuck here and with an idiot like you?"

"No one ever leaves..." the lieutenant whispered as if talking to himself.

***

Ak'Tiul shuffled toward the humans, the MarPul stayed behind him, hiding, but carrying his shock stick and ready to inflict pain should Ak'Tiul try to run.

"I have no weapon, dickface, maybe you give me your stick? Or better, why don't you go first?" Ak'Tiul said, while continuing to slop through the mud.

His answer was the stick jammed into his leg followed by a short burst of voltage. Ak'Tiul spasmed and fell.

Pain and death were becoming one and the same. As he lay there, he saw the few bodies walking across no man's land. The final push. It looked like wayward souls stumbling through the mist of life.

The third level MarPul screamed at Ak'Tiul to get up and keep walking.

Pain and death. He had no incentive to rise. The MarPul stabbed the stick against the prostrate Bazarian's leg and pressed the button, holding it to inflict the maximum punishment.

***

"Shoot them!" the lieutenant screamed fanatically. Chen dropped to his knees and covered his ears. His pinched his eyes closed and rocked himself.

Lance Corporal Riskin Devereaux raised his slug thrower and took aim. *If we win, I get to go home;* he thought as he zeroed in on the one spiker jamming some stick into a second one lying on the ground.

They don't want to be here any more than I do, he thought. *But if we win, I get to go home. Losing is dying.*

No one ever leaves, the lieutenant said. *What the hell?*

"What did you mean by that?" Riskin asked, lowering his slug thrower, which enraged the lieutenant. "What did you mean when you said no one ever leaves?"

The young officer aimed his pistol at Riskin's face. "What I meant isn't for the likes of you. Now raise your weapon, Marine, and get back into this battle. For the glory of the IM and a battle banner for the longest battle ever fought in all the interstellar wars. We must win!"

The whites of the lieutenant's eyes shown as his mouth hung open and he panted like an animal. His pistol shook as his knuckles whitened from his fanatically tight grip.

Riskin raised his slug thrower's barrel and aimed at the Bazarian cajoling the one in the mud.

Sight picture, sight alignment. He focused on the front sight post, positioning the slightly fuzzy silhouette of the spiker in the middle of the rear sight aperture. When everything was aligned, he exhaled and gently squeezed the trigger.

The weapon barked, and the trigger froze to the rear. It cycled uncontrollably like a machinegun, making the barrel jump. The first round hit the Bazarian center mass, in the middle of its chest. As the barrel jumped, the impacts climbed.

The next round hit the enemy in the throat, and the last impact blew a hole through its head. The weapon jumped out of Riskin's hands as it continued to fire.

The lieutenant was too slow diving out of the way, and the last round from the magazine fired and tore through the lieutenant's head.

The slug thrower splashed into the mud beside Chen, followed closely by the lieutenant who toppled over backward.

Riskin stood, eyes wide, shocked at what had happened. He barely breathed. He'd killed his lieutenant.

But it was an accident! He tried to reason. Chen mumbled and whined.

"Shut up, Chen!" Riskin yelled, realizing his mistake. Chen didn't do anything wrong. The man was terrified.

Riskin thought he should have felt worse, but he seemed oddly relieved. He felt free for the first time in a long time. He was out from under someone else's boot, even if only for a short while.

"It's okay, Chen, stand up and let's go. There's no one left to report anything, no one left who knows anything." Riskin looked around and saw a few figures here or there, but wasn't sure if they were human or Bazarian. The enemy closest to him was picking himself up out of the mud.

***

Ak'Tiul heard the sound at the same time he saw the slugs impact the third level MarPul. The officer was close, and Ak'Tiul simply laid there and watched as the Bazarian was torn apart. The dead body flopped like a wet rag, splashing into the mud.

The enlisted Bazarian crabbed backward away from his dead officer. He thought about running for his trench, but if he didn't stand, then maybe they would think him dead.

He remained where he was, but watched the humans closely. Where once there had been three, only one remained standing. Of the other two, one knelt and the last looked dead like the MarPul.

One helped the other to his feet, they turned and walked back to their trench. When they reached it, they stood there, motionless for an interminable amount of time.

He saw his opportunity to return unseen to his trench.

***

Riskin and Chen stood at the top of the wall, looking down at a heavy yellow gas. It rose chest high within, and that's if one knew where the high points were.

"Damn the lieutenant," Riskin said softly, then turned back to the officer's body and screamed. "DAMN YOU!"

Chen was coming back to himself, having raced through the five stages of grief, from denial to anger, bargaining, and depression. He was ready to accept his depression as the final state of his life.

"What if we surrender?" Chen asked. As a Private in the IM, he'd never had to think for himself. Someone else always told him what to do. He needed that in his life. Riskin Devereaux was the opposite; he despised people telling him what to do.

Which is how he ended up as a Marine, to show his father that he couldn't tell him what to do. Riskin had no idea how much freedom he'd had when he lived at home.

The irony wasn't lost on him. The years of being ordered around by an idiot like the lieutenant had convinced him how smart and how wise his father was.

And how young and stupid Riskin had been.

Now I'm going to die for it, killed by my own people because everyone wants this little planet and this little war to go away.

"I wonder…" Riskin started to say. "Come on, Chen, let's see if I'm right."

He turned Chen around, and they started walking toward the muddy Bazarian who was looking at his trench as they'd just looked at theirs.

"You speak Chinese, Chen?" Riskin asked.

"What do you think?' the private replied sarcastically, trying hard not to look at the lieutenant's exploded head as they walked past. He failed miserably as he couldn't keep his eyes off it.

"Tell that Bazarian not to go into the trench, it's poison," Riskin said.

Chen translated the phrases in milliseconds in his head and then spoke Mandarin Chinese in a normal tone of voice.

"Come on, Chen, everyone knows that the spikers don't have ears. You gotta really belt it out!" Riskin threw up his hands in hopeful encouragement.

"You're kidding right?" Chen asked.

"You ask a lot of questions, Private," Riskin sneered. "Why would I kid about something like poison and death?"

"If they don't have ears, why would yelling make any difference?" Chen explained, eyebrows raised.

"Damn straight; maybe he can read lips?" Riskin suggested, then laughed heartily. The Bazarians didn't have lips.

Riskin and Chen kept walking across no man's land.

***

Ak'Tiul looked at the green gas in the trench. He could smell it.

Death.

He thought he heard someone tell him not to go into the trench, but it was in the human Chinese language. He knew the voice spoke the truth, although the truth sounded strange, no matter which language communicated it.

"Hate humans," Ak'Tiul said. He looked back at the dead body of the MarPul. "Hate MarPul more. Sorry, your cerebral supremeness in that I didn't recognize your superiority sooner and raced across the wasteland with reckless abandon to dispatch your enemies."

He saluted haphazardly, then swaggered to the body, picked up the stick and jabbed it against the leg. When he depressed the button, the MarPul's body jumped, but the stick shorted out, sending electricity through the water and into Ak'Tiul's foot.

He dropped the stick and jumped around on one leg, feeling like a moron for shocking himself.

The humans stopped on the other side of the MarPul and stood there watching Ak'Tiul's antics.

He stopped hopping around and stood still, returning the humans' gaze.

"Don't go into your trench. The gas is death," the Bazarian told them in the sing-song language of diplomacy.

***

The creature was the same size as the two Marines, but to Riskin, the Bazarian looked like a cross between a bumblebee and a wasp. When it spoke in Chinese, Riskin was relieved, but still, couldn't understand the creature.

Chen nodded and replied.

Riskin slapped the shorter man in the arm. Chen remembered that the other Marine didn't speak his language. "He said to not go into the trenches."

"We know that," Riskin said.

"That's what I told him." Chen looked oddly at the lance corporal.

"So what the hell do we do now?" Riskin asked. Chen translated the question for the Bazarian.

"Dammit! I was asking you, not him," Riskin clarified.

Chen shrugged.

"Ak'Tiul," the Bazarian said, pointing to himself with one spindly arm.

"Riskin," Chen said pointing to the lance corporal. He said it twice and then pointed to himself. "Chen."

"Who was that?" Riskin asked, leaning toward the Bazarian that he himself had killed.

"The MarPul, an officer, a bad officer," Ak'Tiul said, and Chen interpreted for Riskin.

"Our officer, too, bad and dead," Riskin said succinctly.

"What do we do now?" Ak'Tiul wondered.

"Find a way off this godforsaken mudball!" Riskin exclaimed. Chen smiled before telling Ak'Tiul what the lance corporal had said. The Bazarian bobbed excitedly.

"Like humans," he said, the clicks and whistles of the Bazarian language were lost on his new companions.

The End

Author Craig Martelle

Copyright

The Expanding Universe, an Exploration of the Science Fiction Genre Anthology title is Copyright © 2017 Craig Martelle

The authors of the individual short stories retain the copyright of their work as detailed below.

Defense of the Deep Space Denali - Copyright © 2017 Craig Martelle
Self-Perspective - Copyright © 2017 by Amy DuBoff
Peyton's Legacy - Copyright © 2017 by S.M. Schmitz
Cassowary Raid - Copyright © 2017 by Drew A. Avera
Fox Hunt - Copyright © 2017 by Carysa Locke
Honor Duel - Copyright © 2017 by Kevin O. McLaughlin
A Prayer for the Faithless - Copyright © 2017 by David Bruns
Margolis Space Rescue - Copyright © 2017 by P. Joseph Cherubino
Venusian Uprising - Copyright © 2017 by M. D. Cooper
Destroy the Planet - Copyright © 2017 by T.J. Ryan
Boarded - Copyright © 2017 by Dale Furse
Space Colony One: Night of Flames - Copyright © 2017 by J.J. Green
Pirates vs. Drones - Copyright © 2017 by J.L. Hendricks and S.R. Witt
Space Cadets: Acid Slime - Copyright © 2017 by H.J. Lawson
Nun Shall Pass - Copyright © 2017 by Barry Hutchison
Intuition (A Galactic Warriors Prequel) - Copyright © 2017 by Monica Leonelle
Panic Button - Copyright © 2017 by Sam Maguire
Motherlode - Copyright © 2017 by Bill Patterson
Emergence - Copyright © 2017 by E.R. Starling
Mara's Honor - Copyright © 2017 by Taki Drake
The Drone Pilot - Copyright © 2017 by Brian J. Walton
Operation Solid Iron - Copyright © 2017 by James Osiris Baldwin
Trenches of Centauri Prime - Copyright © 2017 by Craig Martelle

All rights reserved.
ISBN 10: 1547142979
ISBN 13: 978-1547142972
ASIN: B072LMWBWT

Cover Illustration © Tom Edwards
www.TomEdwardsDesign.com

Typography and Book Formatting by James Baldwin
http://www.jamesosiris.com

Printed in Great Britain
by Amazon